DYING TO

REMEMBER

ALSO BY GLEN APSELOFF

Overdose
Lethal Cure

GLEN APSELOFF

DYING TO REMEMBER

fTHOMAS & MERCER

Text copyright © 2015 Glen Apseloff
All rights reserved.

Published by Thomas & Mercer, Seattle

www.apub.com

Amazon, the Amazon logo, and Thomas & Mercer are trademarks of Amazon.com, Inc., or its affiliates.

ISBN-13: 9781477830154
ISBN-10: 1477830154

Cover design by Brian Zimmerman

Library of Congress Control Number: 2014959257

Printed in the United States of America

To the individuals whose tragic poisoning inspired this novel.

Chapter 1

Christopher Barnes awoke in a sweat. In his dream he was about to crack open a patient's chest, and not just any patient—Senator Brown, who needed an emergency bypass graft to save his heart. The OR lights had radiated like sunlamps, making beads of sweat run down Barnes's face and under his surgical mask.

Light from the street filtered through a break between the curtains, illuminating a strip of ceiling and transforming the otherwise total darkness of the hotel room into a menagerie of indiscernible shapes. Beneath him the mattress swayed, as if not on firm ground, while beside him his wife, Elizabeth, slept soundly. Then he remembered. Not Elizabeth. Cheryl—a fellow cardiothoracic surgeon who had sought him out that afternoon at the conference.

He turned to the digital clock. The red numbers glared at him: 1:37.

Something was wrong, something more than guilt about his wife. He had moved out of their Boston home a week ago. Six days, now that he thought about it, although right now he had other things to think about. A malaise coursed through him, as though an internal switch had been flipped, changing doctor Chris Barnes into patient Chris Barnes.

Sitting up, he pushed aside the covers and swung his legs over the side of the bed. The sudden movement created a wave of nausea. He hurried to the bathroom, feeling his way through the darkness. His knee glanced off an upholstered chair, and a Bulgari necktie draped over the back brushed against his ankle as it slid to the floor. The tie cost more than the chair, but he didn't stop to pick it up.

"What's wrong?" Cheryl's sleepy voice trailed behind him.

Barnes concentrated on reaching the toilet. Straining to see through the darkness past the bathroom door, he slapped at the light switch.

Missing.

Missing.

Hitting it.

The overhead light engulfed the room in a blaze. Through squinting eyes he focused on the toilet, stumbled to it, grasped the plastic seat, and retched into it. Gray-yellow liquid with remnants of seafood gushed into the water. His abdomen contracted in spasms, sucking the breath from his lungs, and his world converged on the toilet and the surrounding, unobtainable air.

Then, as abruptly as it began, the vomiting stopped.

Barnes gasped.

The spinning sensation ebbed, and a headache took its place, throbbing in his temples like a hangover. But that couldn't be, not after only two glasses of wine.

He spat into the toilet and grabbed a towel from the rack above to wipe his face. Stomach acid coated his teeth, burned deep in his throat. He forced himself to his feet.

"Are you okay?" It was Cheryl standing naked in the doorway, blonde hair cascading over her shoulders and breasts. Before falling asleep, he'd pressed his face to those breasts, breathing in her scent and feeling the drumming of her heart. Trying to find solace in the closeness of human contact. And trying to get back at Elizabeth.

2

He'd gained little solace, and he'd stopped short of committing adultery.

Now he wanted to be held again, but not by this woman. Cheryl was intelligent, witty, and gorgeous, but she wasn't Elizabeth. Unfortunately, Elizabeth was no longer Elizabeth, either. The woman he thought he'd known, the love of his life, had been incapable of deception. Or so he'd thought. Until last week.

He flushed the toilet and answered Cheryl over the rush of water. "I think I've been poisoned."

Cheryl came to him and put a hand on his chest. "From what?"

"Dinner." He pulled away to rinse his mouth under the faucet. The frigid water washed away some of the bitterness, but not the fear, the deep-rooted anxiety that something worse might be yet to come. Like in the emergency room during his residency training when a local university coed—a cheerleader—walked in with flu-like symptoms that turned out to be sepsis.

"You're going to be all right," Barnes had assured her, even as a dark rash surfaced on her face and neck. Two hours later she died, despite antibiotics, fresh frozen plasma, and every emergency treatment the critical care team could administer.

If he lived to a hundred, he'd never forget that woman's face. When she'd looked into his eyes, he had felt her mortality. Now he felt it again.

This can't be happening, he thought. But that had been the theme of the evening. First flirting with another woman, then crossing the line—taking her to his hotel room. It had all seemed surreal. And so did having some toxin inside him that could cause God knows what.

"It was probably the escargot or the mussels," he said, trying to analyze his predicament. Why couldn't he have ordered something else? The chef's salad, maybe. But a bowl of roughage hadn't appealed to him. So instead he'd ordered escargot in a garlic butter sauce and, as an entrée, North Atlantic mussels in a white wine broth. The mussel shells had been large, and shiny black as though they'd been buffed. Thick and rubbery, the plump mollusks inside had protruded through the open shells like tropical birds' tongues.

Barnes pushed the image from his mind and wiped his mouth again with the towel. Looking at himself in the mirror, he expected to see a haggard reflection. Yet despite his illness and the effect of two decades of smoking, his off-season tan and a full head of hair lent him a ruggedly healthy appearance.

"I'm so sorry," said Cheryl, coming to him and gently rubbing his chest.

Her touch sent an unpleasant shiver through him, and he placed a hand over hers to stop it. "That's okay; I don't hold you personally responsible."

His attempt at humor only made her frown. She stepped back. "What do you think it is? Staph?"

He mulled over her question while steadying himself with one hand against the wall. *Staphylococcus aureus* is a common source of food poisoning, and the toxin produced by those bacteria takes effect within a few hours after a contaminated meal. But his symptoms didn't fit. "Staph would cause vomiting but not this . . . this headache." He took his hand off the wall to squeeze his temples between his thumb and fingers. "I think it's the mussels."

"It could also be something from earlier," Cheryl pointed out. "Something you ate for lunch."

He dropped the towel onto the floor and headed out of the bathroom. "I didn't have lunch."

Taking his arm, Cheryl guided him to the bed. She had turned on a small lamp, and it cast jaundiced light through the room. Above the headboard hung a framed print of a harbor scene with shimmering water reflecting streaks of masts and rusty sunlight. To Barnes the water seemed to ripple within the frame.

"Are you going to be okay?" Cheryl put a cool hand on his forehead. "I think you have a fever. We should get you something."

Barnes shook his head and felt the pounding increase. A resurgence of nausea accompanied it, and he pulled away to stumble back to the bathroom.

Again he threw up, this time mostly mucous and something darker. Bile?

"Maybe we should go to an ER," Cheryl suggested, uncertainty in her voice. She'd put on a bathrobe and was standing in the doorway.

Barnes wiped his mouth with another towel, then tossed it aside. Using the wall to steady himself, he got back onto his feet. "I'm okay." He took a deep breath and ran a hand through his hair, damp with sweat. Putting his head under the faucet, he let water run over his face, then rinsed his mouth. The pounding between his temples eased, giving way to dizziness.

"I don't believe this." Water like icicles dripped down his neck and chest.

"This could be serious," Cheryl said. "We should get you to an ER."

"No. I'll be all right. I don't need some Canadian ER doc to tell me what I already know." He was surprised to sound so self-assured, while inside him fear swelled like an aneurysm. "These things usually run their course in six to twelve hours."

"*If* it's bacterial. It could also be a chemical contaminant or some type of algae."

Barnes wiped his chin and tried to remember the different types of poisoning from seafood. The last time he'd come across anything about that must have been in a journal or textbook during residency training or medical school. The information was somewhere in the recesses of his mind. He reached back into that mental library. Marine plants . . . the ocean's poisons: tetrodotoxin and ciguatera. Both could be lethal, but those came from fish, not shellfish.

Red tide. Every New Englander knew the risks of that, the most common deadly poison in shellfish. But the high-risk period was June to October. This was November. November 22.

"Probably it's *E. coli*," he said finally. "That's the most common contaminant of shellfish, from sewage. I would think if there was an outbreak from algae, somebody'd figure it out before the food ever reached a restaurant. Those things must be monitored."

He was far from convinced. *E. coli* would more likely cause cramping and diarrhea than vomiting and a headache. But algae—that could kill him. The thought of a deadly toxin coursing through his body . . . he pushed it from his mind.

Cheryl came to him and caressed his cheek. "You're probably right."

Her touch sent a cold shiver through him, but he responded by running a hand through her hair. Thoughts of his illness nearly overwhelmed him, but his hands seemed capable of functioning independently, the result of performing thousands of procedures in the operating room. Regardless of where his mind happened to be, his hands knew what to do.

"Let's get you back to bed." Cheryl helped him walk from the bathroom. Barnes stumbled and nearly fell, despite her.

He sat on the edge of the mattress and put his head between his legs, where it seemed to throb and float at the same time. "I feel lightheaded. I need a cigarette."

"You need a toxicologist or an infectious-disease specialist."

"Or maybe an attorney—I should sue that restaurant."

He wasn't sure why, but he suspected the mussels more than the escargot. Maybe it was their sinister appearance in the shells, cloaked in black. At the time they'd seemed innocuous, but his attention had been focused on Cheryl. Sitting across from him in an unbuttoned cardigan and a dress with a low neckline, she'd lifted his spirits with her easy smile, then captivated him by leaning forward to pick up her wineglass and revealing a lacy black bra and the tops of her breasts. She and Barnes had first met a year earlier at the Thirteenth Annual Meeting of the North American Society of Thoracic Surgeons, then again only twelve hours ago when she'd approached him after his symposium on high-risk angioplasty. She'd looked like a college kid off the beach: tanned and supple, with high cheekbones, starry eyes, and legs that beckoned to every man in the room. Now she looked like just another woman.

"Maybe you should lie down," she suggested.

"No, I'm going to get sick again. Help me back in there." He leaned forward in an attempt to stand and nearly pitched onto the floor. With her supporting him, he made his way back into the bathroom.

She returned to the doorway as he vomited. The retching continued for some time.

"I'm going to call an ambulance," she finally said.

Recovering, Barnes held up a hand, then wiped his face on a third towel. "Help me get dressed first." He threw the towel onto the floor with the others.

Cheryl had already picked up the telephone. "In a minute."

While he waited, Barnes felt increasingly heavy—his arms, his legs, even his head. A cloud settled over him, a chilly fog that robbed him of strength and blurred his thoughts. The room no longer looked familiar. How had he gotten there?

A woman was now fussing over him. A friend of Elizabeth's? Yes, that must be it. From seemingly far away, she pushed on his shoes, the way his mother used to on wintry days before sending him off to school all bundled up and warm. Only he wasn't warm. Just the opposite—unable to stop shivering. Maybe in anticipation of the cold outside. He hoped she would give him a scarf.

On the way to the hospital, Barnes fought the thickening fog.

"Hospital . . . Hospital," he repeated out loud, staring at the ceiling of the ambulance and affirming where he was going. Being strapped to a stretcher should have been enough to remind him, but everything was becoming less distinct.

"Hospital . . . Hospital . . . Hospi . . ." The last syllable became lost in the fog. A cloud obliterated his thoughts. Then a bolt of lightning streaked across the expanse.

Barnes convulsed on the stretcher.

A paramedic, who looked too young to handle a real emergency, had just inserted a needle to start an IV in the back of Barnes's hand. Barnes's whole arm jerked with the seizure, and the needle lacerated the vein, spattering both Cheryl and the paramedic with blood.

"He needs IV valium or phenytoin," Cheryl ordered. "Hurry!"

"I'm trying." The paramedic's voice had an edge to it. He snatched a syringe from a medical kit, then held down Barnes's arm, smeared an alcohol pad on the skin, and shoved the needle and drug into a bulging forearm vein.

The seizures stopped.

But Barnes wasn't breathing.

Cheryl grabbed a bag and mask. "I'll give him air."

The paramedic hooked him up to a heart monitor while Cheryl methodically compressed the Ambu bag. She watched Barnes's chest rise and fall to the rhythm of the forced breaths. The mask formed a seal around his nose and mouth, and the air entered his lungs without inflating his stomach.

She stopped long enough to feel for a carotid pulse. Strong. The monitor showed a normal rhythm.

"He's not breathing on his own," she said. She found a laryngoscope and endotracheal tube. "I'm going to put in an ET tube."

"No, I'll do it." The paramedic moved to the head of the stretcher.

She didn't argue. Inserting an ET tube wasn't part of her repertoire as a surgeon, and it was a procedure best performed by someone who did it every day. Inserted improperly, the tube could kill a patient—forcing air into the stomach instead of the lungs, or causing the patient to vomit and breathe in the stomach contents.

The paramedic tilted back Barnes's head, stuck the laryngoscope into the back of his throat, and slid an ET tube along the instrument, down into Barnes's chest. With the Ambu bag on the end of the tube, the paramedic squeezed in air, while Cheryl listened with a stethoscope to verify that the tube was positioned correctly—into the trachea instead of the esophagus, and not past the main windpipe into a branch going to only one lung. The paramedic taped the tube into place, listened to Barnes's chest himself, and put a blood pressure cuff on his arm.

He's probably done this a thousand times, Cheryl reassured herself.

"We're only about a mile from the hospital now," he said.

Cheryl took Barnes's hand in hers. "Hang on, Chris. We're almost there." The ambulance sped through the cold streets of Toronto, lights flashing, siren blaring. "Just a few more minutes." She prayed he would regain consciousness.

But when they finally arrived at the ER of Toronto General, Barnes already looked dead.

Chapter 2

Elizabeth Barnes slept fitfully in her king-size bed, tossing like a child unable to get comfortable. At a distance she could have passed for a child—small, with delicate features and her hair cut in a bob. She wore an oversize T-shirt that nearly reached her knees, and she'd turned so many times it had started to twist around her legs.

She'd gone to bed early that night, only to be awakened by disturbing dreams and two telephone calls. The dreams stemmed from a recent argument with Chris, and one in particular had made her heart pound. In it, Chris had backed her up to a wall and clamped a hand around her throat. In real life he had never harmed her, nor had he ever threatened to, yet in the dream he'd been transformed by rage. The encounter had been so vivid that upon awakening, Elizabeth recalled seeing the reflection of her eyes in the blackness of his pupils. She'd awakened gasping, saved by the telephone.

That first call came from Boston Riverside Hospital, where one of Elizabeth's postoperative patients had spiked a fever. An orthopedic surgeon, Elizabeth rotated being on call with the other attendings in her group. Both Elizabeth and Chris routinely received calls in the middle of the night, and they kept a telephone on each nightstand. Even Rex, their golden retriever, had grown accustomed to the sudden ringing of the phone or the beeping of a pager. Sometimes he wouldn't even turn his head. Usually Rex spent the night on the floor beside the bed, but Elizabeth let him sleep with her when Chris was away.

"Just don't let him put his butt on my pillow," Chris would say.

"No bum on the pillow," she would reply in the British accent she'd retained despite having lived for more than a decade in the United States. Tonight that's exactly where Rex's bum was, with her encouragement. But it gave her no satisfaction. Without Chris, she felt only silence, and that was worse than the pounding drums that preceded it. One bad decision, a mistake of the heart, a foolish fling she had never envisioned. It was an event so unexpected and uncharacteristic it seemed at times that it had never really happened. But it *had* happened, and it had caused more upheaval and heartache than she'd ever imagined.

When the telephone rang a second time, Elizabeth suspected her patient had spiked another fever. But the voice on the other end came from an entirely different hospital.

"I'm calling from Toronto General," the woman said. Elizabeth felt her heart skip. She sat up and switched on the lamp by the phone. Rex turned his head to her, squinting pensively. "Your husband became ill this evening and has been admitted to the hospital here for treatment," the woman continued.

Elizabeth's mouth went dry. "What kind of treatment?"

"A specialist is evaluating him now. The cause of the illness hasn't been determined yet, but he's very sick. How quickly can you come here?"

He's dead or dying, Elizabeth thought. In the United States, hospital personnel are usually instructed not to discuss death over the telephone. The hospitals want to minimize their liability should a family member lose control. The administrators and attorneys are especially concerned that while rushing to the hospital, someone might have an automobile accident and then sue, claiming the hospital inflicted mental anguish that caused the reckless driving. In most US hospitals, when a patient dies, the nurses instruct family members to come quickly but not to rush, that their loved one has taken a turn for the worse. Elizabeth wondered whether the same was true in Canada.

She tried to think of what could have happened to Chris—a perforated appendix, meningitis, food poisoning, a heart attack or stroke. But the woman wouldn't elaborate, except to assure Elizabeth that Chris was indeed still alive, although he had lost consciousness before arriving at the hospital and hadn't regained it since.

Elizabeth canceled her surgeries for the next day and took the first flight to Toronto. At the international terminal, a sea of passengers flooded the customs area.

She stood behind a young couple and their child, a little girl of about two. Bundled in a pink jacket and matching scarf, the girl held her mother's hand and pressed against her leg, but unlike her mother, she faced backward, staring up at Elizabeth, as if wondering about the cause of her frown.

Elizabeth caught the child's gaze and smiled despite herself. She thought of the family she had hoped to have with Chris, and she imagined a little girl like this one gazing up at her. A month ago she would have shrugged off the notion as fanciful—neither she nor Chris had either the time or the inclination—but now she looked forward to it, with all her heart. She wanted to go on walks with Chris, pushing a stroller through the Boston Public Garden. Now that seemed next to impossible.

She'd called Toronto General before boarding the plane in Boston, and the nurse on duty had informed her that the doctors still didn't know the nature of Chris's illness. But the nurse assured her his condition required only medical intervention, not surgical. At least he wasn't going to have to risk an operation and anesthesia.

Several minutes ticked by, with travelers clearing the room only a few at a time. By the time Elizabeth reached the front of her line, the place was nearly empty. She had selected one of the slowest customs officials.

"What is the purpose of your visit?" the young man asked, smiling pleasantly as though trying to endear himself to the pretty American woman.

"My husband is in hospital here," she answered, and her British accent prompted him to look again at the photo in her passport. She was tempted to add that her husband might also have passed away during her wait in line.

"Do you have any—"

"All I have is a change of clothes. Please, I really must go to see him. He's very ill."

He started to say something else, but then, as if sensing the anguish underlying her urgency, decided not to. He simply stamped her passport and handed it back.

Elizabeth exchanged $200, then hurried from the airport and hired a taxi. In silence they drove through the vibrant city of more than three million. Elizabeth had never felt more alone. She'd packed a small suitcase, and she held it in her lap like a stuffed animal. Later she would check into a hotel if regulations at the hospital prevented her from spending the night with Chris.

The taxi left her at the main entrance to the medical complex, and just inside, a receptionist gave her information on Chris's whereabouts. Chris had been admitted to the medical intensive care unit. He lay comatose, hooked up to a respirator, an IV, and a heart monitor. Standing at his bedside, Elizabeth took his hand as the attending physician, Dr. Gallagher, explained the situation. A balding man with large jowls and a broad face, he reminded her of Winston Churchill.

"We're still uncertain what caused it," he said, scowling, "but it's most likely some type of food poisoning. We have a few other patients with similar symptoms."

"Have any recovered?"

He chewed on his lip before answering. "Not completely, but one appears to be improving. We'll know more in a few days."

"Days?"

"Well, maybe less. I'm not sure. We've never seen anything quite like this."

Elizabeth spent the afternoon holding Chris's hand, caressing him, and talking to him. She knew that patients in a coma can sometimes hear and understand people around them. She reminisced about happier times together, including trips to Cape Cod—running with the dog along the beach, picnicking on the Hyannis Port breakwater, and walking hand in hand along the shore as waves lapped at their feet. Sometimes they'd made love on the beach at night. One time early in their relationship, they'd made love in the city, in Cambridge beside the bronze Henry Moore statue in the great court of MIT. The huge abstract figure had shielded them from passersby as she and Chris fervently unbuttoned, unbuckled, and unzipped each other's clothes.

She now felt a yearning as she relived that summer night under the stars. Chris had positioned himself on top of her, and she had reached down to guide him, feeling his excitement pulsate in her hand. Kissing her neck, he'd entered her, tenderly, her flesh yielding to his.

That had been a long time ago, when they still couldn't keep their hands off each other. Now she promised herself and Chris they would make love in that same place, beside the Henry Moore statue.

She touched her husband's lips, parted around the intubation tube that allowed the respirator to breathe for him. She wanted to kiss him, and much more. She wanted to feel him inside her. She longed for that intimacy, that affirmation of life.

Chris was going to die. She knew that the way a migratory bird knows the coming of winter. Yet somehow she would have to prevent it. She was, after all, a physician. What better person to thwart death?

"We can't give up," she said, clasping Chris's hand. "I love you, and I need you. We'll fight this together. Don't leave me."

She told him how he had changed her life and that she refused to spend the rest of it without him. She had moved to the United States after completing medical school in London and had become an American citizen only after marrying Chris. Her parents and brother still lived in Southgate, a London suburb.

She wanted to tell Chris how terrible she felt, how deeply she regretted the course of recent events. But she could say only, "I'm sorry. I'm so sorry."

All that mattered now was getting him back. If she could just get him back, somehow they would work things out.

Somehow.

Chapter 3

Elizabeth spent three days at the hospital before heading back to Boston on the afternoon of Thanksgiving Day. Chris's condition remained the same, and the doctors advised her to go home, promising they would keep her apprised of any changes.

"But there must be something I can do," she'd insisted.

"At this point I don't think there's anything *anybody* can do," Dr. Gallagher had replied.

There was one thing—as soon as she returned to Boston, she would work on the logistics of transferring Chris to Riverside Hospital, where everyone knew him and where he would receive the best possible care. But before that could happen, Dr. Gallagher needed to find a way to wean him off the respirator, and she knew that might never happen. The fact that he'd shown no improvement in three days was an ominous sign. The longer people are in a coma, the less likely they are to recover and the more likely they are to have serious complications if they ever do regain consciousness. Still, she had to start making arrangements for transferring him to Boston. Not doing that would be the same as giving up, and she wasn't going to give up on Chris. Not now. Not ever.

On her first night back, Elizabeth kept to herself. The big Tudor house now felt even bigger, yet less substantial, like an imitation of their home. But at least Rex made it feel less empty, even though the dog hadn't bonded as much to her as to Chris. This despite the fact that she doted on him more. Maybe Rex sensed Chris was the better person. He could be stubborn and demanding, but part of him was also kind and even sensitive. Most people never saw that side of him, especially coworkers at the hospital, but she never lost sight of it.

For dinner Elizabeth made a peanut butter and jelly sandwich and a cup of tea, then headed from the kitchen into the family room, Rex at her heels. He usually didn't follow her from room to room, but perhaps he sensed her anxiety. Or maybe he wanted a bite of the sandwich.

Taking a seat in front of the hearth, Elizabeth set her cup on the coffee table. Rex lay at her feet. She reached down and stroked his fur. He was the best-natured animal she had ever known, a four-year-old, seventy-pound pushover. Children could pull his ears or tug his tail, and he would just look imploringly at her or Chris to make them stop. Sometimes she wished Chris were more like him.

Rex gave a sigh of contentment.

"You're lucky you don't know what's going on," she said to him. "For all you know, any minute now Chris might come in through the garage door." She wished she thought that, too.

How could things have changed so suddenly, so terribly?

She took a small bite of her sandwich. The bread felt like cotton in her mouth, but she forced herself to chew and swallow. *You don't want to look emaciated when Chris comes back, do you?*

She stopped petting Rex to take a sip of tea, and the dog turned to her, head tilted, as if to say, "Why are you stopping?"

"I can't pet you *all* the time," she explained, and put down her cup to tear off a small piece of sandwich for him. "Here you go, baby. Happy Thanksgiving."

Rex wolfed it down.

"Don't tell Chris." He didn't approve of feeding the dog human food.

Elizabeth fought back tears. A few weeks ago, she and Chris had been looking forward to Thanksgiving. Now it was the worst holiday in her life.

She took another bite of her sandwich, and it stuck to the back of her throat. Somehow she forced it down. Starting now, she would have to eat more, not just to maintain her strength for Chris but for the baby.

The pregnancy had come unexpectedly. She had believed that someday a baby would strengthen their marriage, provide more of a sense of purpose and permanence, and enable them to work on more than just their careers. But this pregnancy threatened to tear them apart. In the overall scheme of life, their previous disagreements had been about relatively minor things, but this was huge.

The day she broke the news to Chris, she'd spent much of the morning throwing up, less from morning sickness than from the anticipation of his reaction.

"Do the test again," he'd insisted.

Elizabeth had opened another kit and added another urine sample. When the red line appeared, indicating positive, he turned livid.

"I don't believe this!" he'd raged. "How could this happen?"

"I don't know. I didn't plan it. You know I'm taking the pill."

"I don't believe this!"

The rancor had escalated from there.

Now Elizabeth tried not to think about it. She had never seen Chris so angry. He didn't like things beyond his control, and her pregnancy was certainly that. Still, she'd decided to have the baby, with or without him.

She only hoped it was his.

Chapter 4

Elizabeth had never planned on having an affair, certainly not with a neighbor who lived across the street.

On many occasions she'd seen him walking his dog, a black-and-gold Yorkshire terrier the size of a small casserole dish. The man carried it like one, with both hands, when he crossed the street or traversed a large puddle on the sidewalk. She wondered what he did for a living. Tall and well built, he moved with the ease of a professional athlete, yet she sensed he also carried a heavy burden. His shoulders slumped, and he seemed overly protective of the dog, as if afraid someone or something might snatch it away.

For months when the mystery man and Elizabeth passed each other on the street, they would only nod or say hello. She knew nothing about him, only that he seemed devoted to the dog.

Then one day in October, she found herself on the same street corner with him—both heading home from walking their dogs.

"I'm Marshall," the man said. "Marshall Coburn. And this is Poco."

"Elizabeth Barnes. Nice to meet you." She held out her hand, and he shook it. "And this is Rex. I've seen you more than a few times. I'm sorry I never introduced myself."

"That's okay; I know most people around here tend to keep to themselves. But it's good to meet you and Rex." He flashed a disarming smile, and she suddenly realized how handsome he was, his rugged good looks. Early thirties, she guessed.

"Are you from England?" he asked as they headed across the street.

"Yes. I've been in the States for quite a few years now, but I never picked up the American accent. How about you? How long have you lived here?" She had noticed, as soon as he'd introduced himself, that he didn't drop his *r*'s like a native Bostonian.

"A little more than three months," he said. "But I've lived around Boston and Cambridge for more than ten years. I work in Cambridge."

"What type of work?"

They had reached an intersection, and they turned around to head back, Poco in the lead.

"I teach," he said. "Creative writing."

"Interesting. At Harvard?"

"Actually MIT."

"MIT? Really?"

He smiled. "That's how most people react. They think MIT doesn't even have a writing program. The students tend to be more mathematically than verbally inclined, but most of them are highly creative. They're all gifted intellectually. Some have an impressive command of the English language, but others think a semicolon is part of their gastrointestinal tract. Fortunately they're all eager to learn. That's a luxury many teachers don't have—students who want to learn."

"That must be gratifying. Do you do any creative writing yourself?"

"Now I just teach. I used to write poetry."

"Really?" She didn't think he looked like a poet, although what does a poet look like? "Why did you stop?"

They had reached his front steps. "That I'll save for our next conversation."

A true man of mystery, she thought. "Until next time, then." And she headed across the street.

A few days later, Elizabeth ran into Marshall again as he was walking his dog. Poco scampered along, full of energy, darting back and forth across the sidewalk.

"He seems pretty energetic today," she said.

"Yes, he's a little like an on/off switch. Today he's on." He maneuvered Poco to the grass, where the dog would less likely get underfoot.

They talked about the dogs for a while, and then Elizabeth suggested, "Perhaps now you can tell me why you don't write poetry anymore."

He hesitated but then said, "I lost my inspiration—Abby. She was my wife. The first time I met her was in Lobby Seven, the main building at MIT, when we both reached for the last copy of *The Tech* at the same time. The school newspaper."

Elizabeth thought about telling him she had spent a year at MIT as an exchange student during college, but she didn't want to interrupt his story.

"We decided to share it," he continued. "I've always marveled at that coincidence, the way we were brought together. I discovered she taught there as well—aeronautics and astronautics—and so the next day we met for lunch. After about five minutes, I knew I was going to marry her. She was my soul mate, the love of my life . . . But we were married for less than two years. Ten months ago a reckless driver killed her in a crosswalk."

Elizabeth could feel him struggling with the words.

"She was walking Poco just a block from our house. The car either passed beside him or over him, but it killed her. It didn't even stop."

"That's awful."

"I moved here because I couldn't stand to see that intersection anymore. Anyhow, to answer your question, the last poem I ever wrote was for her, and I'm not ready to write one for anyone else, myself included."

"That's so sad . . . but is it fair to you?"

His eyes looked glazed. "Life is unfair. Otherwise Abby would still be here."

After their third walk together, Marshall invited Elizabeth and Rex inside for coffee. He showed her a framed photograph of Abby, an enlargement on the living-room wall.

"This is my favorite photograph of her," he explained. "There was one shot left on the roll after we came back from a trip to Las Vegas, so I decided to finish it off with a picture of the two of them. She picked up the dog and . . . there you have it."

Abby was holding Poco cheek-to-cheek, and they were both beaming into the camera—Poco showing a little white-toothed grin from the sudden attention lavished on him, and Abby, a petite blonde, relishing the simple joy of being home with loved ones.

"She's lovely," Elizabeth said, making an effort to use present tense.

Later, after they'd finished most of their coffee, he recited the last poem he'd written for Abby. It began:

> *Waxing whispers fill the wings of seabirds sailing south,*
> *Above the Drake, whose waters churn beneath a shroud of clouds.*
> *On ocean's breath they glide across a gray expanse of mist*
> *And gently float awake, asleep, as long as it persists.*

He recited several more stanzas, and although the poem at first seemed to describe petrels soaring over the rough waters of the Drake Passage near Antarctica, Elizabeth soon realized that Marshall was comparing Abby to an updraft that lifted him above the turmoil of daily life threatening to engulf him.

"That's lovely," she said. She and he were sitting on a couch, with Poco stretched out on a pillow between them.

"It's a cliché, but she really was the wind beneath my wings. We used to be a happy family, the three of us. We called him our little hairy baby." Marshall rubbed Poco's tummy. "Now it's just the two of us. I think he understands what happened, and, in a way, I feel as though a part of Abby stayed with him. I like to believe she's not far away."

A glazed look came over him, and in it Elizabeth could sense the magnitude of his loss. Abby had been his light, just as Chris had been hers.

Yet Elizabeth hadn't felt that way about Chris for some time now. She wasn't sure when or why things had changed, but somehow that feeling had slipped away.

Sitting with Marshall, she wondered whether it would ever come back.

After their fourth walk together, Elizabeth and Marshall made love. He'd invited her in for coffee, and afterward, when she was about to leave, she'd kissed him good-bye in the foyer. It had seemed innocent. Just a good-bye kiss, or maybe a "you'll be okay; hang in there" kiss. Not an "I want you" kiss. But it lingered, just a little, and then it was followed by an "I'm here for you" kiss. And her lips just didn't want to leave his. She breathed in his scent, caressed his cheek—that sad, rugged, handsome face—and then she felt his hands on her, touching the small of her back, running his fingers through her hair. She pressed against him, and his heart pulsated against her chest. The bottom of her blouse slipped out of her jeans. His fingers glided down the curve of her back.

Between kisses, she heard herself murmur his name, and then he was undressing her, and she was undressing him. They ended up in his bed, on top of the blankets, Marshall on top of her. Accepting him into her, she felt complete, for the first time in a long time. The sensation made her head swim, released her in a way she hadn't imagined, and in that moment, she wanted him more than she had ever wanted anyone.

They climaxed together. A few heartbeats in time, but with an intensity that took her breath away. She surrendered to the sensation—shudders, then ripples of pleasure that swept over her.

Afterward he stayed inside her. She felt he belonged there, connected to her. He held her close, his heart beating against her breast, and she started to drift off in his arms. But then Poco began barking on the other side of the door.

"I should be going," Elizabeth said. Then she added, "That was a longer good-bye kiss than I had expected."

"I would say I'm sorry I kept you," replied Marshall, "except it couldn't be further from the truth."

She quickly got dressed and kissed him good-bye again. This time she didn't linger.

Crossing the street with Rex, she left behind what had just happened. Already it seemed like a long time ago, as if somehow time had sped up, or maybe all of this had never really happened. But part of her could still feel him touching her, could still feel him inside her. What must *he* be feeling?

For him, she thought, it must have been an escape—an escape from the pain of his loss, however brief. And for her? For her it was a chance to share an intimate moment with a sensitive man not afraid to show vulnerability.

But it couldn't happen again, not if she hoped to keep her marriage. If it happened again, it would happen a third time, and a fourth, and it would keep on happening until she got caught. And she didn't want to get caught. She didn't want to lose Chris.

Two days later she saw Marshall again, and they walked their dogs together. But afterward she didn't go to his place, and she didn't kiss him good-bye.

"I can't do it again," she told him.

"I understand."

She wasn't sure he did. "I just . . ."

"It's okay," he said.

But it wasn't okay.

Two weeks later, Elizabeth's period didn't start when it should have. A week after that, still nothing, and she was feeling tired and nauseated.

It's probably just stress, she tried to convince herself. But to be sure, she took a pregnancy test.

The result left her lightheaded.

Either Chris or Marshall could be the father. Telling Chris would infuriate him. She had no idea how Marshall would react. Regardless, she needed to tell Chris first. That much she owed him.

But how *could* she tell him? "Can I get you some tea, and, oh, by the way, I'm pregnant and the baby might not be yours"?

The shame was overwhelming. She had broken her vows, had betrayed the man she loved, or at least used to love . . . no, still loved . . . yet part of her didn't regret what she had done. What did that say about her? And what would Chris do when he found out?

It doesn't matter, she told herself. *You* must *tell him.*

But she wasn't sure she could.

Chapter 5

Elizabeth finished her peanut butter and jelly sandwich and tried to focus on a couple of books she had purchased in Toronto. The first was titled *Pregnancy and Child Care*; the second, *Brain Pathology*. She picked up the second and began to read.

But her focus kept drifting. She thought about Chris, lying comatose in Toronto, and she wondered what he must be going through. He would probably never recover, and if he did, would he ever forgive her? She had told him about her pregnancy and her affair in order. The first confession had left him furious; the second . . . worse—he'd regarded her with such a menacing expression that the hair had stood up on the back of her neck.

Elizabeth had reread the same page of her book three times, absorbing almost nothing, when the doorbell chimed. Rex got up to escort her to the foyer. The house was equipped with a state-of-the-art security system, and Elizabeth had armed it when she'd first come home. That and Rex provided ample protection, but now the idea of an unexpected visitor made her uneasy. Who would come by unannounced at such an hour, and on Thanksgiving of all days? She hoped it wasn't Marshall.

Turning on the outside light, she peered through the peephole of the front door. She wasn't in the mood for company, especially someone lacking the courtesy to ring her on the telephone first.

Resigning herself to the situation, she entered her alarm code into the keypad on the wall and unbolted the door. She took a deep breath and sighed. This was not her day. Why couldn't it simply be over? Why couldn't the whole year be over?

She opened the heavy door and took a step back as cold air rushed in.

It's okay, she consoled herself. *Barring more bad news about Chris, this evening really can't get much worse.*

But in a moment, it would.

Chapter 6

Eleven days later Barnes opened his eyes to white ceiling tiles and a flood of light. With the light came sounds—beeping, clicking, hissing. He tried to turn his head to get a better look at the source of the noise, but his neck felt as rigid as a pipe. All he could see were heavy curtains and metal cabinets. Beneath him an air mattress massaged his back and legs, inflating and deflating asynchronously, constantly changing pressure. *To prevent bedsores*, he realized. This was the Cadillac of mattresses. Nothing but the best for him.

Barnes managed to turn his head ever so slightly. The top of a heart monitor and respirator came into view. The trappings of an intensive care unit.

He became aware of his physical condition, the little sticky patches on his chest—electrodes from the heart monitor—and the air tube protruding from a hole in his throat. A machine forcibly inflated his lungs in a constant rhythm, reminding him with every inspiration that he had lost control of his basic bodily functions.

He closed his eyes for a moment, and when he opened them, a heavyset nurse in scrubs stood over him. She disconnected the respirator from his tube and instead inserted a suctioning device to clear secretions out of his airway. Gagging, he reached for his throat, but his hands wouldn't move from his sides. Thick strips of gauze bound his wrists to the metal rails of the bed, no doubt to prevent him from pulling out his tracheostomy tube or the IV in the back of his hand. At the moment, all he wanted was to be able to breathe again. Every fiber of his being struggled to do that, to regain control.

"Oh, you're awake!" she exclaimed, looking into his eyes like someone peering into a fishbowl. "You're awake!" She withdrew the device and reconnected him to the respirator. "Don't go anywhere. I'll be right back."

Barnes jerked weakly against the wrist restraints as the machine again forced air into his lungs. Where did she expect him to go, and what was she thinking to leave him still tied up? He wanted to order her to come back and take out the tube, to let him breathe on his own, but until someone plugged his tracheostomy, he wouldn't be able to utter a word. He concentrated on turning his head. Left, right, left. A little farther each time. Then up and down. That's when he noticed his facial hair. He could feel a beard when he rubbed his cheek against the side of his neck and shoulder. Maybe half an inch of growth. That meant nobody had shaved him for two weeks.

A balding man with a stethoscope draped around his neck came to the bedside and leaned over. "Dr. Barnes," he bellowed, "can you hear me?"

Barnes nodded as best he could, wondering why someone would assume that being half-dead meant also being half-deaf.

"Can you hold up two fingers with your right hand?"

He couldn't move his arm because of the restraint, but he held out two fingers.

"Excellent. I'm Dr. Gallagher," the physician enunciated. "In a little while, after we check your blood gases, I'm going to have this respirator unhooked and you'll be able to talk. You're going to be all right. You're a very lucky man."

Barnes didn't feel lucky. He had a tube shoved through a hole in his throat, another running into the back of his hand, and a third he'd just noticed sticking into his chest near his clavicle. The IV line from his chest ran across the bed and up a metal pole to a fluid-filled plastic bag he recognized as an intravenous nutritional solution for patients incapable of eating. Out of his penis ran another tube, a Foley catheter that drained into a bag attached just below the rail of the bed. The bag was outside his line of vision, but his urine in the tube looked normal—no redness from blood and no obvious cloudiness from infection.

Where was Elizabeth during all this? She must have been there earlier, or maybe she was nearby but outside his line of vision. She could be standing on the other side of the curtains consulting with his doctors.

Then Barnes thought about the chronic nature of his condition. He'd been unconscious for quite some time, and eventually Elizabeth would have had to go back to work. That's probably where she was now, repairing someone's hip or knee. But he needed her *here*. She would know how to manage this situation, make everything better. He closed his eyes and pictured her watching over him. If he could just ignore the ventilator and go back to sleep, she would most likely be there when he woke up.

Dr. Gallagher decided to keep the respirator connected for another day. Barnes was still producing excessive secretions that could interfere with his breathing.

"We'll observe you overnight and take it out tomorrow morning," the doctor told him.

Barnes shook his head.

"I know it's uncomfortable, but it's for your own safety."

Unable to talk, Barnes could do nothing but shake his head.

31

The next day he improved, and a surgeon closed his tracheostomy while Dr. Gallagher wrote orders to transfer him from the medical intensive care unit to the internal medicine wing. Barnes also lost the cardiac monitor and the nutrition line in his chest, but not the IV in his hand. As an orderly wheeled him down the hallway, he felt relieved to be out of the intensive care unit. The ICU was like a fork in the road. One direction led to recovery. The other, death. He had just taken the road to recovery. Content in knowing that, he drifted off to sleep.

Sometime later he awoke in a private room. A male nurse stood beside his bed, adjusting an intravenous line.

"What are you doing?" Barnes's throat burned when he spoke, but his concern regarding the nurse's actions overrode any discomfort.

"Just making sure this is working properly." The nurse was tall and prim looking, with sharp features and thin hair. He stepped back to assess the IV line. "That looks about right."

A boat, Barnes thought, noting the Canadian accent.

The nurse addressed the IV bag. "You're going to be fine."

Barnes didn't recognize his surroundings but knew this must be a hospital or similar health-care facility. "Where's Elizabeth?"

"Elizabeth?"

"My wife. What are you doing?"

The nurse was adjusting the IV again. "Just making sure the flow rate is all right."

"What's in the bag?"

"Saline."

Looking at the slow drip and the lack of special labels, Barnes knew it was harmless. He turned his attention to the room, trying to orient himself. "What time is it?" Someone had taken his Rolex.

"Eleven thirty in the morning." The nurse smiled pleasantly.

"What day is it?"

"Wednesday. December 9, 1987."

"December. I don't believe this. How'd it get to be December?"

"I don't know, but it happens every year."

Barnes tried to remember what had caused him to end up in the hospital. An accident? He thought back and remembered a naked woman. Maybe that had been a dream. Certainly he wouldn't have cheated on Elizabeth. But the image seemed too vivid for something imagined: a naked woman in a bathroom doorway.

Cheryl!

He turned back to the nurse. "Did a blonde woman bring me to the hospital?"

The nurse wrote something in the chart at the foot of the bed and replied without looking up. "I wouldn't know that. You've been in the ICU. You should have asked there."

"When are visiting hours?"

"All day until eight this evening."

"Where are my cigarettes?" The nicotine might help him think.

The nurse frowned at him. "There's no smoking here. Besides, you're a doctor. Physicians shouldn't smoke. It sets a bad example."

"I'm not here to set an example." Barnes didn't hide his irritation. "In case you haven't noticed, I'm a patient."

"Yes, and a difficult one."

Barnes raised himself on his elbows. He wanted to sit up but didn't have the strength. The nurse seemed not to notice, just scribbled in the chart.

Barnes lay back. "What time is it?"

The nurse glanced sideways at him. "I just told you. Eleven thirty."

"If you just told me, I think I would have remembered."

The nurse sighed. "I don't wish to argue with you, Dr. Barnes. The time is eleven thirty. Eleven thirty-four to be exact."

"Fine." Barnes sighed, too. "What day is it?"

Chapter 7

The nurse informed Dr. Gallagher of Barnes's short-term memory impairment, and after a brief conversation with Barnes to confirm the problem, Dr. Gallagher consulted Dr. Vincent, a neuropsychiatrist.

Sitting up in bed with the covers over his legs, Barnes was watching *Wheel of Fortune* on television when Dr. Vincent entered the room.

Barnes turned from the television to size up his visitor, a portly clinician with horn-rimmed glasses, a striped polyester tie, and a white coat. The man's face appeared pasty and bloated, and his pointed nose looked out of place with the rest of his features, as though reshaped by cosmetic surgery.

The physician ran a hand through his dark hair, combed over the top from the side to cover a bald spot the size of a coaster. "I'm Dr. Vincent. I'm a psychiatrist with specialized training in neurology."

Barnes motioned to the television. "Do you know the answer to that?"

Dr. Vincent looked at the screen. Vanna White stood beside a phrase with several of the letters revealed: _ E _ E _ B E _ _ _ E _ L _ _ _. He studied it for a moment as a contestant guessed the letter *S* and Pat Sajak replied, "No, there are no *S*s."

"No," Dr. Vincent answered finally. "Do you?"

"'Remember the Alamo.'"

Dr. Vincent pulled up a chair. "That's very good, Dr. Barnes."

"I knew it before they showed the *L*." Barnes turned off the television. "But there's a problem. I remember what I had for dinner last Valentine's Day, yet I don't have a clue what I ate for breakfast this morning."

"Well, the food here isn't very memorable."

Barnes waited for a serious reply.

"Do you recall how long you've been watching television?" asked the psychiatrist.

Barnes thought about that. This was *Wheel of Fortune*, of course, a half-hour show, but had he watched it from the beginning or only partway through?

"I don't know," he said finally. "What's happened to me?"

"You've had a bout of food poisoning." The psychiatrist reached into a manila folder and took out a sheet of paper with several black-and-white photographs on it. "These are pictures of people you should know. Do you recognize them?"

Dr. Vincent was testing for prosopagnosia, the inability to recognize faces. Barnes had seen this disorder once, unexpectedly, in a female patient who'd suffered a stroke following cardiac bypass surgery. For her it had been permanent. And profound. When her husband walked into her hospital room, she couldn't figure out who he was until he spoke to her. This despite the fact that she could describe every feature of his face.

Barnes glanced at the first picture. Yes, he recognized the person. "Abraham Lincoln." He rattled off the others: "Elvis Presley, Marilyn Monroe, Babe Ruth, Albert Einstein . . ."

"Very good." Dr. Vincent seemed pleased, relieved, as he slid the paper back into the manila folder. "We used to have our prime minister on there, but nobody recognized him." He chuckled at his joke.

Barnes said nothing, too preoccupied with his memory deficit to appreciate any levity. He was still trying to remember the beginning of *Wheel of Fortune*.

"I'm glad to see you passed that test," continued Dr. Vincent. "And clearly you also don't have any speech problems. We'd been concerned that your, um, damage might have extended into the parietal lobe. But clearly you don't have a problem with speech. So let's move on, shall we?"

Barnes wanted to move on, and he understood the necessity of neuropsychiatric testing, but he felt uneasy with what they might find. His impairment could be worse than either of them suspected.

"I'd like to try something different," said Dr. Vincent. "I'm going to ask you to remember three objects for me. All right?"

Barnes shifted uneasily. "How about a cigarette first?"

"No, thank you. I don't smoke."

"Not you. Me."

"You don't smoke, either. You quit two weeks ago."

Two weeks? "The only way I could quit for two weeks is if I was in a coma."

Dr. Vincent nodded. "Yes, well, you were. It's now been more than two weeks since you've had a cigarette, and you won't have another one as long as you're in the hospital. You may think you need them, but the fact is you've gotten over your addiction to nicotine, and any need you perceive is purely psychological."

Now that Barnes thought about it, he didn't actually *need* a cigarette. He wanted one to help him relax, to hold in his fingers and distract him, but not to take the edge off the jittery discomfort that used to come over him when he went too long without one. Maybe, at least for the time being, he really had kicked the habit.

"Now, I want you to remember *frog*, *apple*, and *umbrella*." Dr. Vincent enunciated the words as though talking to a child. "Can you repeat those?"

"Frog, apple, umbrella."

"Good, very good."

Barnes knew the doctor was just trying to encourage him, but the man's tone was unacceptable. "Don't do that," he said.

"Do what?"

"Don't patronize me. I speak three languages, I have two Harvard degrees, and I'm a world authority in cardiothoracic surgery."

Dr. Vincent's pasty skin turned red. "I'm not patronizing you. I'm evaluating you." Then, changing the topic, he said, "Let's continue, shall we?" He cleared his throat. "I need you to do an exercise . . . Starting with one hundred, please subtract seven and keep going."

Barnes was tempted to ask why but decided the request was harmless enough. "One hundred, ninety-three, eighty-six, seventy-nine, seventy-two, sixty-five, fifty-eight, fifty-one, forty-four—"

"That's fine," Dr. Vincent interrupted. "Now tell me the three words I asked you to remember."

"Three words?" Knowing how psychiatrists worked, Barnes realized he must have been told those words just a few minutes ago. His heart began to pound, and he suddenly felt hot.

Dr. Vincent seemed oblivious. "Yes. I asked you to remember three words. I said them, and then you repeated them. Do you remember what they are now?"

Barnes concentrated. What had he been doing a few minutes ago? Reading? Watching TV? He glanced at the dark picture tube of the television and thought he remembered watching it, but the program slipped his mind.

"Do you remember any of the three words?" Dr. Vincent repeated.

"Um . . ." Barnes said the only thing that came to mind. "Frog?"

"Yes, that's right." Dr. Vincent smiled.

Barnes felt a rush of relief.

"Do you remember any of the others?"

Remembering another word seemed more daunting than reading the psychiatrist's mind. *It must be a noun*, Barnes thought. "*Pear*, maybe."

"Close. It was *apple*. Do you remember that now?"

The thrill of recalling *frog* had been replaced by the frustration of not recalling *apple*. "No." Barnes clenched a fistful of blanket. "I can't remember anything. I can't even remember what happened the week before I came here."

Dr. Vincent raised an eyebrow. "*Before* the poisoning? Now that's . . . that's unexpected. Your memory of that should be intact."

"Well, it isn't. Bits and pieces—eating mussels in the restaurant, and afterwards. But that's about it. I don't even remember saying good-bye to Elizabeth. What happened to me?"

Dr. Vincent frowned. "We weren't sure until a few days ago. From the start, scientists at our Atlantic Research Laboratory suspected a toxin secreted from a diatom consumed by the mussels."

"A diatom?"

"That's right. A diatom is algae."

"I know what a diatom is."

"Yes, well, fourteen other people from your hotel were poisoned, and two died. Most of the others had a relatively mild course. They were hospitalized for only one or two days and recovered fully. It seems this toxin produces more serious illness in males and also in the elderly, maybe because of increased sensitivity of receptors in the affected areas of the brain. Throughout Canada there were a hundred and seven cases of this food poisoning. The contaminated mussels were cultivated off the shores of Prince Edward Island—the east coast, probably the Cardigan River estuary—and they were flown in the day that you and others at your hotel ate them."

"What type of toxin was it?" Barnes asked.

"At first our scientists guessed paralytic shellfish poisoning, but the symptoms in experiments with mice weren't what you see with that. To make a long story short, you were poisoned by something called domoic acid, produced by a type of blue algae."

"Domoic acid," Barnes repeated, hoping that saying it to himself might help him remember it. "How do you spell that?"

Dr. Vincent spelled it for him, and Barnes wrote it on a piece of paper.

"You probably don't remember," said Dr. Vincent, "but we ran a PET scan on you yesterday. Are you familiar with that technology?"

"Somewhat." Barnes didn't like to admit not knowing a medical procedure, even if it wasn't in his area of expertise. "It's a diagnostic tool in radiology, like a CAT scan or an MRI."

"Yes. We also did a CAT scan and magnetic resonance imaging, and both of those were negative. But a PET scan is different. It measures glucose metabolism in your brain. You know that your brain uses this sugar as its sole source of energy. Therefore, if the brain cells are alive, they must be utilizing and metabolizing glucose. In your case, the cells around the hippocampus and medial temporal lobes don't metabolize glucose."

Barnes felt a knot in his throat. A significant amount of cell death in those regions could cause a permanent impairment. "Why those areas?" he asked.

"Probably because they're located around the ventricles of the brain," said Dr. Vincent. "That region has an incomplete blood-brain barrier, allowing the domoic acid to penetrate."

Barnes knew that the blood-brain barrier is a natural blockade to many drugs and toxins. If that barrier had been a little more effective, the toxin would have been relatively harmless; a little less effective, and he would have suffered massive brain damage. "So this toxin has destroyed much of my medial temporal lobes," he said. "And that may be irreversible?"

Dr. Vincent paused before answering. "That might appear to be the case, but the brain oftentimes compensates in ways that are subtle and poorly understood. When one part is damaged, the surrounding viable cells may take over that function. There's much we don't know about this, but regardless, I would expect your condition to improve somewhat."

"Somewhat," Barnes echoed. He couldn't help but think that meant "very little."

Dr. Vincent regarded him earnestly. "We won't know for at least a couple of weeks and perhaps not for a couple of months. In the meantime, there are things we can do to help, and even if you don't recover more of your short-term memory, we can still improve your level of functioning."

"I doubt that. How can I do anything meaningful without short-term memory? I sure as hell can't perform bypass surgery. What am I supposed to do if I don't remember from one minute to the next what's happening?"

"Perhaps you can assist others," Dr. Vincent suggested.

Barnes remained silent. Of course he could assist. *Anybody* could assist—even medical students who couldn't identify the major branches of the coronary arteries. Assisting in surgery was only a small step above doing nothing at all.

"Regardless, we can work on ways to improve your memory."

"Like what?"

"Like visual rather than auditory encoding. You may be able to remember an image better than a spoken word. If I ask you to remember *frog*, you may be able to recall it for a longer period of time if you form an image of a frog in your mind, rather than just trying to remember the spoken word."

He couldn't believe he'd been reduced to trying to remember the word *frog*. But at least he wouldn't have to face this handicap alone. Elizabeth would be there. He tried to recall his last conversation with her. Nothing came to mind, not even saying good-bye before the conference.

He remembered planning his trip to Toronto several months ago, but he couldn't recall boarding the plane to fly to the meeting. Now that he thought about it, he also couldn't remember giving his seminar at the conference, even though parts of dinner with Cheryl later that day seemed uncannily clear. The mussels—plump and juicy. Coarse strands of dark seaweed-like hair had stuck out of the center of a few of the mollusks, and pulling off the tufts had been difficult.

All these details he could remember—even steam from the white wine broth rising from the bowl—yet he couldn't recall saying good-bye to Elizabeth. His last memory of his wife was of her giving Rex a bath. He'd handed her a towel, and she'd needed it more than the dog. Rex had rubbed up against her and had soaked her oversize T-shirt, and then the dog had shaken himself and spattered water all over her. When was that? Eight days before the conference, he figured. Eight days. He wondered whether the other memories would return.

"Do you know whether my wife was here earlier today?" he asked Dr. Vincent.

The psychiatrist paused before answering. "Let's not talk about her just yet. Let's talk about *you*."

The man was avoiding something. Something about Elizabeth. Had she found out about Cheryl? That was one secret—one mistake—he wanted to keep to himself. All right, he decided. One thing at a time. They could talk about Elizabeth later.

But he couldn't stop thinking about her. *She knows*, he thought. *How could she not?*

He only hoped she would forgive him.

Chapter 8

Elizabeth Kramer Barnes had been gunned down in the front hallway of her five-bedroom house, along with the family dog. Detective Gordon Wright and his partner had been assigned the case, and that was fine with Wright, even though two other unsolved murders currently took up most of his time. This new case would be high profile: a prominent surgeon's wife, herself a surgeon, murdered in her own home. Of course, in these types of homicide investigations, the husband is always a suspect, but his alibi—being comatose in another country—was pretty good. Still, Barnes could have hired someone. He wouldn't have been the first.

Before Wright had come to Massachusetts, he'd been involved in the case of the physician in Ohio who'd cut his wife into pieces and buried her in the basement. That's why the lieutenant had given him this one; Wright had experience with physicians' murdered wives. This despite the fact that he was incapable of understanding how anyone could do such a thing.

Maybe he was becoming too sensitive. Cops are supposed to get hardened by the things they see—the cruelty and senseless homicides—but that hadn't happened to him. Cruelty made him appreciate kindness. Homicides made him value life.

Wright had a lot to be thankful for. He'd been married for seven years, and he loved his wife as much as the day they'd met, despite the limitations and hardship that plagued her daily life. Up until a few years ago, they'd gone hiking, canoeing, and even cross-country bicycling. That was before the accident, before she'd followed Trixie, their cat, out the window onto a ledge to try to rescue her. They'd both fallen, two stories. The cat had walked away, only to get run over and killed by a car during the commotion that followed. Karen broke her back and severed her spinal cord. She would never walk again, never feel anything from the waist down.

Karen was a teacher, an associate professor in the English Department at Boston University. Wright had met her one autumn afternoon climbing Mount Washington in New Hampshire. They'd stumbled along the same path on the way down, after a fog had descended upon the mountain and he could barely see his feet through it. He and his partner, Marty Gould, had heard voices below them, and they'd called back and forth until they met as a group.

Karen had been with Andrea, a friend of hers visiting from Minnesota, but Wright had hardly noticed the other woman. He'd been captivated by Karen's easy smile and carefree nature. She had long, curly hair the color of the red maple leaves that graced the lower mountainside, and hazel eyes that seemed to grab hold of him.

After introductions, they all headed down the mountain together. They ended up on the wrong trail and had to hitch a ride fifteen miles with a couple of college students to get back to their cars. Wedged into the backseat of an old subcompact with worn-out shocks, Wright and Karen fell in love. Even now, he could still recall her animated conversation and the sensation of her hip pressed against his during the bumpy trip to the other side of the mountain.

Ten months later, in a ceremony with half the police in the precinct, Gordon and Karen had exchanged wedding vows. They tied the knot in Boston, on the esplanade along the Charles River near the Longfellow Bridge. Marty Gould served as the best man. Andrea had been there, too, and Gould dated her briefly. He tended to go through women faster than cheap shoes, although Wright had a feeling Gould's current girlfriend, Gloria, would outlast all the others combined. She and Gould had been an item now for three months, and they still hadn't moved past the early romance stage. Gould had even bought a new overcoat and shoes with thicker heels to make him look a little more stylish and a little less stocky, and he'd gotten rid of his lucky hat that was about twenty years old.

Gould had been Wright's partner since two weeks after Wright had transferred to the precinct. They had little in common, but that seemed to work better for them. With "good cop/bad cop," Gould was always the latter. Until he partnered with Wright, he'd typically done just "bad cop," but Wright had convinced him the combination worked better, and that wasn't easy to do, considering Gould had single-handedly extracted a confession from Larry Baxter, the Butcher of Back Bay, a serial killer who'd practiced his profession on stranded motorists. Not only that—Gould had made the man pee his pants during the interrogation.

Now Gould and Wright typically did interrogations together, and Wright usually asked the first question. Like hammering a nail, he would get it started. Gould would pound it in.

Wright couldn't wait to get a crack at Christopher Barnes. He looked at the file on his desk but didn't pick it up. He didn't need to. Everything in it was already in his head.

"Hey, Gordy."

He looked up to see Gould standing there. "Marty."

"Just heard something on our Elizabeth Barnes case." Gould turned a wooden chair around and sat down with the back between his legs. "Our prime suspect just woke up from his coma."

"Well, he's prime only because we don't have anyone else," Wright reminded him. "Being in a coma is a pretty good alibi."

"He did it," Gould insisted. "Nine times out of ten it's the husband. I'd bet my left nut."

"Well, that's one bet I wouldn't want to win. For now let's keep your testicles intact."

"Yeah, well, anyways, there's a problem."

"According to my count, there are three—no prints, no weapon, no witnesses."

"Now there's four."

"Oh?"

"No memory. Seems he got some type of amnesia. You believe that?"

"No." Amnesia was something you saw in movies, not real life.

"Yeah. Me neither. But that's what the doctors say. I think someone smart could fake it pretty good."

"We'll see." Wright leaned back in his chair. "Let's pick him up as soon as he steps off the plane. Find out when that is."

"Yeah. I figure if his memory thing is real, it could give us an up on him—you know, him not remembering everything to hide from us."

Wright thought about that. Maybe Gould was right. With a little luck, they'd wrap things up in a matter of days.

Chapter 9

Dr. Vincent spent more than an hour with Barnes during their first meeting, but when the psychiatrist returned for another visit later that day, Barnes didn't recognize him.

"You're sure it was just three hours ago?" Barnes asked. Possibly the psychiatrist had mistaken him for another patient.

"I'm certain. Try to remember."

Dr. Vincent might as well have said, "Try to levitate." Barnes didn't know where to begin. He couldn't remember *anything* from three hours ago, or even one hour ago. He tried to think back just a few minutes. What had he been doing, other than lying in bed? Watching TV? Reading a magazine? Talking on the phone? Or had a nurse been sticking or prodding him? None of those things came to mind. He wasn't sure he even recalled the moment when this doctor had walked into the room, and that couldn't have been more than a minute or two ago. The exact time when memories vanished was impossible to pinpoint, but it happened quickly. And once they were gone . . .

"Dr. Barnes?" The man in the white coat seemed to be studying his expression.

"What?"

"Do you remember?"

Barnes tried not to show irritation. "Remember what?"

Dr. Vincent came to Barnes's room again the following day. "Good morning, Dr. Barnes."

Barnes was sitting in bed doing a crossword puzzle in the *New York Times*. He'd been avoiding thinking about his predicament, and the puzzle served as a needed distraction. "You know a four-letter word for an Arabian lateen-rigged boat?" he replied.

"I don't even know what *lateen* means." Dr. Vincent pulled up a chair. "Do you remember who I am?"

Barnes focused on the newspaper. "I know who you're not. You're not the editor of the *New York Times* crossword puzzle."

"No. That I'm not." Dr. Vincent leaned forward. "Do I look familiar to you?"

Barnes took a deep breath and let it out slowly. "Dhow."

"What?"

"Dhow. D-H-O-W. A lateen-rigged boat." He wrote the letters in the boxes, then put the puzzle down beside him on the bed.

"Do I look familiar to you?" Dr. Vincent persisted.

Barnes tried to recall. He studied Dr. Vincent's features, his pointy nose, his comb-over. Maybe the nose looked familiar. No, something else. The clothes. "I think I *have* seen you before. You were wearing that same polyester tie."

Dr. Vincent frowned. "It isn't polyester. It's a blend." Then he added, "It isn't identical to yesterday's, although it *is* similar." He became more animated as he spoke. Barnes could tell that on a professional level the psychiatrist was pleased. "Most likely you've retained part of your ability to remember images. The ability to recognize images or faces is much different than the ability to remember spoken words."

"Different *from*," Barnes corrected.

"What?"

"'Different *from*,' not 'different *than*,' although my wife always says 'different *to*.'"

"Different *to*?"

"She's British. They're odd that way. 'Different *to*.' When is she coming here?" He tried to remember the last time he had seen her. Instead he envisioned something completely different—the unsettling image of a plastic cup of urine beside a sink, one of two sinks in the bathroom connected to their master bedroom. It appeared before him like a picture in a slide show, suddenly there. But he didn't know what it meant, only that it made his heart rate increase and his hands sweat.

Dr. Vincent interrupted his thoughts. "Do you remember anything from yesterday?"

"No." The image couldn't have been from yesterday because yesterday he'd been in the hospital.

"Not even bits or pieces?"

"No."

"Well, try to remember. Maybe you can recall a meal you ate or a nurse who visited."

They don't visit, he thought. *They come in to complete orders, armed with needles and thermometers and blood pressure cuffs.* Yet he couldn't remember any of them, or anything they'd done to him. Perhaps that was a blessing.

"Do you remember anything from a year ago yesterday?" Barnes asked. "That's what it's like. Like it practically never happened. It's basically . . . gone."

"Yes. Well, I understand your frustration . . ."

"No, I don't think you do." Barnes now had some idea of how family members of patients must have felt toward him when he would profess to have insight into their anguish. "I'm arguably the best cardiothoracic surgeon in the country, but I can't even remember what I ate for breakfast. Hell, I can't even remember what I did thirty minutes ago. That means I'm incapable of learning. Even pigeons, even *insects*, can learn. But I can't. What does that make me?"

"Brilliant but challenged," said Dr. Vincent, "and we have to meet that challenge head-on. Yes, you have problems remembering things, but by the time I'm done working with you, few people will recognize you have a handicap."

Barnes suppressed the urge to roll his eyes.

"First, I'd like you to help me figure out what parts of your memory are still functional," Dr. Vincent said. "I'm going to show you some pictures and ask you to try to remember them, and I'm going to ask you to try to remember some other things visually, by forming a mental image that connects them. For example, if I ask you to remember the words *frog*, *apple*, and *umbrella*, I want you to form a picture in your mind of a frog eating an apple and holding up an umbrella. Repeat those three words for me."

Barnes shook his head, but he repeated, "Frog, apple, umbrella."

"Close your eyes and form the image. I want it to be crystal clear, as if someone just showed you a photograph."

Barnes felt ridiculous closing his eyes, but he did it.

"Do you see it?"

He formed the image. "Yeah, I see it."

"All right. Open your eyes. Now I want you to begin with one hundred and subtract seven for me, and keep counting down."

"One hundred, ninety-three, eighty-six . . ."

Dr. Vincent let him go down to twenty-three. "That's enough. Now say every other letter of the alphabet as quickly as you can."

"*A, C, E, G, I, K, M, O, Q, S—*"

"That's enough. Now tell me. What were the three words I asked you to recall? I asked you to remember three words for me."

Three words. "Just a minute ago?"

"Yes. I asked you to form a picture in your mind. Do you remember a picture of anything?"

"No."

Dr. Vincent pressed on. "How about a frog? Do you remember a picture of a frog?"

"Not really." *Not at all,* he thought. He wondered how long they'd been playing memory games.

"Close your eyes," Dr. Vincent instructed.

"Maybe you should choose words that are more memorable."

"Close your eyes," he repeated. "Think of a frog and tell me what else you see in the picture."

"What else? How am I supposed to create a picture?"

"Close your eyes and concentrate. Think back, and try to recall a specific image."

Barnes closed his eyes and tried to think back a minute at a time. The last thing he remembered was doing some simple arithmetic.

But then an image did take shape. He opened his eyes. "It's holding a cane and a red ball. Maybe a red rubber ball."

Dr. Vincent beamed. "Very good! The items I asked you to remember were *frog, apple,* and *umbrella.* You retained significant remnants of those items, and that means your visual memory is better than your auditory. With practice, we should be able to enhance that and improve your recall using visual techniques."

"And I'm supposed to apply that to abstract conversations?" Barnes said.

"Let's just take one step at a time."

Barnes knew Dr. Vincent was right. The important thing was that part of his visual memory, however small, remained intact. Somehow he needed to figure out a way to expand that. He wondered whether Elizabeth might be able to help. "Where's my wife? Don't you think it makes sense for her to be a part of these exercises?"

"Ordinarily it would." Dr. Vincent hesitated. "I'll tell you about Elizabeth . . ." He seemed to be choosing his words carefully. ". . . provided you try to remain calm."

"What do you mean by that?" Barnes felt his mouth go dry. Something had happened to Elizabeth. The same thing that had happened to him?

"Your wife is no longer with us."

"With us in the hospital?"

"No. She's no longer alive."

Barnes felt himself trembling—not just his hands but also his chest and head, as though an intense chill had seized him. "Elizabeth is dead? I've forgotten that my wife died?" Even his voice trembled. "Is that why I can't remember the last two weeks?"

"No." Dr. Vincent shook his head. "She was alive then. She died November twenty-sixth, four days after you ate the mussels."

"How did it . . . did she . . ." He took a breath and forced himself to remain coherent. "Was she with me?"

"No." Dr. Vincent put his hand on Barnes's arm.

Barnes drew away. "What the hell happened?"

Dr. Vincent sat back, and Barnes could tell the man was going to unload more bad news. "She was the victim of a homicide. It happened at your home."

"But . . . h-how could . . ." The words ended there.

"I don't know the details," Dr. Vincent said. "It was a shooting."

Barnes forced himself to be calm, even detached, like during a surgery gone bad. While performing routine procedures, he might raise his voice to residents and nurses—and occasionally even an anesthesiologist—but a real crisis always transported him into the eye of the storm. Around him chaos swirled, but it left him unfazed. Now he tried to summon that emotional stillness. "When did it happen?"

"November twenty-sixth," Dr. Vincent said.

"November twenty-sixth. That was Thanksgiving."

"I suppose that's right, in the States. Here we celebrate it the second Monday in October. In any case, she had just returned from visiting you."

"How did it happen?"

"I don't know. I'm sure the police will tell you when you return home."

Why couldn't they tell him *now*? "Isn't there a number I can call to find out?"

"I'll check into it. In the meantime, we need to focus on *you*, on getting you better."

"What's the point? What am I supposed to do? How am I going to live from one day to the next? I don't know that I'll even be capable of taking care of the dog!"

"The dog was with Elizabeth."

Dr. Vincent's reply caught Barnes off guard. "Rex is dead, too?"

"I'm sorry."

"You're sorry? My wife is dead, my dog is dead, my life is ruined, and what? You're sorry?"

"You'll be able to take care of yourself, Dr. Barnes. That's why I'm here, to teach you how to do that."

"Do you think I really give a damn about that?" He didn't wait for an answer. "Elizabeth is dead." The realization sucked all the hope out of him. But not his resolve. "Now I have only one thing to live for."

He clenched a fist. "I'm going to find the bastard who killed her."

Chapter 10

After Dr. Vincent left, Barnes lay in bed contemplating his future—a life without Elizabeth and without a normal mind. Maybe, gradually, part of his ability to remember new information would return, but to expect a complete recovery was unrealistic. In fact, he might not improve at all.

He recalled his third year of medical school when he rotated through psychiatry and interviewed patients suffering from major depression. One had tried to kill himself by firing a shotgun into his mouth. That was about as close to a sure thing as you can get, but Mr. Henry proved to be an exception. He had needed to stretch to reach the trigger, and in doing that, he'd tilted back his head, sending the buckshot upward, instead of straight back, and blowing off everything from the roof of his mouth to his forehead. The force of the blast also destroyed his jaw, leaving him almost entirely without a face. All that remained were his ears, most of his skull, and his brain. In an instant he had blinded himself and disfigured himself beyond recognition.

Medical and surgery residents throughout the hospital came to the intensive care unit at all hours just to get a glimpse of Mr. Henry, until the attending physician put a stop to it. Barnes had interviewed the patient several months later, and he couldn't help but feel that Mr. Henry really would have been better off dead. The man had lost his job and his wife, and then he'd lost his face and his eyesight. As a medical student, Barnes had been unable to say anything positive but had instead focused on the treatment plan—the antidepressant medications, the group therapy sessions, and other activities designed to ease Mr. Henry back into the mainstream of society, if that was possible. At the end of the month, Barnes had rotated onto another service, and he never saw Mr. Henry again. He figured the man had eventually killed himself.

There comes a point when life isn't worth living, Barnes thought, and no doubt Mr. Henry had gone beyond that after losing his face. Now Barnes wondered whether *he* had also passed that point. Tending to patients with Alzheimer's disease during his third year of medical school, he'd assured himself that if the same thing ever happened to him, he would commit suicide. Was this much different? Is life worth living if you can't remember anything you do? Maybe his memory would improve, but probably not by much. When infants and young children suffer major brain damage, they can recover most or all of their lost function, but with adults that's uncommon. And it never happens quickly.

Barnes looked at the window across the room. The blinds were drawn, and he had no idea how high up he was. If he jumped through the window, he might trip over a hedge or he could just as likely plummet a hundred feet.

Thinking about this, about ending his life, made him wonder whether he might be experiencing major depression. Thoughts of suicide are one of the five symptoms. Did he have others? A change in mood—yes. A loss of interest in his usual activities—no. Given the chance, he would still do surgery. A change in appetite? A change in sleep patterns? He couldn't remember enough to answer either of those. A diagnosis of major depression requires three of the five symptoms, and he could have anywhere from two to four. The bottom line was he couldn't even make a simple diagnosis of depression. But one thing was certain—he had already hit bottom.

Or so he thought.

Chapter 11

The next morning Barnes awoke with no memory of the previous day. He thought he recognized Dr. Vincent when the psychiatrist entered the room and came to his bed, but he couldn't recall any details of their meeting, or even whether a conversation had taken place.

After first showing and reshowing Barnes simple drawings and pictures of everyday items to test his visual memory, Dr. Vincent broke the news to him again about Elizabeth. For the remainder of the previous day, Barnes had remembered her murder, even after he'd forgotten Dr. Vincent, because the shock of it had never left his immediate thoughts. But after he fell asleep that night, the memory vanished. Today news of Elizabeth's death caught him off guard. He lay there, too stunned to reply.

"I'm afraid it's something you'll have to relearn every day," Dr. Vincent said, after a prolonged silence. "It won't get any easier, unless you have enough insight to accept it as yesterday's news and force yourself not to dwell on it."

Barnes said nothing. What Dr. Vincent was suggesting seemed impossible, and even callous. Yet the alternative was worse—daily torment.

Somehow he needed to focus on other things. A disciplined mind should be able to do that, and the mind of Christopher Barnes was nothing if not disciplined. The key would be to treat the death of Elizabeth like a major surgery. Focus on the procedure, not the patient. Or, in her case, focus on the crime.

"When exactly did this happen?" he asked.

He followed that with other questions: Where in the house was Elizabeth killed? Had the alarm system been disarmed? Had anyone in the neighborhood reported seeing anything unusual?

Dr. Vincent offered few answers, saying only that the Boston police would have to give him details. Still, Barnes wrote notes to himself. When he finished, the psychiatrist shifted the conversation to discuss Barnes's memory.

"Is there *anything* you can recall from yesterday?" Dr. Vincent asked.

"I don't even remember this morning. How do you expect me to remember yesterday!"

"Don't become angry. Concentrate. Try to remember. Anything. Do you remember this room?"

Barnes looked around. "I don't know . . . It's as though I've been dreaming and then I wake up. My memories fade that fast."

Dr. Vincent nodded. "Well, there are ways to help you remember. We just have to figure out what works best for you. Let's start with some cognitive tests."

"Fine." Barnes had expected this—that's what psychiatrists do.

"I'd like you to repeat three words for me: *frog*, *apple*, and *umbrella*."

Barnes complied.

"Have I said those words to you before?"

"I don't know. Probably, or you wouldn't ask."

"That's right. Now, I want you to form an image in your mind of a green frog eating a red apple and holding up a black umbrella. Okay?"

"Fine."

"Good. I'll ask you about that later."

Barnes jotted something on a piece of paper.

"What are you writing?" asked Dr. Vincent.

"Frog, apple, umbrella."

"Let's not do that. I want you to remember without writing them down."

"Fine." Barnes scribbled over the words.

"I'm pleased to see you're beginning to rely upon notes," Dr. Vincent said.

"Well, I don't have much of a choice."

"It will become an important part of your daily living, but we'll talk more about that later. Right now I'd like to focus on another exercise."

"I'm really not in the mood for these things."

"This is important," Dr. Vincent said, "and it isn't difficult. I'm going to say a series of one-digit numbers, and I want you to repeat them. I'll say them slowly, and I'll start with five digits. Okay?"

Barnes put aside his pen and paper. "What's normal?"

"Normal recall is anything from five to eight."

"Then start with ten."

They compromised and began with seven. Barnes worked his way up to thirteen. Afterward Dr. Vincent asked him to recall the three items from earlier.

"Three items?" Barnes echoed.

"Yes. I asked you to form a picture in your mind of an animal doing something. Try to remember. Close your eyes."

Barnes closed his eyes and tried to form an image. He saw Elizabeth. She was sitting across from him sipping wine over dinner. A candle lit the small table at Anthony's, a seafood restaurant they'd gone to many times, and the flickering light danced across her glass and in her eyes. Elizabeth liked to wear sweaters when the weather turned cold, and Barnes pictured her in a black cashmere V-neck with the sleeves pushed up.

"What do you see?" Dr. Vincent asked.

Barnes cleared the image from his mind. "Nothing."

"Try harder."

He attempted to relax and focus his thoughts at the same time. Another image took shape. Barnes opened his eyes. "A frog."

"Very good. What's it doing?"

He hesitated. "Eating a red ball."

"Close. That's an apple. What else do you see?"

"I don't know. Maybe a parachute."

"Excellent." Dr. Vincent rubbed his hands together. "It's an umbrella. The three words I asked you to remember were *frog*, *apple*, and *umbrella*."

The psychiatrist proceeded with another test, this one involving repeating a series of digits and each time adding another number to the end.

Barnes worked his way up to thirteen. "What's normal for this?" he asked.

"Around twenty, but you shouldn't judge yourself by a single test."

"Let's do it again."

"We will," said Dr. Vincent. "Tomorrow."

Barnes started to protest, then stopped himself. What was the point? They both knew he wouldn't do any better. Not today.

He recalled the final scene of the movie *Gone with the Wind*, when Rhett Butler walked out on Scarlett O'Hara, leaving her utterly alone, her life in shambles. Despite that, Scarlett held her head high and proclaimed to the world, "Tomorrow is another day."

Tomorrow *is* another day, Barnes told himself. He couldn't help but wonder what it had in store for him.

Chapter 12

The next day Dr. Vincent retested Barnes. Barnes's ability to recall the repeated serial digits improved by only one, to fourteen. His recollection of events from the week to ten days before the poisoning remained minimal, but Dr. Vincent assured him much of it should come back with time and therapy.

"Your memory loss before the poisoning almost certainly has a psychological basis," Dr. Vincent said.

"So now in addition to brain damage," said Barnes, "you think I have psychiatric problems."

Dr. Vincent nodded. "It's possible the domoic acid has impaired your midrange memory, but I don't believe that's the case since you can remember events from the evening of the poisoning. We don't know much about domoic acid, but a neurotoxin that affects memory would almost certainly have a more global effect if it caused amnesia; it wouldn't likely spare the events of one evening."

Probably not, but Barnes hesitated to accept the lack of another explanation as a justification for a psychiatric cause. Too often physicians did that with a wide range of ailments, telling patients their pain or their fatigue or their nausea was all in their head. "Do you really know *anything* about domoic acid?" he countered.

"We're learning more every day," said Dr. Vincent. "And you will, too."

That answer was just too pat. "How am I going to learn if I can't remember anything?"

Dr. Vincent had an answer for that, too. "We'll give you a substitute memory."

"A substitute?"

"That's right. You're going to carry a small notebook, and it will tell you what transpired earlier in the day and in previous days, as well as things you'll need to remember to do later."

"I don't do notebooks."

"Then just one sheet of paper. The important thing is that you'll have a written record of what you've done and what you need to do. You're going to be discharged soon, and your notes or your sheet of paper will be your surrogate memory. I've also made arrangements for your follow-up care in Boston." He handed Barnes an appointment card. "You'll be seeing Dr. Parks."

Barnes tried to imagine himself back in Boston without Elizabeth and without even a short-term memory. "How am I supposed to remember this?" he asked.

"Just look at the card."

"How am I supposed to remember I've got the card?"

"You'll write it on your list of things to do."

"How am I supposed to remember I've got *that*?"

Dr. Vincent's face wrinkled in thought. For a moment he looked past Barnes, as though searching for the answer in a far corner of the room. Then he said, perhaps more to himself, "We'll have to figure that out."

Chapter 13

The next day Dr. Vincent visited Barnes again.

"I've changed the face of your watch," he said, handing Barnes's Rolex to him.

Barnes looked at it. In bold black script on a white background it displayed the words "*Examinez votre poche droite.*"

"What have you done to my Rolex?" He had bought it less than a year ago for more than what some people pay for a new car.

"We discussed this," Dr. Vincent explained. "I changed the face to remind you to look in your right pocket."

"*Examinez votre poche droite,*" Barnes read aloud.

"It's French so other people won't know what it means, so you won't feel self-conscious."

"So I won't feel self-conscious. Wearing a Rolex watch with *this* on it?"

"Put it on."

Barnes shoved the watch onto his wrist. "I can't believe I let you do this."

"In your pants pocket you'll keep your list of reminders and things to do," said Dr. Vincent.

"Fine."

"Whenever you happen to glance at your watch, which you'll probably do every few minutes, you'll be reminded to look in your right pocket. Your list will also remind you that you have a tape recorder in your inside jacket pocket . . ." He handed a tape recorder to Barnes. ". . . for when you have things to remember that are too cumbersome to write down."

Barnes put the recorder in his lap. "When am I being discharged?"

"Soon. Maybe the day after tomorrow. We'll have to make arrangements."

Finally some good news. He had no idea the full extent of his problems, or even how long he'd been in the hospital, but right now all that mattered was getting out of there and going home. He imagined Rex bounding toward him, with Elizabeth in his wake. "I should call my wife," he said, "or is she already here?"

"Uh, about that . . ."

Dr. Vincent rebriefed Barnes on Elizabeth's murder, then resumed the conversation about going home. "You should call a relative," he said. "It would be a good idea to have someone come to the hospital to pick you up."

"I don't need an escort. I just need to get out of here." *Anything* would be better than this.

"Believe me; you'll be better off with a relative."

"You don't know my relatives."

"Then perhaps a colleague. There must be someone who would do that for you."

A colleague. Denny Houston, a fellow cardiothoracic surgeon, was his closest friend. The only question was, would Denny do that?

Later in the day, Barnes called Denny's office in Boston. Like Barnes, Houston was recognized as one of the top surgeons in the

country, and their similar skills and reputations had led to a camara-
derie. Denny had grown up in Kentucky, but he fit right in with the
East Coast surgeons, butting heads with the best of them. Barnes
had never asked him for a favor—he'd never needed to—but he
always felt Denny would go out on a limb for him, if it was important. And clearly this was important.

"Hey, buddy," Houston said when he heard Barnes's voice over
the phone. "How the hell are you?" The melody of his Louisville
drawl filled Barnes with a sense of well-being.

"Okay. I'm getting out tomorrow." Barnes was reading a note
he had written to himself. "Looking forward to going home."

"Me, I'd rather be in Miami this time of year, but I know what
you mean."

"Yeah. Listen. I thought, since Elizabeth can't be here, maybe
you could fly over and we can ride into town together."

"Like to, Chris, but you know patients get pissed off when you
tell 'em their bypass or balloon angioplasty has to be rescheduled,
and if they die while they're waiting on you, everybody and their
uncle sues. I've been picking up the slack with your patients, and it's
a bitch getting everything done. Besides, knowing how unpredict-
able the weather is this time of year, it'd be just my luck to get stuck
in Toronto in a blizzard."

"Yeah, well, can you at least meet me in Boston at the airport?"

"Sure thing. When?"

Barnes had the itinerary in front of him. "Two twenty-nine
p.m. Air Canada flight eight-o-five. The day after tomorrow."

"I'll be there . . . You know, considering what you've been
through, you sound damn good."

"Yeah, well . . ." No point discussing the extent of his damage.
". . . it's been unpleasant, to say the least. I can't wait to get the hell
out of here. It feels as though I've been gone for ages."

"Well, you have been. Hey, buddy, I gotta go. I'm backing up the OR."

"All right. I'll see you at the airport."

"You betcha."

"Thanks. And thanks for calling."

"You called *me*, Chris. Take it easy, buddy."

Barnes hung up. Only then did he realize the futility of having anyone meet him at the airport. His car would be parked there, and even though he couldn't remember where, he wasn't going to leave it behind. Maybe he and Denny could look for it together. They could have a drink at the airport bar—talk about old times or current events over a beer—and then go driving around the parking lot.

Denny will help you through this, he assured himself. *All you have to do is ask.*

And the more he thought about it, the more he realized he would need at least a *little* help adjusting to life without Elizabeth and getting through the day without being able to remember anything from one minute to the next. There's no shame in turning to a friend for a leg up.

You can count on Denny, he told himself.

He hoped that was true.

Chapter 14

Twenty-two days after his admission to Toronto General, Barnes walked out of the hospital, unassisted. He took a taxi to the airport and boarded Air Canada flight 805 with a mix of relief and uncertainty. Deep down he sensed that everything would be better once he got home, yet he also knew that Elizabeth had been murdered—he'd relearned this from Dr. Vincent in the morning—and he knew from the list in his pocket that two policemen would meet him at Boston's Logan Airport to question him about her.

He sat in the business-class section of an Airbus A319, thankful that the seat next to him remained vacant. Once the plane reached its cruising altitude, the flight attendants moved about the cabin, serving beverages and snacks. Barnes felt tempted to order a drink, but he reminded himself that if he started, he would quickly lose count.

He put down his tray table as a flight attendant came to him with a plate of cheese and crackers. Despite not having an appetite, he ate anyway. Periodically he glanced at his watch to see the time, and when he did, the inscription prompted him to look in his right pocket. Occasionally the inscription alone was sufficient to remind him about the list, but usually he didn't remember until after pulling it out and looking at it. Written across the top was the date, and across the bottom the words *RETURN TO RIGHT POCKET*.

His list currently consisted of ten items:

1) Elizabeth murdered on 11/26. Rex killed too.
2) You're flying from Toronto to Boston—ticket in jacket pocket.
3) Police will meet you at the airport re Elizabeth.
4) Denny Houston will be at airport.
5) You checked one suitcase, blue herringbone.
6) Dr. Vincent (psych) has arranged follow-up beginning tomorrow at 2:00 at Boston Riverside Hospital Clinic with Dr. Jeremy Parks (617-555-3948).
7) You've lost your short-term memory. Try to remember things as images, but don't expect to recall them after more than a few minutes.
8) Get a handicapped parking sticker.
9) You've quit smoking. Don't start again.
10) There's a tape recorder in your inside suit-jacket pocket. Put a check mark here_____ if additional messages are there.

He read the list again, unaware that he'd looked at it only ten minutes earlier but knowing that Elizabeth had been murdered.

You're flying to Boston. Elizabeth is dead. Denny will meet you at the airport. Elizabeth is dead. You've quit smoking. Elizabeth is dead.

His other notes said she'd been killed in their house with a firearm, but they didn't provide any details—where in the house she'd been killed, what she'd been doing, where anatomically she'd been shot. His mind filled in the blanks, forming multiple images of the murder. He pictured her in the foyer, the living room, the kitchen, and the master bedroom, wearing a business suit, scrubs, an oversize T-shirt, and nothing at all. Each time, covered with blood.

Despite needing to remember, he tried to forget. Yet he couldn't stop forming mental images. As one left, another took its place, a variation on a theme. Regardless of how much he tried not to envision it, Elizabeth's death stayed with him.

He concentrated on the other items in his list. Number ten didn't have a check mark beside it, so there was no point in taking out his tape recorder to listen for a message, but he did pat his jacket pocket to be sure it was there. It was smaller than a deck of cards.

He turned his thoughts to his impending arrival home. According to his list, Denny would be meeting him at the airport. The two of them didn't socialize much—they were both too busy—but they talked frequently in the surgeons' lounge, and they'd been colleagues for nearly a decade. Denny was the closest thing Barnes had to a best friend.

He pictured Denny in the surgeons' lounge, smoking a cigarette between operations. The entire hospital was officially nonsmoking, but the administration had made the surgeons' lounge an exception after a few heavyweights like Denny and Barnes had pressured them into it. Some of the other surgeons had complained, but they'd been told to live with it.

Another image suddenly came to mind. It was a small cup, translucent plastic, half-filled with something yellow. Urine. Barnes sensed he'd seen this image before. The surroundings appeared indistinct, yet the cup stood out like a focal point. As the image sharpened, an odor of ammonia filtered through his memory.

"Coffee, sir?" It was a flight attendant, an older woman with wire-rimmed glasses and streaks of gray in her hair.

The image of the plastic cup vanished. Barnes folded his list and turned to her. "Yes, thanks. Two creams, no sugar."

She poured his coffee on her server and transferred the cup to his tray table. Then she accidentally dropped one of the two small creamer containers into his lap. It hadn't been opened, but the sight of it falling startled him. Acting on reflex, Barnes grabbed it, jarring his tray table and nearly spilling his coffee.

"I'm very sorry, sir," the flight attendant apologized.

In his left hand, Barnes held his folded list, and, distracted, he thrust it into his inside suit-coat pocket rather than his right pants pocket where it belonged. "No harm done," he replied, then turned his attention to his coffee.

The nonstop flight was scheduled to take an hour and a half, but air-traffic control put the plane in a holding pattern over Boston. While they circled, Barnes became increasingly drowsy and eventually, despite the coffee, fell asleep. He awoke only as the tires jolted on the runway. Startled, he looked left and right to get his bearings. Where was he? An airplane, obviously. He leaned over and looked out the window. Nothing but gray runways and, in the distance, a control tower. He could be anywhere.

The hands on his watch pointed to 2:47. Behind them the words *Examinez votre poche droite* jumped out at him. The missing original face had no doubt been worth more than $1,000. He must have had a good reason for replacing it. *Examinez votre poche droite.*

He looked in his right pocket. Empty. He tried the left. That, too, was empty.

The collar of his shirt suddenly felt tight, and his heartbeat pulsated in his temples. What was he doing on an airplane? Where was he, and where had he come from? He didn't even know what day it was.

A scene took shape in his mind: a heaping bowl of mussels on a white tablecloth in a fancy hotel restaurant. Another memory supplanted it—a beautiful blonde woman, naked, standing in a doorway.

Toronto, he remembered. He'd been in her room, or she'd been in his. Naked. What had he done?

He suddenly realized he was hyperventilating. If he kept it up, he might pass out in his seat.

Slow, deep breaths, he told himself. *Don't think about Toronto.* It seemed like a long time ago. Everything seemed like a long time ago. Was that where he was coming from? He had no idea.

"Welcome to Boston's Logan International Airport," a female flight attendant announced over the loudspeaker, "where the local time is two fifty p.m. Please remain in your seats with your seatbelts fastened until we've finished taxiing and have arrived safely at the gate."

Barnes couldn't even remember whether he had any bags. He searched his pants pockets again and looked around in his seat, on the floor, and in the aisle, in case whatever he needed had fallen out of his pocket.

Regardless of where he'd come from, this must be his final destination. When you live in Boston and your plane lands in Boston, that means you're going home. Hurriedly he stood up and opened the overhead compartment. Pushing aside jackets and coats, he looked for a familiar piece of luggage, ignoring the cramping and aching in his legs. He remembered none of the repeated sessions of physical therapy to get his strength back after being bedridden. All he knew was that his muscles felt weak and his joints arthritic.

"Please remain seated, sir," said an unfamiliar flight attendant, an older woman with wire-rimmed glasses and streaks of gray in her hair. "The captain hasn't turned off the seatbelt light."

He sat down, too anxious to argue. The seatbelt sign stayed illuminated like a red light at rush hour, indifferent to his urgency. He stared at the sign and waited until the light went off. Then he jumped back out into the aisle and searched the overhead compartments. He found his carry-on bag and pulled it down. With a little luck, it would have his itinerary and something that might jog his memory. He rummaged through it as passengers filed by.

No itinerary. No claim ticket for checked luggage. Not even a boarding pass. These things must be *somewhere*.

He upended the bag and dumped the contents onto his seat. A shaving kit, assorted papers and journals from work, a throwaway novel, and other clutter, but still nothing to indicate where he'd come from and whether he had any baggage to claim.

Don't panic, he told himself. *Get a grip*.

"May I help you?" It was another flight attendant.

He didn't even acknowledge her. The itinerary or ticket—where could they be? If one of them didn't turn up somewhere, he would leave. After all, he lived here. If he was supposed to go on to some other destination, he could always catch another flight.

Then another thought occurred to him—his overcoat; maybe the ticket was in one of those pockets. He pulled it out of the overhead compartment and turned the pockets inside out. Nothing except gloves. He searched his other pockets again. Front pants, back pants, shirt, jacket.

Jacket. There it was! The receipt of his ticket, a baggage claim check, and the stub of a boarding pass. Also, a folded sheet of paper. He unfolded it and started reading.

Elizabeth murdered on 11/26.

His hand shook, but he kept reading. *Rex killed too.*

"May I help you?" A flight attendant.

He turned to her. "No, I'm fine."

But he wasn't fine. *Nothing* was fine. And it probably never would be. Elizabeth was dead. Murdered!

He finished skimming through the list. Number seven told him he'd lost his short-term memory. That explained the confusion.

What a disaster; he wasn't going to be able to remember *anything*. How was he supposed to function like that? Already he'd been seriously confused, and he hadn't even stepped off the plane! How was he supposed to live in the real world when he couldn't complete a nonstop flight without major complications?

He returned the list to his right pants pocket, then shoved his belongings back into the carry-on bag and picked up his overcoat.

Just go home, he told himself. *Walk out of the airplane, get in your car, and drive home. You've done it a hundred times. How hard can it be?*

He had no idea.

Chapter 15

Denny Houston waited just beyond the row of customs officials that separated the arriving international travelers from the
general public. A tall man who'd played forward on his college bas-
ketball team, he peered over the heads of passersby in an attempt
to spot Barnes. A prominent jaw and muscular build gave him an
athletic demeanor, while gray hair mixed in with his natural sandy
color lent him an air of maturity.

As Barnes cleared customs with his luggage, he and Houston
locked gazes. Like two men on a mission, they strode toward each
other.

"Hey, buddy." Houston held out a large hand, and Barnes
grasped it.

"Damn good to see you, Denny."

At that moment two plainclothes policemen approached,
badges displayed.

"Dr. Barnes?" one of them queried, a taller man with dirty-
blond hair and a no-nonsense demeanor.

Barnes stopped in his tracks. "Yes." Moments earlier he'd been
reminded from his list that the police intended to question him, but
still they caught him off guard.

"Dr. Barnes," the same man continued, "I'm Detective Wright, and this is Detective Gould. We'd like to take you downtown to ask a few questions."

"Horse shit," said Houston. "He just got here."

"What's this about?" Barnes asked as Wright took him by the arm.

"It's about your wife."

"Talk to his lawyer," said Houston. "Dr. Barnes is with me, and I'm taking him home."

"Back off," said Gould, putting a hand on Houston's chest and pushing him back.

"It's okay," Barnes said to Houston. "I want to talk with them."

"As soon as you step off the plane?"

"Whatever it takes."

Houston remained where he was as the police whisked Barnes away. "Call me later, Chris," he yelled after them, "and tell them you want a lawyer."

Those words lingered in Barnes's mind. *Tell them you want a lawyer.*

"Do you have all your luggage, Doctor?" Detective Gould asked. He was a meaty man who looked like the type not to waste words, and he struck Barnes as an unlikely partner for the other detective.

"I'll have to check." He couldn't recall, but his watch reminded him of the list in his pocket.

Number five—luggage. "One suitcase." Now that he thought about it, he could also have verified that from his baggage-claim receipt.

The three of them walked in silence toward the main security checkpoint. As they approached that line, beyond which only ticketed passengers or people with special permission were permitted, Barnes noticed television camera crews and half a dozen reporters.

"There he is!" announced a brunette he recognized from the local evening news.

The two detectives flanked Barnes to isolate him from the reporters.

"How does it feel to be back, Dr. Barnes?" asked the anchorwoman.

Before he could respond, another reporter asked, "Can you tell us anything about your wife?"

"What would you like to say to her killer?" a third added.

Barnes kept walking. The throng followed, inundating him with questions, but he responded with only silence.

"What do the police want to know?" a reporter shouted to him over the din.

Detective Gould answered that one. "The police want to know why you people don't got nothing better to do."

"Let us do our job and talk to Dr. Barnes," said Detective Wright. "Then we'll issue a statement."

Barnes was looking past the reporters. Something had caught his attention—a woman with her back to him. She was seated in a wrought-iron chair, alone at a table outside one of the airport restaurants along an intersecting concourse. From across the expanse, she looked like Elizabeth. Same size, same shade of brown hair cut in a bob. Even the same type of clothes—nondescript shoes, jeans, and a sweater with the sleeves shoved up. In one hand she held a paperback book, in the other a Styrofoam cup. Tea, maybe. Elizabeth would have had tea.

Barnes felt the urge to head down the concourse to get a closer look, to see her face, but he knew that would be a mistake. The woman couldn't possibly be Elizabeth and, up close, would look nothing like her. Confirming that would only heighten the sense of loss. Better to cling to the fantasy than to satisfy any curiosity.

He turned to the tall detective. "Let's get out of here."

Chapter 16

Barnes's ticket from the parking machine indicated the short-term garage, and the detectives cruised up and down the rows looking for a silver Mercedes. By the time they found it, he could no longer recall how long they'd been searching.

Under the eye of the detectives, he slid into the driver's seat and pulled the door closed. Doing that shut out not only the cold but also the uncertainty. The Mercedes was more than just a car; it was part of the orderly world he had left behind. Now he was reclaiming it. His normal life. The car even smelled normal. A lingering odor of cigarette smoke permeated the air. That took him aback. The car must have been sitting there for days, maybe weeks. He hadn't expected to smell anything. Even stranger, the odor didn't cause a craving, and he obviously hadn't just finished a cigarette; there was no taste of it in his mouth. He wouldn't have believed anyone if they'd told him, but the evidence was clear: he had quit smoking. Elizabeth would have been pleased.

He followed the detectives out of the airport to the Sumner Tunnel, where traffic funneled toward the one-way passage. Near the tunnel's entrance, clogged roads intersected and converged on numerous tollbooths before merging into only two lanes. The cars edged forward so slowly that Barnes had time to read the inscription on a large metal plaque mounted on concrete by the right-hand side of the road. It was dedicated to Enrico Fermi, who had played a key role in the Manhattan Project and had been awarded a Nobel Prize in Physics. After coming to America from Italy in the late 1930s, he'd lived in New York and then Chicago. Never Boston.

A likeness of the man's face looked out at the gridlock, and Barnes couldn't help but feel a connection, returning to a world different from the one he'd left. If the real Enrico Fermi had been standing there in the cold, breathing in exhaust fumes, he surely would have asked himself, "Where am I, and what on earth is going on here?"

Barnes paid a forty-cent toll and worked his way to the opening of the tunnel. At the entrance, he passed beneath two cement angels. He'd always liked driving under them, heading into the heart of the city through the grand gateway. Although built in the 1930s, the tunnel had been renovated in the 1960s, and now panels of painted steel covered the cement walls—glossy white with two horizontal stripes of blue, the color of the ocean above. Along the top of each wall, a wide tube of fluorescent light ran the entire length of the tunnel. For most of that, the ceiling was the same glossy white as the walls, and innumerable taillights reflected in shimmering streaks of red along its surface. A tunnel of red, white, and blue. Fitting colors for a city that had played a key role in the American Revolution.

Barnes reflected on this as he edged forward. He also reflected on the amount of time he had spent over the years, during numerous trips from the airport, sitting in traffic along this stretch of road. The speed limit signs of thirty-five miles per hour were a waste of taxpayer money. He could push a hospital gurney faster than they were going.

On the other side of the tunnel, he drove into Government Center. A film of ice and oily water covered the streets, and snow dusted the grass and rooftops. Soon the salt air would turn everything to slush, and the city would change from white to dirty gray. Winters in Boston were usually drab. Still, he felt relieved to be in familiar surroundings, no matter what the weather. Brick buildings dirty with soot, jaywalkers dodging traffic, even orange cones marking road construction—all seemed to welcome him home.

He felt the urge to drive around, zigzagging through the bustle of Chinatown, stately Beacon Hill, and the quaint North End. Boston had everything—the best sports, the best seafood, the best universities and hospitals. Even the best art, and the most unusual, including the largest copyrighted piece of artwork in the world— the 140-foot-high, painted fuel storage tank near the southeast expressway. The abstract rainbow of colors concealed what appeared to be a profile of Ho Chi Minh, although the artist, Corita Kent, claimed the design simply represented hope, uplifting, and spring. Spring was now a long way off, but Barnes did feel uplifted driving past that storage tank.

On the way through town, he tried to recall any recent events. He vaguely remembered driving through the Sumner Tunnel, and he remembered that Elizabeth had been murdered, but everything else from his recent memory seemed to have vanished. Then the face of a man emerged. Broad, almost bloated, with dark hair plastered over a bald spot. The visage smiled—a friend, Barnes guessed, maybe from his hospitalization. He remembered a polyester tie. Then another odd image came to mind—a picture of Kermit the Frog eating a red ball.

At the next traffic light, Barnes turned right. That was the way to get onto Storrow Drive, to go home. Deep down he sensed there was something else he needed to do, some sort of errand, but the nature of it escaped him.

Tires screeched a short distance behind his Mercedes, and in the rearview mirror an unmarked police car swerved into view, a red light flashing on its roof. The car had cut across the intersection he'd just left. Barnes pulled over to let it pass.

But the car didn't pass. Instead it stopped behind him, the red light still flashing, and a man who looked unfamiliar stepped out of the driver's side. Barnes didn't think he'd been speeding, and he'd driven this road enough times to be sure he hadn't made an illegal turn. Could this have something to do with Elizabeth's death? That would explain why the police car was unmarked and the officer wasn't wearing a uniform. Barnes didn't know much about police policy, but he knew it was irregular for a policeman out of uniform to stop someone in traffic. Were they legally allowed to do that?

He lowered his window as the officer approached.

"Dr. Barnes," the policeman said, "I think you may have forgotten where you're going. Do you know where you're going?"

He wondered how the man knew his name. "Home?"

The policeman shook his head, then took out a badge. "I'm Detective Wright. Does that ring a bell?"

"No. Do I know you?"

"We met at the airport. You *do* remember you're coming from the airport."

"Right. The airport." That would explain his suitcase on the passenger's seat.

"You were following me to the police station when you took a wrong turn back there." The detective paused, as if expecting an answer.

Barnes glanced down at his watch: *Examinez votre poche droite.* He reached into his right pocket and took out his list. "Just a second." He unfolded it and read through the items. There it was—the police had met him at the airport. A snapshot of the event formed in his mind. Real or imagined, he wasn't sure, but it seemed real.

"Dr. Barnes," the detective continued, "how about if I ride with you, and Detective Gould follows us?"

Barnes put the list back into his right pants pocket. "Okay." He moved his suitcase to the backseat and opened the passenger-side door.

"Just go straight for now," Wright said, pulling on his seatbelt. "Then take your first right."

"Uh-huh." Barnes put the car into gear. "To the police station?"

"That's right."

"Okay. Sure." Then he asked, "Why are we going there?"

Chapter 17

When they arrived at the police station, Barnes parked his car and wrote the location on the list in his pocket. At the airport he'd already put check marks next to items two, three, and five, indicating that he'd flown from Toronto to Boston, had met the police, and had retrieved his suitcase from baggage claim. Next to item four, which read, "Denny Houston will be at airport," he'd put a check mark and had also written, "Call him later."

At the station, Detectives Wright and Gould escorted Barnes to an interrogation room. There they instructed him to sit in a folding chair at a metal table. It was a narrow table, and the detectives sitting on the opposite side seemed uncomfortably close to him in the windowless room. The place was barren, with nothing on the walls except for a large mirror to his left. Barnes figured it must be one-way glass.

"Dr. Barnes," began Detective Wright, "we'd like to ask you a few questions about your wife. We're hoping you might be able to help us with our investigation."

"Should I have an attorney?" asked Barnes.

"That's your right, of course, but all we're doing is trying to gather information that might shed some light on what happened."

"What my partner means is you don't need one unless you got something to hide," said Gould. "You don't got nothing to hide, do you?"

"No, I have nothing to hide," Barnes answered, "and I don't need the attitude. If you can't be civil with me, I'm not going to have this conversation."

Gould leaned closer. "Civil's in the eye of the beholder. Maybe you being nervous makes us seem less civil, like we're after you or something. I can see how you might think that, you being nervous and all."

"I'm not nervous. I'm annoyed." It was a lie. He'd never been questioned by the police, and who wouldn't be on edge under those circumstances?

"There's no reason to feel uncomfortable, Dr. Barnes," said Detective Wright. "We're here to help you. We understand you've had a serious medical problem, and we know it's difficult for you to remember things. We also know you're probably anxious to get home, so we won't take up much of your time."

"Fine."

"All right, then," continued Wright. "The first piece of information you can tell us is who besides you and your wife has access to the security code on your house alarm."

Barnes reached into his suit-coat pocket for a pen to jot down information and instead felt the tape recorder. Deciding that was even better, he took it out and held it in his hand on the table. "I'm going to record some of this. I want to go over it later, and this way I'll remember it."

"Go right ahead," said Wright. "Now, can you answer the question, please?"

"Just a minute." He turned on the recorder. "I'm being interrogated by Detectives . . . What are your names?"

"Wright and Gould."

"Wright and Gould." He turned off the recorder. The tape probably wouldn't last through the entire interrogation, so he would have to be selective.

"Dr. Barnes, can you answer the question?" insisted Wright.

"What question?"

Gould threw up his hands.

Wright repeated the question: "Who besides you and your wife has access to the security code of your house alarm?"

That was easy. "The maid, Carmen Rodriguez."

"Is she a legal immigrant?" asked Gould.

"I presume she is. I don't ask for work papers when someone comes to clean the house or mow the lawn. She's Mexican, about fifty years old. I think she's been in the US for years, maybe decades, but her English still isn't very good. Elizabeth and I usually speak Spanish to her."

"What's her address and phone number?" Wright asked.

Barnes didn't know her address, but he told them her number. "You haven't questioned her?" he asked.

"Yeah, we questioned her," said Gould. "She's the one that found the body."

"Oh." He envisioned Carmen happening upon Elizabeth lying in a pool of congealed blood. Probably Carmen hadn't needed to call the police; her screams would have alerted half the city.

"We're curious how much *you* know about her," Wright said. "She has the code to your security system, your wife is killed at home, and the alarm doesn't go off. Do you think she could be involved?"

Barnes dictated into the tape recorder, "The security system was disarmed or not armed when Elizabeth was murdered."

"Do you think Carmen could be involved?" Wright repeated.

"I don't think so, but I really don't know her."

"Your wife died at about nine in the evening," said Gould. "Did she usually keep the alarm off at that time?"

Barnes held the recorder to his mouth. "Elizabeth killed at nine p.m.," he dictated. Gould shot him an annoyed glance, but Barnes ignored him. He turned off the recorder and addressed Wright. "She always kept the alarm on in the evening when she was alone. It was like wearing a seatbelt. She always did it."

"So you think maybe the maid told someone the code?" asked Gould.

"I don't know. Elizabeth picked her and checked her references. She's been working for us for about eight months."

"And she got a key to the house?"

"That's right."

"Then she probably ain't our perp. Whoever broke into your house used a glass cutter on a ground-floor window."

Barnes dictated that finding.

"Tell us, Dr. Barnes," said Gould, "who would benefit the most from your wife's death?"

He shrugged. "No one that I'm aware of."

"How much was her life insurance policy worth?" asked Wright.

Barnes figured they already knew the answer to that. After all, they hadn't first asked whether she even had a policy. "I don't know exactly . . . I think it's one and a half times her annual salary." He knew the policy paid at least a few hundred thousand dollars. But it wasn't a policy he had taken out. It came as part of her employment package. Besides, it was only a fraction of her net worth.

"As a couple, would you say you were both pretty well off?" asked Wright.

"Yeah." Barnes wondered whether they knew about his sour investment in the Zeiman Richter Growth Fund. Bringing that up probably wouldn't be a good idea. He'd poured a ton of money into the purportedly low-risk, high-yield mutual fund, only to learn that the corporation operating it was embezzling and defrauding shareholders. He'd lost a fortune, thanks to Denny Houston, who'd recommended it. His only consolation was that Denny had lost even more.

"Or at least your wife was well off," said Gould. "What we want to know is, was there any financial problems you and her had that we don't know about?"

"No," Barnes answered. He wondered what else they knew. His problems stemmed from not only the Zeiman Richter Growth Fund but also from betting on sporting events. He'd never considered it a significant concern, but he'd lost more than he cared to admit.

"How was your relationship with your wife?" asked Wright.

Barnes liked this turn in the conversation even less. "What do you mean?"

"Did you ever argue?"

"Everyone argues." That came out sounding more defensive than he'd intended.

"What did *you* argue about?" asked Wright.

"Nothing in particular. Nothing important."

"You were married how long?"

"Almost five years." He thought of their upcoming anniversary. They'd talked about going back to Hawaii, to the black-sand beaches of Maui where they'd spent a solid week in paradise. Right now, he'd have given anything to be back there with her.

"Did you cheat on your wife?" Gould asked, interrupting his reverie.

The last thing Barnes wanted to do was to discuss Cheryl at the conference. His one transgression. He wished he'd forgotten her along with everything else wiped from his memory, but it seemed he'd been granted only part of that wish. He didn't remember having sex with her, only dinner, and then waking up beside her in bed. She'd been naked—that much he remembered. The police must have known she'd taken him to the hospital, and then they'd connected the dots. "My personal life is none of your business," he said.

"You're wrong about that," countered Gould. "Right now, *everything* about you is our business. We know you cheated on your wife. What we don't know is, was there anyone special, or did you just screw around?"

"The only one special was Elizabeth," he insisted. "That's why I married her."

"So you just screwed around?"

Barnes shifted uneasily in his chair. Better not to answer that.

"Do you have any idea why someone might want to kill your wife?" asked Wright. "Did she have any enemies?"

"No. Everybody liked her."

Gould eyed him skeptically. "And that includes you?"

Barnes pushed back his chair. "I'm done here."

But before he could stand up, Gould lunged across the table and grabbed his shoulder with a meaty hand. "No, you're not. Tell us why someone would want to kill your wife."

Barnes just sat there. What else could he do? He wondered how he'd gotten into this situation.

"Please answer the question," Wright said politely. "You must have some idea."

"I don't," was all he could say.

Gould settled back in his seat. "Why'd you have an affair?" he said. "We know you spent the night with some hottie at your conference."

"I don't know."

"You don't seem to know very much, do you?"

What the hell do you want? Barnes thought. "Look, it just happened. Once. One time. Maybe I had too much wine with dinner. I really don't know. It just happened. I wish I could take it back, but obviously I can't."

"Well, it works both ways," said Gould. "You know that, don't you?"

"What are you talking about?"

"I'm talking about someone pinch-hitting with your wife."

"What?"

"Dr. Barnes," said Wright, "we have compelling evidence that your wife was having an affair."

"What evidence?" He clenched a fist under the table. The thought of Elizabeth with someone else . . . How could she?

Wright removed a piece of paper from a folder and slid it across the table to him.

"What's this?" Barnes asked.

"Just read it and tell us what you think," said Gould.

Barnes read the printed letter into his tape recorder:

Dear Elizabeth,

I apologize for typing this—computers are so imper-
sonal—but I'm in a lazy mood and this is easier for me.
Thoughts of you keep coming to me like butterflies at my
window. I don't know what makes that happen, but I find
myself looking forward to their visits.

Are there butterflies at your window too? I like to
think there are at least a few, and that they brighten your
day as they do mine. I know your life is complicated, with
more stress than you deserve. I hope I haven't contributed
to that by writing this letter, but I wanted to let you know
I've been thinking of you. And us. I can't tell you how
much I've enjoyed our time together and how much I look
forward to the next time I'll see you. You're a special per-
son, and I can't . . .

There was more to the letter, but Barnes couldn't go on. He put it down on the table.

"Finish it," said Gould.

"You finish it."

Gould picked it up and read:

> *You're a special person, and I can't put into words how much you mean to me. I miss holding you, being close to you, feeling your warmth. When I'm with you, nothing else matters, and I find myself looking forward to the next time, and the time after that. My life has become isolated moments in time, shared with you. The days between our meetings have little meaning; they're merely bridges from one shared moment until the next.*
>
> *Please forgive me for putting my thoughts onto paper. I can't promise not to write another letter, but I assure you I'll be discreet. I have no intention of disrupting your life; I want only to enhance it, as you've enhanced mine. I cannot thank you enough for the feelings you've aroused in me, and I cannot thank you enough for the sense of optimism that I . . .*

The letter ended there, at the bottom of the page. Gould waved the sheet of paper in front of Barnes's face.

"Where's the rest of it?" Barnes could hear his voice tremble.

"That's what we'd like to know," answered Gould.

"We found the one sheet in her purse," said Wright, "and we were wondering whether you'd taken the other page or pages."

"Whether *I* did?"

"So you don't know who wrote this?" said Gould.

"Of course not." *Elizabeth had been having an affair.* "I have no idea." *Elizabeth had been having an affair.*

"Maybe you knew but it slipped your mind," suggested Wright. "Maybe if you give it some thought, this letter will jog your memory."

Barnes wondered whether that was possible. Could he have forgotten something so important, so life altering? That seemed like forgetting you have a brother. "I have no idea," he insisted.

"Look, we know this must be difficult," said Wright, "but if there's anything you can tell us, we need to know." He put his hands on the table and leaned forward. "We wouldn't ask if it wasn't vitally important."

Barnes just shook his head. *Elizabeth had been having an affair.*

"Sometimes these things happen in even the best relationships," Wright counseled.

Barnes said nothing. He wondered how long he'd been sitting in the interrogation room. Hours? His buttocks and hamstrings ached from the chair. "I think I need a break."

"We're almost done," said Wright. "Can you tell us what you remember about the last time you saw your wife?"

He wondered whether a cigarette would help. The nicotine might sharpen his concentration. "I can't remember," he said. "Can I have a cigarette?"

"No," said Gould. "Just answer the question. When was the last time you saw your wife?"

"Probably just before I left for the airport to go to the conference," Barnes guessed, "but I don't remember much of anything even a week before then."

"That's convenient, you forgetting all that."

"There's nothing convenient about it." Why had he ever agreed to talk to this jerk?

"So you don't recall anything important that your wife told you before you left for the conference?" asked Wright. "Anything personal?"

He tried to recall his last conversation with Elizabeth. But the memory, if it existed, was buried too deep to retrieve. "No," he said.

"How about her being pregnant?" said Gould. "She told you *that*, didn't she?"

Barnes felt the blood drain from his face. "Pregnant?"

"Yeah. Were you the father?"

An image of a plastic cup of urine suddenly appeared, a translucent cup sitting on a counter beside a sink. Not just any sink—the one in his and Elizabeth's master bath. He had the feeling this wasn't the first time the image had flashed through his memory. Something about it seemed familiar. And now he also pictured something beside the cup. *A pregnancy test.*

A snippet of the memory came back to him. Elizabeth was standing beside the sink, appearing very small in an oversize T-shirt.

"I don't believe this," Barnes remembered saying. "Did you plan this?"

"No, I didn't plan it. You know I'm taking the pill."

"Don't look so surprised," Gould said, driving the scene from Barnes's mind. "She must have told you. We found two pregnancy tests in two different wastebaskets in your house, and a blood test from the body confirmed it."

"If she hadn't wanted you to know," added Wright, "she probably wouldn't have taken the tests at home, or at least she would have disposed of them more discreetly. Since she died on her first evening back from Toronto, and since those urine tests are supposed to be more accurate when you use them first thing in the morning, we have to assume she took one or both of the tests before you left for the conference."

Barnes dictated into the recorder, "Elizabeth died just after returning from visiting me in the hospital. She was pregnant, and the police say I knew about it."

"Why didn't you want her to be pregnant?" Wright asked.

"What are you talking about?" Barnes wiped sweat from the palms of his hands onto his pants.

"You told us ten minutes ago you never wanted to have children." Wright and Gould exchanged glances.

Barnes just sat there. He couldn't believe he'd shared that with them. He'd never even told Elizabeth that. "Later" or "someday," he'd always said.

"Why didn't you want her to be pregnant?" Wright repeated.

"I . . . I never said that."

"Yes, you did," Gould alleged. "You said it sure as we're sitting here. What've you got against kids?"

"Nothing."

They just sat there, as if waiting for a better answer, or more of an answer.

"Elizabeth and I weren't planning on having children anytime soon," Barnes explained. "Not with our careers in full swing. We discussed it, and we decided to wait. That's what we agreed."

The detectives stared silently at him. Barnes looked from one to the other.

"We *both* agreed," he added.

Wright and Gould nodded, as if in understanding. But Barnes knew there was more to it than that.

He had just become their prime suspect.

Chapter 18

Wright and Gould left Barnes alone in the interrogation room while they decided what to do. They left a note with him—*Back in 5 minutes. Don't go anywhere.*—in case he became confused.

"He did it," said Gould, down the hall. "We just got to figure out who he used."

"We can subpoena his bank records," Wright offered, "and see if he made any large withdrawals."

"I say we go for a confession now. Squeeze it out of him."

"Even if we could," said Wright, "I doubt it'd hold up. Not with the way he is. If he can't remember anything, his lawyer's going to challenge what we're doing here. He'll say Dr. Barnes wasn't competent and wasn't aware of his rights. It's better to let him go, and see what he does."

"How about if we skip the confession and go to how he did it?"

"You mean tell him he already confessed?" asked Wright.

"Yeah. If we can get him to buy that, he'll probably cave in and give us the other guy. Then we pick up his accomplice and turn the tables."

"I really don't feel good about exploiting a disability," said Wright.

"You're too sensitive about your wife. He's not your wife. Besides, I bet if you asked her, she'd say it was a good idea."

Wright thought about that. "It's pretty underhanded, even for you. Let's play it by ear."

They headed back to the interrogation room.

Barnes sat in quiet agitation. The door to the interrogation room opened, and two men in sport coats breezed in.

"Do you remember us, Dr. Barnes?" the taller one asked.

He nodded, uncertain.

"I'm Detective Wright, and this is Detective Gould." They both sat down. "We were talking about the death of your wife. Do you remember that?"

He did, only because he'd kept rehashing it. The actual memories had disappeared, but the basic facts remained.

"Why don't you put that away?" said Gould, nodding to the tape recorder. "You don't need it here."

"I may not need it," Barnes answered, "but I'd like to use it just the same." He didn't know what they had in mind, but it couldn't be good if they were asking him not to record it.

"We wanted to ask you some more questions about your wife," Wright said. "Did anyone in the few days before your wife's murder seem upset with you or antagonistic toward you?"

"Toward *me*?" Barnes had no idea. "I can't think of anyone, but I don't remember much from around that time . . ." For a moment he tried to clear his thoughts, to see whether that might help him recall any events, but the only thing to come to mind was an image of Elizabeth dead in their bedroom. "How did you say Elizabeth died?"

"We didn't," replied Gould. "But if you want to know, she was shot point-blank with a 9mm handgun. So was your dog. You want more details?"

He didn't, but he needed to know. "Yeah, everything."

"The perp put three bullets in your wife's chest, then two in the dog."

"It happened in the front hallway," said Wright. "She may have been heading for the keypad or the front door. If she heard the intruder come through the dining room window, it would make sense that she'd try to get to the panic button. If the intruder came around the other side of the foyer, he could have gotten to her first."

Barnes repeated that into his recorder.

"Why are you taping these things?" asked Gould. "Is it so you'll know what to say the next time you get questioned?"

"No, it's so I can figure out what happened."

"How do you expect to do that? You know something we don't?"

"I know a lot you don't. I know Elizabeth and her friends and colleagues. I know the people she associated with and projects she was involved in at the hospital."

"Yeah, but you can't seem to remember anything *important*."

"All right," interjected Wright. "We're all on the same side here. Dr. Barnes, any information you can provide us would be helpful, and we'd appreciate it if you'd call us if you think of anything later. We'll give you both our cards. Now, I'd like to go over just a few more things."

Twenty minutes later Detective Wright escorted Barnes to his car. The wind had picked up, churning a frenzy of snowflakes that forced the men to squint.

"You know, there's one other thing we should think about," Wright said, shivering in the cold.

"What's that?" Barnes asked.

"You," said Detective Wright. "Someone may have killed your wife assuming you were going to be dead in a few days, and now that you're back, they may have a problem with that. Whatever motivated them to kill your wife may motivate them to come after you. I'd strongly recommend a patrol car outside your house."

"No." Barnes shook his head. "What's the point? I've got brain damage, and my wife is dead. I don't think I have a lot to lose."

They arrived at the Mercedes and stopped on the passenger side, where the car partially shielded them from the wind. Nearby, two spindly trees scratched the sky. To Barnes, they looked like lungs without air sacs, missing the basic elements crucial to function. But in a few months, they would sprout buds and their function would be restored. He wondered whether his ever would be.

"Well, call us if you change your mind," said Wright.

Barnes walked around to the driver's side of his car.

"Or if you think of anything that might give us a lead," Wright added. "We'll be in touch."

Barnes didn't say anything. He'd shifted his thoughts to trying to remember the details of Elizabeth's murder that were already slipping away. He opened the car door. Before the detective walked away, Barnes said to him, "I'd appreciate it if you'd notify me when you get a suspect."

Wright seemed to ponder that for a moment. "We'll keep you informed," he said.

Barnes doubted it.

Chapter 19

From the police station, Barnes headed home in rush-hour traffic. Horns blared, and cars cut in front of one another in attempts to gain ground. Barnes wanted no part of that. He called Denny from the road, and they decided to meet for a drink at the Ritz-Carlton. An old luxury hotel situated between Commonwealth Avenue and Newbury Street on the edge of the Boston Public Garden, the Ritz had an air of grandeur, complete with a venerable doorman dressed in a blue uniform and top hat. The bar at the hotel was the perfect place to escape the chaos of rush hour.

Leaving his car, Barnes looked east across Arlington Street, at the Public Garden. Even in the bleakness of December, the Garden beckoned to him, whispering promises it couldn't keep. The Garden held memories of Elizabeth—sitting under a weeping willow and feeding crushed crackers to ducks and pigeons, and walking at his side along the paved path, around the large pond with its paddle-driven swan boats. In the fading light, he imagined her seated on one of the empty benches. But he couldn't bring himself to cross the street and confront his sorrow. He turned his back to it and entered the hotel.

The bar was crowded, mostly with middle-aged men in sport coats, but Barnes found a small table near one wall. The pub had a staid quality, with antique sconces and dark wood. Denny was nowhere to be seen, so Barnes passed the time reviewing his list and trying to remember the events of the day. He pulled out the tape recorder and, holding it to his ear with the volume on low, listened to what he'd recorded from the police interrogation.

When Houston arrived, Barnes wasted no time in bringing up Elizabeth.

"Have you heard anything about her murder?" he asked.

"Just from the news." Houston snapped his fingers at a waitress to get her to take their drink order.

"I wonder if it had something to do with both her and me," Barnes said.

"I'm not sure I follow you, buddy."

At that point the waitress came over. After she left with their order, Barnes continued. "I wonder whether it's possible Elizabeth was killed because whoever did it thought I wasn't going to pull through and wanted both of us out of the way."

"Anything's possible." Houston ate some peanuts.

"Denny, I cheated on her."

"No point in agonizing over it—nothing you can do about it now."

Barnes felt the need to confess, even though Denny didn't seem to want to hear it. "I've never done that before, and you know I've had opportunities."

Nurses and other women flirted with him more than he cared to admit. It was always a strange feeling—both pleasing and distasteful—like a puppy licking your face. It had always been harmless. Until Cheryl.

"In the big scheme of things," said Denny, "the two of you loved each other. That's more than can be said about most couples, and that's what matters."

"I don't know what I was thinking. I met this woman I hadn't seen in a year, another cardiothoracic surgeon, and—"

"What's done is done. Don't beat yourself up."

"I can't help it. My mind's a train wreck. I still can't remember much of anything from the week before the conference, except parts of dinner with Cheryl, the woman I . . ."

"The woman you fucked."

"Yeah. It seems I fucked both of us."

"She must be one hell of a piece of eye candy if she's the only thing you remember from that whole week."

Barnes shook his head. "It figures the one thing I *do* want to forget sticks with me like a botched surgery."

"Shit happens. Forget it."

"Actually, I don't remember all of it. I remember being in bed with her afterwards, but I don't remember the sex. For whatever reason, I've blocked that out. Maybe that's for the best. I don't know why I did it. I . . . maybe I was just trying to fill some void."

"Yeah. The void between her legs."

Leave it to Denny to turn a philosophical comment into something lewd. "Anyway, I can't stop thinking about it. And about Elizabeth."

"Elizabeth was a damn good catch. No doubt about that."

The waitress returned with their drinks. Barnes had ordered a club soda, afraid alcohol might kill off his few remaining brain cells. Also he didn't want to risk losing count and drinking more scotch than he could handle.

"Here's to having you back," said Houston, raising his bourbon.

"Just like old times." Barnes picked up the club soda. He took a swig, and it fizzed unpleasantly in his mouth, then in the back of his throat. He'd never cared for club soda. "How's our research coming along?"

"The atherosclerosis study?" They'd been doing research with an antiarthritis compound that had unexpectedly been found to prevent the buildup of plaque in coronary arteries. Jarrell Pharmaceuticals was the manufacturer, and the FDA had approved the drug that past summer for the treatment of osteoarthritis. Now there seemed to be a huge new market for the drug, to prevent atherosclerosis, and if the results of their study showed what they expected, Barnes and Houston would share in the profits.

"Yeah," said Barnes. "Did you put it on hold while I was gone?"

Houston shifted in his chair. "It's going fine." He took a gulp of bourbon. "Let's talk about that in the office when I can show you the charts. What do you say we turn our attention to those two little ladies over there?" He motioned to two women sitting by themselves, sipping drinks. They appeared to be in their twenties, dressed in business suits. "Bet they'll take your mind off your troubles." Houston waved at them, and they smiled coyly.

"Some other time." Leave it to Denny to prioritize chasing skirts above discussing research.

"I'll bet they're regulars." Houston turned to Barnes. "You remember seeing them the week before your conference?"

Barnes took another drink of club soda. "No. Why would I? You and I were here then?"

"You *moved* here, buddy."

Barnes set his drink on the table before he spilled it.

"Shit." Denny downed his bourbon. "You don't remember."

"No . . . I moved here by myself?"

"Yeah, buddy. By yourself."

"So Elizabeth and I were separated?" A wave of nausea came over him.

"Yeah. Sorry to bring it up. I thought you knew. I mean, why wouldn't you? *You're* the one who moved out."

Barnes wished he had a scotch in front of him. "How long did I live here?"

"Not long. Less than a week."

"Did I tell you why?"

"No, and I didn't ask. You know me. I figured it would blow over. You and Elizabeth—I didn't see that ending."

Barnes figured he'd probably checked out of the hotel before the conference. He jotted a note to verify that at the reception desk. But the real question was, why had he checked in? One way or another, he would have to find out.

What had Elizabeth done to make him want to leave her? Somebody must know the answer to that. But then another thought came to mind—perhaps she hadn't done anything.

Maybe it was the other way around.

Chapter 20

From the Ritz, Barnes drove west, heading home to an empty house. A house without Elizabeth. The familiar streets of Copley Square offered little comfort, although the massive insurance buildings did lend a sense of permanence. His world might be collapsing around him, but nothing could budge the towering Hancock building, or even its brick predecessor reflected in the lower windows of the skyscraper, not to mention the nearby Prudential building with its rooftop lounge that offered the second highest view in the city. On a clear day, the Pru and the Hancock could be seen from as far away as the mountains of New Hampshire. Now, ironically, he was too close for a good view.

The fat antenna on top of the old Hancock building was illuminated in a blue strip, signaling clear skies. The light could shine blue or red and solid or flashing, signaling the weather to those familiar with the code.

Barnes took a detour and headed down Stoneholm Street, a short road off Boylston Street in Back Bay. Many years ago, he'd lived there, at 12 Stoneholm Street. That had been long before he'd met Elizabeth. Now he wondered whether the neighborhood had remained the same, like so much of the city. Gingko trees had lined the street . . . and there they stood, taller than he remembered but still slender, without leaves, poking sharp branches into the night. In late fall the trees turned a brilliant yellow, their leaves as bright as sunflowers. Now they looked like metal-and-wire sculptures.

Barnes passed by his old building, a renovated parking garage that had been converted to small but architecturally unique apartments with high ceilings and not-so-high rent. Seeing it was like visiting a simpler time, but it did little to ease the apprehension of his homecoming.

What are you doing here? he thought. The answer was obvious—postponing the inevitable. "Just go home," he said out loud, as if that would make the drive easier. Yet he couldn't help but think, *Home to what?*

Having made up his mind, he drove quickly. He lived in Brookline, on the east side of the suburb, near Harvard Street. From the road, his Tudor house looked dark and looming, almost like an abandoned building. Pulling into the garage, he felt a knot in his throat at the sight of Elizabeth's car. Her car in the garage meant she should be in the house, and he wanted more than anything to find her there. Maybe his memory was playing tricks on him, fooling him into believing she'd been murdered because a bizarre idea or dream had taken root and convinced him of a false reality. That was possible. Anything was possible. Yet he knew the truth, knew it even without reading through his notes. The thought of viewing the site of the slaying made his stomach turn.

Hesitantly he entered the house, stepping into the family room from the garage. He felt as though he'd been gone for years, and the place seemed eerily quiet without Rex barking and scrambling to greet him. Even the burglar alarm was silent.

Closing the door behind him, he imagined Elizabeth working in her office or cooking in the kitchen. From there she would call out to him in her British accent. But not tonight.

He hung his overcoat in the hall closet. It still held more of Elizabeth's coats than his, and he wondered which she had worn last.

In the kitchen he played back his telephone messages. The machine flashed the number *57*. The tape had run to the end, and there was no telling how many messages had been cut off.

He pushed the "Announce" button and listened to Elizabeth's voice: "Hello, this is 555-1445. We aren't available at the moment, but if you leave your name, number, and a brief message after the tone, we'll ring you as soon as we can. Thank you."

He replayed the announcement and envisioned Elizabeth as she had recorded it. He had come up behind her and kissed the side of her neck, trying to distract her and make her laugh. She'd tilted her head back, allowing him access to her throat, but at the same time, she'd remained focused, even when he pulled her blouse out of her skirt and ran his hands across the smooth flesh of her abdomen.

She had almost started laughing at the "we'll ring you"—when Chris blew into her ear—but she managed to retain her composure until after releasing the "Record" button. Then she pounced on him, and they made love right there in the kitchen, on a throw rug near the sink.

Barnes played the announcement a third time. It was the closest he would ever get to hearing Elizabeth again.

He looked at his watch: *Examinez votre poche droite.* Right pocket. That led him to the list. Item ten on the list led him to the tape recorder. He pushed the "Play" button.

His own voice came from the small speaker, but it was like listening to someone else. This was a dictation taken during a police interrogation. At a police station! When had he been there, and where else had he gone? The fire department? The zoo? The space shuttle? This was ridiculous. He had forgotten the entire event. How can you forget a police interrogation? He'd have to start taking better notes, and he'd have to review them more frequently.

On a clean sheet of paper, he transcribed the tape, relearning the unsettling news about Elizabeth's affair with a mystery lover, and relearning that she'd been pregnant. Had her lover been the father? Most likely. At some point he would have to find and confront the son of a bitch. Who knows where that might lead? Maybe to Elizabeth's killer.

He turned his attention to the fifty-seven messages on his answering machine. With a little luck, one of them would offer some insight into what had happened. He began listening to them, or at least to parts of all of them. Salesmen pitching products, colleagues and relatives sending condolences, even a couple of wrong numbers. Those messages that merited a reply, he jotted down on a piece of paper. Many of the names he recognized, including Shirley Collins and Claire Simmons. Friends of Elizabeth's.

Shirley had a PhD in medical microbiology and immunology and had recently been promoted to associate professor in that department. Barnes didn't know her well, but he knew she and Elizabeth had worked together and had been friends for years. They often met for lunch, and the two had planned to share royalties on a patent involving specially coated screws in orthopedic surgery. The screws promoted rapid healing of damaged bone around sites where they were used to hold plates or rods in place. Fractures healed in as little as half the usual time, thanks to the coating—a solution of gallium, a bisphosphonate, and fluoride, or GBF-complex. Shirley had proposed the initial research and had included Elizabeth on the patent because Elizabeth had coordinated and helped conduct the clinical trials required for FDA approval. The results of their studies had been so compelling that GBF-complex coating would likely soon become the treatment of choice for all orthopedic procedures involving the placement of plates, rods, and other foreign objects for the stabilization of fractures. With that, of course, would come both prestige and money. Elizabeth would still get the prestige, but now her half of the money would go to him.

At the moment, money seemed unimportant. Barnes would have traded any amount, even his house, just to spend a few minutes with Elizabeth. Instead, he would have to settle for her friends. They would be a poor substitute but worth contacting, if for no other reason than to learn more about Elizabeth.

Shirley had left three messages, all asking him to call her. Claire Simmons had left two. Claire was an attorney friend of Elizabeth's who handled many of Elizabeth's legal affairs and had a power of attorney in the event anything happened to both Elizabeth and Chris. In the message, Claire asked him to call her when he got a chance. Her specialty was criminal law rather than tax law, but Elizabeth had trusted her with anything related to the legal profession. He made a note to call her, then pressed the "Play" button again on his answering machine.

The last message to record began. "Hello, I'm calling for Dr. Elizabeth Barnes. You—" And then the tape ran out.

You what? thought Barnes. *You are in danger? You don't know me? You have been selected to win a free pint of Ben and Jerry's ice cream?* The message could have been anything. Vitally important or utterly irrelevant. He would never know. Nor would he know how many others hadn't been recorded. But there was nothing to be done about that.

He looked at his notes. Of the fifty-seven calls, he felt compelled to return only two: Shirley's and Claire's. He would do that in a few minutes, after organizing his notes and trying to minimize the likelihood of misplacing or losing them. The notes would be crucial, his only means of linking thoughts from one day to the next, or even one hour to the next. Losing them would be like losing his mind, literally. At least part of it—his connection to the recent past.

With a notepad, pen, and Scotch tape in hand, he walked around the house, posting messages in many of the rooms, in places where they would be readily noticed. Most he taped to the inside of doors, including his home office and Elizabeth's home office. On each sheet of paper, he wrote the same thing: "Read the notes on the refrigerator!" He even added this message to the list in his pocket. On the refrigerator he taped most of his notes regarding Elizabeth and anything else of importance, including his interrogation with the police, and the telephone messages to be returned.

Then he called Shirley. The last time he'd spoken to her was early November, and then only long enough to pass the phone to Elizabeth. They had gotten together for dinner in October, and it hadn't gone well. Shirley had insisted on sitting in a nonsmoking section. She complained that otherwise smoke permeated her clothes and irritated her eyes. Her boyfriend at the time—hopefully ex by now—was a self-centered research scientist with a myriad of annoying personality traits, including pointing his fork at people when he spoke.

Shirley picked up on the first ring. Barnes recognized her hello and formed a mental image of the woman: early thirties with sharp features but dimples when she smiled. She had shoulder-length blonde hair, and blue eyes that seemed to take in everything.

"Hi, Shirley. Chris Barnes."

"Chris." That single word conveyed both familiarity and sympathy. "How are you? *Where* are you?"

"Hanging in there. I'm back in Boston."

"Back in Boston—that's pretty incredible, considering what you've been through. How are you holding up?"

"To tell you the truth, I'm not sure. It's . . . difficult."

"Everything has been so horrible, but I'm so glad you're back. If there's anything I can do to help . . . Correction: *when* there's anything I can do to help, just let me know."

"Thanks. I appreciate that. At the moment, I'm just trying to sort things out."

"I can imagine. Actually that's not true—I really can't imagine. It must be overwhelming. And so unfair."

Her attempt at empathy sounded genuine. Barnes knew his own was sometimes lacking. "I understand what you're going through," he would tell patients, but of course he didn't understand. It was just something he said. Well, not anymore. The next time a patient or a patient's family suffered a loss or setback, he would offer more than platitudes.

"Yeah," he agreed finally. "Life is unfair."

"But look at you—you're here. The newspapers said you weren't going to make it, that you weren't going to come out of your coma, and then that you'd lost your memory. But here you are, and you sound great."

"I guess it could be worse."

"Ever the optimist, still, I see. We'll have to work on that."

"Yeah, good luck."

"How's your memory? Is that improving?"

He jotted a note to himself that she had asked. "It's um . . . not good."

"That must be frustrating."

"It is."

"But the fact that we're talking means you can still hold a conversation."

"Yeah, but you're pretty easy to talk to. Tell me something—what do you know about Elizabeth, about how she died?"

"Just what I've read in the papers. The last time I saw her was the day before she went to visit you in Canada. She stopped by the office for just a minute or two."

Barnes wrote that down. "How did she seem? Was anything troubling her?"

"Not that I noticed. She was the same as ever. Chris, this came as a complete shock to me. I can't believe anyone would want to hurt her. She was—" Her voice broke off and then became husky, as if she was choking back tears. "Everyone loved her."

"Yeah, I know. I can't even remember the last time I saw her. It must have been the morning I left for the conference, but I can't remember." An image of Cheryl came to mind. Naked. He pushed the thought away and concentrated on Elizabeth. "Do you remember any of your discussions with her that day or the day before?"

"I'm not sure; it's been a few weeks now. My memory of conversations is pretty bad. I've always been more visually oriented than verbally. I don't recall anything specific that she said, although I still remember what she was wearing."

"Well, I don't think her clothes are going to tell us anything," said Barnes, "but if there's anything else you can think of, anything Elizabeth may have said or done, it might help us figure out why someone killed her."

"Believe me; I've racked my brain. But everything was just so ordinary. I really don't think anything was troubling her."

"Well, if you do think of something, let me know."

"You'll be the first. I promise." Then she changed the subject. "Did you just get back today?"

"Yeah." His notes were fanned out in front of him.

"Have you made any plans for this evening? Is anyone keeping you company?"

"No." *Not even the dog*, he thought.

"You do *not* want to be alone your first day back. Have you had dinner?"

"No." At least not that he could recall.

"I'll bring something. What would you like?"

Having company sounded infinitely better than spending an evening alone in an empty house, haunted by visions of his wife's murder. "How about Chinese? We can order it from here."

"I can pick it up on my way over," she offered, and she asked him his favorite Chinese restaurant. "Give me about forty-five minutes," she told him.

"I'll make a note of it." He wrote as he spoke. *Shirley—dinner (Chinese) here at 8 p.m.*

"See you soon," she said.

"Yeah. I'll try not to forget."

As he hung up the phone, he sensed this was the first good thing to happen all day.

Chapter 21

After talking to Shirley, Barnes called Claire Simmons.

"How are you doing?" she asked.

"Okay." He'd never met her, but they'd spoken a few times on the phone, and he recognized her voice. If they ever did meet, that would spare him the embarrassment of having to keep asking who she was. "I'm fine," he added.

"Somehow I doubt that. Nobody could go through what you've experienced and be fine." Her voice was soft and breathy. Barnes always thought that if she ever found herself out of work as an attorney, she could get a job talking on the phone.

"It's been a little rough," he admitted. "I'd like to thank you for the work you did on the estate and funeral and everything else."

"You're welcome. It was the least I could do. I'd like to get together with you sometime to discuss things, whenever you feel up to it."

"Maybe tomorrow." He looked at his list. No plans yet. "We could meet for lunch and then go to the cemetery, if you don't find that too morbid. I'd like to visit Elizabeth."

"That works for me. I'd like to visit her, too." She gave him her number at the office, and he jotted it down. "Chris, I know we've never met, but Elizabeth and I were very close, and I know she would want me to do whatever I can to help. If you need *anything*, legal or otherwise, I want you to call me. Anytime."

"All right."

"How is your memory?" she asked.

Was everyone asking him that? Shirley had posed the same question, according to his notes.

"It's not what it used to be." He wrote down that she'd asked. "But if you don't mind, I'd rather talk about Elizabeth. Can you tell me the last time you saw her?"

"The last time?" She paused. "I don't remember exactly. It would have been sometime in mid-November."

"Mid-November." Barnes jotted that down. "Do you remember the conversation?"

"No, I really don't. Usually we just talked, not about anything in particular. You know, just conversations."

"Can you tell me anything about the circumstances of her death?"

"All I know is what I've read in the newspaper. I can't imagine who would do such a thing."

"I can't, either." He looked at the note regarding his interrogation. Elizabeth had been having an affair. He wanted to ask Claire whether she knew anything about that, but it was too humiliating to bring up, even over the phone. "The police may suspect me," he offered instead. "I'm not sure. They questioned me downtown. I have notes, but I don't actually remember what happened."

"Were you by yourself?"

"I believe so."

"Did they offer to let you call an attorney?"

"I don't know. I don't remember."

"Well, some of them make everyone feel like a suspect. I would think that what they were doing was actually in your best interests, but arguably they violated your rights since it's possible you weren't aware throughout the interview that you could contact an attorney. If they want to question you again, you should call me. Will you remember that?"

"I'll make a note of it." He added that to his list.

Then Claire asked, "Also, as long as I'm offering legal services, I should ask, do you have disability insurance?"

"Yes, fortunately. I never thought I'd need it."

"I'd be happy to take a look at your policy. I know the legal jargon can be daunting."

"Thanks. I'll let you know."

"And do tell me if the company gives you the runaround."

"I will." He hoped that wouldn't be necessary. "Oh, before I forget, was there anything Elizabeth tried to tell you before she died, anything that might have been important or unusual or controversial? Anything out of the ordinary?"

Claire didn't hesitate before answering. "No, Chris. There really wasn't. From what I can recall, she seemed the same as ever the last time we spoke. Her death came as a complete shock to me. I still can't believe it. It's like a living nightmare. I keep hoping I'll wake up and she'll be back, and every once in a while I think I catch a glimpse of her on the street or in a store or in a car. I don't want to believe she's really gone. You probably don't need to hear this from me, but I just can't stop thinking about it, about her. Who would do such a thing?"

"I don't know, but I'd sure like to find out." He wrote down that she had no ideas about what had happened to Elizabeth. "You'll call me and tell me if you think of anything later?" he asked.

"Of course. And if there's *anything* I can do, don't hesitate to ask."

Probably Shirley had said the same thing. According to his notes, she'd offered to help.

"I'll keep that in mind," he said, although right now the only thing he seemed to be able to keep there for any length of time was Elizabeth—the fact that someone had murdered her. *Who would do such a thing?*

He hung up and thought about the types of friends and colleagues Elizabeth had. He really should have found the time and made the effort to get to know them better, but he'd always been so wrapped up in his career and surgeries, and any free time that he could get with Elizabeth was time he didn't want to share with her friends. From what little he could tell, they all seemed genuine. Still, when push came to shove, he wondered whether any of them would really help him.

Chapter 22

As Claire hung up the phone, a flood of memories washed over her. All were of Elizabeth. The two of them had spent nine months together at MIT, their third year in college, when Elizabeth had participated in an exchange program. They'd been roommates at MIT Student House, a coed living group. Claire had lived there since her freshman year. A renovated mansion built around the turn of the century, MIT Student House was a fifteen-bedroom, four-story home to roughly thirty-five students. It had a parlor with ornate woodwork, a library with built-in hardwood shelves, and a dining room with two long tables, a fireplace, chandeliers, and a small adjoining butler's pantry complete with a dumbwaiter to the kitchen in the walkout basement.

Many of the house's bedrooms had been named by previous generations of students, such as Shaft, a two-tiered room on the fourth floor with a connecting ladder and a large skylight; Morgue, a narrow room wedged in a corner of the second floor and, at one time, painted black; and Xanadu, an isolated room perched on top of the back staircase and painted sky blue.

Claire and Elizabeth had shared a fourth-floor room called Inferno, so named because of its working fireplace, small and dark from soot, and also its tendency to be one of the hottest rooms in the house. The room had a small closet near the entrance, and a bunk bed along the wall opposite the fireplace. It also had two wooden desks along opposite walls past the bed and fireplace, abutting the far wall and a solitary window. The room was so narrow that when Claire and Elizabeth studied at the same time, their chairs nearly touched each other.

They had shared many experiences in Inferno, like roasting sausages on straightened wire coat hangers over the fire in the fireplace and getting drunk on cheap wine, oftentimes drinking it straight from the bottle as they sat before the hot orange flames, keeping cool by wearing only underwear or pajamas and opening the window. Other times they stayed up all night to study and, of course, they talked—about things as banal as pop music or as personal as their most embarrassing moments, their hopes, their fears.

Claire had the top bunk, and some nights she and Elizabeth would talk for hours after turning out the lights. Elizabeth understood her in a way that nobody else ever had. Understood not only her worries and dreams but also her very thoughts. Like a twin, only better. In a twin you see yourself. In Elizabeth, Claire saw her own potential. Self-assured, extroverted, content. Claire had the cover-girl face and body, and of course brains, but she lacked Elizabeth's self-confidence and also her ability to connect with practically everyone. Men were drawn to Claire, but they fell in love with Elizabeth. Claire had seen it time and again. Everybody loved Elizabeth. Claire would double-date men she didn't even like, just to spend more time with her.

On their last night together at MIT, they stayed up until the early-morning hours. After finishing their second bottle of wine, Claire gave Elizabeth a back rub in front of the fading flames dancing in the fireplace. That turned into a full-body massage, and although Elizabeth was barely awake at the time, she rolled onto her back. She was wearing her usual nightwear, an oversize T-shirt and panties, and Claire had already lifted up the T-shirt while massaging her back. Caressing Elizabeth's breasts brought no protests, although Elizabeth's eyes were closed, suggesting she wanted to feel this but not see it.

Claire let her fingers wander lower over Elizabeth's abdomen and the top of her panties. Her lips followed her hands, on Elizabeth's abdomen, along the thin waistband, then below it, on the fabric, moving it aside, touching the warmth underneath.

Elizabeth may have been only semiconscious, but the movement of her hips told Claire not to stop, and Claire had no intention of stopping, not until after Elizabeth shuddered to a climax.

Elizabeth let out a murmur of contentment, then fell asleep. Claire pulled down the T-shirt over Elizabeth's hips, and positioned a pillow under her head so she wouldn't have a stiff neck in the morning. After getting her own pillow, Claire lay at Elizabeth's side and watched her rhythmic breathing until the lambent light from the fireplace disappeared and the first rays of dawn took its place.

Hours later when Elizabeth woke up, she seemed immediately focused on getting ready for her trip back to England. "I can't believe that tomorrow morning I'll be on the other side of the ocean," she said, packing her oversize T-shirt into one of her suitcases.

Claire thought about asking to keep the T-shirt, as a memento. "I can't believe it, either." She was sitting on the edge of Elizabeth's bed. "This place is going to seem very empty."

Elizabeth just sighed.

"But we'll always have the memories," said Claire.

Elizabeth smiled. "If they aren't lost in a haze of alcohol."

Could she have forgotten about last night? Claire wasn't sure how to ask. "Well, last night is one night I'll never forget," she said.

"Our last night together in Inferno." Elizabeth zipped her suitcase closed. "I'm going to miss this. Not the hangovers, but Boston and MIT. And, of course, you."

Their eyes met, and that's when Claire knew—Elizabeth really had forgotten. Or maybe she thought it had been a dream. It had felt that way. Surreal. But it *had* happened, and Claire remembered every moment. She didn't ever want to forget.

The two of them kept in touch over the years. They wrote letters, talked on the phone, and then, after Elizabeth moved to Boston permanently, met periodically for lunch, dinner, or shopping. Recently they'd been seeing more of each other, as Elizabeth's relationship with Chris had become strained. Most of the time, they met at Faneuil Hall, a short walk for Claire and a hop on the subway for Elizabeth.

Elizabeth loved the subway, or T, as it was called. Claire did, too. They both agreed it was much more lively than the Tube in London. It didn't travel as quickly or as smoothly, but it merrily screeched and swayed as it lurched from stop to stop. While the Tube was like a greyhound, the T was more like a Jack Russell terrier. The green line of the T, the one that went to Faneuil Hall, was always packed with a culturally diverse crowd of students, businessmen and women, and Asians from Chinatown speaking Mandarin to one another or reading newspapers and magazines covered with calligraphic symbols. The marketplace next to Faneuil Hall was equally diverse, attracting an abundance of entertainers, tourists, and locals. And the assortment of food was unrivaled. Claire recalled the last time she and Elizabeth had met there—their last meal together—in mid-November. Elizabeth had seemed preoccupied. She'd nibbled only the tip off a slice of pepperoni pizza and hadn't even finished her lobster bisque. Afterward, Claire had hugged her good-bye at the T stop.

"Call me anytime, kiddo," Claire had said, taking Elizabeth's hands in hers. They stood so close that Claire could smell her perfume and feel the warm mist from her breath through the autumn chill. Close enough that she could have leaned forward and kissed Elizabeth on the lips. She wished she had.

Elizabeth. Sweet Elizabeth. Gone forever.

If only things could have been different.

Chapter 23

Detective Wright came home early from work. He and Karen lived in an old but well-kept condo on the edge of Back Bay not far from Kenmore Square and Fenway Park, where the Boston Red Sox played. Occasionally Wright went to a game with Marty Gould. That's how he'd found the condo. After an extra-innings game against the Yankees, he'd stumbled across the place when he went home by a different route to avoid traffic. It had a small back porch—to which they'd added a ramp—high ceilings, six-panel doors, hardwood floors, and a fresh coat of white paint throughout.

Wright was met at the back door by their dog, Lizzy, a miniature Schnauzer rescued from a kennel by Wright after its owner died. At first Karen had objected to the dog—she didn't want another pet after her cat, Trixie—but Wright had brought the animal home without asking her.

Karen had thrown up her arms. "How am I supposed to take care of a dog? I can barely take care of myself."

"There are people worse off than you, and they have dogs. Blind people—you never hear them complaining."

"Oh? And our dog is trained to do what? Fetch jars off shelves?"

"No, to eat dog biscuits."

The animal barked, perhaps recognizing the word *biscuit.*

"I really don't want a dog," said Karen.

"How can you say no to that face?"

The dog had cocked its head quizzically. Its ears, which hadn't been cropped, flopped to both sides. Wright had to admit the animal looked ratty—with matted, gray hair and a reddish-brown discoloration around its mouth, extending into its beard. He guessed that something in its saliva had turned the hair that unappealing color.

Karen regarded the animal skeptically. "Is it a boy?"

"Girl."

"That's one ugly girl."

The dog sat quietly, looking back and forth, as if sensing it was the topic of conversation.

"She's getting up in years," said Wright.

"I'm not surprised. How old, exactly?"

"I don't know. Younger than we are."

"I'm guessing not in dog years."

"No, probably not."

"Do you really want a dog that's going to die of old age in a couple of years?" she asked.

"One year, two years—it doesn't matter." Wright took her hand. "It'll be quality time. We'll be a little family."

Karen still wasn't convinced. "Does she even have teeth?" For now, the dog was keeping its mouth shut.

"Of course she has teeth . . . Four or five."

"I don't know, Gordon."

"I do. Trust me."

"I don't know."

Eventually she gave in. Wright let her name the dog, a minor concession considering she would end up taking care of it most of the time. She chose "Lizzy," after Elizabeth Barrett Browning. He didn't tell her it reminded him more of Lizzie Borden.

After a while, Karen even began to feel protective of the pet. Soon it became her child, her hairy baby. This despite the fact that in dog years, Lizzy could have been her mother.

Wright closed the back door behind him, then petted Lizzy to quiet her down. "Yes, I'm happy to see you, too." He took off his jacket and hung it on a wooden peg on the wall. Behind him in a corner of the living room, a Christmas tree blinked colorful lights from beneath evergreen needles. He turned and watched it for a moment. Lizzy avoided the tree, its blinking lights, and hobbled toward the kitchen. Tomorrow the veterinarian would take a look at her front paws. They were both reddish brown from her chewing them, and Wright guessed that some sort of infection had taken root in one or both.

Karen wheeled herself in from the kitchen, Lizzy at her side. At the rate Lizzy was hobbling, pretty soon she might be needing a wheelchair, too.

Wright kissed Karen, then eased himself into a chair and grabbed a small pile of mail off a nearby end table. "How was class?" Karen had taught freshman English that afternoon.

"Challenging." She wheeled herself closer to him.

"Why do I get the feeling you really mean lousy?"

"You're right," she said. "It's just not getting any better." Lizzy looked as though she wanted to hop into Wright's lap, scrunching her haunches as if about to jump, but the dog never got past the scrunching stage. With a soft whimper, she resigned herself to the floor and lay on the hard wood, gazing up at Wright and Karen under bushy eyebrows.

"I don't know what's wrong with these students," Karen said, her voice tinged with exasperation. "I thought I was disadvantaged being in a wheelchair, but the students in this class are truly handicapped. They've learned almost nothing, and the semester is going to be over in a week. What am I supposed to do?"

To Wright the answer was clear. "Give them an F." He dropped a piece of junk mail into a wastebasket.

"Twenty-three out of twenty-five? I can't do that!"

He looked into her eyes, as gorgeous as ever. Kind and bright and honest. "You can do anything." He reached over and ran a hand through the curls of her hair.

"I can't fail ninety-two percent of the class."

"Yes, you can." He returned to the mail in his lap. "If they don't learn, then they shouldn't pass. It's simple cause and effect. Their inability to perform causes them to fail, which in turn will cause them to have to repeat the work and maybe eventually learn something."

"You always have such a logical view of things, but logic doesn't always work. Not in this case."

Wright opened a gas bill. "I'd give them Fs."

She sighed. "Even if I wanted to, the administration wouldn't let me. They'd be concerned it might reflect badly on the department." She shook her head. "Let's not spoil the evening talking about this. Let's talk about your day. How was it?"

"Interesting . . . Marty and I interrogated Dr. Barnes."

"Oh?"

"The man can't remember anything for more than about a minute." Wright discarded another piece of junk mail. "He doesn't even remember faces."

"Does he understand what happened to his wife?"

"Yeah. He's sharp. He can understand anything; he just can't remember it. And he doesn't seem willing to share any pertinent information, like who his wife had an affair with. He seemed surprised when we told him she was pregnant. He might not have known, or he might just be hiding that he had a motive to kill her."

"Do you think he could have hired someone to do that?"

"I wouldn't put it past him. More often than not it's the husband in these types of cases."

"What about the dog?" she asked.

"I think it lacked the manual dexterity for a murder-suicide."

She picked up a letter from his lap and affectionately hit him over the head with it. "You know what I mean. When someone like Dr. Barnes owns a dog for years as an indoor pet, don't you think he'd have a strong emotional attachment to it? Like us with Lizzy. The pet becomes a part of the family. I think he would have given explicit instructions not to harm the dog."

"Maybe he did. People don't always follow instructions. He probably said, 'Whatever you do, don't shoot the dog.' But when a seventy- or eighty-pound canine bares its teeth, all bets are off."

"So what type of person do you think he could have hired?"

Wright put aside another piece of junk mail. "Could be someone who knew her."

"Why do you say that?"

"Well, for one thing, the alarm to the security system didn't go off. That means either it wasn't turned on or Elizabeth Barnes knew her killer, or at least was expecting a visitor. The perp cut a hole in one of the downstairs windows, but I don't think he gained access that way. The dog would have heard him and made a commotion. You can't cut a hole in a window and pop out the glass and then enter a residence without alerting a dog, unless maybe it's deaf."

"So you think someone cut the hole afterwards to make it appear as though they'd broken in?"

"I'd bet on it. Plus we found blood from the victim on the dog's nose."

"On the dog's nose? What does that mean?"

"That means the perp killed her first. He shot her three times. Then the dog came over to investigate. The dog sniffed around and stuck its nose in one of her wounds. Then the perp shot the dog."

"Why does that mean the killer was someone who knew her?"

"Because otherwise he'd have shot the dog first."

"Unless he was instructed explicitly not to."

"Yeah, maybe," Wright acknowledged. "I'll figure that out."

She patted his leg. "I'm sure you will."

"The interesting thing is that Barnes seems to be trying to piece this together himself. I think if he was involved in his wife's murder, there's a good chance he actually forgot about it."

"That would be ironic."

"Yeah. He's our prime suspect for now, so we'll dig into his research and his finances, and we'll talk to his colleagues. If we turn over enough rocks, we're bound to find something under at least one of them, if he did it."

"If he didn't do it, do you think there's a chance he could figure out who did?"

Wright leaned back. "I doubt it. Not unless his memory comes back. In the meantime, we'll keep an eye on him. All our bases are covered—his phone is tapped, and we're intercepting his garbage pickup. If he does figure out anything, we'll know what it is." With that, he turned to the dog. "Am I right, Lizzy? Am I right?" He reached down and scratched her behind the ears.

Lizzy wagged her stump.

Wright took that as a yes.

Chapter 24

When Shirley Collins arrived at Barnes's house promptly at 8:00 p.m., the chime of the doorbell caught him by surprise. He'd forgotten she was coming over, even though the list in his pocket had reminded him every time he looked at it.

Standing in the entryway in a bright red dress coat and a matching beret that complemented her flushed cheeks, Shirley looked up at him with a radiance that seemed to drive away the frigid air. Her eyes showed a hint of tears, and he wondered whether that was from the cold or from emotion—she was, after all, coming to the house where her colleague and friend had been murdered. In one hand she held a bottle of wine, in the other a large carryout bag with Mandarin characters on it.

"Hello, Chris." A puff of frozen breath came out with her words. "I swung by Chinatown and picked up dinner at Shanghai."

He didn't remember having suggested that restaurant to her. The mere mention of it brought back memories of the times he and Elizabeth had ventured into Chinatown for lunch or dinner. Usually they ate at either Shanghai or China Pavilion, but they went there not just for the cuisine. Part of the novelty of eating Chinese food was simply being in Chinatown, seeing the calligraphic symbols on signs everywhere, wandering past stores displaying cooked chickens with the heads and feet still attached, passing by phone booths designed like miniature pagodas. And the smells of spicy beef, pork, chicken, and seafood wafting from the restaurants could make any pedestrian salivate like one of Pavlov's dogs.

She stepped into the front hallway. He closed the door behind her, then hugged her. "It's good to see you," he said.

She kissed him on the cheek. "It's good to see you, too."

He had hugged her every time they'd gotten together, but merely as a courtesy. Now he didn't want to let go. Her embrace felt like that of a long-lost friend.

Finally he stepped back. "It feels like forever since we saw each other," he said.

"It does. I'm glad you called."

"Let me take your coat," he offered. "And of course the wine."

She held the bottle out to him. "It probably doesn't go with Chinese food, but I wasn't about to carry a pot of tea over here, and, no offense, I think I'm really going to need this."

"Yeah, probably me too." He took the bottle and her coat.

She wore a black V-neck sweater-dress that clung to her from static, accentuating a figure that belied her age; she could have passed for early twenties. The hemline fell just below her knees, revealing sheer black stockings and matching pumps.

"You've cut your hair," he said. "It looks good." About four inches had been taken off since he'd last seen her, and it now had more body, bouncing with her movements.

"Thank you. It's nice of you to notice."

He reached into his jacket pocket for his billfold. "Let me reimburse you for dinner." His hand closed on what felt like a tape recorder.

"No"—she waved him off—"put your money away."

126

The wallet must have been in another pocket. No matter. He remembered Shirley wasn't one to give in after she made up her mind. "All right, but don't let me forget that I owe you next time."

"I'll try to remember."

He suddenly felt at a loss for words. Seeing Shirley without Elizabeth made him more aware of Elizabeth's absence and more aware of the fact that she'd been murdered. He wondered whether it had happened close to where they now stood, maybe *exactly* where they now stood. "Let's go into the kitchen," he said.

As soon as they set foot there, Barnes noticed several pages of notes taped to the refrigerator, all in his handwriting. Obviously reminders of some sort. He hoped they didn't contain any information he wouldn't want Shirley to see, but taking them down meant he would probably misplace them, and now seemed like a bad time to start reading them. Instead he took out plates for dinner. "Would you like a fork?" he asked.

"No, I'll give the chopsticks a try." She glanced at the refrigerator.

He rummaged through the silverware drawer and took out a corkscrew. "How about if I open the wine and you serve the food?"

"Sounds like a plan."

She dumped fried rice onto the two plates and covered it with sweet and sour pork, broccoli beef, and Kung Pao chicken. "I got a little of everything because I wasn't sure what you like."

"I always order potstickers. I can eat the rest of this while you go back and get some."

She smiled. "A sense of humor. I'm impressed. I don't remember that from the last time we got together."

"You didn't bring out the best in me then. I think it was that boyfriend of yours."

"Well, I don't think he brings out the best in anyone. That's one of the reasons I'm not dating him anymore." She offered Barnes a plate, then, seeing he was still working on the wine, placed it on the counter.

The cork came out with a pop. He reached above Shirley and retrieved two crystal wineglasses from the cabinet. "Would you like to eat in the dining room or the family room?"

"The family room," she said. "It's less formal." She picked up her wineglass. "I'll try not to make a mess. I usually don't eat with chopsticks, but I think I can keep the food off your carpet."

They carried their dinner and wine out of the kitchen. In the family room the vaulted ceiling reached twenty feet at its peak, and now to Barnes it seemed even higher. Without Elizabeth the house felt cavernous. The chimney of the stone fireplace along the far wall was like an upended road, spanning floor to ceiling.

He turned on the gas flame, and Shirley slipped into a leather wing chair. He sat a few feet away, facing her, both of them angled toward the fire. They set their wine on a coffee table.

"It's good to see you," said Shirley. "And a little surreal. I keep expecting Elizabeth to walk into the room."

He could see tears in her eyes. "I know."

"I hope this doesn't sound selfish," she said, "but I have to admit I came here as much for her, and me, as I did for you. Part of me needed more closure. I went to the funeral, of course, but that wasn't enough. It never is."

"How was it?" Barnes asked.

"Depressing."

"Did you know most of the people there?"

"No. About a third, maybe."

"Did any of them seem unusual?" Barnes asked. He was thinking that her killer might have gone, too.

"I have to tell you, I didn't notice much of what was going on around me. I was in shock the whole time. I . . . I still can't believe she's gone." She wiped away a tear and drank some wine.

"I know. It feels . . . unreal. I'm sure that going back to work will feel the same." He picked up his chopsticks and forced himself to eat. It had been quite a while since he'd used chopsticks, but exercises of manual dexterity came easily to him.

She took another sip of wine. "When do you plan to go back?"

"Tomorrow. First thing in the morning."

"You don't waste any time, do you?"

"No. The longer I wait, the worse it'll be."

"Like falling off a horse?"

"Exactly. I need to get back on. I just hope no one creates any obstacles." He couldn't help but wonder whether the administration—risk management—would try to place restrictions on his OR activities.

Shirley seemed unsure of how to respond. A faraway look came over her.

"What are you thinking?" he asked.

"Just that it seems like forever since you, Elizabeth, and I were together."

The light of the fire reflected in her eyes like a sunset in the ocean. Funny that Shirley should remind him of something so calming. During their last get-together, she'd been more like an impending storm. But then she hadn't had the death of Elizabeth looming over her. Now things like cigarette smoke weren't so important.

Cigarette smoke. Oddly, Barnes didn't have a nicotine craving, and he couldn't remember the last time he'd lit up.

"Where were we then?" she asked.

He'd already lost the thread of the conversation. "I'm sorry. When?"

"When we went out to dinner last time. Was that Mama Maria's?" She took a bite of food.

She was referring to an Italian restaurant in the North End, but that wasn't where they'd gone. "No. Mama Maria's was the time before," he said. "The last time we got together was mid-October at the Union Oyster House."

She smiled, remembering. "You're right. I guess I was blocking that out. It wasn't one of my better nights."

"Not one of mine either," he admitted.

"The four of us would have been better off staying at home—at separate homes. I am sorry about that."

"I was being a bit of a jerk, too," said Barnes.

"Let's blame it all on Peter. He'd been getting on my nerves for a while; we broke up about two weeks after that dinner . . . I wish I'd never met him."

"Well, we all make mistakes." An image of Cheryl flashed before his eyes, tapping her wineglass to his in a toast to "friendship." "Are you seeing anyone now?"

"Not really," she admitted. "I'm playing the field, or, as you men would say, 'being a slut.' Except I'm not doing it very well—I got stood up this evening."

"Oh, well. I have to admit I'm glad that happened; otherwise you wouldn't be here."

"True. And I'll take helping a friend over a blind date anytime."

"Thanks. I appreciate it."

For a while they ate in silence. Then, perhaps compelled by the silence, Shirley said, "I miss Elizabeth so much . . ."

Barnes had been thinking the same thing. "I know. It's hard to fathom." He'd lost his appetite thinking about it, but he forced himself to keep eating. "You two just completed a project, didn't you? A use patent for something?"

She finished a bite of Kung Pao chicken. "That's right. GBF-complex-coated screws. We filed the patent fifty-fifty, so you'll get half."

He recalled a conversation about that with Elizabeth. "What do you think the royalties will amount to?" The extra income would be welcome, considering his uncertain future.

"A lot. This stuff is going to become standard procedure. Orthopedic surgeons across the country are going to be using this every time they put in a screw."

Of course the pharmaceutical sponsor would reap most of the profits. "Jarrell Pharmaceuticals funded the research, didn't they?"

"That's right," she said. "You work with them, too, don't you?"

"Yeah." There was so much research going on in the hospital that he didn't give much thought to the sponsors. Jarrell Pharmaceuticals had just expanded and bought out Kenzelton Laboratories, which had sponsored the coronary-artery research he and Houston were collaborating on.

"The screws are almost certainly going to get approved within the next month," Shirley said.

"Elizabeth would have been pleased."

Shirley looked up at him. "It must be incredibly difficult for you without her."

He drank some wine and wished it would wash away at least a little of his melancholy. "It is, especially with the aftereffects of the food poisoning. But I guess it could be worse. When I was in medical school, we had a lecture in neurology about memory, and the instructor, Dr. Farrow, told us about a patient named H. M."

"H. M.?"

"Yeah. Those were his initials. In 1953 doctors treated him surgically for epilepsy, and they removed part of the medial temporal lobe on both sides of his brain, including some of the structures located in that area, such as the amygdala and part of the hippocampus."

"They used to *operate* on patients with epilepsy? I thought they just gave you medications for that."

"Not always. Some patients have intractable seizures that are unresponsive to every combination of medications. They may have more than a hundred seizures a day even with medical treatment."

"That's terrible."

"Yeah. In those cases surgery may be an option. Sometimes there's a small area in the brain where all the abnormal electrical impulses originate. If you can cut out that area, you can cure the patient. That's what they did with H. M. They got rid of his seizures, but unfortunately they also destroyed his ability to form new memories."

"How awful."

"At the time, we didn't appreciate the importance of the medial temporal lobes. H. M. was eleven then, and now he still thinks he's eleven. If you show him a picture of himself today, he won't recognize it. He's housed in a facility without mirrors so he won't be terrified every time he sees his image."

"So as far as he's concerned, he only just had the surgery and he thinks he'll go home in a few days?"

"Yeah, except if he did, he wouldn't recognize anybody. All his friends and relatives have aged, of course. The only exceptions are people on TV. Everyone he meets in person is a stranger, and he never remembers them after they leave. If he turns his back on anyone for more than a few seconds, when he faces them again, he thinks he's meeting them for the first time."

"That's pretty scary."

"Yeah. Hard to imagine, even for me." He ate a piece of broccoli and had to force it down. "From what I recall, he's kept in a private room under constant supervision. His mother died many years ago, but he doesn't know about it for more than a minute at a time. He forgets everything they tell him. Everything. I'm not quite that bad. I think some things I can remember for an entire day, maybe even longer than that; I'm not sure. But it's frustrating, unbelievably frustrating. It's like I've suddenly become mentally deficient, yet I can still speak fluent Spanish and French, and I still know more about medicine—and certainly more about thoracic surgery—than practically anyone. But an hour from now I won't be able to tell you what we had for dinner, unless maybe I can still taste it."

"When you eventually recover from this, do you think you'll remember anything from tonight?"

"*When?* More like *if*. A full recovery is unlikely. And no, I won't remember tonight. If it takes me two months to recover, then I'll have a two-month gap in my memory. If events aren't stored in the first place, they can't be retrieved."

He thought he saw tears in her eyes. "I'm really sorry you're going through this," she said.

"Yeah, me too."

"It must be awful . . . And this was from raw seafood?"

"No, I never eat raw anything." He took out whatever notes were in his pocket and skimmed through them. "It was from a heat-stable toxin in some mussels I ate. Domoic acid, from algae. No amount of cooking protects you from it. The toxin can accumulate in anything that does filter feeding, like crabs and even some small fish. You could get poisoned just by ordering anchovies on your pizza."

"I always thought those little fish tasted like poison." She shuddered. "Seriously, what are people supposed to do?"

"If you want to be safe, don't eat anchovies or shellfish. It reminds me of a newspaper article I read years ago about someone who created a bizarre art exhibit that consisted of a loaded rifle pointed at a chair. For a small fee, people can sit in the chair for thirty seconds, after they sign a release form. The rifle is connected to a computer that's programmed to fire it at random, at any time during the next several thousand years or more. The chance that it could go off when you're sitting right there is incredibly small, but it's possible. And then you're dead. So if you're smart, you don't sit in the chair. It's the same with anchovies and shellfish. The chances that they'll do to you what they did to me are very small, but if you're smart, you'll eat something else."

"Food for thought." She smiled sadly. "No pun intended."

"I can't tell you how much I wish I'd just ordered a salad . . . Anyway, things don't look good for me, but I'm going to try to go back to work, and if I do nothing else, I'm going to solve Elizabeth's murder."

"Do you think you can?"

"I know I can." Then he added, "I just don't know how, yet."

"Well, if there's anything I can do to help, call me."

He took another sip of wine, then set his glass on the coffee table. "I might take you up on that."

"You should." She kicked off her high heels and pulled her feet up under her legs. For a flash, Barnes saw clear up her dress, to the white flesh above the tops of her black stockings. Despite not wanting to, he felt himself stir. It was not purely a sexual response but also a need for nurturing, and the guilt that came with it was tempered by the conviction that he would never again betray Elizabeth. He might not be able to control his desires, but he *would* control his actions.

For a moment they ate in silence. Then Barnes changed the subject. "You know we used to have a dog, too."

"A golden retriever. Of course."

"The most human dog I've ever met. You could look at him and believe he was capable of conscious thought. There's a reason why they're called man's best friend. You really get attached to them." He gazed into the fire and imagined Rex lying at his feet.

"How did you take care of him with your schedule? Weren't you and Elizabeth both working all day?"

"Carmen, the maid, came by every afternoon to let him out."

"Carmen." She looked into the fire.

"What are you thinking?" Barnes asked.

"I was just wondering how well you know her. Elizabeth never mentioned her."

He shrugged. "Carmen's okay." But now he wasn't sure. He'd never given her much thought, had never taken the time or made the effort to learn some of the most basic things about her. He jotted a note to look into her background.

Having finished her meal, Shirley put her plate on the coffee table. "Chris, Elizabeth was like a sister to me. If there's anything I can do to help you, anything at all, just let me know."

The way she said "anything" brought to mind images of a young OR nurse who'd flirted with him several months ago. A buxom brunette who frequently went braless, the nurse had said, "Is there *anything* I can get you, Dr. Barnes?" with emphasis on the "anything," and the look in her eyes had said, "'Anything' means '*anything*.'" He couldn't help but wonder what "anything" meant to Shirley.

He looked at her sitting demurely in the big leather chair. He wanted to ask whether she found him at all desirable, whether any woman would, given his handicap. Who would tolerate a long-term relationship with someone incapable of remembering even a wedding proposal or a honeymoon? And what about children? If he ever had any and his condition didn't improve, he would watch them grow up without remembering their first steps or first words. He might not even remember their names or know who they were. Would they have to wear name tags? How could a father cope with that? How could his children?

"I'm sorry," he said, suddenly realizing their conversation had turned to silence. "What was I saying?"

She regarded him reassuringly. "Actually I was doing most of the talking. I just said that if you ever need anything, please don't hesitate to ask."

"Thanks. I guess I got distracted."

"What were you thinking?" she asked.

"I'm not sure I should say."

"Oh? Now I'm *really* curious."

At the moment he couldn't think of anything else to talk about, so he told her, "I can't help but wonder whether I'll ever be intimate with anyone again." When she didn't blush at that, he continued. "I don't want to be now, and not anytime soon, but eventually. When that time comes, I wonder whether it'll be possible."

She leaned forward, her face close to his, the scent of her perfume filling the air like fresh-cut flowers. "I'm sure you will be." Then she kissed him. Quickly, tenderly on the cheek. A warmth spread from the touch of her lips, but it vanished when he saw the look in her eyes. She'd kissed him out of pity.

"You should go now," he said.

She unfolded her legs and slipped on her shoes. "I'll help you clean up. Then I'll be off. Maybe you can call me or stop by my office tomorrow and let me know how you're holding up."

"Sure."

"You might want to add it to your list of things to do."

"Right. My list." He stood up. "I'll add it to my list."

He'd already forgotten he had one.

She picked up the plates, and he took the wineglasses and followed her into the kitchen. As soon as he set foot in there, he noticed handwritten notes on the refrigerator. His surrogate memory, no doubt. Strange how he'd spread that information all over the refrigerator. The mind is something meant to be internalized, not displayed like a kid's drawings. Fortunately Shirley hardly glanced at the notes, but she may have read them earlier in the evening. He would have to come up with a better place to keep them.

After rinsing the dishes and putting them in the dishwasher, she turned to him. "I know it must be awful—what you're going through—but you just have to have faith in the future. You're going to be all right, with a little help from your friends." She touched his hand. "Just don't be afraid to ask. Okay?"

"Okay."

They headed to the front door, and he took her coat out of the closet.

"Will you remember that?" she asked.

"I'll try."

After they hugged each other good-bye, he headed back to the family room. The purpose of Shirley's visit and specific topics of conversation had already escaped him. But he still remembered one of the last things she'd said. *Don't be afraid to ask.* The words seemed to resonate in his mind. *Don't be afraid to ask.*

Ask what? he wondered.

He had already forgotten.

Chapter 25

Driving home from Barnes's house, Shirley thought about their evening together. Chris had many good qualities, and she understood what Elizabeth had seen in him. Shirley had known about their separation, although not the details, only that there were some big problems and that Elizabeth was not optimistic about her future with him. Probably Chris had strayed. Men have a way of doing that.

She'd always been cautious about men. Relationships with them usually began better than they ended. Beginnings were inherently exciting—a process of discovery. She liked the passion, of course, but also learning about people, sharing experiences and thoughts, and creating a new bond. But ultimately that bond always weakened, and after weakening, it eventually broke. Too many men were like her brother. She had only one sibling, and that was one too many. Chuck, four years her senior, was a self-centered jerk, and yet their mother loved him. Loved him more than she loved her daughter. And Shirley knew why—because Chuck had been married and had fathered a child. No matter that the marriage had fallen apart after less than two years and Chuck had abandoned his daughter. At least he'd had one.

Shirley could cure the world, and her mother would still consider her a failure. That would probably never change. And she was the one who always took care of their mother. Chuck merely exploited her. He owned a carpet store, and he sold her new carpet she didn't need. Not only had she not needed it, but the fumes had made her so sick she'd been forced to move out for a month. Of course that meant coming to live with Shirley, even though both Chuck and their mother lived in Lawrenceville, New Jersey, hundreds of miles away. Chuck had no room at his place, he'd insisted. What he had was no scruples. He would have carpeted their mother's attic if he thought he could get away with it. And the walls. And the ceiling. The jerk had even sold her throw rugs to put on top of the carpet and what little linoleum and tile he hadn't covered. The last thing she needed was throw rugs. And Chuck probably wouldn't lose any sleep if one of those rugs slipped out from under her or she tripped on it and broke her hip.

At least he didn't sell aluminum siding, Shirley thought, imagining her mother's brick house covered with it. Too bad their father wasn't around to straighten things out. He'd died when Shirley was only seventeen, the victim of a drunk driver.

Shirley stopped for a red light at a deserted intersection. She was tempted to run the light, but her windows were still partially fogged, obscuring much of her view, and she couldn't be sure a policeman wasn't waiting in the darkness for someone like her to give him an excuse to write a ticket. So she waited, and instead worried more about her mother. The woman was only sixty-five years old, but two decades of rheumatoid arthritis had taken their toll, limiting her mobility. Of course Chuck didn't check up on her, except to try to sell carpet and rugs, or to ask a favor. Sometimes she would work behind the counter in his store, and as far as Shirley knew, he never paid her.

When the light turned green, she drove on, and her thoughts turned back to relationships. Failed relationships. Most of the men in her life hadn't been a whole lot different from her brother. They acted considerate when they wanted something, then became self-centered after they got it. Or sometimes they were self-centered from the beginning. Peter, her last boyfriend, had been like that. He'd been too busy trying to further his career at any cost, and he'd resented her success. He should have been pleased that her research was going well and that her future was falling into place, but instead he dwelled on his rejected grant proposals and accused her of not being supportive.

Why couldn't more men be like Chris? He didn't have anything to prove. He was already a nationally recognized cardiothoracic surgeon. Yes, he had brain damage, but he was still intelligent, charming, and worldly. She thought about the fact that if he had fallen in love with Elizabeth, or anyone, just before the food poisoning, that love would have lasted forever. Any arguments would be forgotten as soon as they ended, and the excitement, the newness, of the relationship would never wear off, at least not for him. *Maybe that's the secret to making love last*, she thought wryly—*brain damage*.

Snowflakes suddenly appeared, as if from nowhere, obscuring much of the view as she drove over the Harvard Bridge and the Charles River. Illuminated by her headlights, the flakes looked like shooting stars rushing toward the windshield. The scene took on an otherworldly quality, not unlike her evening with Chris.

The snowfall diminished as she drove past the cement pillars of the main building of MIT just beyond the Harvard Bridge and headed into downtown Cambridge. Housing was cheaper there, near Central Square, than it was in most of Boston. She'd had an apartment in that low-rent district now for longer than she cared to recall—thanks to debts from student loans and caring for her mother—but soon she would be able to move to Beacon Hill or anywhere else in the city. She would be able to buy a house on the Cape, too. She'd always wanted a cottage in Centerville, on the beach. Her mother could retire there, and Shirley would drive down to visit on weekends—it was only seventy-five miles. On sunny days she would lie on a blanket on the warm sand, reading a book or watching people play volleyball. Maybe she would learn windsurfing, too. Thanks to the GBF-complex-coated screws and to Jarrell Pharmaceuticals. Shirley and Elizabeth had signed a licensing agreement with the company, and in turn, Jarrell Pharmaceuticals had provided the funding they needed. After the FDA approved the use of the new product, Jarrell Pharmaceuticals would manufacture and market the screws. She and Elizabeth's estate would split the royalties.

She parked her car on the street in front of her apartment building. Her next house would have a garage. An attached garage. No more walking through snow, slush, and ice every time she came and went in the winter. She hurried from her car to the front door, shivering in the cold. Things were going to change.

Chapter 26

After Shirley left, Barnes read the list in his pocket, to remind himself what had happened during the day. Denny had met him at the airport. Damn nice of Denny to do that. Taking time away from the hospital and fighting the traffic around Logan Airport couldn't have been easy.

Barnes picked up the phone to thank him, unaware that the two of them had met earlier at the Ritz. Although he'd written a note about moving to the hotel a week before the conference, he'd neglected to add that Denny had told him this over drinks at the hotel bar.

"Hello," Denny answered. But this wasn't Denny. It was his answering machine. "If you know my number, then you're probably someone I'll call back. Leave your message after the tone."

"Hey, Denny. It's Chris . . ."

Denny picked up the phone. "Hey, buddy."

"Hey, Denny. Just wanted to thank you for meeting me at the airport."

"No problem. I assume you got home okay."

"Yeah, I'm just trying to get situated now." He suddenly thought about all of the mail that he would need to sort through. Carmen would have put it in boxes in a spare bedroom. That's what she always did when he and Elizabeth went out of town. "That may take me a while," he added.

"I can imagine."

"I just wanted to let you know that I'm planning on stopping by the hospital tomorrow morning. Maybe I'll see you between surgeries."

"Sure thing." Denny sounded noncommittal. "What are your plans exactly, at the hospital?"

"I don't have any yet. I just thought I'd see how everything feels, if you know what I mean. I'm curious what it'll be like to be in the OR again. I feel as though I've been away from it for years."

"Yeah, well, we can talk about that. I should probably go. I was just getting ready to catch some shut-eye. I'll hook up with you tomorrow."

Barnes thought he heard a woman giggle in the background. "Okay. Looking forward to it."

"Take care, buddy. It was good seeing you this evening."

"Yeah." Barnes hung up. *It was good seeing you this evening?* Did Denny mean the airport? That was in the afternoon. Had they gotten together again in the evening? He had no idea. His notes didn't help, either. They mentioned a police interrogation and dinner with Shirley at 8:00 p.m. but nothing in between. In the future he'd have to be better about writing down more information. He jotted a note that he and Denny had talked again.

After that, he began the task of going through his and Elizabeth's mail. Opening her mail felt strange, like looking through her purse. But he had more of a right to it than anyone, and the information might shed some light on why someone had killed her.

Junk mail accounted for three-quarters of everything they received. Most of it went into the trash unopened. The rest ranged from water bills to bank statements to an occasional letter from a friend or relative. All the letters from friends and relatives had been addressed to Elizabeth, and he couldn't help but realize she had considerably more people who cared about her than he did. He'd never concerned himself with that, not before now.

Some of the envelopes contained Christmas cards. Elizabeth had always loved Christmas. To her it was a month-long celebration and an excuse to brighten up and transform the house. She left the exterior to him, but every year transformed the interior into an explosion of ornaments and other decorations, including large wooden nutcrackers, red and white candles, and even rocking horses. At one time they'd had an inflatable Santa, but Rex had punctured it and then chewed it beyond repair. Evergreen swags and garlands with artificial magnolia flowers would cover the soffits and banisters, and the mantel always became an overgrowth of ivy sprouting artificial apples, pears, grapes, and satiny blue bulb ornaments, with a large gold-and-white bow in the center. Beneath this display always hung two stockings, one with an attached cloth reindeer holding a sign that said "Be Merry"; the other—Barnes's—with Santa sprouting a beard of white yarn and holding a sign that said "Ho! Ho! Ho!" Next to the hearth their Christmas tree, which they always selected and sawed down themselves, would stand like a work of art, complete with white lights, angels, candy canes, strands of gold beads, and hundreds of different ornaments.

This year there would be no decorations and no celebration. Barnes wouldn't even display Christmas cards. Not without Elizabeth. There could be no Christmas without her, just as there could be no blinking bulbs without electricity. In so many ways, she was the source of his light. Now he would have to learn to live without that.

Barnes sorted through fewer than half of the letters and packages before putting the rest off until later. The mail worth saving he placed into a separate box and marked the lid "opened—save." The rest he dumped into the trash.

Three other boxes contained all of Elizabeth's papers and notes from work. He opened the largest box and sifted through the contents. Somewhere inside might be a clue to Elizabeth's murder, but she had an intimidating pile of papers. Sorting through all of them would likely take days.

He selected a manila folder at random and read its contents—a protocol and consent form for a clinical trial. Both documents were dated November 5, 1987, three weeks before Elizabeth was killed. The protocol was a ninety-five-page description of a proposed study in patients with scoliosis. Elizabeth had written comments in the margins—recommendations and concerns regarding the eligibility criteria and methodology. She'd never mentioned the clinical trial to Barnes, and nothing in her notes indicated that she had agreed to conduct the study, although more information about that might be filed somewhere else. No matter. Nothing in the protocol or in Elizabeth's comments struck Barnes as noteworthy.

He put the file away and decided to go to bed early. The local news was about to begin on television, but what was the point of turning it on? By morning he would forget it all.

Despair settled over him. It was an alien feeling. Losing Elizabeth. Losing his ability to remember things. Losing control. Christopher Barnes, the great cardiothoracic surgeon, used to be able to do anything, have anything. Now all that had changed.

He wondered how long the neighbor across the street, Marshall, had grieved after the death of his wife. Elizabeth had spoken of him on a couple of occasions and had mentioned that a car had struck and killed his wife in a crosswalk. Barnes had never talked with him, although a few times he'd seen the man outside, walking a little fur ball of a dog. Elizabeth had suggested inviting him over for dinner, but Barnes hadn't thought that was a good idea.

"We don't have anything in common," he'd said. "I'm not into poetry, and I really don't want to talk about his dead wife."

Now Barnes *did* have an interest in such a conversation. But it would do him little good. Any insight he gained would be short-lived.

Still, he couldn't help but wonder. Does the despair ever end?

He rested a hand on one of Elizabeth's boxes. Inside lay count-less hours of her work, but that's all it was. Work. He wanted *her*, or at least a personal connection to her, something that would help him conjure up her ghost, or plant the seeds of a dream. But he had no idea what might do that, if anything. Maybe he would figure that out tomorrow. Now he just wanted to be done with today.

He went to the master bedroom and turned on the lights. The room had never seemed so empty. Carmen had made the bed in her usual fashion, with fewer wrinkles than a sheet of metal, and for once he wished she'd left it messy. It looked overly sanitized, devoid of warmth. He wasn't sure he even wanted to sleep in it.

Above the bed hung a large watercolor by Anatole Krasnyansky—a street scene from Prague, with the sun rising on old buildings and Orthodox churches, casting a bright reddish hue on the otherwise somber structures. He tried to remember a sunrise in Boston, or any-where else. None came to mind. He must have seen hundreds of them, but he'd never committed one to memory. And now he never would. His recollection of it would vanish with the disappearing sun. Like his memories of everything else from the day.

He walked to the dresser along the far wall. This was Elizabeth's dresser, and above it hung a framed photograph from their wed-ding. A photographer from the *Boston Globe* had taken a picture of her kissing him just after the judge had pronounced them man and wife, and Shirley had later called the newspaper and obtained the original. She'd given it to them, framed and matted, when they returned from their honeymoon in Hawaii. They'd spent nine days on the islands of Kauai, Maui, and Hawaii, and those had been as close to nirvana as anything he'd ever experienced. He and Elizabeth had begun each day by making love with the waves from the ocean thundering in the distance. One morning on Maui they drove the narrow, winding road east to Hana. They journeyed along the edges of bluffs and through tropical forests, then emerged at a black-sand beach where waterfalls cascaded down cliffs into freshwater pools. Later they found a more secluded stretch of sand and made love under the stars.

That now seemed a lifetime ago. They'd both looked forward to returning to Maui for their fifth anniversary. Without Elizabeth he would never go back.

He looked at the dresser under the photograph. He'd never opened any of Elizabeth's drawers, but now he did with a sense of anticipation, knowing that each one contained a small part of her— items that had literally touched her.

Her second drawer was full of T-shirts that she wore to bed. He picked up one and smelled the fabric. Detergent. He put it back. The one beside it was a blue shirt with the words "BEACH BUM" across the front. Elizabeth had bought it in Maui. Hesitantly he smelled it. Elizabeth. Faint, but no doubt about it. He had found her.

He refolded the shirt and placed it back in the drawer. Soon he would forget about it, but tomorrow or the day after or the week after, he would probably look again for some trace of her, and he would find it there, in the second drawer down.

He walked to the bed and, from the drawer of his night table, took out a pen and a sheet of paper. In a letter to himself, he summarized his day, using notes from his pocket. Every event and every thought from before he'd entered the bedroom had already vanished from his consciousness, but not the fact that Elizabeth had been murdered. How many times had he forgotten and relearned that during the course of the day? Probably at least a few. Regardless, he would certainly forget it after falling asleep. But in the morning, this letter would reduce his confusion and emphasize the importance of not dwelling on her death all day long. Instead he would try to focus on what he needed to do, taking into account what had transpired the previous day.

He finished the letter and taped it to the center of the bathroom mirror at eye level, where he would be sure to see it the next day. He also taped a small note to the alarm clock on the night table beside the bed, telling him to read the letter on the bathroom mirror. Then he got undressed and crawled into bed. He always slept on the left side, with Elizabeth on the right and Rex on the floor. Sometimes Elizabeth would roll toward the center and take up more than half of the bed, and on those occasions a little prodding would be necessary to get her to relinquish the space that was rightfully his. But now that he had the entire mattress to himself, he didn't want it.

He closed his eyes and pictured Elizabeth at a noon conference he'd attended shortly after they'd met. She had presented a lecture on the advantages of temporary rather than permanent bolts in holding together bones following surgical implantation of a plate to set a spiral fracture. Barnes hadn't known enough about the topic to formulate an opinion, but he'd been impressed by her presentation. This woman, who wasn't much taller than the podium, commanded the audience with authority. When other surgeons asked questions, they were merely searching for answers, not challenging her basic premise, as was often the custom with surgeons. Clearly they viewed her as an expert in the field, and that had attracted him to her even more.

Now with only memories of Elizabeth to keep him company, he fell asleep thinking of her standing behind that big podium. He hoped with all his might that this would transition into a dream about her—anything, just to see her again. Yet even if he did see her, even if he spent the entire night making love with her, he would never remember it in the morning.

Chapter 27

Barnes awoke to his alarm clock at six in the morning. He slapped it off with his left hand and turned to his right to kiss Elizabeth.

She wasn't there. Not a trace of her, not even an indentation in her pillow. No sign of the dog, either, no sound of rummaging and no lingering smell.

"Rex. Biscuit! Rex!" The dog always came for a treat. But not this time. The house remained silent.

Something was wrong. Not just the absence of Elizabeth and Rex. The absence of continuity. Something had interrupted the normal flow of life. Clearly this was his bed in his bedroom, presumably in his house. But *when* was it? What day was it?

Could this be Saturday, and Elizabeth had taken Rex to the vet? That would explain their being gone, but it wouldn't explain vanishing without a trace.

He tried to think back—when had they last been together? All that came to mind was a dinner of escargot and mussels in a fancy restaurant. Large, black, hideous-looking mollusks served in white china on a white tablecloth. Canada, he remembered. But the woman across the table hadn't been Elizabeth. Instead she'd been a blonde eating shrimp fettuccine.

He turned his head to look at the alarm clock. A note taped to the top hung over the front, its bottom edge just above the digital readout. *A message from Elizabeth*, he thought. But when he turned on the lamp, it revealed his own handwriting: "Read note on bathroom mirror." His throat tightened. Why would he write a note to himself, and why couldn't he remember having written it?

As much as he tried, he could recall nothing from last night. Now that he thought about it, he couldn't recall anything from the entire previous day. What *was* the last thing he could remember? The blonde in Canada. But without an anchor in the present time, he had no idea how long ago that was. It could have been days or weeks.

He hoped that a medication he'd taken last night was interfering with his memory. The alternative was much worse: a stroke or some other injury, or a disease, had damaged part of his brain. Could that have happened in Toronto?

He threw back the covers and headed to the bathroom mirror. A letter of some sort was written on a sheet of paper taped to the glass. He turned on the vanity lights to read it. But before he could focus on the print, he saw his reflection in the mirror. The sight made him gasp. His neck. The *center* of his neck. He moved closer to the mirror for a better look.

A circular, indented scar reflected back at him. A gunshot wound? That's what it looked like, but a bullet there would have paralyzed him. Or killed him. No, a scar of that shape in that location could be from only one thing—a tracheostomy.

He touched the normal skin of his neck, then the smooth connective tissue that had formed the scar. It was pink but well healed, probably a couple of weeks old. What on earth had happened to him?

He read the note on the mirror:

> *Don't panic. Your ability to form new memories has been impaired (but not completely ablated) since you*

ate contaminated mussels in Toronto on November 22. Don't expect to remember anything from yesterday, and don't expect to retain new information for more than a few minutes. Today is December 16, your second day back home. Elizabeth was murdered on 11/26—shot in the foyer—and you're going to figure out who did it.

He stopped reading. Elizabeth had been murdered! He pictured her lying in a pool of blood, and he imagined the police taking photographs, then stuffing her into a body bag to be carted off to the morgue—alone, without him. He hadn't even gone to her funeral. Instead he'd spent days, maybe weeks, lying in a hospital bed, probably comatose, certainly brain damaged. And now he was going to solve her murder? He read on:

Last night you had dinner with Shirley, Elizabeth's friend. She got rid of her annoying boyfriend. You agreed to call her sometime today, maybe for dinner again. You also spoke to Claire, Elizabeth's attorney friend. Consider meeting her at the cemetery when you visit Elizabeth.

The cemetery? He didn't even know where Elizabeth had been buried. He would have to call Claire or Shirley to find out.

He read the remainder of the note:

At 2:00 you have an appointment with Dr. Parks, a psychiatrist in the clinic building.

Yesterday the police questioned you regarding Elizabeth's death, and they told you she was pregnant. On the refrigerator you have notes about this and details of the murder. Elizabeth had an affair shortly before she died. Don't get too worked up about it because you cheated on her, too. You moved out (to the Ritz) almost a week before the conference.

In the front right pocket of your pants is a list of things to do today. Keep this with you at all times.

You slept with your watch on last night, and you need to do this every night so you don't misplace it. You <u>must</u> <u>not</u> lose your watch because it reminds you to look at the list in your pocket.

When you've finished reading this letter, leave it on the bathroom mirror. This evening write another note to replace it.

Have a good day.

"Have a good day?" What kind of mood had he been in to write that? Elizabeth was dead. She'd cheated on him. He'd cheated on her. And he had brain damage that could condemn him to spend the rest of his life trapped in the present, living moment to moment with no link to the recent past.

He remembered as a child in first grade walking through an autumn fog on his way to school early one morning. He was shivering, not just from the cold. What had always been so familiar, now seemed alien. Trees and houses receded into the mist, dissolving into a gray shroud. As the fog grew thicker, the sidewalk behind him disappeared after only a few steps, and nearby objects faded only moments after they appeared.

Now his memory was like that, events fading into a mist. And once they entered the mist, they wouldn't come back. His notes could serve as a surrogate memory, but they couldn't help him remember, only retrieve information. Retrieve only to forget again. A never-ending cycle.

"*Je ne le comprend pas,*" he said, speaking French to assure himself that at least his intellect remained intact. He repeated the sentence in English. "I don't understand it." Yet he did understand, all too clearly. Elizabeth had been dead for weeks, and he would have to rely on his notes to relearn this every day and to try to figure out who'd killed her. The notes would have to be brief, only the essentials, like details of Elizabeth's murder in a condensed format so he could see the whole picture at once. He would need to be organized, and he would need to make an effort not to dwell on the same things day after day.

Having resolved to move forward this way, he got ready to take a shower. He placed his clothes on a chair beside the bathroom door, where they'd be in plain sight afterward, and laid his watch conspicuously on top. Forgetting to put that on after his shower would mean losing the link to his list of things to do, and only the list stood between him and chaos.

He closed the bathroom door and stepped into the shower. The hot spray pelted his face and head, drumming in his ears and running in rivulets over his shoulders and down his back. As it streamed off him and into the drain, he hoped his anxieties would follow, washed away like silt, and with them, thoughts of Elizabeth dying, alone in a pool of blood.

He closed his eyes and pictured her on their honeymoon, in the hotel on the island of Maui. Moments after arriving at their suite, she came up to him while he was starting to unpack. She took his face in her hands and kissed him softly on the lips, once, twice, then longer and harder, with a passion that took his breath away. The intensity in her eyes fueled it, a look of omniscience and desire that said, "I can have anything, but I want only you." And he wanted only her—emotionally, intellectually, physically. Only her.

As thoughts of his honeymoon came back to him, so, too, did memories of other shared moments, streaming through his consciousness, first in a trickle, then in a torrent.

With them came sadness. And regret.

Chapter 28

After his shower, Barnes read through his notes again. They looked vaguely familiar, like something he'd written a long time ago. Since his last reading, the only fact that had stayed with him was Elizabeth's murder.

According to his notes, Shirley was being a much-needed friend, and she'd gotten rid of her intolerable boyfriend who had ruined their evening at the Union Oyster House. He would call her later. Right now all he could think about was Elizabeth. Why would anyone want to kill her? And then he thought about another possibility. Maybe that hadn't been the plan. Maybe *he'd* been targeted but something had gone wrong, and Elizabeth had died because of it. This would mean that someone would need a motive for killing *him*. Plenty of people disliked him, but wanting him dead was another matter.

What could be a possible motive? His research with Denny? The two of them had been working on preventing recurrences of atherosclerosis following coronary-artery bypass surgery. Many patients spend sixty or seventy years building up plaque in their coronary arteries until the constricted vessels have to be surgically replaced, but after the procedure, the grafted vessels become blocked in only five years. For decades researchers had been trying to figure out why the new grafts clog so quickly, and Barnes had joined Denny in the race for an answer. Admittedly it was a slow race—the eligibility criteria for the study were so restrictive that enrolling patients was taking more than twice as long as they had originally projected— but could somebody now be trying to keep them from completing that clinical trial?

It seemed an unlikely motive for murder. Common sense dictated that Elizabeth's death more likely had something to do with her research with Shirley on the GBF-complex-coated screws. But if someone had wanted to stop that research, they should have killed Shirley, too, and they shouldn't have waited so long. The screws would almost certainly be approved by the Food and Drug Administration within the next month. Killing one of the researchers after the project had already been completed made no sense, and it wouldn't alter the flow of money, except that Elizabeth's share of the profits would now go to him.

Given that his own research was a work in progress, the more he thought about it, the more he became convinced that his atherosclerosis study could be a possible target. But if someone had wanted to kill him, why hadn't they also tried to get rid of Denny? After all, either one of them could do the research without the other.

Still wondering about that, Barnes left home to drive to work. After being away for the better part of a month, he knew he wouldn't have any patients to see or even charts to review. No doubt Denny had taken care of everything, including collecting the fees. Barnes didn't care. At least the patients had been treated by a skilled surgeon. Now he just wanted to get to the hospital and see how everything was going, see whether it still felt like a second home. He missed the coffee in the surgeons' lounge and the nurses in the ORs, but most of all he missed the exhilaration of surgery—holding a beating heart in his hands and literally giving new life to patients. He couldn't wait to do that again.

The sun still hadn't risen as Barnes drove through the city streets on his way to the hospital. He took Storrow Drive along the winding Charles River, past the Harvard Bridge and then the Longfellow Bridge. Traffic was light at this hour. Setting his cruise control, he looked to the left at the placid water separating Cambridge from Boston. Robert F. Kennedy once said that when you fall into the Charles River, you don't drown; you dissolve. With continued cleanup efforts, the Charles might someday be safe for swimming, but Barnes would always think of it as it was now, just as he would think of everything, frozen in time.

The snow from the previous day had melted, leaving the road shiny black like the river. At the hospital he eased his Mercedes into his reserved parking space in the main physicians' lot, appreciating that amenity more than he'd ever anticipated. Thanks to assigned parking, he wouldn't have to worry about misplacing his car.

Shaking from the cold, he hurried along the cement walkway to the Whittaker Building, the main entrance of the eight-building complex. A bitter wind pressed his overcoat against his legs and blew his hair into disarray. The sun had finally risen, but it wasn't showing itself.

He entered the main lobby, and a blast of warm air enveloped him, carrying with it Christmas Muzak piped in from ceiling speakers. In front of him stood the information desk, staffed by four women and decorated with holly. None of the receptionists greeted him. He'd never paid attention to anyone at the information desk, and now he realized they'd never paid attention to him, either.

He walked past Christmas decorations and down the hallway to the Braddigan Building, then rode the elevator to the eighth floor, the surgical wing. There, the nurses, technicians, and unit clerks all knew him.

"Welcome back, Dr. Barnes," a couple of them chimed. Normally they avoided him. He had a reputation for being brusque and hard to please, mainly because he expected everyone to give his patients the highest priority. And when they did, he seldom thanked them. But why should he? His demands were for the patients; the *patients* should thank the staff.

He continued down the hallway and passed through a doorway marked "Restricted Area. Authorized Personnel Only." Beyond that, he walked down a short corridor. To the right was the entrance to the men's locker room, the *only* locker room. Female surgeons were relegated to the nurses' changing room. They were permitted in the lounge, but most avoided it. The room had the aura of a men's club, and the women didn't feel welcome. Even Elizabeth had seldom set foot in there.

Barnes stuck his head into the locker room. He didn't know when Denny's first surgery was scheduled to begin, so he didn't know where to look for him—the locker room, the lounge, or the OR.

The locker room was smaller than the one at the gym where Barnes worked out, with only three rows of benches and lockers. He looked down the first row, toward Denny's locker, but Denny wasn't there. Barnes recognized other surgeons getting changed, but he turned and left before they noticed him. In the lounge an OR schedule would be posted, and that would tell him where to find his friend.

He entered the lounge at the far corner, near the coffeemaker. Straight ahead on the opposite wall stood the door leading to the operating rooms and the recovery room. Barnes had walked through that doorway more times than he could count, without ever really thinking about it, but now he eyed the metal door with uncertainty. It was a passage back to his normal way of life; yet somehow it had changed, become more imposing, more of a barrier than an entryway. Now it might be off-limits.

Even if the hospital administrators allowed him to continue performing surgeries, he wondered whether he could maintain his train of thought throughout an operation. The types of procedures he performed always took hours, and although one step logically followed the next, every operation was different. How would he be able to keep track of all the details, like where every sponge had been placed? The nurses do sponge and needle counts at the end of each operation, but the chief surgeon is responsible for keeping track of them during the surgery. Of course he would always have assistants, but would that be enough?

He turned his attention to the interior of the lounge. It was a large room with two couches, a conference table and chairs, and two vending machines. One of the couches spanned half a wall, and the other stood near the center of the room, facing a television mounted on the wall. Four surgeons sat in the lounge—two chatting on the couch in the center of the room, a third watching television in a nearby chair, and the fourth reading a newspaper at the conference table. They all wore scrubs and head covers, and the two on the couch also wore paper shoe covers. Surgical masks dangled around their necks.

Barnes poured himself a cup of coffee, dumped in powdered creamer, and stirred the concoction with a wooden tongue blade. Then he dropped the tongue blade into the wastebasket and headed across the room. The place smelled of cigarette smoke. The smokers, himself included, usually sat in the far corner near an ineffective portable filter, and the other surgeons tolerated them, grudgingly. Now, like those other surgeons, Barnes found the odor unappealing.

"Hey, Christopher! Welcome back." It was the surgeon watching television, Ian Williams. Williams was an ear, nose, and throat specialist, or ENT man. Although only a couple of years younger than Barnes, he had a mop of curly hair and a boyish face that made him look more youthful than some of the residents in training. He also had a reputation for being the best, especially with throats. He and Barnes spoke only infrequently, although Williams was always cordial. The man got along with everyone.

Barnes nodded to him. "Thanks."

The other surgeon sitting alone, Nate Billings, the lone black member of the Division of Cardiothoracic Surgery, put down his newspaper and acknowledged Chris. The two of them rarely spoke. Barnes never felt comfortable with him. He'd always had the impression that Billings wasn't up to speed; he was too tentative, too reserved. On the surgical highway, the man puttered along in a golf cart.

Barnes nodded at Billings, then pulled up a chair next to Williams. The other two surgeons on the couch kept talking. Barnes didn't know either of them, although he'd seen them around.

"Is Houston here?" he asked.

"Not yet," said Williams. "His first case isn't until eight thirty. How have you been?"

"All right. Actually shitty, but I don't want to talk about it. I tell you, it feels great to be back."

"Yeah, well, you should have come in ten minutes earlier. One of the guys brought in a dozen doughnuts. They went fast. Billings over there just had the last one."

Yet another reason to dislike Billings. "Well, at least he didn't drink all the coffee." Barnes took a sip of the scalding brew. "What's on the tube?"

"Nothing. I'm just killing time. Got about ten minutes. Then I have to do a T and A."

Barnes remembered relatively little about ENT surgery, but he knew that a tonsillectomy and adenoidectomy was as routine as getting an oil change. "You ENT guys must be really stressed by all those complicated life-and-death procedures," he said.

Williams grinned. "We leave the big organs like hearts for you old-timers who can't handle the more intricate structures."

Just then the door behind them swung open. Barnes felt it more than heard it. Then, "There's the man!"

Denny Houston. Dressed in street clothes and with a lit cigarette dangling from the corner of his mouth, he stopped at the coffee pot to pour himself a cup. He took the cigarette from his lips and said, "How goes it?"

"Good." Barnes went over to join him. "How about you?"

"Can't complain." He took a drag on his cigarette.

"It's good to see you, Denny."

"Good to see you, too. Can't talk long, though. Someone else's patient canceled in OR six, so I'm moving up to eight o'clock. Got an aortic aneurysm to repair on a guy named Castleman. That name ring a bell?"

"Castleman, Gross, and Meyers?" Barnes guessed.

"You got it. If this guy croaks, his partners are going to sue the pants off me. But at least there'll be one less lawyer in the world."

"Who's first assisting?"

"What's his name—Willard, the chief resident."

Barnes nodded. "You know, I wouldn't mind getting my hands wet this morning. If you want to tell Willard to stay on the floor, I could scrub with you."

"Thanks for the offer, buddy, but we're all set." He flicked ashes off his cigarette into the wastebasket.

"Uh-huh." Barnes felt his face flush. Houston had just chosen a resident over him. A resident! "Listen, can we step into the hallway for a minute?"

"Yeah, okay." Houston snuffed out his cigarette on the sole of his shoe and dropped the butt into the trash can. Coffee in hand, he headed down the corridor out into the hallway of the main floor.

Barnes dumped his coffee into the trash and followed.

"What's on your mind?" asked Houston.

They turned away from the nurses' station. "You just chose a resident over me," said Barnes. "Are you serious?"

Denny sipped his coffee. "He's assigned to the case."

"Look, I need to get back into the OR. That's where I belong." When Houston didn't say anything, Barnes added, "If I can team up with somebody like you, I'll be fine. I just need to get back into a routine. If you take me into your practice, you won't be losing anything because you'll get all my patients. I just need someone I trust in the OR with me, for part of the surgery, to make sure I remember everything."

Houston cleared his throat. "Chris, don't take this the wrong way, but you're a liability. What happens if you forget what you're doing halfway through a surgery? What if you do a double instead of a triple bypass? Or a triple instead of a double?"

"That won't happen. I just need—"

"No, *anything* can happen. What if you're doing a sequential graft and you connect it in the wrong places? In this business there's no margin for error. If you're not a hundred percent, forget it."

"Hell, at fifty percent I'm better than—"

"Buddy, I'm not gonna argue with you. If it was me, I'd file for disability."

"Yeah, right." Barnes shook his head in disgust. "After two weeks you'd be climbing the fucking walls. Let's face it, Denny. You and I are two of a kind. We'll never retire. Most people go to the office and push papers. We split open someone's chest and hold their beating heart in our hands. I need to do that, Denny."

"I hear you, buddy. But I work alone. If I'd wanted a partner, I'd have teamed up with you a long time ago. But it ain't my style. You need to give serious consideration to retiring. Before you're *forced* into it."

"Are you kidding?" The only people in a position to force him out were his own colleagues, all of whom were well aware of the revenue and recognition he'd brought to the hospital.

"There's going to be a meeting sometime next week about your privileges. Administration's concerned about liability."

He felt himself flush. "I don't believe this. I've brought millions into this place, *tens* of millions, and they have the gall to consider me a liability?" He knew his voice carried all the way down the hall, but screw decorum. "*I'm* the reason this is a world-class cardiac unit!"

"Keep it down, buddy. It's not that simple."

"Not that simple? Those sons of bitches."

Denny glanced at a clock on the wall. "Listen, buddy, I need to get back to the locker room. My first case has been moved up half an hour."

"Fine." He forced himself to be calm. "Who's assisting?"

Houston raised an eyebrow. "Willard. I already told you."

"Yeah, right." Barnes returned his gaze. "Don't look at me that way. I remember."

But he couldn't remember, and he knew Denny was observing the signs of his disability. Now Barnes understood how patients in the early stages of senility must feel when they begin to lose their mental faculties but try to conceal it from their loved ones. Barnes could conceal his disability only as long as people let him. A few simple tests and he would be stripped of his facade, and stripped of his dignity.

Gazing past Denny, he looked at the picture windows behind the nurses' station. How easy it would be to walk over there and fling himself through one, into oblivion. The pain would be brief.

Denny draped an arm around him. "Look, buddy, you only just got back. You can't expect to just pick up where you left off.

You should go home and catch up with things from when you were gone. Just take it easy."

He shrugged off Denny's arm. "Screw that. I need to be here, *working*." Even if it's just pushing papers, he thought. And that reminded him of their research. "How's our atherosclerosis study going? Anything happening, or did you put it on hold?"

"We talked about that yesterday."

"Refresh me."

"Everything's going great." Denny looked at his watch. "I don't have time to get into this now with my case coming up. Let's talk about it later."

Barnes didn't want to let him off the hook that easily. "Later *today*. I want to know everything that's going on with that. Don't think you can take it away from me."

"Don't be paranoid, buddy. I'm not trying to steal your thunder. Look me up later, or maybe tomorrow, and we'll talk about it again. Right now I have to go to the OR." Houston opened the door, and they entered the hallway to the surgeons' lounge.

"I'll do that," said Barnes.

Denny turned his back on Barnes and headed into the locker room.

Barnes just stood there in the hallway, then took out his list. He added a note: *Houston doesn't want to work with you.*

Chapter 29

Barnes left the surgeons' lounge. He didn't belong there. No cases had been assigned to him, and nobody would share any. Not today and probably not ever. Why should they? Surgeons just don't do that. It's like asking a pilot to let you fly the plane.

He went to the nurses' station and walked behind the main desk, heading for the nearest picture window—the solution to his problems, clear as glass. The unit clerks, nurses, and other staff members might just as well not have been there. He saw only the window.

He steeled himself and took a last breath. *Like jumping into a swimming pool,* he told himself. You make up your mind; then you do it. Only a different kind of splash.

"Dr. Barnes?" The feminine voice interrupted his thoughts, temporarily broke his resolve. He turned from the window.

It was Stella Laskin, a third-year student. Her straight hair hung limply and accentuated a long but pleasant face. "I'm sorry to bother you, Dr. Barnes, but I was wondering whether I might ask you a medical question."

He remembered grilling her a few times in the OR during her surgery rotation in September; she'd surprised him with mostly correct answers. Now she'd surprised him even more simply by being there. Medical students seldom sought him out. "What is it?" he asked.

She looked up at him, her eyes filled with sorrow. "My father went to see our family doctor for what he thought was laryngitis, and the doctor told him there's a tumor on his vocal cords. I know that's not your area of expertise, but I was hoping you might recommend a specialist."

That was easy. "Ian Williams."

She wrote the name on an index card. "He's here at this hospital?"

"Yeah. He's the best. Anything else?"

"No." She put the index card in the pocket of her lab coat. "Thank you, Dr. Barnes." She hesitated, as if about to say something else, then turned and walked away. Even when Barnes was helpful, medical students found him intimidating.

Barnes looked around him, wondering what he was doing behind the nurses' station. He must have come here to look at a patient's chart, but who was the patient? Maybe one of the nurses knew and would hand him the chart or lab report or other information. But all of them seemed occupied with other things. He glanced at his watch. *Examinez votre poche droite.*

The list in his pocket didn't help. Instead it informed him that Denny didn't want to work with him. He thought he recalled a piece of that conversation from not long ago, here in the hospital, but it had become clouded almost to the point of obscurity.

He headed back to the surgeons' lounge—he didn't know where else to go—and poured himself another cup of coffee. Taking a seat near the television, he tried to figure out what to do next. More than anything, he wanted to be in the OR, but that wasn't going to happen anytime soon.

Billings hadn't moved. When he saw Barnes sit down, he folded his newspaper on the conference table and turned to him, catching his eye. "The man wants nothing to do with you, does he?"

The baritone voice, as much as the question, startled Barnes. "What?"

"Your *friend* . . . Houston. Acts like you've got the plague." He spoke slowly, deliberately, almost as though translating the words from another language. At the same time, his large forehead wrinkled into dark crevices, and his eyes reflected such a dark shade of brown they looked black.

"He's just busy," Barnes replied.

"He's a jerk is what he is."

"What's it to you?"

"To me it's just an annoyance. But to you . . . it's a big problem. You associate with him."

Barnes took a long drink of coffee. Billings was right, but what could he do? It was too late to make new friends.

Billings added, "I hope you're not counting on him."

Barnes avoided the man's gaze.

Billings picked up his newspaper. He talked to it rather than to Barnes. "Houston would let pneumonia into his OR before you."

"Yeah, well, I don't see *you* jumping at the opportunity," Barnes countered.

Billings put down the paper and glared at him. "Why the hell should I?" Those words came faster than his others.

"Because I'm the best—" Barnes cut himself short, deciding to take another tack. "No, because you don't like Denny, and you and me working together will piss him off."

Billings frowned. "Can't argue with that."

"Hell, it may even improve race relations."

Billings said nothing, and Barnes knew the man was wrestling with the decision. He was probably weighing personal factors, such as whether working with someone more experienced than a resident would free up more time for him with his wife and kids—if he had any—or give him extra time to do Christmas shopping.

"I've got a double bypass with a skip graft," Billings said, "coming up in fifteen minutes. The skip is for the left anterior descending artery. The patient has a small proximal obstruction . . . and a larger distal one."

Barnes had performed more skip grafts than he could count. It involved connecting a bypass graft to two parts of an artery instead of just one, to bypass two separate obstructions. "No problem. I'll be ready in five." He stood up to go get changed.

Billings raised a hand. "Hold on . . . First let's get something straight . . . I don't *want* you to scrub with me. I'm *allowing* you to scrub with me . . . Don't think *you're* doing *me* a favor."

"You're right," Barnes conceded. "You're doing *me* a favor." Yet he couldn't help adding, "I never figured you as the altruistic type."

Billings stood up—tall and muscular. "You don't know Jack shit about me, Barnes. If you want to be in the OR, this is your chance. You assist *me*, and that means . . . I'm going to micromanage you; you're not going to start any procedure . . . without my okay. You're going to follow my every direction and my rules. Otherwise . . . I'll throw you out."

"What are your rules?"

"My rules are . . . you act civilized and treat everyone with respect—nurses, residents, even medical students. You do what I tell you, and . . . you don't raise your voice. You don't make others uncomfortable."

The way you are now? thought Barnes. "Anything else?"

"Yeah. I play classical music . . . on the radio. You have a problem with that?"

Barnes shrugged. At least it wasn't Christmas Muzak. "I can live with that."

As if on cue, two residents and two medical students entered the lounge.

"Change of plans, Walt," Billings said to the less senior resident. "Dr. Barnes is going to scrub with me on this one. You'll do the next . . . I need you to follow up on Mr. Jansen's X-rays. See if they're done . . . and see if they're clear. We want to be sure he isn't getting pneumonia. And check on Mrs. Wilson's labs. They should be back any time."

Walt tucked his chin to his chest and headed out of the lounge.

The other resident, Peter Findley, approached them. He was a tall, angular man with a large nose and thick glasses. Barnes had worked with him before and knew him to be competent.

"Welcome back, Dr. Barnes."

Barnes grunted a thank-you. He remembered the last time Findley had assisted him. Barnes had been in a bad mood and had chewed out the resident for everything from being too slow to making incisions that weren't straight enough. Barnes had a reputation for never being satisfied with the help he received. The residents used to say, "There are two ways to cut suture on Barnes's cases: too short or too long." The residents had come to accept the notion that on Barnes's cases they couldn't do anything right. Findley was no exception. He was quieter and more polite than the other surgeons—he seldom spoke unless prompted—but Barnes figured that underneath the silence and obsequiousness, Findley hated him.

That was okay. Barnes wasn't there to please residents. Surgical procedures were performed for patients, period. And patients would be a hell of a lot better off if all surgeons had that attitude. Too many placed too high a priority on teaching, or worse—making money. Hell, some surgeons let residents operate unsupervised. That was legal because the consent forms said Dr. So-and-So "and/or his associates." "Associates" could be residents, and "and/or" could be simply "or." So residents performed some procedures unsupervised, and the staff surgeon got paid for the work. A surgeon could make hundreds of thousands of dollars a year that way, having residents do the work, and as far as Barnes was concerned, that was immoral. Others might consider him arrogant, but nobody could accuse him of being lazy or immoral. No one could accuse him of giving anything less than the best possible care to every patient. He wondered what kind of care Billings gave.

Two medical students stood a few paces back. They knew their place. During surgery they would hold metal retractors to keep skin, fat, and muscle out of the way, and they would speak only when spoken to.

"Why don't you go get changed, Chris?" Billings suggested. "We don't have much time."

"Yeah. I'll do that."

Barnes hurried to the locker room. Like all the surgeons, he had an assigned locker. Finding his clothes later would be no problem. As he took off his watch, the French inscription caught his eye. He suddenly remembered the list in his pocket, without having to reach in and discover it. That meant his loss of short-term memory wasn't complete. There must be some functional cells in that part of his brain, and although those cells would probably not multiply, they could create new links and maybe even recruit other cells to assist in the repair process. In a few weeks he should have a better idea about where things stood. Who knows—he might even make a comeback as chief surgeon.

Anything was possible.

Chapter 30

After changing into scrubs, Barnes pulled out his list for a final review before putting away his clothes. He'd placed his watch and wedding ring in his right front pants pocket—no watches or rings are allowed in the OR—and in a moment his all-important list would go back there, too.

He still couldn't believe he was about to do a bypass surgery. Back in the OR, scalpel in hand. His fingers itched to hold the steel instrument. The nagging fear of never being able to come off the disabled list had been replaced by the thrill of anticipation.

He unfolded the paper to refresh his memory one last time before the surgery. He remembered nothing on the page, not even item one. Elizabeth had been murdered!

In his excitement over the upcoming surgery, he'd forgotten the fact that someone had killed his wife. He'd been thinking about her murder all morning, but it had slipped his mind long enough for it to disappear. The fact was, the prospect of doing surgery had, however briefly, overshadowed the loss of his wife.

He put away the list. Thoughts of Elizabeth now filled his head—everything they'd done together, and everything they would never do again. He *had* to solve her murder, even if that became his sole purpose in life. This much, at least, he owed to her.

He slammed his locker shut. Nobody turned a head. The reverberating clamor of metal on metal, and even fists on metal, was routine in the surgeons' locker room.

He headed out to the lounge. Then another unsettling feeling came over him. What exactly was he doing there? Surgery, yes, but with whom, and on whom? He looked around the lounge. It offered no insights—no gestures or even nods from the few surgeons there. Someone had asked him to assist on a case. That much he remembered. Most likely Denny, but Denny wasn't anywhere to be seen. In fact, there was only one surgeon Barnes even recognized, an old-timer named Brennen, and the man's specialty was head and neck.

Barnes walked along the wall to the OR schedule posted near the door. Houston was scheduled to start on a repair of an aortic aneurysm in OR 6. But Barnes had been thinking about a bypass graft; that meant most likely someone had asked him, or assigned him, to assist on that particular surgery. Could the schedule be wrong?

"You ready?" The baritone voice came from over his shoulder.

He turned to see Billings, who'd just come in through the door to the operating rooms.

"We're going to start . . . in five minutes." Billings was talking to *him*. "OR 9. You ready?"

"OR 9. Yeah." He tried to sound self-confident, but he felt his face flush. *Billings*, not Houston, had offered to let him assist. Barnes remembered nothing about that, and he wasn't sure why he'd accepted. He would have to trust his previous judgment, go with the flow. Best not to ask about the case. No sense taking the risk of appearing clueless if they'd already discussed it.

He put on a head cover and paper shoe covers from boxes on the table by the door, then followed Billings out of the lounge and down the stark corridor, past the recovery room and a nurses' station and past one operating room after another. Billings stopped at OR 9 and stuck his head in the door. Outside, Findley and the medical students had just finished scrubbing; they turned off the water faucets by moving knee-operated levers under the sink. For a moment Findley stood there with his hands at shoulder height, water dripping off his elbows into the sink. Then he walked a wide circle around Barnes. The medical students followed. Billings moved out of the way, and they walked backward past him. Findley pushed open the metal door to the OR with his buttocks and backed into the room.

"Let's go in and take a look at her films," Billings said to Barnes.

In the OR, they went to the viewing boxes along the wall. The patient's X-rays looked unremarkable, but on the arteriograms, Barnes could see obstructions in the coronary arteries.

"This is what we're dealing with," said Billings. "The patient's name is Mrs. Rigsby, Dorothy Rigsby. I'll get the graft from her leg while you open her chest with Findley."

Barnes preferred the chest, although he knew the most important part of the procedure was obtaining the bypass graft. This Billings would do by removing part of the greater saphenous vein from the inside of the leg, starting near the ankle. Even microscopic damage to the vein would compromise the entire procedure. Barnes found working in the leg to be tedious, but he always did it himself on his patients. Now Billings was going to assume that responsibility. Hopefully that wouldn't be a problem.

They exited the OR to scrub in preparation for the surgery. Barnes joined Billings at the wide metal sink, grabbed a scrub brush, and broke open the plastic package. Inside, an iodine and chemical solution created a brown froth. Billings held the brush under the running water of a faucet, then, in the presurgery ritual practiced by all in their profession, methodically rubbed the plastic spicules along his fingers, scrubbing every surface again and again, before advancing to the palms and backs of his hands, then the wrists and forearms. Barnes was doing the same.

"Just so you remember," Billings reiterated as they scrubbed, "I make the rules around here . . . I know you're used to being the boss in the OR when you're chief surgeon, but not today. If you give me any lip, I'll . . . throw you out. Understand?"

"Yeah." For a moment he resented Billings, his slow authoritative manner, but the man had a point. You can't have two chief surgeons. "I hear you," he added. "Just remind me if I forget."

"Don't worry. I will."

Barnes entered the OR behind Billings, and they gowned and gloved with the assistance of a nurse. Everything was already in place: the anesthesiologist with all of his equipment, the perfusionist with the heart-lung machine, and the nurses with their trays of instruments, including scalpels, a saw, electrocautery, and numerous hemostats, scissors, retractors, and other specially designed instruments. The patient, a youthful forty-six-year-old Caucasian woman, had already been prepped and sterilely draped.

"She's under," announced the anesthesiologist, writing vital signs and other notes on a sheet of paper attached to a clipboard near Mrs. Rigsby's head. "You can start whenever you're ready."

"Scalpel," Barnes and Billings said in unison, and scrub nurses picked up the instruments from a sterile tray. Barnes held out his right hand, palm up, and felt the handle of the scalpel slapped into it.

"Here we go," he said. For a moment he hesitated, wondering whom he was about to cut into, knowing only that it was a female who looked too young to be having coronary artery disease. She should be at home playing with her children, or maybe doing paperwork in an office in the financial district. Anywhere but on this table. Most of Barnes's patients were much older, the majority men, and all of them he knew well from their hospital charts and office visits. Yet he identified with this woman, this complete stranger, more than with any of his other patients. Through forces beyond her control, she had ended up on this table, and she had probably never seen it coming.

If all went well, this patient would leave the hospital a cured woman. Maybe her arteries would eventually clog again, but for a while at least, she could return to her role of mother or wife or businesswoman. Back to normal.

Barnes made an incision down the center of the chest, from just above the top of the sternum to the abdomen, extending an inch below the xiphoid process at the bottom of the sternum. At the same time, Billings was working on the leg. Barnes didn't even notice. He focused solely on the chest, maintaining a dry operative field by electrically cauterizing even the small bleeders while Findley retracted the skin. At this point, the patient was simply an object, a chest, and the resident and medical students across the table were merely pairs of hands. Almost. Findley was also a reminder of Barnes's status as an assistant—every few minutes the resident updated Billings on exactly what Barnes was doing.

Barnes cut through the sternum lengthwise with an electric saw and opened the chest with a sternal spreading retractor, exposing the beating heart. He'd done this more times than he could count, but it never failed to inject him with a rush of adrenaline. Denny always said it was like lifting a skirt over the hips of a woman, and Denny had a similar analogy for touching the organ, but to Barnes the experience was more spiritual. To him, it was an opportunity to preserve the soul. The human brain holds that—our very essence— but it's dead without a heart. The heart keeps everything alive. Even when the brain dies, the heart can prevent the rest of the body from shutting down.

The fate of such an incredible organ shouldn't be entrusted to anyone but the most skilled surgeons. That's why Barnes didn't trust medical students, or even most residents, to do anything except minor procedures—and that's why medical students and residents resented him. They didn't appreciate his reverence for the organ, or the magnitude of their obligation to the patient. They viewed this woman as a teaching tool, not a desperately ill person entrusting them with her life.

Barnes examined the heart through magnifying surgical glasses, as it beat, inspecting the outside of the coronary arteries. Next he would lower the temperature of the heart with a cold potassium solution and would work together with Billings to reroute the blood flow through it.

A radio on the far counter played classical music, and this, along with Findley's intermittent updates to Billings, reminded Barnes that someone else was the chief surgeon. Had *he* been in charge, rock 'n' roll would have filled the air. Classical music was too sedate for open-heart surgery. But it seemed fitting for Billings. The man, like the music, was clearly different.

Barnes could no longer remember the chain of events that had led him to assist in this surgery, yet he was pretty sure Billings was doing *him* a favor, rather than the other way around. The man might have had an ulterior motive, but right now Barnes didn't care.

"You remember what you're doing?" Billings asked, breaking his train of thought.

"Hysterectomy," Barnes replied.

Billings was right to ask, but Barnes didn't need any help, at least not yet.

"Double bypass," Billings said, obviously not in the mood to make light of the situation. He moved from the patient's leg up to the chest, beside Barnes. "I'll show you which vessels."

Barnes gave him some room but said nothing. He'd never deferred to another surgeon in the OR, not since his days as a resident.

He couldn't decide whether to be annoyed or grateful.

Chapter 31

After checking on Barnes, Billings focused on dissecting around the greater saphenous, the longest vein in the human body. He'd done the procedure enough times that it was like brushing his teeth, but a sense of urgency still tugged at him. The patient's life rested in his hands, and he felt uneasy having that power. For most surgeons it was a rush. Not for him.

He knew that with Findley keeping an eye on things, he could rely on Barnes to manage the other half of the surgery. The son of a bitch had the best survival record in the history of the hospital, despite taking the most complicated cases. That had been a major consideration in letting him assist—having Barnes instead of a resident was in the patient's best interest.

But Barnes was abrasive and arrogant. Why should anyone help a jerk like that? If things had been reversed and Billings needed help, would Barnes have offered to let him assist? Not a chance.

On the other hand, Barnes's illness and the death of his wife had reduced him to a manageable state. Not surprising, considering that either of those tragedies would prompt any normal person to take stock of his life and change his attitude and priorities.

Barnes did have redeeming qualities, Billings conceded, but then so did almost everyone if you looked hard enough. It would take more than that to make working with him palatable. Of course, this might be their first and last time as a team. If Barnes behaved the way Barnes usually did, Billings wouldn't invite him back.

Too bad the man didn't have any real friends to help him, but that's not surprising when you treat everyone as though they're inferior to you. What had Elizabeth ever seen in him? Billings had liked her, despite her poor choice in a husband. Unlike Barnes, she would say hello to him and sometimes chat with him when their paths crossed on rounds or outside the operating rooms. Of course nothing could be done to help Elizabeth, but certainly she would have wanted him to help her husband. Maybe he could do that, in part, for her.

And there was one other thing—Denny Houston. Houston was a bigot, and you could bet he'd be infuriated to see his former friend working under the direction of a black man.

Billings had endured racism nearly every day of his life, much of it subtle or hidden. He especially hated that type, where people act collegial but block your promotion or pay raise, act neighborly but try to keep you from buying a house in their white district. His father told him not to resent those people, to look past the injustices, but Billings couldn't help it. His father had been an associate professor of political science. For thirty years the man taught classes, conducted research, and wrote papers, but he never got promoted to full professor. Bad luck? Billings didn't think so. More like the wrong skin color. His father had since retired and now received a pension, but it was less than he deserved.

Despite the unfairness, though, his father enjoyed retirement while Billings staved off an ulcer. Maybe there was a lesson in that. Maybe he should spend a little less time working and a little more time enjoying life outside the hospital, with Priscilla—his wife of sixteen years—and their daughter, Maria, who was rapidly growing up without enough of his guidance. She'd just turned fifteen and already had acquired her mother's charm, ethereal beauty, and self-confidence. Against his better judgment, she'd started dating, and in another year she would be asking to borrow the car. At least he didn't drive a Mercedes or a Jaguar like most of his colleagues. He would feel a lot better letting Maria borrow the three-year-old Buick.

Billings suddenly felt sorry for Barnes. More likely than not, the man would never know the joy of having a family—never see a child's eyes light up when he came home from work, never have a little girl or boy call him "Daddy."

Billings glanced over at him again. Barnes seemed intent upon his work. He would help save this patient's life, but in a few hours he wouldn't remember anything about it. Yet Billings knew this was important to Barnes. Maybe on some primitive level he would learn from his experiences, even if he couldn't remember them. Or maybe he would learn to compensate. The brain sometimes has a miraculous ability to adapt. Billings had seen patients recover from worse.

He knew all about Barnes's condition. So did everyone else at the hospital. It's hard to keep a secret when the story is printed in every major newspaper in North America. He didn't know the full extent of Barnes's memory impairment, but he'd read that the domoic acid in the shellfish preferentially destroys the temporal lobe regions of the brain, and he knew the ramifications of that.

Helping Barnes wasn't easy, but it was the right thing to do. His father would be proud of him. That alone might be reason enough to do it. But there was a more compelling reason that he chose not to contemplate—a humiliation he'd endured for most of his life.

Damn Barnes for making him think of that. Some things you should be able to put out of your mind. Some things are best forgotten.

He forced his focus back on the patient.

Chapter 32

Barnes and Billings emerged from OR 9, the surgery completed. Barnes had already forgotten most of what they'd done, but he had been surprised by Billings's skill in handling the greater saphenous vein. They'd worked together in attaching portions of the vein to the coronary arteries, wearing magnifying glasses to see while they sutured the small vessels. None of the segments of the grafts appeared kinked, twisted, or stretched, and Barnes knew the patient would likely recover without complications.

"That went all right," he said as they walked down the corridor to the surgeons' lounge. They'd left Findley and the medical students to accompany the patient to the recovery room and write the orders for her nursing care.

"You're welcome," replied Billings. "I assume that's your way of saying thank you."

"I probably need a little practice with that," he admitted.

"If you want to operate again tomorrow, stop by before my first case."

"Really?" Barnes had figured it would be a one-shot deal.

"No, I'm just being polite. I figure . . . you'll forget in a few minutes."

"Very funny." Under different circumstances he would have told Billings to screw himself, but that wasn't an option if he wanted to get back into the OR.

"You can assist," Billings said, "as long as you do exactly what I tell you . . . and treat everyone with respect."

"I can do that." Then he added, "Can you remind me about this later when I've got a pen to write it down?"

"I'll stick a note in your locker."

They had reached the surgeons' lounge, and Barnes felt like his old self—ready to take on whatever anyone could throw at him. He pushed through the door ahead of Billings.

". . . bricks short of a full load! He doesn't deserve a break!"

Apparently he'd walked into a heated debate, but the conversation abruptly halted. Then he realized why—they were talking about him. Carl Milligan, the chairman of surgery, had just hurled the insult. The old jarhead had been talking to Denny Houston and Ralph Manning, another surgeon. The only question was who, if anyone, had defended him.

Milligan cleared his throat and collected himself. Nodding an acknowledgment, he said, "Hey, Chris, Nate." Then he turned back to Denny and Ralph and said, "I'll catch you two later." And he hurried out.

Billings headed back to the locker room, shaking his head. Manning joined him. Barnes stayed behind in the lounge and asked Houston, "What was that about?"

"Nothing. Milligan's just being an ass. You know how he is. You just come from the OR?"

"Yeah. I did a case with Nate."

"Nate?"

"Yeah, Nate Billings."

Houston shook his head. "I'm surprised at you, buddy, working with that guy. He's not in your league."

"I'll take what I can get." He could recall only fragments of the procedure yet sensed it had gone well. All he knew for sure was that he wanted to do it again. "Don't judge Billings till you've shared a case with him."

"I wouldn't share a case of *beer* with him."

"You wouldn't share a case of beer with *anyone*," Barnes said. "Sharing's not something you do."

"Horse shit. What about that nurse, Kitty what's-her-name?"

"That was seven years ago, Denny. Can't you think of anything more recent?"

Barnes could see Houston's jaw clench. Then Denny said, "That's beside the point. The point is you don't belong with Billings."

Barnes shrugged him off. "I'm going to get changed. If you're still here when I get back, I'll talk to you then." He started for the locker room.

Houston called after him, "You can do better than Billings."

Opening his locker, Barnes saw a note scribbled on a piece of paper wedged in the door: *You're scrubbing with me tomorrow at 7 a.m.* Signed *Nate*. Putting the note into his pants pocket, he remembered that Billings had offered to let him assist. Billings. Who would have thought?

He changed back into street clothes and put on his watch and wedding ring. As the gold band slid onto his finger, it brought back memories of Elizabeth—his marriage proposal to her. He'd popped the question at the end of the Hyannis Port breakwater, the longest rock jetty on the Cape. They'd hiked out there at low tide, climbing over massive boulders that had shifted and fallen from years of pummeling by ocean waves. Standing on the last rock in the late-afternoon sun, surrounded by glistening waters and curious seagulls, he'd pulled a diamond engagement ring out of the pocket of his swim trunks.

He held it out to her. "This is for you."

"Oh, Christopher." She looked at him with disbelief.

"Will you marry me?"

For a moment she said nothing, just looked into his eyes. Then, "Do you really want to be with me forever?"

"Longer. If you can tolerate me."

As if in slow motion, she took the ring. "Yes. I'll marry you."

He might not remember anything now from one day to the next, or even one hour to the next, but he would never forget that afternoon, that proposal to Elizabeth.

He glanced at his watch to see the time, and the inscription on the face reminded him to check the list in his pocket. He unfolded that paper, and the first item jumped out at him: *Elizabeth murdered . . .*

It wasn't as much of a shock as it should have been. Some part of him must have remembered. That would explain why he'd thought of the marriage proposal. In the back of his mind, he knew she was gone. What he'd learned about Elizabeth, and even some of the morning's events, must have left impressions, however faint. Was this an improvement over the day before? Most likely. And tomorrow, or the day after that, should be even better.

He read through his notes. Nothing shed light on what had happened to Elizabeth. There wasn't much about Denny, either, at least nothing good. No mention of the atherosclerosis research the two of them had done together. Barnes wondered what was happening with that. He vaguely recalled having seen Denny in the surgeons' lounge. That could have been hours ago, but it was worth checking out. He finished getting changed, then threw his scrubs into a hamper and headed to the lounge.

Denny was sitting on the far end of the long couch, smoking a cigarette and reading a newspaper.

"Hey, Denny?" Barnes said.

Houston looked up, then back at the newspaper. "Yeah."

Barnes sat beside him and took out a pen and paper. "Can you give me any insight into what happened to Elizabeth?"

"All I know is what was on the news." He put the newspaper on the arm of the sofa and took a drag on his cigarette.

"I'm trying to approach this thing from every angle, and I was wondering whether there might be any connection to me. You know what I mean?"

"I'm getting this feeling of déjà vu," Houston replied. "We already had that conversation. Yesterday at the Ritz."

Barnes recalled nothing about that. "Humor me. What if whoever killed Elizabeth really wanted to kill me instead?"

He took another drag on his cigarette. "Then they really fucked up. You weren't even in the same country."

"Yeah, but not everybody knew I was going to that conference. It's *possible* that someone was after me instead of her."

"Anything's possible." Denny flicked his cigarette over an ashtray balanced on his thigh.

"You haven't had something happen to you, have you?"

"What do you mean?" Houston looked at the clock on the wall.

"I mean nobody's tried to kill you, have they?"

"Other than the usual maniacs on Storrow Drive?" He paused, as if debating whether to mention something, then added, "I doubt it, but somebody did try to break into my house."

"You're kidding." Barnes almost dropped his pen. "When did that happen?" He wrote down the information.

"Thanksgiving night. Around one in the morning. They cut a hole in my dining-room window and set off the alarm. Maybe they wanted what was left of my turkey."

Barnes scribbled more notes. "I can't believe you didn't tell me this already. I assume the police came."

"Damn right they came."

"And?"

"And what? They didn't find squat. No fingerprints or fibers or whatever the hell else they look for. The police are useless. You remember last summer when some lowlife broke into my car? He left fingerprints all over the outside door and one of the windows, but the cops said they wouldn't be able to arrest anyone because the fingerprints have to be on the *inside*."

Barnes shuffled through his notes. "The Boston police never mentioned anything to me about this. I would definitely have written that down. I write down everything that's important."

"Maybe they don't tell you everything they do, especially when it makes them look like they don't know their ass from a hole in the ground."

"More likely they didn't know about it. You live in Weston, and all you reported was a robbery. The Weston police probably never informed the Boston police. It's not only a different department but a different city."

Houston flicked ashes off his cigarette. "I don't know, buddy. That's pretty basic police work. If they couldn't put together something that obvious, nobody's ever going to figure out what happened."

"Why didn't *you* tell the Boston police?"

"Look, I *did* tell the police. If they don't know in Boston, they're morons. Besides, I didn't know what happened to your house at the time."

"I can't believe this. Weren't you worried that somebody might be trying to kill you?"

Houston waved that off. "Not hardly. First they'd have to get past my Glock."

"Glock?"

"Yeah, my 9mm." Houston held up his hand like a gun. "On the streets they're called 'cop killers.' If it's good enough to kill cops, it's good enough to kill any idiot who comes at me."

Barnes had no idea Denny owned a handgun. It had never come up in conversation. He added the information to his notes.

Houston continued. "They hold seventeen rounds, and you can kill a whole roomful of people even if you can't aim worth a damn. So to answer your question, nobody scares me."

"I guess that doesn't surprise me." Barnes looked through his list and saw a question mark next to their research. "Where are we with the Jarrell Pharmaceuticals study? Is that on hold?"

Houston shook his head. "No, it's not on hold. It's done."

"Done? You finished it?"

"Yeah. That's what *done* means."

"How's that possible? At the rate we were going, we were months away from completing that."

"I work faster without you."

"Less carefully . . . You didn't file the patent yet, did you?"

Houston shifted, and he had to put a hand on the ashtray to keep it from sliding off his thigh. "As a matter of fact, I did."

Barnes suddenly realized why Houston appeared uncomfortable. "I'm not on it, am I?"

Houston avoided eye contact and took a drag on his cigarette. "We can change it. It's no big deal."

"No big deal?" Barnes felt his face flush. "It's a *huge* deal. I can't believe you did that. We *are* going to change it."

"Of course we are. Look, buddy, I'm sorry. It's easy to correct. I'll do it this week."

"You'll do it *now*."

"Now's not really possible. I'll do it tomorrow."

Although Barnes wanted it corrected immediately, one day wouldn't make any difference. "Fine." He jotted a note to himself. "Tell me something, Denny. How'd you pull it off so fast?"

"We only needed two more patients," he said. "Found one, and used Reston for the other."

Barnes wrote that down, too. "William Reston, the AIDS patient?"

"You may recall we did a triple on him."

"I recall he was a protocol violation. He shouldn't have been included."

"Well, he was, and the statistics are clean. We'll get the patent—both US and international."

Denny was leaving something out. He wouldn't have used Reston except as a last resort. "What was so urgent that you had to enroll a patient who didn't meet the eligibility criteria?" Barnes asked.

"Nothing was *urgent*."

"Don't bullshit me, Denny. Why were you in such a hurry to apply for the patent?" Then he realized—Houston must have sent off the preliminary results for publication. If the patent application wasn't filed before the publication came out, the information would be considered public domain, meaning they would lose the right to apply for the patent. "You went and wrote a paper, didn't you?"

Houston snuffed out his cigarette. "No, it was just an abstract. For the San Francisco conference."

"Son of a bitch. Am I even on it?"

"Course you're on it," Houston replied. "I'd have put you first, but you'd have had to present it, and at the time, you were in a coma."

"That's just great, Denny. You cut corners and slap everything together while I'm in a coma."

"Bullshit. I finished a project that needed to get done. That's all. If you'd had your way, we'd be working on it through half of next year."

"I'm going to check everything in the analysis," said Barnes, "and if it isn't a hundred percent accurate, we're retracting it."

Houston regarded him coolly. "You do that, buddy. It's all legit."

Barnes stood up. "We'll see about that."

Chapter 33

From the surgeons' lounge, Barnes went straight to Houston's office. First he had to get past Marcie, Denny's secretary. A bespectacled woman of about fifty, she sat behind a large desk and looked up passively at Barnes.

"I need to see all the files on the Jarrell Pharmaceuticals project," he said to her.

"Well, hello, Dr. Barnes. Welcome back." She smiled pleasantly. "I just received a call from Dr. Houston. He instructed me to make copies of that file by the end of work today. I'll have it on your desk first thing in the morning."

Barnes didn't want to wait until morning. "That's *my* study," he said. "*I'm* the principal investigator. I should have access to the data immediately, not tomorrow."

"I understand, Dr. Barnes. Dr. Houston hasn't given me the file yet. I can't give you something I don't have, but I assure you I'll provide you with a copy, a complete copy, by tomorrow morning."

"It *better* be complete," he said. "And I expect a revised copy of the patent application, too. By eight a.m. tomorrow." He took out his list and jotted a note. "Otherwise both of you are going to wish you never knew me."

Leaving Marcie, Barnes headed to his own office down the hall. Even though he'd been gone for weeks, he knew that his secretary, Kristine, would still be at her desk. Like Marcie, she was old school. Some of the other surgeons liked to hire younger secretaries—office candy—but Barnes and Houston knew the folly of that. An inexperienced secretary or office manager can turn a ten-hour day into a fourteen-hour day. Kristine had more than twenty years of experience, and Barnes could trust her to keep on top of things, even under the current circumstances. He knew, without asking, that she'd canceled everything noncritical and had rescheduled or reassigned everything else.

As he walked past her desk on the way into his office, she looked up. "Dr. Barnes!" A genuine smile lit her face. "Welcome back."

"Thanks." He kept walking into his office.

She jumped up and followed. "At your convenience I can fill you in on everything that happened in your absence."

"Tomorrow." He took out his list. "Also tomorrow make sure I get all the Jarrell Pharmaceuticals files from Houston, including a revision of the patent. Call Marcie if they're not on my desk by eight a.m."

"Yes, Dr. Barnes. Anything else?"

"No, that's it. Thanks. Please close the door on your way out."

She left him alone, and he settled into the armchair behind his desk. The supple leather, molded to his contour from the countless hours he'd sat on it, seemed to embrace him. In front of him, stacks of papers, journals, and notebooks cluttered a seventy-two-inch mahogany desk, hiding much of the dark surface. In contrast to the clutter, the rest of the office appeared well organized. Signed lithographs of harbor scenes adorned two walls, and behind his desk more than a dozen framed certificates displayed his credentials, including training at Harvard and Mass General, specialty certifications, and certificates from memberships and fellowships in professional societies.

From his desk, he phoned Shirley Collins. His other calls—administrators, colleagues, and everyone from stockbrokers to headhunters—could wait. If anything had been urgent, Kristine would have told him.

Shirley wasn't in. The departmental secretary told Barnes she was teaching a class across the street. He walked over there, to the main building of the college of medicine. Cracking open the side door to the auditorium, he saw her finishing a lecture to the second-year medical students. More than a hundred of them scribbled notes as she made her concluding remarks.

". . . and remember, osteoclasts, which break down bone, are of monocyte lineage, meaning they're derived from the immune system. That's likely to be on your test." She noticed Barnes at the door and smiled, then turned back to the class. "If you have any questions, feel free to come up here now or stop by my office later."

In an instant a drove of students surrounded the podium. Shirley was obviously a popular instructor; after lectures, medical students usually bolted from the auditorium.

The crowd dispersed in a few minutes, and she collected her notes. Barnes walked over. Her hair was shorter than he remembered from October, and she looked more confident, more energetic.

She held out her arms and hugged him. "It's good to see you, Chris."

"I was in the neighborhood. Just finished assisting on a bypass." He hoped she wouldn't ask for details. What he recalled was so vague it could have been a figment of his imagination.

"Congratulations. I have to admit I was concerned that some administrator there might try to prevent that."

"Assisting in a surgery? Not a chance. Residents with minimal training assist in major surgeries every day. Those with more training act as chief surgeons on a regular basis, usually when patients don't have insurance."

"Is that really true?"

"It is. And I can tell you that even if I can't remember what I'm doing, I'm still the best cardiothoracic surgeon in the state, if not the entire country."

"I don't doubt that."

"So . . ." He looked at his notes. ". . . are we having dinner tonight?"

She smiled and showed her dimples. "Are you asking me because you'd like to or because your notes say you should?"

"Both," he decided. "I have to trust my notes."

"I actually got a call from Richard asking me to reschedule after he stood me up last night. He wants to go out tonight."

Barnes didn't know who that was, but he didn't see the point in asking. "So are you turning me down, or are you double-booking him and me?"

"Neither. I told him *maybe*. He's my backup in case you change your mind."

"I won't do that. It's in my notes."

"All right, then."

"So you'll call me later?"

She closed her folder of lecture notes and took his arm. "I will. Friendship always trumps a blind date."

Maybe for Elizabeth's friends, he thought. Not for his.

"Please make a note in your list that we're confirmed," she said. "I don't want to cancel Richard and then have you cancel me."

He wrote *confirmed* on his list. "Done."

"Okay, then. We're all set."

He wished everything could be that simple.

As if reading his mind, she said, "You're going to be all right, Chris."

"I know." But he didn't believe it. Things might get better, but they would never be all right.

Chapter 34

Shirley went to her office to prepare another lecture, and Barnes left her to go to the medical library. There he reviewed his notes on Elizabeth's murder, including the portion of the letter he'd transcribed, the one without a second page. Something about the letter struck him as odd. The tone? The wording? He read the transcription again. Something wasn't right. It was like a painting with a skewed perspective. Yet the nature of the problem eluded him.

He set the letter aside and reorganized the rest of his notes into a concise outline. Elizabeth would have been proud. She was always trying to get him to be more organized. Until the food poisoning, he'd rarely written notes to himself, and he hardly ever filed anything in any logical order. Now circumstances had forced him to do both—to be more like Elizabeth.

These are the facts, he thought. *Some person or persons killed Elizabeth along with Rex in the early evening after the security system was turned off. A few hours later someone broke into Denny's house.* If it was the same intruder, and if the break-ins had something to do with the research he and Denny were working on, then why had the killer murdered Elizabeth and the dog? And how had this person gotten past the security system? Elizabeth wasn't one to keep the alarm off when she spent the night home alone. She could have opened the door for someone she knew, but then why the hole in the window?

Barnes tried to picture Elizabeth's murderer. Chances were it was someone she knew, possibly the same person who had written the love letter. Maybe it was someone he knew, too, someone from the medical college or the hospital. The fact that the intruder had shot Rex suggested the killer hadn't come to the house before. Anyone who'd been to the house would have known that Rex wasn't a threat. His size would intimidate a stranger, but not anyone who knew him.

Another question also nagged at Barnes—if the killer had murdered Elizabeth by mistake, why go on to Houston's house and try to break in after botching the first job? Why not wait for another opportunity to do it right?

Barnes wrote down every scenario and motive he could think of, but none seemed likely. Something always failed to make sense: the hole in the window or the alarm turned off or Denny's house being targeted.

Eventually he gave up trying to figure it out, for the time being. He gathered his notes and headed to another library—the Boston Public. A short drive from the medical complex, it was a massive structure with a facade that spanned an entire city block. The front entrance consisted of an expanse of cement stairs leading to three enormous arches with four overhanging clusters of serpentine wrought-iron sconces. At the top of the stairs, between huge cement blocks and flanking the entrance, sat two larger-than-life bronze women, green with age. Sculpted by B. L. Pratt in 1911, the young women in flowing robes possessed a grace and grandeur befitting the enormous building. Barnes recalled that the bronze woman on the right, holding a painter's palette in her left hand and a paintbrush in her right, represented the arts. The other one represented the sciences. In her left hand, she held a bronze crystal ball. Too bad it didn't offer a glimpse into the future. He could have used that now.

Once inside the library, he found the microfiche section and viewing machines, and he reviewed back issues of the *Boston Globe*. He searched for anything of substance that a reporter might have uncovered, beginning with the headline story the day after Carmen had happened upon Elizabeth's body:

PROMINENT SURGEON SLAIN

Dr. Elizabeth Kramer Barnes, an orthopedic surgeon and the wife of cardiothoracic surgeon Christopher Barnes, was found shot to death in their Boston home early yesterday morning. Her body and that of their dog were discovered in the foyer by Carmen Rodriguez, a maid of several months. Both Dr. Barnes and the dog sustained multiple gunshot wounds from a medium-caliber handgun. Police estimate the murder took place the previous evening, but the coroner's office has not yet released any findings. Police also confirmed evidence of forced entry, although they have not released any details. There was no apparent sign of a struggle, and a motive has not yet been determined.

At the time of the murder, Dr. Christopher Barnes lay comatose in a Toronto hospital, the result of an outbreak of food poisoning. Doctors describe his condition as poor.

The article went on to discuss Elizabeth's professional and personal background. Barnes moved on to the next one after making a note about the handgun. His list indicated that Denny owned a 9mm handgun, and he wondered what caliber had been used in Elizabeth's murder.

After Barnes finished reading the next article, he moved on to another, then another. Most of what appeared in print, the police had already told him. Nothing seemed enlightening, but he took notes anyway. Maybe later some detail might take on added significance.

He could only hope.

Later, Barnes met Claire for lunch at Mississippi's, a deli in Kenmore Square, not far from Fenway Park. The restaurant offered dozens of sandwiches on eight different types of bread. Named after famous Americans, the sandwiches included every imaginable deli meat and vegetable, and toppings ranging from marshmallow fluff to caviar.

"When we're done here," Barnes said, setting their tray on a small table, "I'm going to go to the cemetery to visit Elizabeth." He handed Claire her plate and drink and sat across from her. She wore a gray business suit with a pink blouse that brought out the color in her cheeks. She was the type of woman men notice, and although that was immediately obvious to Barnes, the other male patrons confirmed it for him. She had hair the color of Elizabeth's, but much longer, and her aquamarine eyes seemed to reflect both intellect and compassion.

"Would you like for me to come along?" she asked, and she took a sip of tea. Her voice had the same breathy quality he'd always noticed over the phone.

"That would be good if you can find the time." He unfolded a napkin. "It's going to be depressing as . . ." He suppressed the profanity. "It's going to be hard."

"I know." Her eyes looked deep into his, and her gaze felt, for an instant, like Elizabeth's. Comforting. "How well did you know Elizabeth?" he asked.

She took another sip of tea. "Very well. We would finish each other's sentences. There were times when we wouldn't see each other for many months, but I've known her since college."

"It seems strange that you and I never met."

"I know. That's my fault."

"How is it your fault?" he asked.

"Elizabeth suggested it several times, but I just . . . well, it doesn't matter. It was just me."

"What does that mean?"

She looked at him earnestly. "You didn't come here to talk about me, did you? I'm really not that interesting."

"If you say so." He didn't want to press her, at least not about this. Better to focus on more important things. "Did you know many of the people at the funeral?"

"No, but I introduced myself to many of them."

"Were any of them, I don't know, suspicious or noteworthy?"

"Nobody seemed suspicious, but I did meet a neighbor of yours."

"Really? I don't know my neighbors. Who was it?"

"A man named Marshall. I can't remember his last name."

"Coburn," said Barnes.

"Yes, I believe that's right. So you do know at least one of your neighbors."

"No. I've never met him. Elizabeth did once or twice, walking the dog." Why would the man come to her funeral if he met her only once or twice? Barnes wondered. He wrote a note and added that he should find out more about how well Coburn knew Elizabeth.

"Did you meet anyone else noteworthy?"

"Not that I can remember. People in the orthopedics department. Medical students. And patients—a lot of them."

"Well, let me know if you think of anyone else who might have any insight into Elizabeth."

"Of course."

"On a different note, can you tell me where Rex is buried? Eventually I'd like to try to get some closure with him, too, if that's possible."

She frowned. "I guess no one told you."

"Told me what?"

"I had him cremated. I didn't know what you would want, and that's what my veterinarian suggested."

"Uh-huh." What veterinarian in his right mind would recommend *that*, he thought. You don't cremate an animal when it can provide evidence in a murder investigation. If it's buried, the pet's remains can always be exhumed if necessary. He'd hate to see that happen with Rex, but it could provide key information if the police decided to look for gunshot residue or if they wanted to study the trajectory of the bullets.

He took out a pen and paper and jotted down what Claire had told him.

"Was that a mistake?" she asked.

"I'd have preferred a burial."

"Well, I did what my veterinarian recommended."

Your veterinarian is an idiot, Barnes thought. "How about what the police recommended?"

"The police didn't say anything about it. I assumed they took photographs of the crime scene, examined Rex's body, and that was all they needed."

He said nothing and instead continued taking notes about Rex.

"Do you mind my asking why you're writing that?" Claire asked.

"Because otherwise I'll wonder about it later."

She hesitated, then said, "I'm sorry if I made the wrong choice. Personally I don't think it matters what you do after they die. What counts is how you treat them when they're alive."

Barnes said nothing.

"It's the same with people. You loved Elizabeth, and she knew it. That's what matters. Not the funeral or her headstone or all the flowers people sent. Simply the fact that you loved her and she loved you. Nobody can take that away."

He wasn't so sure. "Did she talk to you about any problems she was having with me? I can't remember anything specific, but apparently just last month I moved out of the house for a short while."

"Oh, I didn't know that, but it would explain why she seemed preoccupied. I remember she threw away most of her lunch."

"So she didn't say anything specific, like 'Chris did whatever' or that we argued about, I don't know, having a baby?"

"No, I wish I had tried harder to find out, but I can tell when Elizabeth wants to talk about something, and she didn't seem to want to talk that day. Maybe that's when you moved out."

He just nodded.

Her eyes glazed over. "I miss her."

"I do, too . . . more than I've ever missed anyone." That much was true. "I don't know whether I can function without her."

"After what you've been through . . . What a horrible situation. But you should have faith in yourself, and you should lean on your friends. It's times like these when you learn who they really are."

"That's probably true."

"It is. And I'm sure you'll find you have many."

Not likely, he thought, but he said simply, "We'll see." He took a bite of his sandwich. At the moment he couldn't think of any, except for one. Maybe Claire was right. Maybe he should lean on Denny.

Chapter 35

After lunch, Claire drove Barnes to the cemetery. They took her car. The drive was only a short distance, but to Barnes it felt interminable. Sitting next to Claire, he tried to imagine Elizabeth in the backseat. He needed to picture her somewhere other than in the ground. Yes, he was heading to her gravesite, but he didn't want to think of her buried there. The last place she belonged was in a coffin under six feet of cold dirt.

They finished the drive in silence. Barnes no longer felt any emotional support having Claire with him. She might as well have been a taxi driver.

At the cemetery they walked the lonely stretch of blacktop from the parking lot to the stone-marked fields, their silence broken only by the rhythmic clapping of their footsteps and the mournful whistle of wind through barren trees—nature's dirge.

Claire guided Barnes to Elizabeth's gravesite. They stood together before her headstone, braving the gusting wind and freezing drizzle. The inscription on the white marble read: "In loving memory of my wife, Elizabeth Kramer Barnes."

"I didn't know what exactly to write," Claire said, looking at the words. "I hope this is okay."

"It's fine." A sense of loss weighed on him like the earth over Elizabeth.

"You can replace it with something else if you like," she offered.

"No, it's fine." He'd never had a chance to say good-bye, not even at her funeral. Only now. He reached out and touched the etched stone. "Elizabeth always liked white. Thanks for this."

"It was the least I could do." Her voice was trembling, and she crossed her arms, as if to hold herself together.

He turned to her. "When was the last time you saw her?"

"Last month." Then she added, "You already asked me that, and you wrote it in your notes."

"Oh." He took out his list and, reading it, shielded the paper as best he could from the wind and spattering of rain.

"We ate at Faneuil Hall."

"I can't remember the last time I saw her," he said. "It must have been the day I left for the conference in Toronto, but no matter how hard I try, all I recall are bits and pieces of that day and the day before."

"That must be frustrating."

"You have no idea. It's like I'm disconnected from the rest of the world. With this memory problem, in some ways I feel like an outcast."

"I can relate to that."

"You? I find that hard to believe."

"Obviously Elizabeth didn't tell you much about me."

He said nothing, waiting for her to explain.

"I'm in a profession that's an old-boys' network, and my situation is complicated because I have a nontraditional lifestyle. Some people have a problem with that, which means *I* have a problem with some people. So I can relate, at least a little, to what you're saying about being an outcast."

"Nontraditional lifestyle," he said. "What does that mean?"

"It means . . ." She was trembling, he guessed from the cold. ". . . I have a same-sex partner."

Barnes tried to wrap his head around that—not the notion that Claire was a lesbian but the fact that Elizabeth had hidden this from him. He didn't like secrets. Often, behind them was something bigger. He now wondered whether he was seeing only part of the picture with Claire and Elizabeth. "Were you and Elizabeth ever, you know . . . Is that why we haven't met?"

"No." She answered too quickly, as if anticipating the question. Then she added, "Elizabeth was always more interested in men."

"Uh-huh." He jotted a note—*Claire, Elizabeth's attorney friend, is gay.* He wanted to write that Claire might have been involved with Elizabeth, but the paper was getting damp and the pen wasn't working well. He folded up his list and returned it to his pocket.

"I hope this doesn't change your opinion of me, Chris."

"No, it doesn't." But that didn't sound convincing, even to him. He dug into his coat pocket for a cigarette. Nicotine always had a way of sharpening his focus. No luck. He tried his other pockets. No cigarettes anywhere. "I'm just a little surprised," he added.

She forced a smile. "Well, you're not the first." She looked back at the tombstone. "One of the things I loved about Elizabeth is that she wasn't judgmental."

"No. I try not to be, either."

He shouldn't have invited her along. This time should be spent alone with Elizabeth, engaging her in silent conversation, not talking to Claire about her sexual orientation.

"I need a few minutes by myself," he said.

"Of course. I'll wait in the car." She touched his arm. "Whenever you feel like it, just come to the parking lot and we'll leave. Take all the time you need. I don't have any meetings scheduled."

He thanked her and watched her walk away, then when she was out of earshot, turned back to Elizabeth's grave. "I miss you," he said to her. He touched the inscription carved in the cold marble, and for a moment it became blurry as he fought back tears. "I'll find out who did this to you. I promise."

He wasn't a religious man, but he said a silent prayer. He hadn't prayed since elementary school when Brillo, the family's cocker spaniel, was diagnosed with cancer and given less than a month to live. When his mother told him the news, he prayed every night for two weeks. Then his father took the dog to the vet to be put down.

Barnes knew his prayers wouldn't be answered this time, either, but desperate moments offer limited options. He prayed that there had been some sort of mix-up, that somehow Elizabeth had survived and someone else had been mistaken for her. After all, he had never seen her body after the murder. Anything was possible.

This could even be simply a nightmare. He'd certainly had bizarre dreams before, and they were often as believable as real life. This could be another, induced by sleeping pills or happenstance. He prayed for that, prayed he would wake up to find everything back to normal.

But he knew that would never happen. Elizabeth would be alive again only in the moments when the memory of her death escaped him. Perhaps, in a small way, his inability to remember was a blessing. But then he would have to relive the loss. Every day.

He spoke to Elizabeth silently for a while, then touched her tombstone one last time before turning away from the gravesite. "I'll be back," he promised.

The cemetery suddenly appeared vast and unfamiliar, as though it had grown and reshaped itself.

A knot formed in his throat. How was he supposed to get back to the car, if there even was a car to get back to? He shuffled through the notes in his pocket. Nothing useful.

Out of the corner of his eye, he caught movement, and he turned to see a vortex of starlings swirl skyward like autumn leaves caught in a whirlwind. How different this was from where Elizabeth would have chosen to be. Overlooking a beach—that's where she belonged. She'd always loved the sand and the ocean. Even in the rain.

The starlings vanished as quickly as they'd appeared, and in their place Barnes pictured solitary gulls in the gray sky, floating like kites in an updraft. Elizabeth would have liked that.

Then he remembered his predicament, being stranded in a cemetery. His car must be parked nearby. How else could he have gotten there? Probably not by taking the subway. A graveyard wouldn't be a logical stop for a transit system. Except in Paris. In that city, he recalled, the Metro did stop at the Père Lachaise Cemetery on the outskirts of town. But regardless of which cemetery this was, he would have needed directions to find it, and there weren't any in his pockets.

"It's not a problem," he said out loud, forcing himself to think of alternatives. Chances were someone had accompanied him. One more time he sifted through his notes. *Lunch with Claire.* That must have been recent. Most likely she was sitting in his car or hers, waiting for him nearby.

He followed a winding path over a hill and came across a parking lot with only a half-dozen cars in it. None of them was his, but in one he saw movement, and he headed toward it. A woman sat in the driver's seat. He tried to convince himself that he recognized her, that it was Claire. But it could have been anyone. *She* would have to recognize *him*.

He approached from the front. And then she saw him—a wave and a smile. She leaned to her right and opened the passenger-side door.

Getting into the car, Barnes wondered whether Claire had noticed his confusion. "I hope I didn't make you wait too long," he said.

"No, that's okay. I was just catching up on work."

He recognized her voice.

She took some papers and a legal pad off her lap and put them into a briefcase. Her head bowed, she seemed to be avoiding eye contact. "How are you holding up?" she asked. "Are you okay?"

"Yeah. It's just hard to get used to."

"I know." She started the car and put it into gear, still not looking at him.

And then he realized why. Her eyes were filled with tears.

"You know she valued your friendship," he said. "And I'm grateful for that, too."

She started driving out of the parking lot, eyes front. A tear rolled down her cheek; she took one hand off the steering wheel to wipe it away. Then, in a voice as faint as a whisper, she said to him, or to herself, "I know."

After Claire dropped off Barnes at his car, she drove back to the office and tried to make a dent in the pile of papers on her desk.

How do I ever get anything done here? she asked herself, looking about her cluttered cubicle. She worked as an associate in a firm with six other attorneys who were senior to her, and a lot of the research and background assignments for cases ended up on her desk. That was all right. Litigation and the limelight didn't hold the allure for her that it did for the others. She preferred working behind the scenes.

Of course, litigation did have its rewards. That's how she'd met Darcia, arguing a case of a woman arrested for assaulting her boyfriend with a crowbar. She lost the case but won the judge. That had been both good and bad.

The bad came when Darcia felt threatened, and that happened most of the times when Claire went to lunch with other women. Especially with Elizabeth.

"If we're a couple, you shouldn't need to go out with other women," Darcia argued.

"I'm not going out with them like a date. We're just having lunch. I don't see anything objectionable about having lunch with a friend."

"A young *female* friend who just happens to be a size two?"

"Most of my friends are female and about my age. Yes, that makes them younger than you. I admit it. I have friends who are younger than you."

Age was a touchy subject. Darcia had turned forty over the summer, and although she dyed her hair the color of her judge's robe, she couldn't hide the crows' feet around her eyes, or the extra ten pounds on her hips.

Claire loved her despite her wrinkles, muffin top, and temperament. And recently, with the death of Elizabeth, Darcia had offered a much-needed shoulder to cry on.

She wondered who would do that for Barnes. He had lost a big part of who he was, and coming to terms with that would be no small feat. He probably wouldn't be able to do it alone, and even with help it probably wouldn't happen anytime soon. But she had to try to be there for him. She *would* be there.

She owed at least that much to Elizabeth.

Chapter 36

After returning from the cemetery, Barnes drove back to the hospital for his 2:00 p.m. appointment with Dr. Parks in the clinic building down the street from the main hospital. He rode the escalator to the second floor and entered the waiting room marked "Psychiatry: E. A. Winslow, MD, K. L. Hubbar, MD, R. Kaplan, MD, C. B. Bardles, MD, J. L. Parks, MD, PhD." He was just enough of an elitist to think that having two degrees might make his physician better than the others.

He turned in the usual medical history forms, and the receptionist showed him to the psychiatrist's office. Stepping inside, Barnes suddenly felt confined. The room had no windows and only the one door. Why would a psychiatrist have a windowless office? Probably either to avoid distractions or to avoid tempting suicidal patients.

Half a dozen framed certificates hung on the back wall behind the psychiatrist's desk, and along the walls on either side stood bookshelves filled with journals and textbooks, all neatly arranged. On top of one of the bookshelves, an antique clock ticked away like a metronome.

He suddenly noticed the color of the carpet—a light gray. It reminded him of fog. That, along with the ticking clock, reminded him of his disability, the way time slips by and events get lost in the fog. He wondered what effect the room had on other patients.

The walls were devoid of artwork with one exception: a framed print of a painting by Andrew Wyeth. Barnes recognized it as *Christina's World*, from the late 1940s, a somber work in mostly brown hues. The slender woman in it was sitting awkwardly in a field, propped up by a thin arm and looking away from the viewer, toward a distant farmhouse. Barnes had recently read that Christina was a neighbor of Wyeth's and that she'd been afflicted with a degenerative muscular disorder, leaving her unable to walk. After Barnes learned about her disability, the painting was never the same. Instead of a girl sitting in a meadow, Christina became a cripple struggling in isolation. People would now view him the same way.

He turned his attention from the artwork to Dr. Parks. The psychiatrist struck him as remarkably average—average height, average weight, even average age, about forty. His brown hair receded at the temples, and his pale eyes appeared neither blue nor brown.

The two of them exchanged handshakes, and Dr. Parks motioned Barnes to an easy chair. "Have a seat, Dr. Barnes."

Barnes sat with his back to the clock, facing the Wyeth painting, and took out his notes and a pen. Parks took a seat opposite him in another easy chair.

"I've spoken to Dr. Vincent in Toronto," the psychiatrist said, "and he's apprised me of your situation."

"Good." Barnes remembered no Dr. Vincent. "Then maybe you can tell me why I'm here."

"Why do you think you're here?"

Barnes wasn't in the mood for guessing games. "I don't know, but what I need is for someone to improve my memory. Can you do that?"

Dr. Parks folded his hands in his lap. "I believe so, at least to a limited degree. First I'd like to ascertain for myself the extent of your impairment and the manner in which you're compensating. I know the strain on you must be immense. You've suffered two separate tragedies—the loss of your wife and the loss of your capacity to encode new information. I can help you more with the former."

"That doesn't surprise me."

"Yes, well, with that in mind, let's talk about your wife, Elizabeth. Did you love her?"

What an offensive question, thought Barnes. "Of course I loved her."

"I don't ask that lightly. Many men don't love their wives. There's nothing unusual about that. Sometimes when a sudden, unexpected loss like this occurs, it's the men who *don't* love their wives who suffer the most. Sometimes they feel guilty that they didn't love them. They focus on the things they didn't do, the emotional support they didn't provide. These men need to come to terms with the fact that life isn't perfect and that bad things happen to people irrespective of how we feel about them. That's why I'm asking you, did you love Elizabeth?"

"Yes, I did." Then suddenly he pictured her in the bathroom of their master bedroom, showing him her positive pregnancy test. He remembered the sense of betrayal and the rage that had overcome him. He'd felt an urge to put his fist through the wall, despite the risk of a hand injury. More than anything, he remembered Elizabeth's expression—wide-eyed and tremulous, she believed that he might hurt her. Was he capable of that?

"All right." Dr. Parks jotted a note. "I won't belabor the point. As you probably know, people go through a fairly well-defined grieving process after the loss of a loved one. For you that may not be possible, considering your memory impairment. Do you remember from one day to the next whether Elizabeth is gone?"

"I doubt it," said Barnes, "but I don't recall enough to be able to answer that. I think of her all the time, but I don't know how long specific thoughts of her stay with me."

"I see." Dr. Parks jotted another note. "I understand that your memory of the events shortly before your food poisoning is a problem. Tell me about that."

"I remember parts of that night—I can see the mussels as clearly as if they were sitting on a plate here. But I can't remember much in the days before that, including even before I left for the conference. I can't even remember saying good-bye to Elizabeth." He skimmed through his notes. "Apparently I moved out of the house shortly before the conference, but I don't know anything about that. Why would I remember eating mussels in the restaurant but not moving out of the house?"

"It's possible that from one day to the next you may be going through a process of repression, in which your subconscious keeps you from recalling unpleasant events."

Barnes doubted that. "The night I ate those mussels was the worst day of my life, and I remember practically every bite I took."

"You may think it was the worst day of your life," Dr. Parks said, "but another part of you might believe otherwise. A part of you might think that losing Elizabeth, including whatever occurred that estranged you from her, was the worst thing ever to happen to you."

"And you believe I'm suppressing those thoughts?"

"No. Suppression is a conscious effort not to remember. I believe you're *repressing* those memories. I believe that your inability to recall at least some of what happened is entirely unconscious and not linked to the food poisoning."

Barnes had never considered that, but repression made sense. It seemed the most logical explanation for why some memories were lost and others around them weren't. "So you don't think it's just brain damage?"

"Not entirely. We can test that. I'd like you to start doing an exercise for me at home. When you wake up first thing in the morning, write down everything you remember from the previous night and from anytime since your illness, including whether you remember that Elizabeth is gone."

Barnes made a note to himself.

"And write down anything that you may recall from the time period of memory loss before the food poisoning. If you can't remember from one day to the next what happened after the food poisoning but you do begin to remember some previously forgotten events from before the food poisoning, then you're repressing the earlier lost information."

Barnes finished writing. "Is that good or bad?"

"In general it isn't good. Repressing an event is sometimes necessary for a while—it's a defense mechanism that enables us to go about our lives without being overwhelmed by something we're unable to confront—but ultimately the solution is direct confrontation, facing the problem and finding a resolution. Sometimes the solution is simply an acceptance of the fact that there is no solution."

"That doesn't sound very satisfying."

"Not superficially, but at a deeper level, perhaps."

"Well, the fact is I can accept that Elizabeth and I had some major disagreement, and even that she's dead."

"Yes, but you can't resolve it. In part your problem is that you can't remember, but I think you also don't *want* to remember. In those moments that you forget, Elizabeth is still alive to you and you're both still a happy couple, and you want that very much."

"Of course I want her to be alive and I want us to be happy," Barnes said. "That doesn't mean anything."

"It means there's a reason for your forgetting. Repression is a crutch. It takes your mind away from something unpleasant and helps you focus on other things. The first step in overcoming this problem is to recognize that it exists. For the time being, there's no urgency in finding a resolution, although ultimately one of our goals will be to allow you to conduct your life with as few crutches as possible. We won't try to take them all away at once. We'll work on solving the problems one at a time."

"Let's solve my memory problem first."

"We'll work on that. Maybe during our next session I'll hypnotize you, although I usually wait until the patient knows me better."

"Given my condition, I may never know you better than I do right now."

"Perhaps, but *I'd* prefer to know *you* a little better. I don't believe hypnosis has much to offer during an initial visit. It may confirm that you're repressing memories of Elizabeth, but that's relatively unimportant at this time."

"So what do you suggest we do?"

"Let's talk about Elizabeth. What effect do you think her death has had on your overall state of mind, emotionally, intellectually?"

"Other than the obvious overwhelming grief?" Barnes thought about that. "I don't remember enough from moment to moment to answer that, and I can't separate all of the effects of losing her from the effects of the food poisoning. For example, I've become more organized, like her, but that's necessary to avoid confusion."

"Are you *thinking* more like her?"

He hadn't considered that. "I probably am. I'm more organized and methodical, and my guess is I'm less critical of others, given my condition. Do you think that has a deeper meaning?"

"What do you think?"

"I think you're not answering my question."

"I think you know the answer. You're internalizing a part of her. It's a common phenomenon. When we admire others, we tend to acquire some of their characteristics. When we're younger, that's what shapes who we become, and that's why there's so much controversy about who should be role models in schools. The same thing happens to adults, although they usually aren't as impressionable. Nevertheless, adults frequently change their behavior after they associate for a time with someone they admire. I believe that, for the most part, you're becoming more organized because you have to—to cope with your disability—and you're becoming less critical of others because of the different perspective you now have, again as a result of the food poisoning. But I also believe that you're internalizing a part of Elizabeth because you admired her and because you want to hold on to part of her."

"I guess that's possible," Barnes conceded, "but she was very different from me, or as she would say, different *to* me. She was British. I think about her much more now. I'm not sure how much, given my difficulty remembering things, but I get the feeling it's practically all the time. Before, I took her for granted; I tended to focus more on work."

"We all do that to some extent," Dr. Parks said. "Other people in our life are ultimately what's most important, but our career defines who we are, and most of us need that framework to feel we have a direction, if not a purpose, in life."

"Yeah, well, my life is in shambles, and I may never get back my career, but one thing I do have is purpose. I'm going to live from day to day by doing the one thing I *have* to do."

Dr. Parks raised an eyebrow. "And what might that be?"

Barnes was surprised the man didn't know. "I'm going to solve Elizabeth's murder."

Chapter 37

Barnes spent much of the afternoon running errands, including going shopping and going to the gym for an abbreviated workout. At the gym he sometimes placed bets with Burt Fielding, a stockbroker who served as a bookie for anyone with a penchant for wagering on sports. Barnes had placed more bets with him than he could count, but not anymore. Now the added confusion and stress from not knowing whether he owed or was owed money would be a sufficient deterrent.

After returning home, he spent some time opening his and Elizabeth's mail, including letters of condolence from people he hardly knew. The ringing of the telephone interrupted that chore just when he was thinking about taking a break.

An unfamiliar woman's voice asked, "Christopher Barnes?"

"Speaking." He prepared to interrupt a telemarketer.

"You don't know me," the woman began. "My name is Darcia. I'm a friend of Claire's."

Claire? He pulled the notes out of his pocket and skimmed through them. "Elizabeth's attorney friend?"

"That's right. I understand you had lunch with her this afternoon."

Barnes said nothing. He was busy looking through his notes.

"I'm calling to inform you that she was distressed by your comments."

"Oh?" His notes didn't seem to offer any hint of what she was talking about.

"You criticized her for cremating your dog."

There it was: Claire had instructed the vet to cremate Rex. "Well, if I did, she deserved it," he said. "It's common sense not to destroy potential evidence in a murder investigation."

"She was trying to do you a favor at a difficult time," the woman said, an edge to her voice. "You shouldn't have expressed a lack of appreciation. You—"

"She doesn't even know me."

"Don't interrupt me. She *does* know you, through Elizabeth, and you've upset her. Claire cared deeply for Elizabeth and is still grieving for her. She doesn't need any additional stress in her life."

Tell me about it, he thought. "What did you say your name is?"

"Darcia Parker. You don't want to hear from me again."

He wrote that down. "Are you an attorney?"

"I'm a judge."

Suddenly he remembered her. The woman had run commercials on television, campaign ads for a local election. *Elect Judge Parker.* He may have even voted for her. In her advertisement, she'd looked like a thirty-something librarian—glasses, hair up in a bun. Nothing like the shrew he'd envisioned from this conversation. "Did you know Elizabeth?" he asked.

"Don't change the subject. I'm calling about Claire, and specifically to tell you that if you can't show some appreciation for her, then stay away. Am I making myself clear? *Stay away.* Write a note to yourself so you don't forget. If I hear another complaint about you, you'll regret it." And she hung up.

Barnes did write a note to himself: *Claire had feelings for Elizabeth. Darcia (Claire's overly protective significant other) threatened me. Did Darcia know Elizabeth?* Then he added, *Ask Claire about that.*

Elizabeth's relationship with Claire could have been more complicated than he'd thought. According to his notes, Elizabeth had been unfaithful. But with whom? The police didn't know, and neither did he. Could it have been with Claire?

Somewhere Elizabeth had likely kept evidence of her infidelity. He decided to conduct a search, starting with the most likely place—her office.

Entering her room, he felt out of place, even guilty. This was Elizabeth's personal and professional space, and she wouldn't want him snooping around in it. But the truth was more important than propriety.

He sat at her desk, in the chair she had occupied countless times, yet he felt no closer to her. His intent here was to gather information, not to reminisce. But then a small framed picture next to her computer monitor caught his attention. It was a photograph of the two of them with her parents, taken shortly before their wedding. They'd eaten at a small place on Newbury Street, dining outside under an umbrella just a couple of feet from the sidewalk. Elizabeth's parents liked to people-watch, and Newbury Street was an ideal place for that. Lined with shops, art galleries, and restaurants, it attracted locals as well as tourists. Everything from tuxedos to tattoos. Long dresses, short shorts. Bald heads, spiked hair. And multiple piercings. Elizabeth's parents also enjoyed making fun of the Boston accents. He could still hear them imitating, "Pock the cah."

Barnes looked up from the photograph. What was he doing in Elizabeth's office? How long had he been there? Her computer was right in front of him, so that must mean he'd intended to look for something on it.

He pushed the computer's power switch. Nothing. Was the CPU unplugged? He looked under the desk. No, the surge protector had been turned off. He turned it on, and the computer whirred to life.

Elizabeth didn't store much research or other work-related material on her hard drive at home—she usually saved it only on her computer at work and on disks as backups—but he listed every document file on the computer. Not surprisingly, most of them were months old and contained information unrelated to clinical research. That was just as well. Her disks alone could take weeks to review. He would need to prioritize them, in part by subject but mainly by date. The most recent ones would likely be the most meaningful. He just needed to be methodical. Like Elizabeth. Already he'd forgotten the letter the police had shown him suggesting that she'd had an affair, and that he'd been intent upon uncovering the details. Instead he was focusing on being organized and thinking about how well everything was falling into place, how applying simple logic could guide him through whatever activities needed to be done.

He had no idea how wrong that was.

Chapter 38

Barnes left Elizabeth's office and decided to open the day's mail. A business envelope caught his attention—a plain white envelope without a return address. It was postmarked in Boston on December 15 and addressed to "Chris Barnes," not "Dr. Barnes" or "Christopher Barnes, MD." The address was printed in capital letters, childlike, with a black felt-tipped pen.

He opened the envelope and took out a folded sheet of typing paper. Something about it sent a shiver down his spine.

He unfolded it, and bold, black letters jumped off the page. Capital letters—the same handwriting as the address.

YOU STILL OWE ME $10,000. DEPOSIT IT BY NOON SATURDAY.

Unsigned.

The implications of the letter were clear. He owed somebody a chunk of money, and that person expected to be paid. But who, and why? Had he lost a bet on the New England Patriots? It wouldn't be the first time, but nobody had ever notified him via an anonymous letter. Burt, the bookie from the gym, would never do something like that. Any reasonable bookie would just call him. Besides, they always dealt with cash in hand, not bank deposits. And his bets were never that large. At least, almost never. The World Series—once—and last year's Super Bowl. But those were exceptions.

What debt could be worth more than $10,000? Nothing that Barnes could recall. Obviously whoever wrote the letter didn't want to be implicated in the transaction. Yet that person had assumed Barnes would know what the note pertained to.

He had no clue.

He tried to concentrate, to summon memories buried in his subconscious from the days before his trip to Toronto. Some people claim to be able to remember events from a previous life, from hundreds of years ago. If they can do that, it shouldn't be asking too much for him to remember back one or two months.

He concentrated on recalling events that must have taken place. Saying good-bye to Elizabeth. Packing for the conference. *Thinking* about packing for the conference. Nothing registered.

Then another thought dawned on him. He got out his checkbooks—four, counting a joint money market account—and looked for large withdrawals. If he *still* owed someone $10,000, that meant he'd made some sort of previous payment.

He flipped through all the pages. Nothing unusual. Nothing that could explain the anonymous note.

He tried to remember sporting events, games he may have bet on in the past couple of months—football, hockey, even golf. Instead, his mind formed the image of a cup of urine and, beside it, Elizabeth's positive pregnancy test.

He'd been furious about that. Why, he wasn't sure. Nor could he recall what had happened next. He'd never wanted children, but now the thought of having a baby with her seemed not only acceptable but appealing. A child would be a part of her. A part of both of them. It didn't make sense that he would react with rage.

At that moment the doorbell rang, interrupting his thoughts. He walked to the foyer and peered through the peephole. Two middle-aged men in overcoats stood outside, one stocky, the other tall. Both strangers.

"Open the door, Dr. Barnes," the stocky one ordered. "We see you looking through the hole."

Why were they demanding that? Did he owe them money? "Who are you?"

"Detectives Wright and Gould," said the other one, taking out a badge and holding it up to the peephole. "We interviewed you when you came off the plane from Toronto. We'd like to ask you a few more questions about your wife."

Elizabeth? In his confusion over the uninvited visitors, he'd forgotten everything about her. He also forgot about the note in his hand. He opened the door. "Come in."

They quickly stepped inside, and he closed the door behind them.

"You don't mind if we sit down for a few minutes," the taller one said, stamping his feet and unbuttoning his coat.

"Is Elizabeth all right?"

The two officers exchanged glances; then the taller one said, "Let's sit down."

Barnes suddenly noticed the letter in his hand—some sort of threat or maybe a ransom note. He folded it quickly and shoved it into his back pocket. Leading the men into the house, he glanced at his watch and noticed the inscription—*Examinez votre poche droite.* He reached into his right front pants pocket and retrieved a folded-up sheet of paper, but before he could open it, they'd entered the family room where he was taking them. The stocky policeman plopped down on the couch with his partner, while Barnes sat in a chair.

"Dr. Barnes," said the stocky one, "what do you remember about your wife?"

What kind of question was that? "She's an orthopedic surgeon," he said. "Has something happened to her?" He finished unfolding the paper.

"Is that a list of things to do?" asked the tall officer.

Barnes glanced at it, and the first item jumped out at him: *Elizabeth murdered on 11/26.* He recalled that now, or at least he thought he did. How could he ever have forgotten? "Elizabeth was murdered," he managed to say.

"That's right," said the stocky cop.

"You don't remember us, do you, Dr. Barnes?" asked the other one.

Elizabeth was murdered. "No."

"We met yesterday," said the stocky one. "You remember anything from yesterday?"

They must already know his mind was a sieve. "No," he said. "I don't remember much of anything since . . . maybe the end of November." His Toronto conference had taken place then.

"I'm Detective Wright," said the taller cop, "and this is Detective Gould. We're from homicide. What was that letter you put in your back pocket?"

He had no clue what they were talking about, but he reached back and put his hand in the pocket. Sure enough—a folded sheet of paper. He unfolded it but not in a way that let the detectives see what had been written on it. Then he remembered—someone was demanding money from him. That couldn't be good. He folded the paper again and put it back in his pocket. "It's personal."

"People write letters to you in black magic marker?" asked Detective Gould.

"I said it's personal." He looked at his notes but saw no mention of it there.

"We're here to help," said Detective Wright. "If you don't want to show it to us, you don't have to." Then he changed the subject and asked whether Barnes was having any problems settling in and adjusting under the circumstances.

Barnes wondered whether the man was just biding time, waiting for him to forget about the letter so they could ask to see it again.

In your back pocket is a letter demanding ten thousand dollars, he said to himself, hoping the silent words would help him remember. *Keep it there until they leave.*

But remembering the note while carrying on an unrelated conversation was a lot to expect.

"Are you getting any counseling?" asked Detective Wright.

In your back pocket is a letter demanding ten thousand dollars. "I don't know." Barnes added a hasty note to his list: *Letter in back pocket.*

"Why don't you put that away and just talk to us?" Wright suggested.

"I don't think so." As he read through his notes, Wright and Gould exchanged glances. "I keep notes on everything," he said, "including my meeting now with you." He jotted that down.

"How about sharing that with us?" asked Gould. "It might help us solve your wife's murder. You want to help with that, don't you?"

Barnes didn't dignify the question with a response. He kept reading and came across an entry about Denny Houston's place being broken into. *That* he could share with them. "Dr. Houston, a colleague, told me that his house in Weston was vandalized the night Elizabeth died."

Wright took out a notepad and jotted down the information. "Was anyone arrested?"

"No, not that I'm aware of. I imagine you'll want to call the Weston police."

"Obviously," said Gould.

"What's your colleague's address?" asked Wright.

Barnes gave it to him.

"I'm surprised we haven't heard about this from the Weston police. Communications are usually better than that. Tell me, Dr. Barnes, what exactly is your connection with this Dr. Houston? Is he a surgeon, too?"

"Yeah, the *second* best surgeon in the hospital. He and I also do research together."

"What kind of research?"

"We're working on a way to make coronary-artery bypass grafts last longer."

Wright took more notes. "What do you mean 'last longer'?"

"They get clogged in about a tenth the time it takes to fill up your original arteries with plaque. If we can come up with a way to make them last as long as the original blood vessels, then people won't need repeat surgery or angioplasty five or ten years down the road."

Wright nodded. "That makes sense. Can you think of any reason why someone wouldn't want you to conduct this research?"

"No. This is one of those things you'd think everyone would want. Like a cure for cancer. Who wouldn't want that?"

"Maybe the cancer doctors," offered Gould, "if it cuts into their profits."

Barnes said nothing.

"Who would benefit from stopping *Elizabeth's* research?" asked Wright.

"Nobody," Barnes said. "It's already done."

Wright and Gould looked at each other, as if deciding what to do next. Then Wright stood up. Gould followed suit.

"We'll check these things out," offered Wright. "We don't need any more of your time right now. You've been very helpful." He took out a business card. "We gave you our cards yesterday, but here's another in case you misplaced them. Give us a call if you think of anything else. Don't just write it down on your list. Okay?"

"Okay." Barnes took the card, then walked them to the door.

"Oh, I almost forgot," said Wright, his hand on the doorknob. He turned to face Barnes. "You were going to show us that letter."

"What letter?" He wouldn't have been surprised if he had a pile of about a thousand of them.

"In your back pocket. You said you wanted to show it to us."

He didn't recall putting anything there. He reached inside. The detective was right—a folded sheet of paper. He began to open it. A single page with large black letters from a felt-tipped pen. When he saw the lettering, he visualized the note, and the memory of what it said returned in a flash.

He refolded the page. "It's personal." Putting it back in his pocket, he opened the door for them. "Thanks for stopping by."

"Almost," Wright said to Gould as they walked from Barnes's house to their car.

"We should've just taken it," said Gould. "By the time he got around to filing a complaint, he wouldn't have a clue what it was about."

Wright resisted telling his partner how much he'd wanted to do just that. "It would be thrown out of court," he replied instead. "An illegal seizure isn't going to do us any good."

"Then we should've just looked at it and gave it back. I'd bet my left foot it had something to do with the murder."

"Which one?"

"Which murder?"

"No. Which left foot?"

"Very funny. I think there was a dollar figure on that letter."

"I didn't see it." They had reached the car, and Wright walked around to the driver's side.

"We'll get him," said Gould. "It's just a matter of time."

"If he did it," added Wright.

They got into the car. Wright started the engine and pulled out into rush-hour traffic.

"You think there's any connection with his pal Houston?" asked Gould.

"Most likely." But Wright doubted it was anything direct or simple. High-profile murder cases are usually more complicated than they appear. "Or it's possible somebody just wants us to think there is," he said. "Hard to tell."

"Maybe we should lean on him, too."

"Yeah, we'll do that. In the meantime, we'll wait to see if the phone tap turns up anything. It's just a matter of time before we know everything Dr. Barnes does. He's always writing notes to himself. Sooner or later most of them will end up in the trash, and then they'll be ours. We'll figure things out soon enough."

"Yeah . . . Kinda spooky how he didn't even recognize us. The guy must be really gorked out."

Wright stopped the car at a red light. "I don't think that's the medical term," he said, "but Dr. Barnes has a real problem. For his sake I hope it isn't permanent."

"That would suck big time."

Wright edged the car forward. "That's an understatement."

Chapter 39

Karen Wright's last class ended at 3:30 p.m., leaving her plenty of time to prepare dinner for herself and Gordon. She liked to cook, even though friends teased her about being too domestic. The only thing she didn't like was having to reach for things. Much of the kitchen wasn't accessible to people who couldn't stand up, and she needed to resort to a specially designed retriever to get items from all but a couple of the cabinets. The retriever was a metal pole with a pistol grip at one end and a clawlike hand at the other. Rubber covered the claw so that glass and other slippery objects would be less likely to fall through its grasp, but over the years, she'd dropped and shattered more than a few jars and bottles.

Karen had just finished cooking—Italian—when Gordon walked through the door.

"Something smells good," he said, hanging his coat on the peg near the door and petting Lizzy, who had hobbled over to him and was wagging her stump. She'd survived her trip to the veterinarian and had returned with only one paw bandaged, wrapped in gauze and a rubber material that would protect it from being chewed. Fortunately the paw showed no signs of being infected, just a small cyst that needed time to heal.

"Italian?" he guessed, entering the hot room redolent of garlic and oregano. Pots, pans, trays, and dishes covered much of the counter space.

Karen gazed up at him from her wheelchair. "That's right. Is that why they made you detective—your incredible deductive skills?"

He bent down and kissed her on the lips. Even spattered with spaghetti sauce and sweating from the kitchen heat, she looked beautiful. He wanted to pick her up and hold her, but that always irritated her, being treated like a child or, worse, an object, albeit the object of his affections. So he settled for a long kiss.

"How was your day?" he asked.

"The usual. Nothing exciting. How about yours?"

"Interesting. The Barnes case is getting more complicated. Just when I think it's going to stall, something else turns up. But it's never anything that can break the case. Just bits and pieces that don't seem to tie anything together."

Karen opened the oven and reached in with two pot holders, leaning forward in her chair. "Well, isn't that usually the way these things work?" She picked up a pan of lasagna and put it on top of the stove, then closed the oven door and turned off the heat.

"Yeah, you've got that right. You know, I'm pretty sure Barnes still believes he's innocent, but I get the feeling he's holding out." Wright shoved his hands into pot-holder mittens and carried the lasagna to the table while Karen wheeled herself to the refrigerator to retrieve a salad.

"Did he tell you *anything*?" asked Karen.

"Well, he told us the house of a colleague of his was broken into. Turns out it was the same MO. Most likely the same perp, but I don't know that it'll lead us anywhere except further astray. I read the report from the Weston police. No fingerprints, footprints, or any other material. Nothing."

"But the report must tell you *something*."

"Yeah, that more than one house was broken into that night. Assuming it was the same perp, either there's a connection between Dr. Barnes and Dr. Houston, or somebody wants us to think there is, in which case there really isn't one at all. I'll talk to Dr. Houston again tomorrow to see if he can tell us anything else. I wonder why he didn't mention the break-in when we talked to him last month."

"Unless maybe he didn't want you to know."

"Maybe. The fact is we should have known. It's bizarre that this could happen just down the road and we're not informed. Talk about poor communication!" He went to the refrigerator for salad dressing. "And I get the feeling Dr. Barnes is more interested in trying to figure this out than in helping us. I don't understand that."

"I do. He needs to do things for himself."

"You mean he really thinks he can solve this case on his own?"

"It's not a matter of *thinking* he can," said Karen. "It's a matter of *needing* to. He has to empower himself. He has to do something on his own that shows him he's capable of overcoming this challenge. If he can't do that, then he can't begin to recover. It's like when I went up the ramp to get into the apartment the day I came home from the hospital. I wouldn't let you help me up the incline. It was a simple thing for you, but for me it was a challenge and I had to do it myself, for my own self-esteem. Dr. Barnes isn't any different. He probably sees solving the case as a way of redeeming himself. If *you* do it, he's going to feel impotent." She wheeled herself up to the table and transferred herself to one of the dining-room chairs. "Doesn't that make sense?" She put a napkin in her lap.

"No." Wright served salad to Karen and himself while she cut the lasagna. Lizzy stood nearby. Wright refrained from adding that whatever Barnes felt the need to do, clearly exceeded his ability to do it. Wright had sometimes felt that way about Karen. He didn't understand why she wouldn't let him help her more.

"What do you mean 'no'?" she said.

"I mean his wife's been murdered, and he should do whatever he can to help Marty and me crack the case. Anything else is counterproductive. Investigating homicides is what we do, and we're damn good at it. Having a heart surgeon try to solve a murder doesn't make any more sense than having a homicide detective put in one of those heartbeat-regulator things."

"A pacemaker?"

"Yeah, a pacemaker. People should stick to what they know, and Barnes doesn't know anything about investigative work."

"Does Marty have any ideas?"

"Not really." Gould wasn't much of an idea man.

"We should invite him over again. It's been ages."

"Yeah, well, ever since he's been seeing Gloria, he hasn't had much time for anything else, and he still hasn't gotten to the point of wanting to share her with anyone."

"That sounds serious."

"It might be. Ask me in another month."

"Maybe then you two will have solved the case and we can celebrate it over dinner."

"Yeah, if I can just get Barnes to back off and help us."

"You shouldn't count on it." She stuck her fork in her salad. "Keep in mind it's his wife who was killed."

"So what do you suggest?" he asked. "How do I get Barnes to cooperate?"

"Make him feel important. Make him feel needed." She took a bite of her salad. "Don't treat him as though he's helpless."

"You're saying I should stroke the ego of a heart surgeon?"

"Either that or don't expect much help from him. It's like trying to take a sock out of Lizzy's mouth. You can yank it out and prove that you're stronger, and probably tear it in the process, or you can pet her for ten seconds and she'll drop it at your feet." Karen reached down and rubbed Lizzy's hairy chin. "It's up to you."

Wright mulled that over while he ate a forkful of lasagna. "You may be right," he decided, "but . . ."

She looked up at him. "But what?"

He picked up another forkful of lasagna. "But I think I'll still yank it out."

Chapter 40

After the detectives left, Barnes reviewed Elizabeth's files and other work-related items from her office at the hospital. Reading through all of her papers would take days, if not weeks. Then there were her computer disks, holding hundreds of additional files of information. He took a container of the disks to his office.

He had a second-floor office similar in size and layout to Elizabeth's. They each had their own computer, bookshelves, file cabinets, and fax machine. But there the similarity ended. Her office always looked as though a maid had just cleaned it, whereas his looked as though it had been ransacked: notes, journal articles, and open books strewn all over his desk and some even on the floor, and computer disks scattered around the computer.

He sat at his terminal, switched on the computer, and inserted one of Elizabeth's disks. A list of fifty or more files appeared on the screen. He would enter them through the programs used to generate each, and then go through them one by one, taking notes on anything unusual or unfamiliar. For all he knew, Elizabeth could have been working on dozens of different projects. He wished she had talked to him more about her work, but that wasn't their nature. They both liked to get away from their jobs once they left the hospital. Ironically, he would now learn more about her work after they could no longer discuss it.

He read through Elizabeth's files until his vision blurred. Then, at seven thirty, he answered his doorbell to find Shirley with three Styrofoam cartons of food in hand. She hugged him and kissed his cheek. This was not the Shirley Collins of a few months ago. Apparently they'd become better acquainted. She looked different, too. Her hair was fuller and about four inches shorter than the last time he and Elizabeth had gone to dinner with her.

"You look good," he said. "I like your hair." He didn't add that he preferred it longer.

"Thanks. You look well."

Was she politely lying, too?

She unbuttoned her overcoat, revealing an aubergine dress with a plunging V-neck. Obviously silk, from the way it rippled, and underneath, barely discernible, the dark shadow of a bra. As she took off her hat—a red beret that matched her overcoat—he noticed little gold grand-piano earrings. He wondered whether she played the piano and whether they'd already had that conversation.

"Nice dress," he said.

"Thanks, but for the sake of full disclosure, I have to admit I didn't wear it for you. I met Richard for coffee instead of canceling my date with him."

"Richard?" That must be a new boyfriend.

"Yeah, Richard, my blind date. Except he wasn't really blind. That would have been an improvement. Then he wouldn't have spent our entire time together conversing with my breasts."

"Well, maybe you shouldn't have worn that dress."

"Maybe not. Not for him, anyway."

"So I'm guessing Richard is history."

"Richard is a dick, no pun intended."

"Well, I think we can improve on your evening. Let's go into the kitchen." He took the food from her. "If nothing else, I should be able to find a good bottle of wine."

"Tonight I'll take large over good."

In the kitchen he asked, "Where would you like to eat? Here, the dining room, or the family room?"

"Let's do the family room like last night."

"Sure. Whatever you like. What have you brought here?" He opened the Styrofoam containers.

"Cannelloni, spaghetti carbonara, and lasagna."

The two of them bustled around preparing their takeout dinner—opening wine, reaching for glasses and plates.

Just like a married couple, Barnes mused. Like what he and Elizabeth used to do. Yet it felt strange without Elizabeth there. Shirley had always been *her* friend, not his. But that seemed to be changing.

Barnes felt something in his back pocket. He reached in and found a folded sheet of paper. As soon as he opened it, the bold print struck a chord of fear—he remembered. As quickly as possible, he refolded the paper. But Shirley was standing only a few feet away. Had she seen the message? He looked at her, and their eyes met, but her gaze gave no indication she'd seen anything out of the ordinary.

"Something you need to do?" she asked.

"No. I just have to jot another note to myself. You can head into the family room. I'll be right there."

She left the kitchen, and he put the paper back into his pocket. He wondered how many times in the past half hour he'd pulled that out and unfolded it.

He looked at his list and noticed he'd already mentioned the letter in his back pocket. To decrease the risk of overlooking it later, he underlined the item and added the fact that whoever wrote the letter was demanding $10,000. Then he joined Shirley in the family room. They sat in what he guessed were the same chairs as the previous night.

Sipping the wine seemed to trigger a flash of déjà vu, but nothing specific. It was just a feeling, a sense that they had shared a similar time.

"How about a fire?" she asked.

He dimmed the lights and started the gas fireplace.

"Thanks for coming over," he said after returning to his chair. "The house feels less empty with you here."

"You're welcome, but you don't have to thank me. It isn't a chore."

He took a sip of wine. "I never used to mind being alone because I never *felt* alone. I'm not sure I ever really knew what it was like. But now, even with you here, I still feel it. That's nothing personal, of course."

"I know. We'll have to work on that."

"I like having you here. But at the same time it seems pointless. By tomorrow I probably won't even remember you came over."

"You don't know that," she said. "Not for sure. Do you remember anything from yesterday?"

"I don't know." He tried to think, oddly not just for himself but also for her. He sensed that she genuinely cared, that they were trying to achieve a common goal. "Maybe some images," he said, "but I'm not sure they're actually memories."

"What sort of images?"

They flitted before him like fish in a murky lake, coming into view for just an instant before disappearing back into the depths. "I remember eating with chopsticks, but I don't know if it was lunch or dinner, and I couldn't say for sure that it even really happened."

"It did," she said. "We had Chinese food for dinner."

"What did my fortune say?"

233

"Hmm." She seemed to be studying him. "I think it said, 'Seize the moment.'"

He doubted that but nonetheless asked, "Did I?"

"Not really, but there will be other moments." She smiled.

"My memory is a huge problem, but my number one concern is finding whoever killed Elizabeth."

She pulled her chair closer to his, until they almost touched. "I can understand that, but you should leave it to the police. That's what they're trained to do. Have you found out anything that might help them?"

"I've taken notes." That much he remembered. "Not for them. For me. If I remember, I might translate them tonight or tomorrow."

"What do you mean 'translate'?"

"Rewrite them in French."

She gave him a puzzled look. "Why would you do that?"

"Because," he explained, "whoever killed Elizabeth probably knew either her or me, or both. If they come over here, I don't want them reading my thoughts. Did you see all the notes I have on the refrigerator?"

"Yes, I did. I didn't read them, but they're hard to miss."

"Well, I also have them in my pocket, on the side door to the garage . . ." He pointed in that direction. ". . . and I'm sure more are upstairs in different places I don't remember. I'm surprised I can recall the list in my pocket, considering how many other things I forget. That's the reason I have notes scattered around, in case I lose a set or forget where I've put them. I have a fax machine in my office upstairs, and it doubles as a copier. I'm going to start copying my notes with it and leaving them everywhere. That way I'll never lose track of what's going on. And I'll write them in French."

"Do you mind telling me what you've learned so far?" She took a sip of wine.

"Yeah, I'll tell you." He balanced his plate on his lap while he retrieved the list from his pocket and skimmed through it. "Denny Houston's house was burglarized that same night." He looked up at her. "Do you know Denny?"

"Not personally, but I know who he is. A heart surgeon, right?"

"That's right." Barnes turned his attention back to his list and read about the letter demanding $10,000. No need to mention that.

"How well do you know him?" she asked.

"We're best friends."

"Oh, yeah? Then why isn't he here?"

"He's a busy man."

"Right. If you think he's your best friend, but he's not spending time with you when you need him the most, you may not be a very good judge of character. What else is on your list?"

He read more of it to himself. *Houston doesn't want to work with you.* Below that . . . "Something about Claire." He took a last bite of his meal and set his plate on the coffee table.

"Claire?"

"Elizabeth's attorney friend. Do you know her?"

"Yeah, the lesbian."

"Am I the only one who didn't know that about her?"

"Probably. I don't know her well. And I definitely don't want to know her partner."

"Oh?"

"Her girlfriend is a judge—Darcia Parker. A friend of mine used to work for Darcia and said she's a psycho bitch. Those were her exact words. Why are you interested in Claire?"

His notes seemed to confirm Shirley's assessment of Darcia. He added the characterization of "psycho bitch." His notes also questioned whether Claire should be trusted. "Just wondering. I've met her and talked to her on the phone, but I don't remember her the way I do you." He looked at his list again and saw that he and

Elizabeth had been separated before the conference in Toronto. "Did you know that Elizabeth and I were separated?"

She nodded but said nothing.

He could see the hurt in her eyes. Was that for him, he wondered, or Elizabeth? "Do you know why?" he asked.

"Not exactly. She told me that she was pregnant and that you were being a jerk but that mostly everything was her fault. Those weren't her exact words, of course. I inferred that everything was your fault, but that's just how I felt at the time. I don't think she felt that way. She said it was complicated, but when I asked what she meant by that, she didn't say . . . What happened?"

He shrugged. "I don't know. I don't remember." He folded up his list and slipped it back into his pocket. "I was hoping you could tell me."

"Whatever it was, I'm sure it wasn't all your fault, and I know she loved you." She reached over and put her hands on his thighs, just above his knees, then leaned forward, her face only inches from his. Her eyes regarded his intently, and then she closed the distance and kissed him softly on the lips. He kissed her back. At first it was a kiss of comfort and friendship, perhaps deep affection, but it quickly grew.

As if on cue, Barnes's hands took over. They glided up her arms to the back of her neck. He pulled her closer, breathing in the fragrance of her perfume as he pressed his lips to hers, first feeling, then tasting. He sensed this was wrong, that it was too soon, but what's too soon when you have no concept of time? A month or a year or even a decade later might still feel too soon. And a decade later she might not be available.

Shirley seemed conflicted, too, shifting herself to sit on his lap, straddling him, yet saying, "Do you think this is a good idea?"

When he didn't answer, she kissed him again deeply. Her hands pulled up his shirt and reached underneath, held his lower back, then slid under his belt and pants.

He pulled up her dress and felt the warm flesh above her hose.

Her lips moved across his cheek and found their way to his neck. "I'm not sure we should be doing this," she said.

That makes two of us, he thought, yet he didn't stop. Her breath on his neck was mesmerizing.

She kissed him again, then stood up and slipped off her dress.

She stood before him in a black bra, black panties, black garter, and black hose. In a moment he would ease her to the floor, unfasten her garter straps, and slide her lace panties down over her hips.

She unfastened his belt.

That's when he stopped her. "No." He put his hands over hers.

She didn't say anything, just looked at him, as if asking whether he was really serious.

"I'm sorry," he said. "I can't do this."

She ran a hand through her hair, then backed away and sat by the fire. "That's probably for the best." She looked up at him, her face glowing in the lambent light. "I really shouldn't make love with my best friend's husband."

"I'm sorry," he said again.

"Don't be. You made the right call." She began putting her dress back on.

"Let's just sit by the fire for a while," he said.

"Sure."

He pulled two cushions off the couch and put them on the floor in front of the fireplace, and Shirley dimmed the lights more. They sat down next to each other, but not holding each other.

"So now we're pajama buddies?" she said, laughing.

"I guess so."

"Life sure is strange."

"Tell me about it."

The two of them stared into the fire for some time, alone with their thoughts. He soon felt himself nodding off, and although he didn't fall asleep, he did forget the chain of events that had led to this point in time.

He looked at his watch. *Examinez votre poche droite.* Maybe that would tell him how he'd ended up on cushions in front of the fireplace with Shirley, whose lipstick was smeared. Smeared onto his own lips—he could feel it.

He reached into his pocket and found the list. Shielding it from her, he read through it by the light of the fireplace.

Elizabeth is dead.

The words caught him off guard. He'd forgotten. The realization brought shame. Here he was with Shirley, doing who knows what, and Elizabeth was dead.

He looked at the list again and saw farther down on it that he and Elizabeth had been separated. Still that did little to ease the guilt. What had he done here?

He read through the rest of the notes and realized he would need to write a reminder to himself, something to tape to the bathroom mirror for tomorrow morning. Otherwise, everything from tonight might just as well never have happened.

He looked into Shirley's eyes, and she reminded him of Cheryl in Toronto.

"What's wrong?" she asked.

"Nothing. I've just got a long day ahead of me tomorrow."

"Is that your way of asking me to leave?"

"Yeah. I really do need to get up in the morning."

"Do you feel guilty about us?"

"Yeah."

She put a hand on his thigh. "Elizabeth is gone. You aren't betraying her, no matter what you do with me or anyone else."

"I don't know what I'm doing."

"I don't, either," she admitted.

He looked at his list and thought he should write this down. But he wasn't sure what "this" was. He thought he remembered her naked, standing in front of him, her panties on the floor. Or was that merely imagined?

He hesitated. It seemed rude to ask whether they'd had sex, or had stopped at second or third base, yet he could still taste her lipstick and smell her perfume on him. He decided to write simply, *You and Shirley Collins have become more intimate.* That was sufficiently vague to cover just about anything.

Feeling guilty about asking her to leave, he offered to get together again with her the following evening.

"A third dinner in a row?" she said.

He'd forgotten about yesterday.

But then she added, "I actually have another date. I'm not sure I want to jinx it by saying this, but I'm really looking forward to it."

"What makes this one different?" asked Barnes.

"I've already met him once," she said, "and he's intelligent, personable, and handsome. That combination is hard to find."

"True. You don't want to pass that up." He was surprised to feel a tinge of disappointment.

"If I get home early, I'll call you," she said, and she kissed him on the cheek.

Driving home from Barnes's house in the cold darkness, Shirley replayed in her mind their evening together. She hadn't planned to get physical with him, and now the experience took on an abstract quality. She felt no regrets about the turn of events. Dr. Perry, her biochemistry professor in college, had once said to her, "I never regret the things I do, only the things I don't do." That conversation had taken place behind closed doors in his office when she came to him for help before the final exam. He followed that remark by leaning forward and putting a hand on her knee, then saying, as he slid his fingers upward, "You should live that way, too."

She'd slapped him hard across the face. "Then I shouldn't regret *that*."

The professor, fifty and married, had taken the rebuff in stride.

Afterward, the more Shirley thought about what Dr. Perry had said, the more she agreed with it.

Especially now.

Chapter 41

After Shirley left, Barnes turned off the fire in the fireplace. The image of Shirley standing naked before him still lingered. Regardless of whether it was real or imagined, he knew that his relationship with her was evolving into more than just friendship. But how? He could no longer recall either the events or the passion that had brought them together. Shirley was simply a friend of Elizabeth's, and he felt no closer to her than to the nurses at work.

In all likelihood the situation would repeat itself. If it happened once, it was bound to happen again, especially since he wouldn't remember enough to stop it. He made a note to discuss this with Dr. Parks at their next session.

After cleaning up, Barnes organized his notes and rewrote all of them in French. He had no idea whom he was hiding things from, but chances were the murderer would eventually visit the house again. It could be anyone—even Shirley—and although he had no compelling reason to suspect someone that close to him, he wouldn't take any chances.

Then there was the mystery lover. Why hadn't Elizabeth saved the second page of the letter? Had she lost it? Had somebody taken it? And who would write a letter like that?

He reread it and focused on the more personal parts: "You're a special person, and I can't put into words how much you mean to me. I miss holding you, being close to you, feeling your warmth."

Something about that seemed odd. He turned to his French translation: "*Tu es une personne speciale.*" "You're a special person." For some reason it sounded better in French.

Then he realized why. In French the word "person" is always feminine. Saying "*personne*" is more like saying "woman." If *he* were writing a love letter to Elizabeth, he would have said, "You're a special *woman,*" not, "You're a special person." It was a subtle difference, but as he reread the letter, other nongender-specific sentences became apparent: "I miss holding you, being close to you, feeling your warmth." There was nothing odd about that by itself, but combined with references to butterflies, it created a message with an effeminate quality. Maybe he was overanalyzing it, but the more he studied it, the more that seemed to be the case. This was most likely written by a woman.

He shuffled through his other notes.

Claire?

It made sense. She was one of Elizabeth's best friends, and Elizabeth had never told him the woman was a lesbian. Why hadn't he thought of her earlier? Of course, he had no hard evidence to back his suspicions, but Claire seemed the most likely person to have written that letter. And apparently Claire was in a relationship with an overly protective judge who had threatened him and who had been described as a "psycho bitch." Did this judge, Darcia, know Elizabeth, and if Elizabeth was seeing Claire, what would Darcia have done if she'd found out about it?

He jotted down these thoughts while they were still fresh, then rewrote the main note on the bathroom mirror, incorporating every relevant happening since the morning. He could no longer remember what he'd expected from today, but this series of events certainly wasn't it. He wondered what he would think when he read about everything in the morning.

Chapter 42

Barnes awoke to the drone of his alarm clock at 6:00 a.m. He slapped the "Off" button with his left hand, then turned to his right to kiss Elizabeth before crawling out of bed.

She wasn't there. He lay still for a moment, wondering what day it was and trying without success to recall the night before. A touch of a dull headache lingered in his temples. Too much alcohol? Sedatives? Either could cause memory loss. Something had disconnected him, something more than just deep slumber.

What had happened last night? He vaguely recalled making love to Elizabeth in front of the fireplace. Or was that a dream? Yes, it must have been. The image in his mind didn't make sense. The woman by the fireplace, the woman he'd made love to, had been blonde.

A sinking feeling came over him, a vague sense of dread rooted in the loss of something vital. Elizabeth. He sensed she'd left him. That might explain his confusion—severe emotional turmoil. Extreme mental anguish *can* cause amnesia. Yet the physician part of him searched for a more plausible explanation. Then he remembered the mussels in Toronto. And Cheryl in Toronto. Had she also been in his house last night? Her blonde hair drifted through his consciousness like a flower's scent in a breeze—faint but discernible, then gone the next moment.

He rolled onto his back and noticed now for the first time a note taped to the alarm clock. It hung down over the top and covered part of the digital readout. A message from Elizabeth? He switched on the lamp.

Read note on bathroom mirror. It was his own handwriting.

His mouth went dry. Something terrible had happened. Something life-changing. Yet nothing came to mind except images of a woman, perhaps from the night before. His pulse pounded in his temples as he tried to remember more details from yesterday, the day before that, or even the week before. Nothing. Then he pictured Nate Billings in scrubs. Why, he had no idea. Nate was never someone he thought about.

He threw back the covers and headed to the bathroom mirror. A lengthy handwritten note was taped to the glass. He turned on the lights to read it. The message was in French, and he translated as he read:

> *Don't be alarmed. Your ability to form new memories has been severely damaged since you were poisoned by mussels in Toronto in November. Don't expect to remember anything from yesterday, and don't expect to retain new information for more than a few minutes. If you do remember anything from yesterday, write it down <u>immediately</u> on a piece of paper; this may mean a significant improvement.*

He found a pen on top of Elizabeth's dresser and jotted down on a scrap of paper the vague recollection of having sex by the fireplace with someone other than Elizabeth. He also jotted a note about the image of Nate Billings, on the off chance it might have some significance.

He continued reading:

> *Today is December 17, your third day back home. Eliza-*
> *beth and Rex were murdered on 11/26, and you're going*
> *to figure out who did it.*

He stared at the note for some time. Not reading. Just staring. "Get a grip," he finally said out loud.

And he began reading again. The letter continued for another five paragraphs, describing the pregnancy and death of Elizabeth, consultations with a female attorney who might have been Elizabeth's lover, rejection by Denny, and an anonymous note demanding $10,000. Not to mention possible sex with Shirley.

You and Shirley Collins have become more intimate, the note said. What did that mean? Coupled with the dream or the vague recollection of a naked blonde in his family room, and the dream or the vague recollection of making love to that woman, it most likely meant they'd had sex. He and Shirley.

How had that happened? Regardless, he had to acknowledge it. His notes were his memory, and there was no point in being vague about what he'd done. He changed the note to read: *You and Shirley Collins had sex.* He was tempted to add: *That may have been a bad decision.* But what mattered were his feelings at that time, not now. Now he was thinking of her as the old Shirley Collins, Elizabeth's friend and colleague, with the arrogant boyfriend at the Union Oyster House, but last night she had likely been someone completely different. He thought of the paradox, that events from his recent past were closer to the present than his perception of things at this moment.

Of course, it was still possible that he was making bad decisions. Assisting Nate Billings in surgery might have been one of those. What had possessed him to do that? If the note hadn't been written in his own handwriting, he would never have believed it. But he *had* to believe it. This was the only way he could ever learn—to trust his notes from day to day. Those notes would be his surrogate memory, and they might even enable him to grow emotionally if not intellectually. In theory he could develop a meaningful relationship with another woman, although letting go of Elizabeth would be impossible.

He remembered a ski trip they'd taken in Vermont three years ago, his first-ever attempt at downhill skiing. In contrast to him, Elizabeth had once been an instructor. She accompanied him to a bunny hill, yet even with prime snow conditions on a gentle slope, he couldn't maintain his balance.

"Are you okay?" She looked down at him, her breath coming out in puffs of mist. She wore a mostly white ski suit, and to Barnes she looked like an astronaut.

"I could use some snow tires or chains on these." He tried to stand up, but his skis slipped out from under him again.

"I wish I'd thought to bring a camera. This would make a wonderful photograph—world-famous cardiothoracic surgeon on his bum, or 'butt,' as you would say."

He tried to stand up again. No luck. "Damn. How do you do this?"

"Stick your ski pole in the ground here . . ." She pointed with her own pole. ". . . and push yourself up."

He tried but lost his balance again. "Forget it." In frustration he reached back with his pole to release one boot from the ski.

Elizabeth parried his pole with hers. "Don't do that. That's cheating. Pull your legs up more, and stick your pole right here in the snow."

"I can't believe you're doing this to me."

"*With* you, not *to* you. Now come on, Christopher. Get up."

"You're enjoying this, aren't you?"

"Perhaps a little."

"I thought so." He struggled to his feet, leaning on his pole the way she'd instructed.

"There you go . . . Now that wasn't so bad, was it?"

"I'll bet you say the same thing to your hip-replacement patients." He brushed himself off. "But at least you're cute when you're sadistic."

"*I'm* cute? I'm not the one doing an imitation of a powdered doughnut." And she kissed him on the nose.

Most of that vacation was now a distant memory, except that afternoon on the bunny hill. When Barnes closed his eyes, he could still see Elizabeth smiling down at him in the snow. He didn't ever want to forget.

Barnes got dressed, then looked through his notes again. According to what he'd written, solving Elizabeth's murder was his number one priority, yet he was also supposed to go to work and do surgery with Nate Billings. Being in the OR seemed more appealing than undertaking the daunting task of solving a homicide, no matter how personal, so, after promising himself not to forget about Elizabeth, he hurried through his morning coffee, then headed off to work. On the passenger's seat in his car lay a framed photograph of him and Elizabeth, and his list reminded him that he had decided to put a picture of Elizabeth on his desk at work, not just to remind him of her and their life together but to remind him of his highest priority.

In silence he drove through the dark streets of the sleeping city. When he arrived at the hospital parking lot, the sun had risen, bathing the buildings in a reddish hue. The hospital complex loomed over the main lot like a guard tower, and he imagined how depressing it must be for a patient to enter that huge, somber building, which served as the main entrance.

He walked through the automatic doors and hurried down the hall, past the Christmas decorations, to the elevators in the Braddigan Building. There he got off at the eighth floor—the surgical wing.

As he walked past the nurses' station, a woman behind the counter chimed, "Good morning, Dr. Barnes." She was a thirty-something unit clerk whose name he'd never bothered to learn.

"Good morning," he replied. Unit clerks usually didn't greet him, and he'd never given that any thought. Yet now, receiving a salutation felt validating.

You're still Dr. Barnes, it said to him.

He entered the surgeons' lounge and poured himself a cup of coffee. An elderly physician whose name he couldn't remember sat at the conference table reading a journal. The man ignored him. On the couch in front of the television sat Denny, his legs stretched across two cushions. He looked up from a newspaper. "Hey, Chris. What are you doing here?"

"Same thing you're doing." In one hand Barnes carried the note Nate had written for him the previous day.

"Uh-huh." Denny sounded unconvinced.

Barnes went to the OR schedule and looked up Billings. A case for him was coming up in fifteen minutes, a quadruple bypass. Barnes also noticed Houston had been scheduled for a mitral-valve replacement at the same time. Given the choice, Barnes would have taken the bypass.

"Have you seen Nate?" he asked.

The elderly surgeon glanced up from his journal to verify that Barnes wasn't addressing him, then returned to his reading. Denny looked up from his newspaper as though the question had caught him by surprise. "Billings? Don't tell me you're going to work with *him* again."

Barnes wasn't in the mood to take any lip. "You have a problem with that?"

Houston folded the paper dramatically. "You do what you want."

"I will, Denny." Barnes turned from him and headed to the locker room.

Houston started to say something, but Barnes wasn't listening.

In the locker room, he ran into Billings. Houston had always been annoyed by the fact that Billings's locker stood only ten feet from his and Barnes's. Barnes had never cared one way or the other, but now it seemed like a stroke of luck.

Barnes grunted and nodded, not comfortable enough to address Billings by name.

"Morning to you, too."

Barnes turned his combination lock. "We're scrubbing together. Right?"

"That depends . . . You remember the rules?"

"Rules?"

"You treat everyone with respect, and don't forget . . . *you're* assisting *me*."

Barnes opened his locker. "Right."

"We've got a quadruple bypass on a sixty-six-year-old Caucasian male . . . Vessels are so occluded . . . I'm surprised he can squeeze blood through them. He put off getting a physical till it almost killed him." Nate pulled a scrub shirt over his head and down past his dark chest and abdomen.

Barnes's own physique wasn't as good as Billings's, but he was certain his skill as a surgeon was superior. "Any other health problems?" he asked.

"Only hypertension. Should be fine if we can just get him to the recovery room."

Barnes took off his shirt and reached for a pair of scrubs. "We'll do it."

"You know your buddy Houston is hoping we don't."

Barnes opened his mouth to defend Denny, then decided not to. Billings was probably right.

Using glasses that provided threefold magnification, Barnes sutured blood vessels onto the patient's heart with a precision that comes from innate talent and years of experience. With needle holders like forceps, he grasped the eyelash-sized needle and guided it through the delicate walls of the blood vessels. The special vascular suture was stuck directly to the blunt end of the needle and filled each hole exactly as it passed through, preventing leakage of blood from the procedure.

Barnes believed that even on a bad day, he could suture blood vessels more skillfully than anyone. Even under magnification his hands had no perceptible tremor, his motions entirely fluid.

"With hands like that," Billings said, "you should take up target shooting . . . or biathlon, if you can ski."

"I can't ski to save my life," said Barnes, "but I used to shoot in college."

"I assume you mean targets . . . and not classmates or teachers."

"Just targets. I shot pistol, and I can't tell you how many hours I spent at the range." Barnes grasped the tiny tip of his needle with the metal needle holders and pulled it through the thin wall of the vessel, completing the attachment to the left anterior descending coronary artery. "Now I don't even own a gun."

After the bypass operation, Barnes and Billings walked to the surgeons' lounge.

"Looks like Mr. Parsons is going to see Christmas," said Billings as they passed the recovery room.

"Yeah." Barnes had long since forgotten the patient's name, although he knew what Billings was talking about. "Thanks for letting me help." Barnes yanked off the surgical mask that dangled around his neck and dropped it into a wastebasket as they walked by.

"No problem. I'd ask you to assist me again . . . tomorrow, but I don't schedule surgeries on Fridays."

They'd reached the surgeons' lounge. It was empty, and they headed to the coffeepot.

"I suppose . . . we could do lunch instead," said Billings.

Barnes was caught by surprise. "Lunch?"

"It's that meal between breakfast and dinner."

"Uh-huh. Sure. I guess if we can stand each other for, what, four hours in the OR, we should be able to do lunch. Where are you taking me?" He poured himself a cup of coffee.

"Oh, now suddenly I'm buying? How did that happen?" Billings poured himself a cup, too.

"*You* asked *me*, right?"

"Yeah . . . but it's not like a date." Billings took a sip of coffee. "All right. If I'm paying, I'll take you to McDonald's. After you forget, I'll tell you we went to L'Espalier. How does that sound?"

"Sounds like something Denny would do."

Billings let forth a resonant laugh. "You got that right. Pencil us in for twelve o'clock . . . in your notes, and meet me in my office in the clinic building. I'll be through seeing patients by then . . . And don't be late. I don't like waiting for people. You got that?"

Barnes wrote it down. "Yeah. I'll try to remember."

"You better."

"Are you going to bring your wife along?"

"I don't know. You think you'll remember afterwards if I do?"

"Probably not."

Billings shook his head. "Yeah, just you wait. She's the prettiest woman you'll ever meet. Except she's not white."

"You think that matters to me?"

"I'm not sure. I know . . . it matters to your friend. Houston."

"Yeah, well, he and I aren't the same."

"I hope not," said Billings. "Otherwise I'm making a big mistake."

Chapter 43

After leaving the surgeons' lounge, Barnes followed the instructions on his list. He went to his office, framed photograph in hand, and asked Kristine, "Did Denny's secretary give me the files on the Jarrell Pharmaceuticals study?"

"Yes," she said, "this morning. They're on your desk. Also, Marcie asked me to inform you that Dr. Houston called the patent attorneys to have your name added to the application."

"Thanks. Get the name of the attorney handling it, and ask for a copy ASAP. They'll need my signature. Be sure to remind me to take care of that."

"Certainly."

He started for the office.

"From your honeymoon?"

"What?"

"The photograph."

"Oh." He looked at it. "Yeah."

"It's a lovely picture."

"Thanks." He placed it on the corner of his desk, in clear view from his chair. The files from Jarrell Pharmaceuticals sat in the center of the desk. For an hour he pored through the papers, taking notes, occasionally looking up at the picture of Elizabeth. Except for her, he didn't like what he saw.

He went out to talk to Kristine. "I need you to call the American Society of Cardiothoracic Surgeons. Here's the number." He handed her a memo. "Tell them I'd like to withdraw the abstract Denny sent to them. The data's flawed." He handed her a second sheet of paper. "This is a letter I drafted. They'll want the request in writing, on letterhead, of course. Sign my name and fax it to them as soon as you finish typing it."

"Yes, Dr. Barnes."

"And don't mention this to anyone."

"Of course not, Dr. Barnes."

"When Denny finds out, I want him to hear it from them, after the deadline for resubmission. There's no way he's going to present that data. And when you're done with that, I need you to draft a letter to the office of technology transfer: 'Dear So-and-So. This is to inform you that the patent filed on behalf of Dr. Houston, entitled blah blah blah, should list me as the principal inventor. Please instruct the patent attorneys to make the proper corrections.' Something like that. Make sure I read it and sign it within the next day or two. Okay?"

"Yes, Dr. Barnes." She beamed, and he wondered whether she was happy to see him back at work or whether she just liked the idea of putting Houston in his place.

Back in his office, Barnes called Claire and asked to meet her for lunch again at Mississippi's. Having reread his notes, he was inclined not to see her, but she might be able to tell him more about Elizabeth.

When he arrived at the deli, Claire was already seated at a table. He didn't remember her from the day before, but something about her seemed familiar, and when she looked up at him, her eyes registered recognition and a warmth reserved for friends.

She waved. He approached her and guessed by her flushed cheeks that she'd only just come in from the cold.

They hugged. Then she asked whether he recognized her.

"More or less," he hedged. "I have to admit I don't remember faces the way I used to. Or events." He set his coat on the back of a chair opposite her. The restaurant didn't look even remotely familiar.

They walked to the counter to order and, a few minutes later, carried a tray of food to their table.

"I'd like to apologize for the phone call you received from Darcia yesterday," Claire said, unfolding a napkin in her lap.

"What was it about?" He took out his notes.

"She overreacts sometimes," Claire explained. "She thought you were ungrateful for my help. But I know that isn't the case."

Barnes found it in his notes. "Does she usually call people on your behalf?"

"No, that's really not her. She's just sensitive about you and me."

"And Elizabeth?"

"Yes. But I've spoken to her, and it won't happen again."

"How well did she know Elizabeth?"

"I think they met only once. Maybe twice. They really didn't know each other."

Barnes jotted down the information. "Was she jealous of Elizabeth?"

"She didn't know her."

"Uh-huh." Barnes took that as a yes.

"Is that French?" Claire had leaned forward and was pointing to his notes.

"Yeah. I do that so other people can't read it, although with my handwriting, that's probably not necessary. Do you speak French?"

"No. I had a year in high school, but I've forgotten most of it."

So she said, but she didn't take her eyes off the notes. He gathered the papers together.

"How have you been getting along today?" she asked. "Any problems?"

"None that I recall." He forced a laugh. "I guess that's one advantage of not being able to remember things."

She touched his hand. "Well, if you have any, let me know . . . What are your plans for the rest of the day?"

"I'm not sure. I don't plan very far ahead." He took a bite of his sandwich.

"So you probably haven't thought about Christmas."

"No. I guess I could visit Elizabeth's parents, but without Elizabeth . . . I don't know." He wondered whether they knew about his affair in Toronto with Cheryl.

"What about *your* parents?"

"I'm not close to them. And they're divorced. I talk to them once or twice a year; that's it."

"That's a shame. Do you have any brothers or sisters?"

"No. Do you?"

"I have a sister. She's married and they have a two-year-old. They invited me to visit this year, but they live in Los Angeles. That's a little too far to go for just a few days. Besides, what's Christmas without snow, or at least slush and freezing wind?"

"Yeah. So you'll be by yourself?"

"I'll be with Darcia. I've been seeing her for about three years off and on."

He wrote that down in French. "Did you spend Thanksgiving with her?"

"Yes."

"Here in town?"

"Yes. Why?"

He didn't want to tell her that he was trying to see whether Darcia had an alibi for the time when Elizabeth was killed. "No reason. I'm just asking. I was in a coma then, so I missed it." He jotted a note that Darcia was in town then. Maybe he would pass that information along to the police, although how seriously would they investigate a judge when he had no facts to back up his gut feelings?

"Um, about Christmas," said Claire. "Darcia and I talked it over this morning, and we'd both like you to join us for part of the day if you haven't made other plans."

"I appreciate the offer." Barnes jotted that down, too. "You're sure Darcia won't mind having a man around?"

"I'm certain she'd prefer it to another woman." Claire blushed. "Forget I said that."

"Just wait a couple of minutes, and I will." In his notes he underlined *jealous* after Darcia's name. "Let me know if you change your mind, if you decide it's not convenient."

"I will," she said, "but I'm certain it won't be a problem."

He tried to imagine spending Christmas with Claire and her potentially hostile partner instead of with Elizabeth. Probably he would be better off alone. Or with Denny. But if he didn't solve Elizabeth's murder by then, it might be an opportunity to gather more information, assuming Darcia was still a suspect. Of course, Darcia could also have some ulterior motive in inviting him.

He took a bite of his sandwich and thought about Christmas with Denny. That would be a first, despite their long friendship. But Denny probably had other plans. If he didn't spend the holidays with family, he would probably find a nurse to take to bed. Or some woman at a bar. The more special the occasion, the less particular Houston became.

Barnes suddenly realized he'd forgotten his conversation with Claire. "I'm sorry," he said. "I lost my train of thought. What were we talking about?"

"The holidays. I invited you to spend Christmas with Darcia and me."

"Right. I'll let you know. I'm not planning that far ahead now. I'm just trying to get through one day at a time." *One hour at a time*, he thought. He didn't want to admit, even to himself, that it was sometimes just one minute at a time.

"If there's anything that I can do to help," said Claire, "please don't hesitate to ask."

He looked at his notes again about Darcia. If push came to shove, Claire would almost certainly help *her* over him. He wondered whether someday soon she might be faced with that choice.

Chapter 44

Detective Wright walked to his partner's desk. Gould's was more Spartan than his—devoid of clutter and lacking any personal touches except for a small picture of Gloria and him in a plastic frame. The picture looked as though it had come from an automatic photo booth at a shopping mall—grainy with a white background. The two of them were sitting close together, almost pressed together, probably because the booth was intended for only one person. They were both grinning.

He must be in love to be smiling in a photograph, thought Wright. To Gould, photographs of people were all mug shots.

Gould was rifling through a report when Wright interrupted him.

"What have you got there?" Wright asked.

"Transcripts of the phone tap on Barnes." Gould held out the papers. "Not much yet except he talks with Shirley Collins more than anyone else, and they get together at his place for dinner. Can't say I blame him—she's a looker."

"And the colleague of his dead wife. We need to rule out a love triangle."

"You think? Their conversations don't sound lovey-dovey."

"Do any of his conversations?"

"No. He's not the warm-and-fuzzy type."

"No," agreed Wright. "Do you feel like going for a ride?"

"Yeah. I need a break. Where to?"

"Houston."

"Kind of far, ain't it?"

"Not the city, the surgeon."

Gould stood up. "I'm a step ahead of you. Called his office an hour ago. Talked to Marcie someone."

"That makes two of us. Let's see if Houston knows something we don't."

They put on their coats.

"What's that I smell?" asked Wright, catching a strong whiff of musk.

"Cologne. Gloria bought it for me. You like it?"

Wright chose not to answer that.

"Yeah, I'm still trying to get used to it myself."

They headed out of the station into the cold. "I gotta say I don't see a motive for Houston murdering our vic," said Gould, facing into the wind to look at his partner. "Why would he want to get rid of Barnes's wife?"

"I don't know. Maybe we're overlooking something."

"Tell me about it. You know, I keep thinking about the dog, it not being shot first."

Wright recalled his conversation about that with Karen. "That doesn't necessarily mean anything."

They walked faster, in a hurry to escape the wind.

"Yeah, well, it makes me think the perp was somebody they knew. Makes me think again about that Collins chick. She is a hottie. I have to say, if I wasn't seeing Gloria, I'd offer that woman some personal protection in a heartbeat."

"You're probably not her type. I picture her with a professor in a cardigan." They got into Wright's car.

"I could wear one of them."

"Please don't, or I may have to look for a new partner." Wright closed the door. "That cologne is bad enough."

Wright sat on a leather sofa in Denny Houston's office, waiting for the surgeon to return from a meeting, while Gould, who couldn't sit still that long, was examining a multicolored, multifaceted piece of glass from one of the bookshelves. The piece was the size of a soccer ball, and he'd picked it up and was turning it like a child with a new toy.

"What do you think you're doing?" demanded Houston. He had materialized at the door.

Gould set the artwork back on the shelf. "Just looking."

"That piece of glass is worth more than the car you drive."

"So's the watch you're wearing. What's your point?" Gould glared at him. "You wanna get in a pissing match with me?"

Neither said anything, like two dogs about to go at each other. Wright wouldn't have been surprised if one or both of them had started growling. He stood up next to his partner. "We won't take up much of your time," he said. "We have just a few questions to ask."

Houston strode to the chair behind his desk and took a seat. "You can have three minutes. I've got patients to see." He took a Montblanc pen from the pocket of his white coat and jotted a note on a chart he'd brought in.

"We want to know why you didn't tell us about someone breaking into your house," said Gould. He moved closer to the desk, reached over, and took a handful of jelly beans from a bowl on the corner.

"I don't remember offering those to you," Houston said.

Gould ate one. "Seems everybody's got memory problems these days. Answer the question. Why didn't you tell us?"

Houston moved the candy bowl away from the detective. "The police came and filed a report, so I figured you knew about it. I can't help it if you all don't communicate."

"What sort of research were you doing with Dr. Barnes?" asked Wright.

"I don't have time now to discuss my research."

"*Your* research?" said Gould. "I thought you and Barnes did it together."

"I'm not going to argue semantics. Talk to Dr. Barnes about it."

"You and he must be pretty close," Wright said, "doing research together."

"What's that supposed to mean?"

"I was just wondering whether you do other business-related things together, like investments."

"We keep our finances separate."

"But you both lost big in the Zeiman Richter Fund. Separately."

"What's your point?"

"We're just trying to figure out your relationship," said Wright.

"Probably the same as you two. We work together, and sometimes we socialize."

"So you would know if he was cheating on his wife?" Wright asked.

"You'll have to ask him that."

"But we're asking you," said Gould.

"And I'm telling you to ask him," Houston insisted.

"Well, we already know the answer," said Gould. "What we want to know from you is, who was it?"

"You'll have to ask him that."

"Do you know a Shirley Collins?"

"No."

"You're sure?"

"Yes, I'm sure."

"What about Barnes's wife?" asked Wright. "You knew her, right?"

"Of course I knew her."

"She was a looker," said Gould, and he ate another jelly bean. "You ever do more than look?"

"We're done here," said Houston. "Get out of my office."

"Actually we're not quite through," said Wright. "Do you own a 9mm handgun?"

Houston scowled. "I own a Glock, and I have a license for it."

"A 9mm Glock?" asked Gould.

"That's right."

"We'll need to see it," said Wright. "Elizabeth Barnes was shot with a 9mm handgun."

"Yeah, and Ronald Reagan was shot with a .22-caliber revolver. I've got one of them, too. You wanna test that for ballistics?"

"We'll need to see the 9mm," said Wright. "Today."

"And what am I supposed to use for protection after you take it?"

"The .22," said Gould.

"That's bullshit."

"We should be able to return the weapon to you in a day," Wright assured him, "provided the ballistics tests don't show a match."

"Do you think I'm an idiot?" said Houston. "Do you think if I used that gun for anything illegal, I'd keep it? No wonder you can't solve crimes. You don't think."

"Just get us the gun," said Gould.

Under the threat of a search warrant, Houston made arrangements for them to pick up the weapon.

"If you want to ask any more questions," he said, "call my lawyer."

Gould ate another jelly bean.

"Have a good day," said Wright, and they left the office.

Out of earshot, Wright turned to Gould. "I think Houston's hiding something."

Gould popped the remaining jelly beans into his mouth. "Ain't they all?"

Chapter 45

After his lunch with Claire, Barnes returned home and pored through his notes. He spread out the pieces of paper on the dining-room table and organized them, then rewrote them concisely. He'd already summarized and resummarized the notes as he'd gathered information over the past day, trying to condense everything into as little space as possible. That way he would be able to digest the maximum amount without forgetting what he'd just read. A number of facts disturbed him but none as much as the letter demanding $10,000. The other evidence suggested that someone close to him or Elizabeth may have been involved—Claire and Darcia, Shirley, Denny, or another colleague from the hospital—but the letter implicated him.

He tried to focus on other suspects. Logic dictated that Elizabeth had been killed by someone who knew her. The fact that the alarm hadn't been set meant that either Elizabeth had forgotten to turn it on or she'd disarmed it to invite someone inside. More likely the latter. Elizabeth wasn't one to forget things.

Denny's house had been broken into later that night. This suggested a possible connection between Denny and Elizabeth or, more likely, Denny and himself. Almost certainly the same person had broken into both homes—a glass cutter had been used on a window in both cases, and neither forced entry had resulted in detectable fingerprints.

Denny hadn't reported his break-in to the Boston police after reading about Elizabeth's murder. Was he just being self-centered and lazy? Probably. He hadn't been much of a friend lately, but the two of them went way back.

Barnes reminded himself of that—Denny was his best friend. Not even money had come between them. And they'd certainly had their share of financial setbacks. Especially Denny. He'd sunk a lot into the fraudulent Zeiman Richter Fund that at one time had seemed like such a great investment. Yet Denny never mentioned money problems. With all the surgical procedures he did, he should be making enough to maintain his lifestyle.

If Denny wasn't involved, then who were the remaining suspects? Shirley? Certainly Elizabeth would have let her into the house, but Shirley had no motive to hurt her. Their project together was finished, and any surprises with that were unlikely. GBF-complex had already been used for years to treat toxic calcium levels in cancer patients, in much higher doses than were present in the coated screws used for orthopedic surgery, and the drug had been shown to be safe and effective.

Maybe Carmen, the maid. She had access to the house, but her only likely motive would have been money, and nothing appeared to have been stolen.

Then, of course, there was Claire, or more likely Claire's significant other, Darcia. Would Elizabeth let Darcia into the house? Even if Elizabeth didn't know her personally, she probably wouldn't turn away a judge. If Elizabeth had been having an affair with Claire, that would give Darcia a motive to kill her. But that seemed pretty extreme behavior for a judge, even one characterized as a "psycho bitch."

Finally there was Jarrell Pharmaceuticals. Was it just a coincidence that this corporation happened to be funding both his research *and* Elizabeth's, just a coincidence that both research projects could generate billions of dollars for the company? Probably, but it was still unusual. And what would Jarrell Pharmaceuticals gain from her death? Maybe the company needed to hide something she'd discovered. Even so, Barnes couldn't think how that would work to their advantage. If Elizabeth had discovered anything potentially dangerous in the GBF-complex-coated screws, even an unethical corporation would want to scrap the project before sinking more money into it. The last thing a pharmaceutical company would want would be to conceal something that could damage them down the road, that could not only tarnish their image but generate massive lawsuits. Unless . . .

He shuddered at the thought. A pharmaceutical company would never benefit from concealing a major flaw during drug development *unless* they intended to sell the product not to patients but instead to another drug company. That wasn't unusual in the pharmaceutical industry, but most of the time, it happened earlier in development, not when the product was this close to being approved by the FDA. If a company managed to sell a defective but promising product, they could make a small fortune and, at the same time, severely damage their competition. Of course, the key to doing that would be to conceal the problem. Yet it seemed unrealistic that Jarrell Pharmaceuticals would murder a medical doctor to enhance their profits or avoid a financial loss. They might allow patients to die, but that's very different from killing an investigator. And what about all the other investigators? The GBF-complex-coated screws had already been tested on thousands of patients in hospitals throughout the country. If the screws were defective, surely other investigators would have noticed as well.

Barnes made a note to ask Shirley whether Jarrell Pharmaceuticals had indicated they intended to sell the GBF-complex-coated screws to another company. Even if she was somehow involved in a conspiracy, he had nothing to lose by posing the question. He could also ask his contacts at the company.

But a more troubling question was whether he personally might have been connected to Elizabeth's murder. He and Elizabeth held most of their assets separately, and the fact was he would now make a fortune from her research. And this at a time when his own research had been stalling, and when his own finances were problematic.

But money wasn't the only possible motive. Murder is often a crime of passion. That could have provided an incentive for Darcia, but it could have also provided an incentive for him. A wife's infidelity and resultant pregnancy are undeniable motives for murder.

That put him on both lists—money and passion. Two possible motives for him but only one for each of the other suspects.

What if he *had* hired someone to kill Elizabeth? If she'd told him she was pregnant with another man's baby, in theory that could have pushed him over the edge. And it would explain the note demanding a final payment of $10,000—hiring someone would almost certainly cost double that or more. Also, the alarm wouldn't have gone off because he would have told the intruder the code to disarm it.

In theory that was all possible, but harming Elizabeth wasn't something he would do. To plot her murder—or *anyone's*—was unfathomable. Sure, he had a temper—most surgeons do—but you need more than that to conspire to commit murder. He loved Elizabeth. He would never harm her.

Yet part of him wanted a second opinion. That's what he always recommended when a patient was ever in doubt, and if it was good advice for his patients, it should be good for him, too. But only one person knew him well enough to give him a second opinion about his relationship with Elizabeth: Denny.

Barnes gathered up his summaries and threw away his older notes, then picked up the phone.

"I have to ask you something," he said after apologizing for bothering his friend.

"Go for it, buddy." Denny sounded annoyed, but then he often sounded that way.

"Did I seem . . ." Barnes tried to choose his words carefully. ". . . *different* after I moved into the Ritz before I left for Toronto?"

"You were moody as hell, but that's understandable. You really didn't talk about it. Least not that I recall."

"Yeah. I was just wondering whether I seemed, you know, really pissed off."

"Not enough to kill her, if that's what you're driving at."

Barnes was taken aback by how quickly Denny surmised the purpose of his questions. Of course, Denny was no idiot, but Barnes hadn't expected him to pick up on that. "There are some things I probably haven't told you," Barnes admitted.

"I'm not sure I want to hear 'em."

"Well, let me—"

"Look, buddy. Unless your bank account shows a large, unexplained cash withdrawal, I wouldn't lose any sleep."

Barnes unfolded the letter demanding $10,000. "I don't have that. But maybe something worse."

Denny said nothing in reply, and Barnes decided not to elaborate. "Never mind. Forget I said it."

"Already forgotten."

"Change of topic: Do you remember the last time you and I bet on a football game?"

"Yeah. The Patriots' season opener. You got lucky in the last quarter, and I dropped a G."

"Yeah, I remember that. It was a good game. I picked up another thousand from Burt at the gym."

"I won't tell you what else I lost. That wasn't a good weekend. But, hell, easy come, easy go."

"Yeah. You know whether I've bet on anything since then?"

"I don't keep tabs on you, buddy, but you didn't mention anything as far as I recall. Why? Somebody hitting you up for money?"

"No. I just want to be sure I'm square with everything."

"You're square with me."

"That's good to hear. Sorry I bothered you with this."

"No problem."

"I guess I'll let you go, then. I'll talk to you tomorrow."

"Take care, buddy."

Barnes hung up. He wished he had never called.

Down the street outside Barnes's house, an unmarked van sat parked at the curb. Inside, among elaborate recording equipment, two men wearing headphones listened to the telephone conversation.

"Sounds pretty damn incriminating to me," one said, removing his headphones after Barnes hung up.

"Toast," said the other. "The guy is toast."

Chapter 46

Sitting at his desk in the station, Wright played the tape for Gould. "I don't have that," Barnes's voice said on the recorder. "But maybe something worse."

Wright turned off the tape.

"Time for a search warrant," said Gould, chewing noisily on bubble gum and smelling strongly of the cologne Gloria had given him. "Let me hear the rest of it."

Wright played it for him.

After the tape finished, Gould said, "Let's haul his butt in."

"Not just yet." Wright scooted his chair back to escape the fumes. "Barnes doesn't know if he did it. Otherwise he wouldn't be talking about it with his friend."

"We don't give a rat's ass if he knows." Gould moved closer. "All that counts is, did he do it? And if he's still trying to figure that out, then he didn't pitch that letter yet, or nothing else."

"Yeah . . ." Wright debated whether to say something about the cologne. "But if he doesn't know, we probably can't find enough against him to convict. Besides, it's not like he's a flight risk. He can't remember anything from one day to the next, so there's no way he can skip town and start over somewhere else. Let's just wait. In the meantime, he's writing down everything he needs to remember. He probably rewrites his notes every day, maybe even more often than that."

"So we search the premises and take all his scraps of paper, everything we can get our hands on. If we can't nail him for murder one, we can still book him for illegal gambling."

Wright edged back a few more inches. "Let's wait a day or two. Tomorrow is trash pickup, and we can look at the lists he throws away. In the meantime, maybe he'll figure out he's guilty. If he does, we'll find out, too." He pushed his chair back some more.

"You afraid of something on your desk?"

"What?"

"You keep scooting away from your desk. What's with that?"

"Actually it's not my desk. It's your cologne."

"Maybe if you wore some," Gould said, "you'd get used to it."

"Yeah, but what about everyone else?"

"Very funny." Gould smelled his shirt. "You think I'm putting on too much?"

"I think if I lit a match, you'd go up in a ball of flames."

"All right. I can take a hint. Let's get back to Barnes. What do you think he'll do if he figures out himself that he did it?"

"Hard to say." Wright reflected on the impact that the realization might have. For Barnes to discover that he'd orchestrated the murder of his wife—the woman he probably still loved and now needed more than ever—would be devastating. "Obviously, for him, flight isn't an option."

Gould moved closer. "So you think he might turn himself in?"

Wright held his ground. "No." Then he added, "More likely he'll kill himself."

Despite mounting evidence against him, Barnes couldn't believe he would harm Elizabeth. There must be some other explanation for the letter demanding $10,000. A gambling debt of some sort—that must be it. He would have to wait until Saturday, two days, to find out. Then, hopefully, the author of the letter would contact him after he failed to deposit the money by noon as instructed. If push came to shove, he could always show the letter to the police, but now that didn't seem like a good idea.

The more he thought about everything, the more convinced he became that solving this case was going to require a major break. With no clear motives and no obvious suspects, he needed some way of finding more clues. The logical thing to do was to resume looking through Elizabeth's papers, notes, and computer disks from work. According to his notes, he'd already reviewed several of the files on her computer disks but had found nothing useful. Many of them had turned out to be progress reports of research, but none of them seemed to contain anything controversial or otherwise problematic. He was amazed at the volume of work his wife had done. While most researchers focus on one project at a time, she seemed to have been involved in at least three or four simultaneously.

After a couple of hours, Barnes took a break and had a can of ravioli and a cup of coffee for dinner. Then he resumed looking at Elizabeth's various projects from work. He put a disk into the disk drive and listed the files. One was a large text file. He opened it and found a progress report on Elizabeth's research with Shirley, labeled "Summary of GBF-complex-coated screws in phase II/III."

If nothing else, at least this would give him a better understanding of what exactly her most important recent project had entailed. But before he could read it, the telephone rang.

It was Shirley. He remembered her and her boyfriend from dinner at the Union Oyster House, and he fished through his pockets for a note to see whether he might have written something else about her.

Then he saw it—*You had sex with Shirley last night.* Maybe she didn't have that boyfriend anymore.

"How are you doing?" he asked, not sure what tone or direction the conversation should take.

"Good. I had a pleasant relaxing evening, and that doesn't happen very often when I'm on a first date. I just got back. We met for dinner in Harvard Square."

Apparently whatever had happened last night couldn't have been too serious if she was going on a date with someone else and telling him about it. "So you might have a second date with this person?" he asked.

"Maybe. We don't have much in common, except chemistry—he's quite a hunk."

"What does he do for a living?"

"He teaches humanities."

"Humanities? Somehow I can't picture you with a humanities teacher."

"No, neither can I, but, like I said, he's a hunk. I met him at Elizabeth's funeral."

"So you pick up men at funerals?"

"Hey, I'll take them wherever."

"How did you meet him at the funeral?"

"He spoke there briefly, to the mourners, and read a poem he'd written—about death, very sad but in an uplifting way. Afterwards I ran into him and asked how he knew Elizabeth. He said that she gave him poetry."

"Really? What does that mean?"

"He said he'd been unable or unwilling to write after the death of his wife, but that Elizabeth gave that back to him."

"Was this recent?"

"I guess."

Barnes suddenly saw an image of a urine container on the bathroom counter, with Elizabeth standing next to it and holding a positive pregnancy test. He looked through his notes for more information. "Did you get the impression they were . . . Could they have been having an affair?"

"Oh, I don't think so. I don't think Elizabeth would do that."

He wondered whether she would tell him if she knew. Shirley and Elizabeth were pretty close. Then he saw in his notes that Claire had mentioned that his neighbor, Marshall, had gone to the funeral. "Is his name Marshall?" Barnes asked.

"It is. How well do you know him? Please don't tell me I'm dating a drug dealer or an embezzler."

"Maybe both. I don't know him." He jotted notes while he talked. "What else did he say about Elizabeth?"

"Not much. We talked mostly about each other."

Could Elizabeth have been having an affair with him? Did that man write the love letter mentioned in his list? Barnes felt the urge to run across the street and confront him, but instead he just took notes.

Then he saw something else in his notes, a question about Jarrell Pharmaceuticals and the research Elizabeth and Shirley had been doing. "On an unrelated note," he said, "do you know whether the sponsor of your research intended to sell the GBF-complex-coated screws to another pharmaceutical company?"

"That's an odd question," said Shirley. "What makes you ask that?"

"I don't remember. It's in my notes."

"Not that I'm aware of. It would be unusual this late in drug development. Usually companies do that before they get to the expensive multicenter studies. Besides, I think if they were going to do that, they would have to notify me, or at least the university . . . You really don't know why you want to know?"

"Maybe I'll figure it out later," he said. "I'm not all that well organized."

"Well, I can tell you anything you like about the research. If you don't have plans, we can talk about it tomorrow over dinner."

He thought about that. Probably more questions would come up between now and then that she might be able to answer, including about Marshall, and he really didn't like eating alone. No matter how busy he and Elizabeth were, they always tried to have at least one meal a day together, and usually it was dinner.

"All right," he said. "Does seven o'clock work for you?"

"It does. I'll stop by with something from somewhere, if that isn't too specific."

"That works for me. Thanks."

After talking to Shirley, Barnes returned to his computer and the summary of GBF-complex-coated screws in clinical trials. He was reminded of the work only because it was right in front of him. Even before his conversation with Shirley had ended, he'd forgotten that she was dating Marshall, and that Marshall had likely been involved with Elizabeth. A residual anger lingered, but he didn't know the source of it. The distraction of talking about Jarrell Pharmaceuticals and then scheduling dinner with Shirley had been sufficient to push Marshall from his thoughts.

Elizabeth's notes began with an overview of the research. She described the background, then the actual studies. Most drugs and devices in development are first studied in healthy volunteers, but not GBF-complex-coated screws. The FDA granted permission to skip that first step because the procedure for testing would require the insertion of metal screws into bone, and that's something you can't do to healthy volunteers. This meant, Barnes realized, that the file in front of him was likely the summary of everything Elizabeth and Shirley had been involved with, including maybe a review of results from other clinical trials throughout the country.

This was the type of information he'd been looking for. The file showed that Elizabeth had recruited patients for the early studies and had then reviewed much of the data from the later ones at other research centers. She'd coordinated the studies, but that didn't mean the information in her files was complete. She would have received only summaries. Yet even if Barnes had every piece of relevant information, it probably didn't matter. In all likelihood this project had nothing to do with her death.

He scrolled down and began reading a summary of results from a study in Minneapolis. Elizabeth had written: "The following pertains to results of a phase III trial in patients with GBF-complex-coated screws inserted for a minimum of one year. Demographic data is shown below in table I." The table listed the age, sex, height, weight, body frame, and race for each of the patients enrolled in the study. The summary continued: "To date, two hundred forty-five of the two hundred sixty-three patients are being followed with no significant adverse events. Fifteen patients were lost to follow-up, and three died eleven, fourteen, and sixteen months after their surgery: one of an automobile accident, one of a gunshot wound to the head, and one following a bout of bacterial meningitis. The autopsies were unremarkable, suggesting the toxicity of the GBF-complex-coated screws was not significant and not different from patients who received plain screws."

Barnes reread the end of the last sentence: ". . . the toxicity of the GBF-complex-coated screws was not significant and not different from patients who received plain screws."

Elizabeth hadn't written that sentence!

He read it again. Someone had altered the summary. Unlike her American colleagues, Elizabeth would never have written "different from." She always said "different to."

Maybe she'd had some sort of lapse, he thought. As she was becoming more Americanized, the word *from* could have slipped out. But he knew she proofread everything she wrote, and the likelihood that she would use that word in the first place and then not notice it in rereading was next to impossible.

This raised the possibility that one or more of the autopsies cited in the summary held clues to Elizabeth's murder. Somehow he needed to get those reports. The three cases might have some abnormality in common. On the surface they appeared unrelated—an accident, a homicide or suicide, and an infectious disease—but one or more of them must have contained something that somebody wanted to hide. He just had to figure out what that something was.

He made a note to himself. Tomorrow, first thing, he would call around to get the reports. Elizabeth must have had them in her possession at one time, but like her computer disks, they had probably been altered, or stolen or discarded. He wondered what the reports contained that could be worth her life. Maybe something unrelated to her research, an incidental finding. If it *was* related to the GBF-complex-coated screws, she could have discovered a problem that jeopardized their clinical utility. But that seemed unlikely. If the screws weren't holding properly, or if the bone around them was eroding, those findings would be readily apparent on X-rays of all the other patients enrolled in the study.

Nothing he could think of that related to the screws or the surrounding bone could be discovered on autopsy but not by routine examination of the other patients. Also, in a clinical trial involving such a large number of patients, certainly some of them would have had their screws removed, either because of complications like the shaft of a screw breaking or because some of the screws and bolts were meant to be only temporary. So a problem with the screws would more likely be noticed in the living volunteers than in those few who died. Now that he thought about it, the screws probably weren't even examined on autopsy. After all, when someone dies of a gunshot wound to the head, a coroner doesn't dig around his ankle or back or forearm to look at screws or rods or a metal plate. Medical examiners value their time as much as everyone else.

Most likely Elizabeth had uncovered something unrelated to the screws and her research. It could have involved the patient who'd died of the gunshot wound to the head. If the death had been ruled a suicide, she might have discovered evidence to the contrary.

Another thought occurred to Barnes: maybe she hadn't uncovered anything at all. She could have been murdered simply because someone was afraid of what she *might* find. That meant that by pursuing this, he might risk becoming a victim himself. But at least that would eliminate him as a suspect.

Then he considered a more innocent explanation for the apparent alteration in the file: someone else could have written the summary, or at least part of it. After all, Elizabeth's name wasn't on it. Anyone involved in the study—even someone at another medical center or at Jarrell Pharmaceuticals—could have sent her the report on a disk.

The more he thought about it, the less the finding seemed to be any sort of breakthrough. Still, he would follow up on it. He wrote a separate note in French and taped it to the refrigerator.

The discovery could turn out to be nothing, but there was only one way to find out. And pursuing this might just lead to the break he'd been looking for.

He summarized his findings and lack of findings, then wrote a note of instructions to put on the mirror for the morning. Half-asleep, he got undressed and crawled under the covers. The bed felt large and empty without Elizabeth.

He lay there in the darkness. It seemed to fill not only the room but also his entire being. Soon he would fall asleep, and when morning arrived, he would have to relearn the terrible things that had happened to him and Elizabeth. Already he'd forgotten most of the day, remembering neither sunrise nor sunset, nor anything in between.

Under these circumstances, life didn't seem worth living. But if that was the case, why hadn't he already ended it? He knew the answer—Elizabeth.

Before turning out the lights, he had looked at the framed picture above her dresser, the black-and-white photo from their wedding. He pictured it in his mind. But then an image of Cheryl in Toronto flashed before him. How could he ever have cheated on Elizabeth?

She deserved better, he thought. But he took some solace in recognizing his shortcomings. Maybe that was a sign of improvement. He had never felt that way before. Remorse was an entirely foreign emotion to the old Christopher Barnes.

"I'll make it up to you," he said in the darkness. "I promise."

Chapter 47

Barnes awoke to the sound of his alarm clock and slapped it off with a heavy hand. Exhaustion lingered like a hangover. How late had he stayed up? Looking at the clock through bleary eyes, he discerned a handwritten message taped to the front: "Read note on bathroom mirror."

He suddenly noticed that Elizabeth wasn't there, and an unsettling feeling came over him. He had no idea where she'd gone, and he had no recollection of the night before. Now that he thought about it, he couldn't remember much of anything. The day of the week? The month? November, he guessed. He remembered sitting in a restaurant across from a blonde woman, a heaping plate of mussels in front of him. That had been November. It felt like a long time ago.

He lifted the note on the clock and looked at the time: 8:01. Why had the alarm been set so late? Didn't he have surgery? Today must be Saturday, or Sunday. The morning paper would tell him.

He went to the mirror and read his message:

> *Don't be alarmed. Your ability to form new memories has been severely damaged since you were poisoned by mussels in Toronto in November. Today is December 18.*

December. He had the feeling he'd read this before, but neither a note nor déjà vu was necessary to remind him of the poisoning: the fancy restaurant with obsequious waiters in black suits; the tables covered with white tablecloths, adorned with fine china; his blonde dinner companion and soon-to-be after-dinner companion; and most of all, the mussels—dark, ominous, steeped in brine.

He continued reading. The next paragraph described his coma and the protracted hospital stay. Then Elizabeth's affair and her death.

Thoughts of Elizabeth came back to him, multiple images like photographs flung into the air: Elizabeth at home in front of the fireplace, reading a medical journal with Rex at her side; in a fondue restaurant, dripping chocolate onto the tablecloth; in the OR wearing bloody scrubs and replacing a hip; and in the Museum of Fine Arts posing between two Van Goghs. One memory in particular stayed with him, suspended in the air, while the others flitted away. It was the recollection of a picnic on a July weekend a year and a half ago, one of the hottest days of the summer. Early that afternoon Elizabeth had suggested—no, insisted—they have a picnic on the esplanade along the Charles River. Barnes remembered sitting on a blanket she had spread on the grass about ten feet from the water.

"It's way too hot for this," he'd complained.

She wore a straw hat, sandals, and a sky-blue sundress with little yellow sunflowers on it. Despite the oppressive heat, she looked comfortable, although tiny beads of sweat had formed on the tip of her nose.

"Christopher Barnes, the great cardiothoracic surgeon, can't take the heat?"

"It's hot as hell out here."

"You just have to chill, no pun intended. Have some iced tea." She'd brought iced tea, sandwiches, fruit, and Twiglets. Resembling straight pretzels in shape and consistency, Twiglets were junk food imported from England. They were coated with a yeast extract that most Americans, Barnes included, found foul tasting. Elizabeth loved them.

"There isn't even a breeze out here," Barnes complained. That was true. Only a couple of sailboats had ventured onto the water, and they didn't appear to move much faster than the scattered clouds overhead.

Elizabeth blew in his face. "How's that?"

"Don't stop."

She handed Barnes a cup of tea. "You didn't dress properly. You shouldn't have worn trainers."

"Trainers?"

"Sneakers. You should have worn sandals instead. They're much cooler."

"I don't wear sandals. Besides, they're not going to cool off the rest of me. My clothes are practically dripping. Maybe you don't have that problem with a dress, but doesn't your underwear stick to you in weather like this?"

She smiled and squinted at him in the bright sunlight. "I'm not wearing any underwear."

"Really?"

"Really."

He wondered whether she was just saying that. "Show me."

She shook her head like a child. "Show me yours first."

"Show you my underwear?" He was wearing short pants.

"No. Show me what's underneath." She smiled mischievously.

"Are you trying to get me arrested?"

"No, but if you expect me to lift my dress, you should be prepared to drop your shorts."

He thought about that. "You're really not wearing anything underneath?"

She scooted on the blanket to face him and looked around to make sure no runners or bikers were passing by. Then, quickly, she lifted her dress.

He could see under the garment for less than a second, but with her sitting like that—knees apart—the sight left an indelible impression. "If you're trying to arouse me, it's working."

She leaned forward, put her hand on his thigh, and slid her fingers upward, reaching under the leg of his shorts.

"Too bad you wore underpants," she said, caressing him through the cloth. She withdrew her hand.

"Don't stop."

"Later. Have a sandwich. If you finish your lunch, you can have me for dessert."

She teased him for more than an hour before they headed back. When they arrived home, they made love before Elizabeth even took off her straw hat. On the living room floor. She sat on top of Barnes, having pulled his shorts around his ankles. He could still picture her looking down at him.

He and Elizabeth would never have another picnic, never make love again. Yet he mustn't allow himself to dwell on that. Right now he needed to finish reading the note on the mirror, to find out what else was happening in his life.

Your number one priority today is to obtain the autopsy reports from the three people who died after receiving GBF-complex-coated screws. See the note on the refrigerator for details. One or more of these cases may be connected with Elizabeth's murder.

Your next priority is to investigate Claire's lover, Judge Darcia Parker—the jealous type. Find out about her relationship or interactions with Elizabeth.

He needed a cigarette. Not just to calm his nerves but to sharpen his focus, to help him try to remember any details from the past day or two.

Then he read he'd quit smoking. The rest of the letter contained other unexpected news: lunch plans with Nate Billings, dinner with Shirley Collins. What turn of events had led to this?

He tried to remember the day before. Certainly *something* memorable must have happened to result in lunch and dinner with Nate and Shirley. Had Nate assisted him in surgery? And what about Shirley? He'd *slept* with her. Yet he could conjure up no memory of that, not even an image of her in his house.

How had he managed to do so much when he could remember so little? At least it meant he wasn't just sitting around moping. And it gave him an incentive to do more. Already he might have made significant headway in solving Elizabeth's murder. Focusing on that would be paramount.

After getting dressed, he fixed himself a cup of coffee, took out the garbage—it was trash-pickup day—and then started making phone calls.

His first task was to figure out the names of the people who had died in the clinical trial with GBF-complex-coated screws. The patients hadn't been identified by name but rather by their initials and an assigned number, to maintain their privacy. To get the names, he called the orthopedics departments at the participating hospitals and asked to speak to the investigators conducting the studies. He identified himself as Elizabeth's husband and a medical doctor, and the clinical investigators at two of the three sites revealed the information necessary for him to obtain autopsy reports. The third site was in California, three time zones away, and he would have to wait at least two hours before calling them. From the other two sites, he obtained autopsies of a twenty-nine-year-old black man who'd died in an automobile accident and a fifty-four-year-old Caucasian who'd died of a gunshot wound to the head. Both were faxed to him in his home office. He looked at the gunshot victim first.

Leslie Martin Dobson, subject LMD-019. Dobson had undergone surgery to have a plate with a bolt and six screws placed in his right ankle, according to Elizabeth's case summary. The autopsy report didn't even mention it except in the general findings, in which the coroner had described a well-healed scar from a surgical incision along the lateral aspect of the lower left leg. The gunshot wound was determined to be self-inflicted from a 9mm handgun fired into his mouth. The bullet had passed through the base of the brain, and the cause of death was ruled to be the destruction of the respiratory center in his brain stem.

Barnes read and reread the report of the examination of the various organs, but he found no abnormalities that he could attribute to GBF-complex-coated screws. The patient had an obstruction of three major coronary arteries and moderate emphysema, probably from cigarette smoking. The liver was entirely normal—no congestion or necrosis or other pathology. This was significant because if substances produce toxins, they often damage the liver as it tries to break them down. But the liver in the autopsy had no abnormalities.

From what Barnes could tell, the screws in this man's ankle had no bearing on his death or any other medical problems. He moved on to the next case.

Melvin Carl Brooks, subject MCB-031, appeared to have been in good health until the time of his death. He hadn't been wearing a seatbelt and had suffered multiple rib fractures, one of which perforated his left lung. The cause of death had been ruled massive hemorrhage from a ruptured spleen.

Barnes read through both autopsies a second time but found no additional information. Maybe the remaining report from

California—the patient who'd died from bacterial meningitis—would be more useful. Elizabeth had most likely uncovered *something*. He just needed to figure out what it was. If she'd found it, eventually he would, too.

As Barnes studied the autopsy reports, a large van rolled up to the curb in front of his house. Two gloved men stepped from the rear.

Garbage cans lined the street for refuse collection, and Barnes had set out two tall cans along with several boxes full of letters and other papers. The men hurriedly loaded the boxes into the van and dumped the contents of the trash cans into a bin. After setting the empty cans beside the curb, the men hopped back into the rear of the vehicle, and it pulled away from the curb.

Chapter 48

Barnes stayed home all morning. According to his notes, Billings didn't have any surgeries scheduled and Houston wouldn't let him assist in the OR. Going to work would be pointless. At least Billings had let him assist with cases during the previous two days. That was hard to believe, but perhaps not as hard to believe as some of the other things in his notes, like sleeping with Shirley. Apparently Billings and he worked well together, and maybe they even liked each other. Otherwise, why would Nate have asked him to lunch? Life seemed to be taking a series of unusual turns, but that was okay. All he needed to do was to trust his notes.

At eleven thirty he tried calling California to get the last autopsy report, but the person who could give him that information hadn't arrived at work yet. The report would have to wait until after lunch. He poured the remainder of a cup of coffee down the kitchen sink and headed out the door.

Traffic was light on Storrow Drive along the Charles River. Barnes set his cruise control and relaxed. By the time the Harvard Bridge came into view, he no longer remembered why he was going to the hospital, but he knew the reason could be found on the list in his pocket, and he would relearn it soon enough.

At the hospital, he found Billings's office and knocked on the open door.

Sitting behind his desk, Billings looked up from a hospital chart. "Hey, Chris, have a seat. I'm just wrapping up here."

Barnes sat in a leather chair and waited for him to finish.

"Priscilla should be here any minute . . . She's looking forward to meeting you."

"Priscilla?"

"My wife. You'll like her."

Just then he heard a knock at the door. He turned as Priscilla entered. She looked like a model—tall, elegant—with just a hint of gray in her jet-black hair.

"Hi, hon." She smiled at Nate, then turned to Barnes. "You must be Christopher Barnes, the bypass wizard." She extended a dark hand. "I'm Priscilla."

He grasped it gently. "Chris. Nice to meet you."

"I've heard a lot about you, Chris. I know if Nate ever needed a bypass, he'd want you to do it. Of course that's only because he can't do it on himself."

Barnes couldn't help but smile.

Priscilla turned to Nate. "Are you ready to go, hon?"

He closed the chart on his desk. "Yes, ma'am."

Priscilla let Barnes sit in the front while Nate drove them to a nearby Indian restaurant. Seated at a booth, they looked through menus and decided to share entrées. Barnes felt uncomfortable eating family style with these virtual strangers, but he figured it was better than taking the risk of ordering a single entrée that might turn out to be inedible.

Throughout the meal, Billings and Priscilla kept a conversation going. Mostly they talked about their daughter—their pride and anguish. It was a topic as foreign to Barnes as needlepoint, but the challenges involved in raising her made for good conversation.

"We should have taken her to your wife . . . last year," said Billings. "She broke her ankle. Needed a plate and screws put in."

"Who did you send her to?" asked Barnes.

"George Gainer. I've known him for years, and . . . I've always trusted him. But in retrospect that was a mistake. The ankle got infected, and . . . it was a mess." Billings spooned curried vegetables onto his plate, over a small mound of rice.

Barnes didn't know anything about Gainer. "Is she okay now?" he asked, accepting an entrée of tandoori chicken that Priscilla passed to him.

"Yeah. It just took about three times as long for her to recover."

"How old is she?"

"Fifteen," said Priscilla.

"She's at that age where all the boys are chasing her," said Billings. "If you had a fifteen-year-old daughter, Chris, would you let her go out with a boy . . . to a movie that doesn't end until eleven thirty?"

"That's out of my league," said Barnes. "I don't know the first thing about raising kids."

"Nobody really knows," said Priscilla. "You just do the best you can. I think it's fine to give them a little freedom, within reason."

"Eleven thirty isn't within reason," countered Nate, "especially if . . . she's with a sixteen-year-old boy." He speared a curried carrot with his fork.

"I'd have to agree with Nate," said Barnes. "Sixteen-year-old boys have got only one thing on their minds."

"It's hard to remember back that far," said Priscilla. "Were we ever that young, Nate?"

"I don't know, but . . . you'll always be young to me."

She kissed him on the cheek. "Nate always knows what to say."

"Yup, he's quite a guy." Barnes no longer recalled where the conversation had started, but that didn't matter. Despite everything, he felt at ease.

"Um, Chris," said Nate, taking on a more serious tone, "there's something . . . I should tell you."

So much for feeling at ease.

"There's going to be a meeting this afternoon . . . in the surgery conference room at four o'clock. It's to discuss your future . . . in the surgical program."

"They don't waste any time, do they?" That jarhead chairman, Carl Milligan, was probably behind it.

"No. I'm telling you because . . . I don't like it when people do things behind someone's back." Billings took another bite of curried vegetables and waited for a reply.

"Yeah, I appreciate it." Barnes didn't know what else to say. At least Billings had told him. He wondered whether Denny had, too.

"Let me make a suggestion," offered Billings.

"I'm listening."

"Don't go to the meeting. Let me handle it."

Barnes wasn't so sure that was a good idea, trusting Billings, or anyone, with something so important—his entire career. "If you don't want me to go," he said, "why'd you tell me about it?"

"Because you have a right to know. But if you show up there, they're going to pick at you till you bleed. Then they'll all attack you like . . . turkeys."

"Turkeys? You mean maybe sharks?"

"No, turkeys. Sharks tear you apart, but turkeys, when one of them starts bleeding, the others gang up and peck him to death. Not a pretty sight."

"I have to tell you, Nate, I'm not afraid of turkeys."

"You know those guys. You don't want to be there. I'm going to tell them . . . you and I are working together and you're still the best pair of hands in the hospital . . . or maybe second best. Then I'll recommend we keep working together . . . for the next month. After that, they can call another meeting . . . to assess the situation. Considering you're still in the early stages of recovery, it would be reckless for them now to pass judgment . . . on your future. I don't think they'll do anything rash . . . if it might come back to haunt them."

Billings was probably right.

"They need to consider," he continued, "that this is uncharted territory. You could recover most of your ability to remember, and . . . they'd look pretty stupid if they got rid of one of the most high-profile cardiothoracic surgeons in the country. Not to mention the fact that they'd want to avoid a lawsuit."

"*That* I don't doubt." For the administration, covering their behind was always priority one.

Billings put his napkin onto the table. "With your okay, I'll pick up your cases . . . and we'll do them together. You'll get paid for the operations, but the patients will see me in the office before and after their surgery. You can be there if you like. I'll extend my office hours to fit them in."

"I don't know." Nate was going out on a limb for him, increasing his own workload and his liability. "Seems like a lot of effort on your part. I won't argue, but I'm not sure I'd have done the same for you."

Nate shook his head. "Probably not, but don't try to talk me out of it. It's the right thing to do."

"Is it really that simple?"

"No. It's the right thing to do . . . *and* I know how you feel. I know what you're going through."

"How can *you* know what I'm going through?"

"I've had people ostracize me. I've had people, even family, treat me like I was . . . damaged goods."

Barnes didn't know how to respond to that. What about the man was damaged? Physically he was like a professional athlete, and mentally . . . well, he obviously wasn't a slow learner.

Billings continued. "You probably wonder why I talk the way I do, so . . . deliberately. It's because . . . I used to stutter. It was bad, real bad. I'm told it didn't start until I was five, but I don't ever remember not doing it. It would take me thirty seconds just to . . . spit out a sentence. I'd try real hard not to stutter, but the more I tried, the worse it got. I became what they called an . . . advanced stutterer. I had repetitions, prolongations, and blocks. You name it. I repeated parts of words . . . a lot. Especially if a word started with *de*, like *de . . . cide* or *defense*. I still don't like saying them."

Barnes now understood, however briefly, where Billings was coming from.

"Growing up was no picnic. I had a lot of . . . shame. The kids in school teased me. They imitated me. They called me stupid. I had to take speech therapy . . . and it didn't help. When anyone visited my parents, before they arrived, my father would take me aside and remind me not to talk to them. 'Just shake hands and go into the other room,' he would say."

Billings was trembling, and Priscilla took one of his hands in hers.

"So how did you overcome that?" Barnes asked.

"I just did. On my own. But not until college, and I still have to fight it. So I know how you must feel at times: self-conscious, isolated. That's . . . a lot of the reason why I'm offering to help you, why I'll pick up your cases and work with you."

"I appreciate it."

"You're welcome."

Priscilla beamed, as though Barnes had just been accepted into the family. "Nate will take care of you," she assured him.

Barnes believed her.

Chapter 49

Wearing latex gloves, Wright and Gould sifted through Barnes's trash in a back room of the station. Both of them had hoped the ballistics test on Houston's Glock would turn up a match to the bullets that had killed Elizabeth—then Barnes's garbage wouldn't be so important—but the results had come back negative; the gun was definitely not the same weapon used in her murder. That didn't eliminate Houston as a suspect, but it made Barnes's trash more important.

A drop cloth covered the floor, and they stood in the middle of it, reading scraps of paper and letters. Food products, napkins, and other useless refuse accounted for much of the trash, and they discarded those items into large cardboard boxes lined with plastic bags. On a sheet of paper on a clipboard, they took notes of anything that might provide insight into Barnes's lifestyle, his friends, or his finances. This information they obtained from not only his personal correspondence but also credit card bills and business mail.

"I wonder if this stuff is any good," Gould said, holding up an empty bottle of Pinot Noir. "Maybe I should ask that Collins chick—she probably drank two-thirds of it."

"Are you thinking of buying some?" Wright glanced at the label. French. Probably expensive.

"What I buy comes in a can. You think he's screwing her?"

"It may be the other way around." Wright thought about Barnes, mentally disabled and trying to cope without his wife. Would someone with his disability, yet also his reputation and resources, be appealing to a woman like Shirley?

"I don't trust that Collins chick," said Gould. "Or Barnes."

"You're not the trusting type," said Wright.

"You got a point there. I sure as fuck don't trust Denny Houston. I wonder whether he was screwing Elizabeth Barnes. We know she let Marshall Coburn into her panties, and he hardly even knew her. I'll bet he put a loaf in her oven and it pushed Barnes over the edge. Only question is, why didn't Barnes kill him too?"

"Well, we can't arrest Barnes on a hunch or even on motive and opportunity. We need evidence."

Gould tossed the wine bottle into a trash box. "Evidence is overrated. He did it. He was looking at big money problems, and his wife was a cash cow who was going to have a kid he didn't want and that probably wasn't even his. Meanwhile he's fucking some blonde at a conference."

"Just find us some evidence," said Wright.

Gould had moved on to other garbage. "This is disgusting." He held up an empty carton of Chinese food. "How do people eat this crapola? Smells like paint thinner."

Wright was surprised his partner could smell anything through Gloria's cologne.

Gould threw the carton into the trash.

"Some people think hot dogs are disgusting," Wright pointed out.

"Yeah, foreigners."

Wright didn't say anything to that, and for a while they sifted through trash in silence. Then Gould said, "Looking through all this is gonna take a week."

Wright glanced at his watch. "We'll finish today. Captain says he'll try to get two men to help us."

"Yeah? You believe that and I got some real estate to sell you. I'd bet my left arm nobody helps us."

"I'm not sure what I'd do with your left arm, although, come to think of it, Karen and I have been looking for something to put over the mantel."

Gould threw a handful of coffee-stained napkins into the trash. "I hate this part of the job. I didn't become a cop to look through garbage."

Wright hated it, too. Yet looking through garbage might be the key to cracking the case. Both he and Gould knew that. Gould just liked to complain.

Wright looked at his watch. He hoped the other two cops would get there soon.

Chapter 50

Barnes returned home after lunch and walked in on Carmen, the maid. "Buenas tardes, Dr. Barnes," she said, turning off the vacuum cleaner.

Barnes spoke to her in Spanish, and before she could offer her condolences, he said, "What are you doing here?"

"Today is Friday," she explained. "I clean the house on Fridays."

"The house doesn't need cleaning. There are no dishes to wash; there's no laundry; there isn't even any dust. You're vacuuming a carpet that's clean enough to eat off of."

"Yes, Dr. Barnes, but Miss Claire told me to keep coming and make sure the house stays clean."

"It's clean now," he said, suppressing the urge to ask her who Miss Claire was and why she would ask anyone to clean a house that was already spotless. "Please go home. I'll still pay you." He threw his overcoat onto a chair.

"Yes, Dr. Barnes." She unplugged the vacuum cleaner and started to wrap up the cord.

A sudden thought occurred to him. "Can you tell me anything about Elizabeth?" He took out his notes and started looking through them for ideas about what questions to ask her.

"God bless her, she was a special woman. It's terrible, terrible what happened to her."

"Yes, it is, but what I mean is, is there anything specific you can tell me about her, or about the house?"

"Specific?" She seemed evasive, focusing more on the vacuum cleaner than on him.

"Is there anything you can think of that you haven't told the police?" He saw in his notes that she had found the body. "Was there anything unusual when you found Elizabeth or when you cleaned the house after the murder?"

"No, Dr. Barnes."

"Take a minute to think." He tried not to sound condescending. "Elizabeth cared about you very much, you know, and anything you can tell me that might help me figure out who did this would be something that Elizabeth would want. Do you understand what I'm saying?"

"Yes, Dr. Barnes."

"Was there anything unusual you may have found or seen when you were cleaning up, anything out of place?"

"Not really."

From the way she avoided his gaze, he figured there was something. "Please tell me, Carmen. For Elizabeth."

She stopped fidgeting with the vacuum cleaner. "I'm not sure it means anything, Dr. Barnes, but the thing the computer plugs into, that metal thing that goes into the wall . . ."

The surge protector. "Yes."

"It was turned off. She told me that it protects the computer and I shouldn't turn it off, but the last time I cleaned, it wasn't on. I know because otherwise I'd see the little orange light. I didn't know what to do, so I left it off. I hope that was right." She wrung her hands.

Barnes didn't care how anxious Carmen felt. All he could think of was Elizabeth. She may have accidentally turned off the surge protector, but more likely someone else had. He wrote a note to himself.

"Does that help?" Carmen asked.

"I'm not sure, but thank you for telling me." He shuffled through his notes again and saw he'd suspected someone had altered the text in one of Elizabeth's computer files, a summary of clinical trials with GBF-complex-coated screws. Carmen's observation now lent more credence to that. He turned his attention to her again. "Is there anything else?"

"No, Dr. Barnes."

"All right. Thank you, Carmen." He put his pen and paper back into his pocket. "If you think of anything else, call me. Okay?"

"Yes, Dr. Barnes."

He doubted she would.

While Carmen finished putting away her cleaning supplies, Barnes called California for information on the patient who had died of bacterial meningitis. The principal investigator of the study had left town on vacation, and the only coinvestigator who could help, Dr. Kapryn, had managed to tie himself up in meetings until at least four thirty Pacific time. That meant Barnes would have to wait until after seven thirty in the evening. He gave the secretary his telephone number and the number of the fax machine in his office upstairs. She assured him Dr. Kapryn would return the call.

Barnes jotted down the information. On his list he saw a note about dinner with Shirley and a reminder to call Claire, to try to find out more about her significant other, Darcia.

He called Claire at work.

"A couple quick questions," he began, after apologizing for the interruption. "I have in my notes that you and Darcia invited me over for Christmas."

"That's right. We're hoping you'll join us."

"According to my notes, Darcia met Elizabeth a couple of times."

"Yes. Once or twice." She sounded distracted. Papers rustled in the background.

"What court is she in?"

"Common pleas."

He took notes.

A muffled male's voice said something, followed by a second male voice, this one more strident. "Could we perhaps talk about this another time?" Claire said. "You caught me in a meeting."

He apologized again and let her go. In his notes he wrote, "Common pleas—common criminals." Maybe it was reaching, even paranoid, to suspect a female judge of committing murder, but presiding in a common-pleas courtroom, she might have access to convicted felons who could be manipulated to do her bidding. If, God forbid, Elizabeth was having an affair with Claire, Darcia could have found out. In a jealous rage—or perhaps a calm, calculated rage—Darcia could have arranged for someone to kill Elizabeth. Barnes would have to find out more about her.

He called Shirley at work. One of the research scientists in her lab answered the phone and paged her for him.

"Hi, Chris. What's up?" She sounded pleased to hear from him.

"I called to see whether we can move dinner up to six o'clock."

"All right. I'll bring Chinese again. I might be a little late, but I'll be there."

"Thanks. I'll make a note of it."

"How's everything going?" she asked.

"Slowly. Just working on things related to Elizabeth."

"You don't give up, do you?"

"No. I should go now, but I'm looking forward to seeing you later." He wasn't really sure about that, but his notes suggested it was the right thing to say. He might not understand why he'd written half of what was there, but he understood the importance of relying on it as a surrogate memory. The bottom line was that he had to follow his notes.

Even if he didn't agree with them.

Wright and Gould continued to sift through Barnes's garbage, just the two of them. It turned out the captain couldn't spare anyone else. They hadn't spent the entire afternoon there—they'd managed to squeeze in a late lunch and some other work—but it was now after five thirty, and a substantial pile of unsearched trash remained.

They'd uncovered several pages of shredded notes, presumably written by Barnes, but they would have to be pieced together, and the ones that they'd started taping didn't appear to have been written in English. To Wright it looked like French. To Gould it was gibberish.

"At least it was a strip shredder and not a crosscut," said Wright.

"Why the hell can't he write in English like a normal American?" said Gould.

"He doesn't want someone reading it," said Wright. "We need to get a translator in here."

Wright asked the captain. The captain said he would look into it.

In the meantime, Wright kept taping shreds of paper and searching for more evidence.

Gould continued to complain about items in the trash. "Look at all this crap! I said it before, and I'll say it again: I didn't join the force to dig through some guy's garbage. Barnes is gonna pay for this."

An hour later Wright and Gould were still looking, and an hour later they still didn't have a translator. Wright was mainly taping strips of paper, while Gould was finding more strips for him to tape. Wright passed some of the time by thinking about the holidays. He wondered what Gould would get for Gloria and, more important, what Gloria would get for Gould. He hoped it wouldn't be anything annoying, like shoes that squeak.

"I'm getting the feeling we're not going to figure this out tonight," said Wright.

Then Gould thrust his hand into the air, clutching a scrap of paper. "Bingo!"

Chapter 51

Shirley arrived promptly at six, and Barnes took her coat. Wearing a sapphire-colored dress and matching stud earrings, she appeared more radiant than he'd remembered. In one hand she carried a bottle of wine, and in the other, dinner from Shanghai.

"Potstickers, Szechuan chicken, broccoli beef, and fried rice," she announced.

Barnes wondered whether he'd told her that potstickers, and in particular potstickers from that restaurant, were his favorite appetizer. Most likely. Otherwise the woman had read his mind. Clearly their relationship had evolved since the last time they'd had dinner at the Union Oyster House.

He went to hug her before taking her coat, and she kissed him on the cheek. What if she had kissed him on the lips instead? How would he have reacted to that? Someday it could happen, as they spent more and more time together. But although his list could tell him what to do, like "Kiss Shirley hello," it couldn't change the way he felt. Somehow he would need to do that on his own.

In the kitchen, Shirley served Barnes while he worked on opening the bottle of wine she'd brought. "You probably don't remember much of the time we've spent together," she said, "but I do think that will change."

"I wish I shared your confidence," he said.

"You might if you spend a little more time with me." Then she asked, "Do you remember anything from when we had dinner the day before yesterday?"

He shook his head. "No, but I keep notes."

She rubbed his shoulder. "We'll have to work on that." Her touch spread in soothing ripples.

Just then, the cork slipped out of the bottle with a hollow pop. Barnes filled two glasses. As he put down the bottle, the telephone rang.

"Probably a telemarketer."

He tried not to sound too annoyed when he answered it.

"Hey, buddy." It was Denny. "How's it goin'?"

"Okay, but I'm kind of in the middle of something."

"I won't keep you. Just called to talk about our research, the abstract I wrote."

Barnes searched through his notes. "What about it?"

"Just wanted to make sure you don't have any problems with it. The deadline for changes is coming up."

Barnes found what he was looking for, a note that he'd withdrawn the abstract and hadn't told Denny. "I can't remember. You know how I am."

"Yeah, well, okay," said Houston. "Let me know if there's a problem."

"Sure thing. Talk to you later."

Barnes hung up.

"Dr. Houston?" Shirley asked.

"Yeah. Good of him to call."

She shook her head. "Chris, that man is not your friend. I can't believe you still talk to him."

"Denny's okay."

"Yeah? I called him yesterday and asked him to at least act like he cared and spend a little time with you, and you know what he said?"

"What?"

"He said, 'Let him have sex with you. He'll like that a helluva lot more than spending time with me.'"

"That sounds like Denny."

"The man has no concept of empathy. He's not your friend. Friends don't abandon you when you need them. They don't make excuses to avoid you. If he calls again, you shouldn't even answer the phone. Or better yet, you should take the phone off the hook."

"Let's forget about Denny and go into the other room."

She picked up Barnes's plate and wineglass and handed them to him. "After you."

He led her to the family room, and they sat in front of the fireplace.

"How about a toast?" Barnes lifted his glass.

She didn't have hers. "Oh, I left mine in the kitchen." She set her plate on the coffee table and stood up, smoothing out her dress. "I'll be right back."

He watched her walk into the other room. Something about that dress drew him in, like a deep blue sea. Within it her legs and buttocks shifted and slid against the thin fabric.

He wondered whether she knew the effect it created.

In the kitchen, before retrieving her wineglass, Shirley took the telephone off the hook and put it in a drawer under a stack of dish towels. Then she returned to the family room. Barnes had already started eating.

"You didn't wait for me," she scolded playfully.

"I forgot you were here."

She shook a finger at him. "You're getting a sense of humor. I like that."

Billings pushed the "Disconnect" button on his telephone. He was pacing the family room but trying not to obstruct the big-screen television. Priscilla had just turned on the news. Their daughter was upstairs on her own telephone, talking to her sixteen-year-old boyfriend whom Billings trusted about as much as a cat with a field mouse.

Sitting on the couch, Priscilla looked up at Nate. "The line's busy again?" she asked.

"Yeah. Maybe he . . . forgot to hang up." Billings felt guilty as soon as the words came out. "I can't believe I just said that."

"You didn't mean anything by it, baby."

"Remind me to call him again in ten or fifteen minutes. I know he'll be relieved to hear they're keeping him on staff."

"Sure, hon."

Ten minutes later the line was still busy.

"I wonder if his phone *is* off the hook," Billings said.

"Call the operator and ask."

He dialed the operator. Afterward he said to Priscilla, "Either the phone is off the hook or there's . . . something wrong with the line."

"Maybe you should go over there and see if he's all right."

"Are you serious?"

"Of course I'm serious. He doesn't live that far away."

"He doesn't live that close, either."

"Suit yourself, hon."

Billings grumbled to himself, then went to get his coat. "I'm probably going to . . . regret this."

Chapter 52

Barnes and Shirley finished their dinner and relaxed in front of the fireplace.

"This is so peaceful," Shirley said. She kicked off her shoes and let the flames warm her outstretched feet.

Upstairs a telephone rang, the one in his office. It rang twice, then stopped.

"What was that?" she asked.

"My fax machine. Somebody's sending me something."

She touched his arm. "Please don't get up. Read it later."

Reluctantly Barnes got to his feet. "No, if I put it off, I'll forget. It's probably something I'm expecting."

"But—"

"I'll be back in a minute."

"In a minute you'll have forgotten about me."

She was cute when she pouted. But the fax could be important. "I won't forget. Don't go anywhere." And he headed up to the office.

The fax machine had already printed a cover sheet from Dr. Kapryn in California, with a note scrawled across the bottom:

I tried calling, but your line was busy. We had two deaths among the study participants at our center, not just one. The medical examiners were reluctant to fax the reports directly to you, so they faxed them to me instead. Here they are. I hope they're what you're looking for.

In the bottom right-hand corner, Dr. Kapryn had written *page 1 of 12.*

Barnes skimmed through the list in his pocket, looking for a reference to Dr. Kapryn. Who was this man? His notes answered the question. These were autopsy reports that might be relevant to Elizabeth's research.

More pages emerged from the fax machine. Two autopsy reports: those of a nineteen-year-old woman who had died of meningitis and a forty-six-year-old man who had died of Alzheimer's disease. The latter patient was a white male with a history of degenerative disk disease and an old fracture in the thoracic region of his vertebral column. Nothing suspicious. Barnes had hoped the extra autopsy report would reveal something more striking, like massive liver damage or sudden kidney failure.

Alzheimer's disease wasn't very exciting, even in someone as young as forty-six. Usually it afflicts the elderly, typically people in their seventies and eighties, but sometimes younger adults are stricken, and in those cases the disease often progresses rapidly. From his childhood Barnes remembered a next-door neighbor, Mr. Mallory, who'd succumbed to it in his forties. The man would sometimes throw a football with him and talk to him about his work as an architect and the importance of getting a good education. But Mr. Mallory began getting confused and wandering the neighborhood late at night. His wife put him in a nursing home, and before he passed away not long afterward, he didn't even know what a football was.

Barnes reflected on whether the GBF-complex-coated screws had somehow caused or contributed to Alzheimer's disease, especially considering that this autopsy appeared to have been deleted from Elizabeth's files. But how could he or anybody else prove that the disorder had been caused by the screws? The man had died eighteen months after having two rods and several screws inserted along his spine in the thoracic region.

Barnes skimmed the autopsy report again, looking for something out of the ordinary. Anything. He found nothing. The brain showed neurofibrillary tangles and plaques, microscopic changes typical of Alzheimer's disease, although occasionally older people will have these findings without any apparent damage.

He reread the section on the gross appearance of the brain. It was normal size. That struck him as unusual, now that he thought about it. Typically with Alzheimer's disease, there's shrinkage of the cerebral cortex, the largest part of the brain. The sulci, or spaces, become wider, and the gyri, the brain matter between the spaces, become narrow. He couldn't remember how common this was, but he remembered it as being typical of the disease. Yet it was also typical of old age, and most people with Alzheimer's disease are old. Since this patient was relatively young, maybe a normal-size brain wasn't so unusual.

He put down the report and turned his attention to the other autopsy results still printing from the fax machine. The nineteen-year-old with meningitis had died more than a month after the onset of her disease. Apparently the bacterial infection had been misdiagnosed and mistreated. She'd received an insufficient dose of penicillin, and the meningococci bacteria had resisted the treatment and subsequently multiplied. The exact cause of death was ruled a basal adhesive arachnoiditis—the obstruction of the space around the base of the brain. From what he could tell, this nineteen-year-old had died horribly and needlessly.

He pored over the report. In the external examination of the teenager, the pathologist described a white, plastic identification band encircling her wrist and a red band above it with the word *Sulfa*, indicating that she had been allergic to sulfonamide antibiotics. The pathologist then described her general appearance, skin, head and neck, thorax and abdomen, back and anus, extremities, external genitalia, and hair in enough detail that Barnes could form a mental picture: a five-foot, 105-pound, blonde-haired, brown-eyed, freckled young woman with pierced ears and red fingernail and toenail polish.

In his internal examination, the pathologist described all the girl's organs and body systems including her brain. The brain weighed 1,710 grams—more than normal—and appeared markedly swollen. The gyri had widened, and the sulci between them had narrowed.

Barnes skipped down to the microscopic findings. Large areas of the brain had filled with white blood cells—an indication of inflammation—and the brain had developed a mild vasculitis, inflammation around the blood vessels. The girl even had microinfarctions, tiny areas of dead brain tissue resulting from the obstruction of small blood vessels.

She'd been incredibly unlucky, he realized. People who die from bacterial meningitis usually succumb to it in a day or two. The progression of the illness is rapid and can be fatal if not treated with antibiotics. But if it *is* treated in time, the patient usually recovers without problems. This nineteen-year-old had received treatment, but not enough and too late. How that had happened, he didn't know, but it certainly had nothing to do with GBF-complex-coated screws.

Buried within the microscopic report, Barnes read about an incidental finding that the pathologist described in a single sentence: "Neurofibrillary tangles and plaques of unknown significance were identified in the frontal, parietal, and occipital lobes using Bodian and Bielschowsky stains." Barnes had no idea what Bodian and Bielschowsky stains were, but that didn't matter. His mouth went dry. The patient had neurofibrillary tangles and plaques in her cerebral cortex, a characteristic finding of Alzheimer's disease. Why did a nineteen-year-old have findings of a disease that typically afflicts people in their seventies and eighties? This must have been what Elizabeth had wondered, too.

Barnes thought about the implications of his and Elizabeth's findings. Two young people afflicted with a disease that has a predilection for the elderly. Either one of these cases by itself would probably have been overlooked as insignificant or considered, at most, a finding of mild interest without clinical relevance, but together they suggested something ominous. The likelihood that these changes in the brain had occurred merely by chance in two of four cases was vanishingly small. Something had caused the changes to happen, and the only thing these two patients had in common was their GBF-complex-coated screws.

But that raised another question. If the screws caused something similar to Alzheimer's disease, why had only these two patients gotten it? Of the hundreds or thousands of people who had received the screws, why hadn't any of them died of Alzheimer's or at least showed some of the symptoms of the disease?

And then he understood. The realization took his breath away. GBF-complex was destructive to the brain only if it could *reach* the brain. In his own condition, the key factor determining the extent of damage had been the blood-brain barrier, the natural filter that prevents many drugs and toxins from entering either the spinal canal or the brain. According to his notes, that's what had saved his life—his blood-brain barrier had filtered out most of the poison from the mussels.

But the blood-brain barrier isn't perfect, and certain conditions can weaken it. That's what the forty-six-year-old man and the nineteen-year-old woman had in common: their blood-brain barrier had been compromised—his probably by the insertion of the screws along his spinal canal, allowing the substance to gain access to his cerebral spinal fluid, and hers as a direct result of the inflammation caused by meningitis. Barnes recalled that patients with bacterial meningitis respond well to treatment with large doses of penicillin, even though that antibiotic doesn't normally cross the blood-brain barrier. In patients with meningitis, the barrier is compromised and the penicillin is able to enter the brain and spinal fluid and thereby fight off the infection. Similarly, in this patient the GBF-complex had gained access to the brain and caused the neurofibrillary tangles and plaques observed during the autopsy.

The ramifications of Elizabeth's findings were alarming: patients who had received the GBF-complex-coated screws were walking around with time bombs in their bodies. These bombs might never go off, but if they did, the patients would become senile, just like someone with Alzheimer's disease.

"I don't believe this," Barnes said out loud, and he began scribbling furiously on a sheet of paper from the fax machine. First the key information—*GBF-complex causes Alzheimer's, blood-brain barrier must be compromised, evident in a 19-year-old girl with meningitis, killed a 46-year-old man.* He needed to get the essentials onto paper before anything interrupted his train of thought. To forget a discovery of this magnitude would result in God knows how many deaths.

Everything finally made sense. The motive for Elizabeth's murder—to silence her and cover up the damage caused by the screws. And the identity of the killer—Shirley Collins.

Chapter 53

Barnes said her name out loud—Shirley Collins—to reinforce the revelation and make it less likely to slip away in an instant.

The sound of a throat being cleared startled him. He thought he'd been alone, yet someone was standing in the doorway.

Shirley!

Wineglass in hand, she looked down on him. Where on earth had she come from?

"We were having dinner," she said in answer to what must have been a dumbfounded look on his face. "I guess you forgot."

Dinner! "Yes, of course . . ." *With her? Here?* "I guess I ran out on you."

She said nothing, just looked at him with eyes that pierced.

"You've cut your hair." He was trying to fill the silence with something, anything. "It looks . . . short."

"I presume you've figured out what happened."

He looked down at his notes, to confirm what he knew. "You killed Elizabeth. You *killed* her. How could you do that?"

She set the wineglass on a bookshelf. "I did it for the money. Why do you think?"

"For *money?*"

A look of resolve came over her. "That's right. It doesn't mean much to you because you have it. I'm still paying off student loans, I can't afford to take care of my own mother, and I can't even rent a decent apartment in a safe neighborhood. GBF-complex-coated screws would have changed all that. I staked my career on those screws, and then Elizabeth had to stumble across this obscure adverse event that might not even be related to the GBF complex. She insisted on reporting it, even though it was sheer speculation. I tried everything I could to talk her out of it, and any reasonable person would have agreed with me, but she wouldn't listen. And the FDA would have put a hold on the approval, just because of a finding that happened in only two patients and likely had nothing to do with the screws."

"Of course it has to do with the screws! The GBF-complex crossed the blood-brain barrier and caused the neurofibrillary tangles and plaques. Those screws cause Alzheimer's disease."

"You don't know that."

"Christ, Shirley. Open your eyes!" He stood up. That's when he noticed the firearm in her hand.

With surprising swiftness she pointed the barrel at him. "Sit down."

In an instant his anger disappeared. Like flipping a switch—anger, fear.

His life was about to end. Worse, his discovery would be meaningless. Shirley would shred the papers, and no one would know. His heart pounded so hard he felt it in his throat.

He eased himself back into his chair. This woman was going to kill him, and he had no idea how to stop her.

"Empty your pockets onto the floor, and stay in that chair."

He stared at the barrel. What was it—a 9mm? Head on, it looked like a cannon, and it was pointed right at his heart. In an instant he pictured the organ, its delicate electrical nodes and branching nerve fibers, its thin papillary muscles holding the valves in place.

The barrel of the gun drifted a few inches higher, now aimed at his aorta, the largest blood vessel in the body.

"Everything!" she ordered. "Turn your pockets inside out. I want all of your notes."

Without leaving his chair, he emptied his pants pockets. Papers. Change. Car keys. He put them in a pile at his feet.

On one piece of paper, he'd written, *Denny has a Glock*. Why couldn't he have asked Denny to lend it to him? Of course, Denny would probably have told him to buy his own.

He finished with his pants and reached into his sport coat. In the pocket normally reserved for his billfold, he felt something entirely different—a tape recorder, the type used to dictate operative reports. He pressed what he hoped was the "Record" button.

From the pocket with the tape recorder, he removed only a pen. From his other jacket pocket, he removed his wallet, then placed both items on the floor with his other personal effects. As he did this, he tried to figure out a way to remember what he'd just learned, to tie everything together before it slipped away. He created a mental image of Shirley wearing a T-shirt with "GBF Alzheimer's" emblazoned across the front. In one hand she held a stack of autopsy reports; in the other, a smoking gun.

If he could just remember that image, he could forget everything else and still solve the case again. Even if he could remember only half of it, he might still be able to piece everything together. He concentrated in an attempt to etch it into his mind.

Shirley took the wineglass from the bookshelf and walked a wide circle around him. Still training the gun on him, she placed the glass on the edge of his desk. Before Barnes could even think about trying to disarm her, she had returned to her position near the door.

"Now drink that." She motioned with the gun.

"What is it?" He looked at the wineglass but still saw the mental image of Shirley that he had created.

"A sedative. To be sure you forget everything. I can't take the chance that some fragment of tonight might lodge somewhere in the recesses of your mind."

So much for the mental image, Barnes thought. He wondered what she would do if he spilled the wine. Probably kill him. She had already murdered her best friend. How hard would it be to kill again?

He leaned forward and picked up the wineglass. It was half full. "What type of sedative?"

"Just drink it!" The look in her eyes told him her patience had run out.

Holding the glass in his hand, he wondered, *Is this how Socrates felt drinking hemlock, knowing that death—slow death—awaited him?*

No. Socrates had accepted his fate. Barnes couldn't do that.

The wine was close enough that he recognized the smell—a Pinot Noir. "You don't want to do this." His mouth had gone dry, and he had to force the words out.

"Drink it. I'm not going to ask again."

No, he didn't expect she would. His hands had always been steady in surgery, in any crisis. Now they trembled. In the OR they could function independently, but at this moment the simple act of bringing a glass to his mouth seemed daunting. Yet Shirley was giving him no choice.

The glass touched his lips. Then the wine. Never had a Pinot Noir repulsed him so much. His throat constricted.

Just drink it, he told himself, and he upended the glass. Wine streamed down his throat in burning gulps.

"Now put the glass down," Shirley said.

He placed it on the desk. "I hope you get the death penalty for this." He was surprised to hear himself say that. The words bolstered his courage.

"Aside from the fact that the death penalty in Massachusetts was abolished three years ago, I'm surprised you would say that, after all we've shared."

"I don't remember sharing anything with you."

"Perhaps not, but you did. And we're going to share more. Much more."

"What does *that* mean?"

"I'm going to get rid of your notes and type new ones for you. When you wake up tomorrow, with me at your side, you'll read what I want you to believe. You'll read that you love me."

"I'll never love you. You killed Elizabeth."

"You'll love me, and you'll trust me. I'll become a part of you. I'll give you your own memory. After I get rid of your notes, you'll be less obsessed with Elizabeth. I just have to stay close enough to you to keep all this from happening again. And of course I'll have the financial resources to hire people to keep an eye on you."

He pictured himself trapped in a relationship with her, sharing a bed and a life with the woman who had murdered Elizabeth and who would knowingly inflict premature senility and death on unsuspecting patients. To be dependent upon this woman, manipulated into believing her wishes were his truths, would be worse than death. Yet the prospect of death, of a bullet ripping through his heart, kept him planted in the chair.

"I hope there's a special place in hell for you, Shirley. Elizabeth was your friend."

"Yeah, and Denny Houston is yours. We sure know how to pick 'em."

"You even killed Rex. He was harmless."

"I couldn't take the chance he'd throw a fit the next time I came over."

"How did it happen?" Barnes leaned forward and looked at his notes on the floor.

"I don't want to talk about it."

"You knocked on the door, right, and Elizabeth turned off the alarm and let you in?"

"That's how it started."

He moved the notes around with his feet, then looked up at her. "You killed her and the dog, then cut a hole in the dining-room window to fake a burglary, and you did the same thing to Denny's house so the police would think it involved him and me, not just Elizabeth."

"Something like that. And I put the love letter in her purse."

"The love letter . . ." He looked down at his notes. "She didn't . . . she wasn't . . ."

"Not that I'm aware of. As far as I know, she loved you, even when you were a self-centered jerk who didn't want to father her child."

Barnes didn't say anything.

She continued. "I sent the other letter, too, the one about the ten thousand dollars."

He saw a mention of that letter in his notes as well. "To implicate me?"

"That's right. It wouldn't have been necessary if you hadn't recovered from your coma. But with you digging around in Elizabeth's files, that extra measure seemed prudent."

When he didn't say anything in reply, she asked, "How did you know to look for the autopsy reports? Those don't go to the FDA, and even the investigators at the site didn't see anything there."

He tried to recall, but the sequence of events had escaped him. "I don't remember."

She laughed. "That's pathetic. You solve the big mystery, but you can't remember how you did it?"

"I figured it out. That's what counts."

"Yeah. Well, not for long."

He didn't like the sound of that. "So you're going to kill me."

"No," she said condescendingly. "Can't you remember *anything*? I put a sedative in your wine."

"Right." He thought he remembered that. Certainly he should have; the fear of what it was doing to him should have kept it in his consciousness. He felt the drug already taking effect, causing a weariness to settle over him. Was it chloral hydrate? "You should turn yourself in," he said.

She scoffed. "Then Elizabeth's death would be for nothing."

"It *was* for nothing. If those screws cause Alzheimer's—and we both know they do—then it's just a matter of time before the FDA realizes that and takes them off the market." Anger seemed to stave off the weariness.

"Maybe. But it'll take years for them to do that, and by then, I'll already be rich. Jarrell Pharmaceuticals will be sued, but all I did was obtain the patent. I'll be out of the legal loop."

"Don't you have *any* morals? Don't you care if people die?" His tongue felt thick. Words were beginning to slur. He had to do something to stop her. *Something*.

"Of course I care," she said. "But I also care about *me*."

The room began to spin. Subtly. As though he had a mild inner-ear problem. Soon it would get much worse. Then everything—including hope—would fade away. He had to stay awake. Sleep now would be worse than death. To succumb to sleep would be to surrender his humanity, to become forever enslaved to the woman who had killed Elizabeth. Living her fantasy at the expense of innocent lives.

But how could he not sleep? Staying awake was like treading water in the middle of an ocean. The waves were growing, and his body was getting heavier.

How could he think of a plan now? Even clearheaded, he hadn't been able to come up with anything.

Stay awake!

He kept treading water, unwilling to yield to the sea of dreams. Yet the water was pulling him under. His mind seemed to float in another direction, drifting away from the crisis.

Somehow he had to concentrate.

At that moment the doorbell rang. A faraway chime so distant it could have been only a memory.

"Don't make a sound," Shirley warned, "or I'll kill both of you."

The bell rang again, two pitches reverberating through the house and through Barnes's mind. A rescue ship. Yet if he didn't signal it, the ship would pass him by.

The window, he thought. He could throw something through the window to alert whoever was there. But that would achieve nothing. Shirley would kill him. She'd already murdered his wife.

He had to think of something else. Now!

He stood up. The room swayed, but he stayed on his feet.

Shirley trained the gun on him. "Sit down."

He raised his hands in a conciliatory fashion. At least that's what he thought. He couldn't tell for sure what he was doing. The room was beginning to blur, although his thoughts seemed to be more focused, maybe clearer from the exertion of standing.

He knew what needed to be done.

He took a step toward the window at the rear of the house. Another step put him in front of it. The drawn metal Venetian blinds hid him from view to anyone outside, but being seen wasn't the plan.

"Get away from the window," Shirley warned, urgency in her voice, "and keep your hands where I can see them. I *will* shoot you."

The doorbell chimed again, and she glanced in the direction of the sound.

Barnes hurtled himself at the window.

With luck the metal blinds would shield him from the shards of broken glass that might otherwise kill him. He'd seen people who had gone through windows, and it wasn't pretty. Not like in the movies where cowboys stand up and brush themselves off. Usually people suffer disfiguring wounds and severed arteries. But in his case the blinds offered a protective screen of sorts. He only hoped he'd generated enough force to carry him all the way through.

The window shattered. Taking the blinds with him, Barnes plummeted toward the wooden deck in a tangle of metal and a shower of glass. As he fell through the cold darkness, he thought, *I can't believe it worked.* He hadn't seen, heard, or felt a gunshot. Maybe Shirley had hesitated to shoot because he was moving away from her rather than toward her and she didn't feel threatened, or maybe she cared for him after all and couldn't bring herself to do it. Or maybe she simply couldn't make up her mind that fast.

Barnes crashed to the deck. He landed with his feet underneath him, although he fell to one side, hitting his hip, arm, ribs, and finally his head on the unforgiving cedar. All thoughts of Shirley, the autopsy reports—everything from the entire evening—exited him upon impact. His world turned white, like the bursting brightness of a camera's flashbulb, then faded to darkness. In the confused moment before losing consciousness, he wondered, *Where's Elizabeth?*

Chapter 54

Shirley put the gun back inside her purse. She turned out the light in Barnes's office and rushed to the broken window. Taking care not to cut herself on the jagged glass, she stuck her head out and squinted into the frigid night. Darkness and snow flurries obscured the view, transforming everything on the deck below into poorly defined shapes. The outline of a dark mass directly below appeared to be Barnes, but she couldn't be sure. Nothing moved.

She strained to see more, and her eyes adjusted to the darkness. The shape on the deck came into view. Definitely Barnes, partially draped in the metal blinds. Probably the fall hadn't killed him—it was only two stories—but that didn't matter. He appeared to be unconscious, and she knew when he woke up, he wouldn't remember anything. *If* he woke up. Even without the windchill factor, the temperature outside was well below freezing, more than cold enough to kill him if he didn't regain consciousness soon. Of course he could be faking it, but that didn't make sense. If the fall hadn't knocked him out, he would certainly have tried to scramble off the deck to safety. Lying there and risking a bullet would be foolish. He must be unconscious.

Shivering, she backed away from the window, then flipped on the light again and quickly surveyed the room. She had to get rid of anything that might help Barnes or the police implicate her again, and she had to do it in a hurry, before anyone saw her standing there or moving about. She pulled the disk out of the computer and shoved it into her purse, along with the faxed autopsy reports and the note Barnes was writing. She also gathered up the notes from his pockets. Thank God he'd emptied his pockets before going through the window.

She picked up his wallet and placed it on the desk, then wiped her fingerprints off it.

Where else would her fingerprints be? All over the downstairs, of course, but that was okay; he'd invited her over for dinner. Fingerprints in his office would be harder to explain.

She wiped the doorknob, took the wineglass off the bookshelf, and left the room. Rushing from one room to the next, she looked for more notes that Barnes had posted on the walls, mirrors, and furnishings. She gathered the scraps of paper and shoved them into her purse, including the note that had been taped to the alarm clock.

Satisfied that she'd gotten rid of anything that might incriminate her, she carried the wineglass downstairs to the kitchen, rinsed it, and put it in the sink. She put the other wineglass and dinner dishes there, too, and rinsed them. Time to go.

She grabbed her coat from the front hall closet. What else? Purse, hat, gun. Time to go.

Her hand on the front doorknob, she suddenly remembered . . .

The telephone!

She rushed to the kitchen and took the phone out from under the pile of dish towels in the cabinet drawer. Leaving it there would have been a major blunder. Possibly a fatal one. She wiped it down with one of the dish towels.

What else was she forgetting? Her mind went over every detail of the evening. *Last chance to cover your tracks.* Everything seemed in order.

She returned to the front door and looked through the peephole to see whether whoever had rung the doorbell was in sight. The fish-eye covered the entire entryway, but beyond that, darkness and snow obscured much of the view.

You have to go, she told herself, realizing that every moment spent in the house increased her likelihood of being caught.

Steeling herself, she opened the door and slipped outside. Only after she pulled the door closed did she dare look around.

Nobody.

She hurried straight to her car at the curb. Snow crunched under her feet, leaving behind footprints. Evidence she had been there.

It's irrelevant, she assured herself. *You were invited to dinner.* Besides, in half an hour or less, the footprints would be obscured by wind and new snow.

A car sped by. She strained to see whether the driver appeared to notice her. Probably not, but impossible to tell for sure. The street was always at least half full of parked cars, although she appeared to be the only pedestrian. She threw herself into the driver's seat and shoved her key into the ignition. The engine whined, then turned over. The windshield had fogged and iced up, but waiting for the heater to defrost it wasn't an option. She rubbed a knothole with a gloved hand, then put the car into gear and stepped on the gas.

Time to go home.

Chapter 55

Billings heard glass shatter, followed by a crash that sounded as though a piece of furniture had been thrown through a window and onto something hard. He hoped the noise had come from a neighbor's house, but it sounded more like the other side of Barnes's place. Barnes was known for having a temper. Throwing a TV or a chair through a window wasn't beyond the realm of possibilities for him. Billings hoped that was what had just happened. The alternative was more troubling. If Barnes had gone through the window, he was probably lying in a heap, half-dead, bleeding out.

Billings ran around the side of the house, through snow and over bushes. A chain-link fence seemed to appear out of nowhere, and with it the nagging fear that a large dog might be behind it. He would have to take that risk. He stuck the toes of his shoes in the diamond-shaped holes, pulled himself up, and hauled himself over. At least this wasn't a wrought-iron fence with spikes. A man could get impaled on something like that.

Landing in a shrub on the other side of the fence, he lost his balance and fell to one knee, muddying a pant leg and glove with dirty snow.

Barnes, you are not worth this, he thought. But he got up and ran to the back deck.

A figure there lay motionless, surrounded by broken glass and entangled in Venetian blinds.

Barnes.

Kneeling beside his unconscious colleague, Billings pulled off and pushed aside the metal blinds.

Airway, breathing, circulation, he remembered—the ABCs of emergency care.

Barnes's airway appeared unobstructed—no broken teeth or anything else in his mouth—and his breathing seemed regular, although shallow. No profuse bleeding, either—no deep cuts from the glass—and no signs of major trauma, no obvious broken bones. Yet Billings couldn't risk moving him. If Barnes had an injury to his spine, any movement might paralyze him. Instead he took off his coat and draped it over his colleague.

"You're going to be . . . okay," he said, although Barnes remained unconscious. "I'll get help." Already Billings was shivering in the cold, despite having just run around the outside of the house. He rubbed his arms to keep warm. "I'll be right back."

Retracing his footsteps, he headed back to the street.

He had just reached the front of the house when a police car pulled up to the curb.

Chapter 56

"Everything's going to be all right," Shirley said to herself, gripping the wheel of her car, squinting through the fogged-up windshield. "Just stay calm."

As she drove, the car warmed up. The events of the evening, like Barnes's house, soon seemed far behind her. She couldn't believe she'd had dinner with him less than an hour ago. Too bad he'd been so obsessed with solving Elizabeth's murder. Too bad he couldn't just go on with his life.

She spotted a Dumpster at a gas station and stopped to throw away Barnes's computer disk, his notes, and the faxes of the autopsy reports. Then she made a second stop to get rid of her handgun. For that she chose the Charles River. In another month it would freeze over, but this early in the season, only a thin shelf of ice had formed along its banks. She threw the gun from the Cambridge side of the river, where passing cars wouldn't notice, and she hurled it far enough from shore that no one would ever find it.

Losing the 9mm was a shame, but the chances of getting caught with it had become too great. She'd made the right decision. Her heart stopped pounding. Her hands stopped shaking.

By the time she got home, the events of the past hour seemed so distant they almost could have happened to someone else. She poured herself a glass of wine, put a movie into the VCR, and, kicking off her shoes, relaxed on her sofa in front of the TV. Everything was under control.

She watched *Dr. Zhivago*, a story of love, war, and adultery. She'd already seen it twice and had fallen in love with Omar Sharif. Then there was Julie Christie, who played a character even more admirable—stunning and intelligent, driven by passion, although plagued by injustices. The cast, the script, the editing, and the directing—all had come together perfectly to create this cinematic masterpiece. But now it was just a distraction.

Despite the tensions of the evening, she felt herself start to drift off. Then, during Omar Sharif's first strained encounter with Sir Alec Guinness, the doorbell jarred her back to reality.

Who would come to her place, uninvited, after dark? Better not to find out.

The doorbell rang a second time. Still she ignored it.

It rang a third time, and a man's impatient voice yelled, "Open up. Police."

"Just a minute," she answered finally. Were they here to make an arrest? How could she have become a suspect so quickly? Her mind reeled as she slipped her shoes on. Maybe the police were only going to question her. They probably just needed information. After all, Chris couldn't possibly have told them anything incriminating. There wasn't a chance he could have remembered anything after being drugged and after that fall, even if he *had* survived.

The police might somehow have placed her at his house, but that didn't mean anything. She and Chris had spent part of the evening together. She was just being a friend. Maybe he'd become so despondent afterward he'd jumped through the window. Stranger things had happened, and certainly he had every reason to be suicidal—his wife had been killed and he'd suffered major brain damage. Who wouldn't be suicidal after that?

Opening the front door, she willed herself to be calm. Two plainclothes policemen crowded the entryway. She recognized them from a few weeks earlier when they had questioned her regarding her relationship with Elizabeth.

"Shirley Collins," one of them stated. Clearly he remembered her, too. He was tall and slender with sandy hair and an unpretentious demeanor.

"Yes?"

"You're under arrest for the murder of Elizabeth Barnes and the attempted murder of Christopher Barnes."

The other one, more stocky and smelling strongly of cologne, took out a pair of handcuffs.

"You've got to be joking," she said, but the tremor in her voice belied any indignation.

"You have the right to remain silent . . ." the stocky one began. Just like on TV.

She couldn't believe this was happening. "Why do you think I did those things?"

"We don't *think*, ma'am," said the tall one. "We know. Now put on a coat and come along with us."

She turned from them, and they followed her to the hall closet. "This is a mistake."

"Put your coat on, ma'am," said the stocky one, dangling the handcuffs from one finger.

She took her coat from the closet and put it on.

"Button it up. It's cold outside."

"I don't believe this," she muttered, her fingers trembling with the buttons.

"Believe it," said the tall one. "It's over."

Chapter 57

Barnes awoke late the next morning with no recollection of what had happened. The last thing he remembered was eating mussels in a Canadian restaurant in the company of Cheryl. No, the last thing he recalled was seeing Cheryl naked in a hotel room. He hoped with all his heart that Elizabeth would never find out.

Was he still in Canada? And what day was this? What month? November, maybe. He wondered whether some sedative or other medication had caused a temporary amnesia.

A movement at the foot of the bed caught his attention. A woman reading a magazine. She wasn't someone he recognized, and a woman like that—with flowing chestnut hair and delicate features—wasn't someone he would forget.

He noticed railings on the bed. And controls for raising and lowering its head and foot. This was a hospital room. Yet his visitor didn't appear to be any sort of employee or nurse. She wasn't wearing scrubs or a uniform.

She set down her reading material and came to his side. "Don't try to sit up," she said in a breathy voice that sounded familiar. She looked to be in her late twenties. "You've had a concussion, but the doctors say you're going to be all right."

"Where's Elizabeth?" he asked.

"That's a long story. Do you know who I am?"

"I'm not sure." Something about that voice.

"I'm Claire, Elizabeth's friend."

He remembered. "The attorney."

"That's right."

"What happened to me?"

"That's a long story, too. It's understandable if you don't remember. You've been through quite a lot. We can talk about it later. Right now you just need to get better."

I need to know what's going on, he thought, but fatigue and apprehension drained him of the strength to argue. Part of him suspected something terrible had happened, like a car accident that Elizabeth hadn't survived. He wasn't ready to face that just yet.

He closed his eyes and tried not to think about it.

After Claire left, Detective Wright visited Barnes at the hospital and briefed him on the events leading to the arrest of Shirley Collins. He and Gould had taken her into custody after playing back the tape recording Barnes had made. The recorder had fallen from his jacket pocket when the emergency medical technicians had lifted him onto a stretcher, and Wright had noticed it on the deck in the snow.

Wright told Barnes that apparently Shirley hadn't wanted to risk killing him in his backyard where someone might witness the event. He didn't mention that he and Gould had driven to the house to arrest him rather than rescue him. In their search through the piles of garbage, Gould had discovered a crumpled note that happened to be in English and that described the letter demanding $10,000; it also indicated that with Elizabeth's death, half the profits from her research would go to Barnes. Logically they concluded that Barnes had hired a professional to solve his financial problems and at the same time eliminate the woman who was threatening to have a child from another man.

Wright also neglected to mention that only a few hours ago, they'd decided not to turn over to the district attorney the tape of the wiretap in which Barnes discussed his illegal gambling on football games. They didn't throw it away—that would be destroying evidence—but they might as well have. By the time anyone with authority happened upon that information, filed away with piles of other documents in a closed case, the statute of limitations would long since have run out.

Wright concluded by saying, "We didn't know it was Shirley Collins until after we played the tape, but we would have figured it out on our own pretty soon."

Barnes raised the head of his bed.

Wright had to admit that "pretty soon" was a stretch. Regardless, he'd wanted to figure it out himself, but Barnes had done it instead. Now he understood how Karen felt when he did things for her that she wanted to do herself.

"You can have the next one," said Barnes.

"Yeah. Maybe it's better this way, but it would have been nice if you could have solved the case before we spent an entire day going through your garbage, although I have to say it smelled better than my partner's cologne."

Barnes didn't say anything to that.

"Well, I guess I should leave you alone. You need your rest."

"What I need is to get out of here. I told them I want to sign out, but they stall until I forget. They think I'm not onto their game, but I know what they're doing. *Some* things I can remember for more than five minutes."

"I'll see what I can do," Wright replied. "I think they want you to stay until tomorrow."

"I want to leave today."

"I'll see what I can do. The good news is they say you're going to be fine. They tell me you had a concussion and that's it."

"That and preexisting brain damage."

"The doctors say that may get better, too. You just have to give it time. In a few days you'll be over your bumps and bruises, and I'll bet pretty soon you'll be back to normal."

"Back to normal," Barnes echoed. "That would be nice."

Chapter 58

Four months later

Barnes awoke to the drone of his alarm clock. He'd been dreaming of Elizabeth, vacationing on Maui in celebration of their five-year anniversary. They'd cast aside their clothes and were making love between two blankets on a black-sand beach, under the stars, while rhythmic ocean waves crashed to shore in tempo with their movements. Behind them a waterfall cascaded into a freshwater pool, and the thundering water had translated itself into the sound of his alarm. He slapped the "Off" button and, as the memory of the dream slipped away, looked at the time: 6:00. He wanted to go back to sleep, to recapture that fleeting dream, but it was time to get up and start his day.

He rubbed his eyes, then looked again at the clock. A message in his own handwriting, taped to the top, hung partially over the digital readout: *Read note on bathroom mirror. Surgery at 7:30 with Nate Billings.*

He remembered Nate now, not just as the deliberate and cautious black surgeon he and Denny Houston had avoided but also as the surgeon who had helped him, who had befriended him. He vaguely recalled having scrubbed with Nate on a case, or was it several cases, and he thought maybe he'd had dinner with him and his family, although he couldn't remember how many children Nate had or even what his house looked like. But one thing was certain: Nate was a friend.

Barnes rolled out of bed and sat on the edge of the mattress, trying to recall the previous night. Dinner, a movie, a conversation, anything. Instead he remembered mussels in November in Toronto. That was the dinner that had changed his life, and opposite him had sat the woman with whom he'd eaten that fateful meal. He pictured her for the umpteenth time, in her dress with the neckline that gapped and revealed the tops of her breasts. She still had cascading blonde hair and sparkling blue eyes, but her face and her body no longer appealed to him.

Her image transformed to that of Elizabeth the last time he remembered seeing her, through the rearview mirror of his Mercedes as he drove to the airport on his way to the conference. He had left the Ritz-Carlton early that morning and had stopped by the house to drop off some clothes. He and Elizabeth had spoken only briefly. Then they left for the airport and work. He remembered that she'd waved good-bye to him wistfully from her car before turning off Harvard Street to head to the hospital. He'd regained that memory many weeks earlier and now had no recollection of ever having lost it. He also recalled her being pregnant, and fragments of their fight about the pregnancy, although the details escaped him.

He forced himself out of bed and headed to the mirror to read a note he presumed he'd drafted the previous night. He didn't remember having written anything but now realized his retentive skills were minimal. Still, he couldn't help but wonder whether the note on the mirror might jog his memory, enabling him to recall events from the days and perhaps even weeks before. He stretched and turned on the light near the dresser. It filled much of the room with a harsh glare. Turning away from it, he felt empty, as though a part of him had taken flight, never to return. At the moment, he didn't know whether months or years had gone by since the food poisoning, but he sensed that enough time had elapsed for things within him to stabilize. His memory would not improve.

He had nearly reached the bathroom mirror when he looked back at the bed and, for the first time, realized Elizabeth was gone. Her work schedule was usually lighter than his, but she sometimes got up early and left for the hospital before he did, almost always without waking him. Apparently today was one of those days.

He wondered when she would be back.

Epilogue

The November 1987 outbreak of domoic acid in mussels killed three people and left a dozen with permanent memory impairment. As a result, officials in Canada took measures to reduce the risk of a recurrence of poisoning by shellfish contaminated with domoic acid. Batches of mussels are labeled with their location of origin, and before commercial distribution they are spot-checked by laboratory tests for the presence of domoic acid. The last reported case of poisoning by domoic acid in Canada was December 1987.

In September 1991 the first reported marine outbreak of domoic acid in the United States occurred in Monterey Bay, California. Hundreds of cormorants and brown pelicans were found dead or dying, and analyses of their stomach contents revealed anchovies containing domoic acid. Analyses of mussels from Monterey Bay also revealed domoic acid.

Within two months another outbreak traced to razor clams afflicted twenty-one people in Washington State, and shortly thereafter, domoic acid appeared in Dungeness crabs along the coast of Oregon and Washington and in other edible marine species in the Gulf of Mexico.

Despite these events, the United States government did not institute federal regulations mandating routine testing of shellfish or other seafood for domoic acid.

To date, there is no antidote.

Bibliography

Anonymous. "Domoic acid intoxication." *Canada Communicable Disease Report* 18, 15 (1992): 118–20.

Department of Fisheries and Oceans, Canada. "Fish inspection regulations—amendment." *Canada Gazette*. Part I. Ottawa, Ont.: Government of Canada, April 29, 1989: 2145–8.

Dickey R. W., Fryxell G. A., Granade H. R., and Roelke D. "Detection of the marine toxins okadaic acid and domoic acid in shellfish and phytoplankton in the Gulf of Mexico." *Toxicon* 30, 3 (1992): 355–9.

Gjedde A. and Evans A. C. "PET studies of domoic acid poisoning in humans: excitotoxic destruction of brain glutamatergic pathways, revealed in measurements of glucose metabolism by positron emission tomography." *Canada Diseases Weekly Report* 16, S1E (1990): 105–9.

Kizer K. W. "Domoic acid poisoning." *Western Journal of Medicine* 161, 1 (1994): 59–60.

Perl T. M., Bédard L., Kosatsky T., Hockin J. C., Todd E. C. D., and Remis R. S. "An outbreak of toxic encephalopathy caused by eating mussels contaminated with domoic acid." *New England Journal of Medicine* 322, 25 (1990): 1775–80.

Squire L. R. *Memory and Brain.* Oxford University Press: New York, 1987.

Teitelbaum J. S., Zatorre R. J., Carpenter S., Gendron D., Evans A. C., Gjedde A., and Cashman N. R. "Neurologic sequelae of domoic acid intoxication due to the ingestion of contaminated mussels." *New England Journal of Medicine* 322, 25 (1990): 1781–7.

Todd E. C. D. "Domoic acid and amnesic shellfish poisoning— A review." *Journal of Food Protection* 56, 1 (1993): 69–83.

Wekell J. C., Gauglitz E. J. Jr., Barnett H. J., Hatfield C. L., Simons D., and Ayres D. "Occurrence of domoic acid in Washington state razor clams (Siliqua patula) during 1991–1993." *Natural Toxins* 2, 4 (1994): 197–205.

Wright J. L., Bird C. J., de Freitas A. S., Hampson D., McDonald J., and Quilliam M. A. "Chemistry, biology, and toxicology of domoic acid and its isomers." *Canada Diseases Weekly Report* 16, S1E (1990): 21–6.

About the Author

 Glen Apseloff won first place at the international SEAK medical fiction competition for his novel *Dying to Remember*. He is also the author of the medical thrillers *Overdose* and *Lethal Cure*. A medical doctor with expertise in drugs and toxins, he draws on his clinical experiences and training to generate ideas for his novels. He is also a nature photographer who has published numerous calendars and two books: *Backyard Birds—Looking Through the Glass* and *The Chipmunk Book*. He lives in Ohio with his wife, Lucia.